THE UNIVERSE BOX

MICHAEL SWANWICK

The Universe Box

Interior and cover design by Elizabeth Story
Cover art "All We Have Is Now, if any" copyright © by Inktally
Author photo by Beth Gwinn

Tachyon Publications LLC
1459 18th Street #139
San Francisco, CA 94107
415.285.5615
www.tachyonpublications.com
tachyon@tachyonpublications.com

Series Editor: Jacob Weisman
Project Editor: Jaymee Goh

Print ISBN: 978-1-61696-450-4
Digital ISBN: 978-1-61696-451-1

Printed in the United States by Versa Press, Inc.

First Edition: 2026
9 8 7 6 5 4 3 2 1

Praise for *The Universe Box*

"Swanwick is a great science fiction writer. His stories are brilliantly inventive, often hilarious, often profound, and always heartfelt."
—Kim Stanley Robinson, author of *The Ministry for the Future*

"Virtuoso Swanwick delivers a microcosm in every story of this immaculate collection."
—Cat Rambo, Nebula Award–winning author of the *Tabat* Quartet

★"Five-time Hugo Award winner Swanwick (*Stations of the Tide*) swirls together myth and science in this wildly inventive collection. A frequent theme is the interaction of humanity and technology, which is probed poignantly in the bittersweet 'Artificial People,' narrated by a newly sentient robot who falls for one of the scientists on her team, and 'The White Leopard,' about a man who is able to see through the eyes of his leopard-shaped military drone. In 'Requiem for a White Rabbit,' animatronic escapees flee a life of misery in an amusement park. The epistolary 'Timothy: An Oral History' imagines the consequences of a scientist in an all-female society engineering a male child in a lab. Swanwick's wry humor comes through in 'The Warm Equations,' a space exploration story helmed by the arrogant Dr. Osborne, and in 'The Star-Bear,' about a Russian émigré poet who meets a bizarre celestial being. All of Swanwick's stories awaken insights into the mystery of being human in an increasingly mind-bending technological world. This is an author at the height of his powers."
—*Publishers Weekly*, starred review

"At this advanced stage of the game, I'm in no way surprised to find that Swanwick has produced a story collection that rivals his classic, *Tales of Old Earth*.... SF short fiction lovers and beyond will relish this new collection."
—Jeffrey Ford, author of *A Natural History of Hell* and *The Shadow Year*

"Brilliant, multilayered, breathtakingly imaginative, these stories surprise, delight, sometimes shock, and always reward with their insightful humanity."
—Nancy Kress, the multiple award–winning coauthor of *Observer*

"If Michael Swanwick had never been born, it would have been necessary to cobble him together in Victor Frankenstein's workshop, so that the SF and fantasy fields might be enriched…."
—James Morrow, author of *The Last Witchfinder* and *Shambling Towards Hiroshima*

"Every Swanwick collection is a reminder of how much he has taught me, and how much I have yet to learn. He is truly one of the all-time great writers of short sf."
—Andy Duncan, author of *An Agent of Utopia*

"Swanwick's wondrous tales climb every imaginable rung of the cosmic distance ladder leading to our innermost constellations."
—Alvaro Zinos-Amaro, author of *Being Michael Swanwick*

"Swanwick's natural storytelling ability and wonderful imagination made these tales of strange and fantastic sing, irrespective of their genre."
—*Advance the Plot*

MICHAEL SWANWICK

TACHYON

SAN FRANCISCO

Other Books by Michael Swanwick

Novels

In the Drift (1985)
Vacuum Flowers (1987)
Stations of the Tide (1991)
The Iron Dragon's Daughter (1993)
Jack Faust (1997)
Bones of the Earth (2002)
The Dragons of Babel (2008)
Dancing with Bears (2011)
Chasing the Phoenix (2015)

Collections

Gravity's Angels (1991)
A Geography of Unknown Lands (1997)
Moon Dogs (2000)
Puck Aleshire's Abecedary (2000)
Tales of Old Earth (2000)
Cigar-Box Faust and Other Miniatures (2003)
Michael Swanwick's Field Guide to the Mesozoic Megafauna (2004)
The Periodic Table of Science Fiction (2005)
The Dog Said Bow-Wow (2007)
The Best of Michael Swanwick (2008)

CONTENTS

INTRODUCTION
THE HOUSE OF SKULLS AND MASKS

by Michael Swanwick

ONCE UPON A TIME, my wife, Marianne Porter, spontaneously asked, "How did I come to live in a wizard's den?"

"The masks are my doing," I reminded her. "But the skulls are yours." Marianne is a biologist.

A friend, newly welcomed into our house, looked around and exclaimed, "You live in a Cornell box!"

Okay, yes, our house is a cabinet of curiosities jam-packed with items to engage the mind: a plastic orrery mounted sideways on the wall as if it were a fifties starburst, the head of the Virgin from a cement *Pietà*, original comic strip art, a cover painting by Robert Walters for *Asimov's Science Fiction* depicting me being menaced by a tyrannosaur, a West African spear that was in the Centennial Exposition, Chesley Bonestell lithographs, a photograph of the first footprint on the Moon, a Moebius serigraph, a San Ildefonso pot, a Kiyochika triptych from the Sino-Japanese War, a bottle of cat whiskers, and another bottle containing several years of melted snow and hand-labeled *Les neiges d'antan.* Among very much else.

But skulls and masks are endemic, ubiquitous, everywhere: a fossilized cave bear skull, a plague doctor mask from Venice, an impala skull bought in New York City that made the natives gape and stare when Marianne waltzed it down their streets, an art mask that Gardner Dozois held when M. C. Valada photographed him in our library, a 3D-printed wolf's skull from Yellowstone National Park, a life mask of Marianne with an unpublished flash fiction pasted across it in a kind of demi-mask, a bowl of mink skulls intended for a future Dragonstairs Press project, tourist slum from Africa and Indonesia, a delicate egret's skull, a vintage catcher's mask, fantasy skulls of creatures that never were, Marianne's old fencing mask . . . The list goes on and on.

If you sat within our house and were inclined to do so, you might well imagine it as a memory palace, with masks representing appearances and skulls as essences.

So too, it may be, with this book.

This is the fifth summary collection of my short fiction as it came out: *Gravity's Angels, Tales of Old Earth, The Dog Said Bow-Wow, Not So Much Said the Cat,* and the volume you hold in your hands. They are milestones of my life and career. (There were many more collections along the way, but these are the core.) All but the first, published by Arkham House, are available from Tachyon Publications.

And the life and mind that this book perhaps reveals? Well . . . it would be tedious to go through this collection story by story. So, instead, I'll give you some of the highlights.

"Starlight Express" is typical of far too much of my fiction in that it took forever to write. It is no easy thing to come up with something genuinely original. The premise came fast, but the conclusion . . . ? God help me! The late Gardner Dozois, who was possibly the best story doctor in the history of science fiction, told me there were only two possible endings, neither of which I found acceptable. Forgive me, Gargar, but they felt trite. After so promising a beginning, I was not willing to settle for a conclusion the reader had seen a dozen times before. So the story waited for inspiration. And waited. And waited. Years after I began the story, I finally found its proper ending.

If a lifetime of reading has taught me anything it is that when a good story is going to fail, it's the ending that will do it. My theory is that when this happens, the author just slapped on whatever seemed to work, because they were unwilling to wait another year or two for something better.

Some stories are enormous fun to write. "The Last Days of Old Night" was one of them. It came about because I went to Iceland to attend Icecon, that country's only science fiction convention, and stayed afterward to see Snorri Sturluson's homestead, Thingvellir, Geysir, and a great deal more. Near the southernmost village of Vik lies the black sand beach of Reynisfjara, by which three sea stacks rise from the ocean. There is a legend that two of them were trolls and the third a boat they were pulling to shore when the sun rose and turned them all to stone.

So far, so good. But there the legend stopped. It felt incomplete. So I set out to create a more satisfying tale of who those trolls were, what they were like, and what they hoped to accomplish. I set it before the creation of daylight because not enough stories are set so far back in the mythic past. I threw in anachronisms because fantasies should be free in their invention. Mischling popped up of her own accord and took control of the tale, and I was grateful to her for that. I gave her a difficult life and a chance to better it. And the world she helped create was, as I said, enormous fun.

When I first shared "Ghost Ships" with Marianne, she said, "This is an essay."

"Eh?" I replied.

"I've heard every one of these stories from you. There's not a word of fiction in here."

It is notoriously difficult to define what is and is not necessary for something to be a "story." Beginning, middle, and end. Moral or emotional change in the protagonist. A problem to be solved. Catharsis.

The only commonality all the definitions have is that it should be fictional. "Ghost Ships" is by all appearances fiction. It was written as fiction. It *functions* as fiction. Yet every word of it—save for the proper names, which I changed—is true.

I did say that in the story. But when was the last time you read a story in which the author assured you that "this really happened" and believed it? If you're like me, never.

If I hadn't told you its origins, you would not for an instant think "Ghost Ships" anything but fiction. And if you decide that I am lying, then you have no choice but to consider it a story.

Which demonstrates how fast even the simplest aspects of a writer's craft turn strange. Personally, I feel that, no question about it, "Ghost Ships" is not an essay but a story—an improper story maybe, but a story nonetheless. But decide for yourself. Once a story is written, it belongs as much to the reader as it does to the writer.

"Requiem for a White Rabbit" was solicited by Sheree Renée Thomas for the 75th anniversary issue of *The Magazine of Fantasy & Science Fiction*. I have a particular fondness for that magazine because its very first issue—the one that was titled *The Magazine of Fantasy*—came out in the year of my birth. Also, the several major anniversary issues I have seen all contained spectacular stories by major writers. I wanted to join that confraternity. So I did my best to live up to their example.

Alas, as of this writing, *F&SF* is going through a rough patch, and it is not at all certain whether or not that anniversary issue will ever appear. You who live in my future know its fate better than I. It would be a pleasant thing, however, for that particular publication to sail on to a centennial celebration and beyond.

I do not know if "Requiem for a White Rabbit" has a happy ending or a terribly sad one. I do know, however, that I greatly enjoyed the trip it took to reach that ending and that I liked the characters in it very much indeed.

Russia is one of my enthusiasms. Another is Hope Mirrlees, author of the 1926 fantasy classic *Lud-in-the-Mist,* whom I esteem so much that I wrote a slim book on her life and works. One of *her* enthusiasms, and a friend, was the expatriate Russian modernist-surrealist-fantasist Alexei Mikhailovich Remizov. Reading of his life in Paris led me to write "The Star-Bear." It is explicitly not about Remizov, however, because he was married—which was inconvenient for my purposes, since the facts of his life did not fit the story I wanted to tell.

The central truth of being an émigré writer, however, was the same for all. They missed their homeland horribly but knew that returning to it could mean imprisonment or death and certainly the loss of the freedom to write whatever they wished. The Soviet Union in the first half of the twentieth century was hard on its creatives. To this day, Russians have a low regard for those who fled rather than staying and suffering persecution. It is this last fact that made me want to write about Remizov and his fellow exiles.

Alice Sheldon, who dazzled the science fiction world as James Tiptree, Jr., was notorious among her close friends for midnight phone calls when she was sitting with her loaded shotgun, contemplating suicide. In a letter to one such friend, she compared her longtime depression to two vultures perched on her shoulders. She clearly spent a lot of time thinking about her impending death. So it was not entirely a surprise that her last story, "In Midst of Life," published only a few months after she killed her husband and then herself, was a posthumous fantasy. Unhappily, it was neither revealing nor particularly good.

I never met nor corresponded with Ms. Sheldon, but as an admirer of her fiction, I felt that her final horrifying act deserved something better. Then a friend—I shall withhold her name—shared her theory that Alice Sheldon was not gay but rather an untransitioned trans male, and that set me to thinking. I gave the vultures names and wrote "Huginn and Muninn—and What Came After."

Sheldon remains a controversial figure in the field because no one knows if her husband was a willing participant in a suicide pact or was murdered. But she was one of the best short fiction writers of her time.

This story is laid, like a rose, on the grave of her brilliant career.

Another strikingly dark story, "Cloud," had a lighthearted origin—years of staring down at clouds from airliners and imagining what it would be like to walk on their surfaces and to meet the mist giants who live there and visit their huts and castles and hear their stories. But my concerns when I came to write the story were dark and my judgments stern.

I combined the whimsy of the setting with memories of New York City at its low point in the seventies, when it could be a very frightening place indeed, and a few glancing encounters I'd had with the genuinely wealthy and those who aspired to become them. It's not that my worldview is as bleak as "Cloud" would make it seem, but that stories demand to be told true to their inner essences. To make one more optimistic than it wanted to be would be to perform a violence upon it.

The structure of the story I took from John Cheever's "The Swimmer," though that might not be obvious to the casual reader. Of late, several of my stories have tended to have a mainstreamish streak, and this is one of them.

Considering all of the above, it seems particularly appropriate to close with "Universe Box." Marianne's one-woman imprint, Dragonstairs Press, publishes handcrafted, limited-edition chapbooks, usually but not always written by me. After seeing an exhibit of Joseph Cornell's assemblages, she decided to make something similar. She modified thirteen cigar boxes with star charts and Charles R. Knight illustrations of megafauna lining the insides. Then she gathered strange and evocative items to place within them: antique taxidermy eyes, vacuum tubes, red coral, a tektite, and the like. Several items were common to all the boxes, but each contained things the others did not. She commissioned me to write a story, which I did, and she made that into a stab-bound chapbook which was included inside the boxes. Ten of them were made available for purchase with the buyer's name and address on a label on the outside along with a variety of hand-canceled stamps, and the whole tied up with string. The original drafts of the story were put through a shredder and used as packing material.

Do I need to say that "Universe Box" was terrific fun to write? It was. I began with the biggest heist in the history of the universe, threw in a protagonist who had no idea what a loser he was, gave him a girlfriend who was better than he deserved, and set out to violate every trope and expectation of conventional fiction possible. A story with Trickster at its heart could do no less.

As a former citizen of Vermont, home of beautiful if sometimes deadly winters, I was particularly happy with the story's conclusion.

So that's what I was up to with this collection: evoking a world of skulls and masks—and the faces in between them. It is that region midway between essence and appearance that I try to write about. I really can't put it any simpler than that.

STARLIGHT EXPRESS

Flaminio the water carrier lived in the oldest part of the ancient city of Roma among the *popolo minuto*, the clerks and artisans and laborers and such who could afford no better. His apartment overlooked the piazza dell'Astrovia, which daytimes was choked with tourists from four planets who came to admire the ruins and revenants of empire. They coursed through the ancient transmission station, its stone floor thrumming gently underfoot, the magma tap still powering the energy road, even though the stars had shifted in their positions centuries ago and anyone stepping into the projector would be translated into a complex wave front of neutrinos and shot away from the Earth to fall between the stars forever.

Human beings had built such things once. Now they didn't even know how to turn it off.

On hot nights, Flaminio slept on a pallet on the roof. Sometimes, staring up at the sparkling line of ionization that the energy road sketched through the atmosphere, he followed it in his imagination past Earth's three moons and out to the stars. He could feel its pull at such times, the sweet yearning tug that led suicides to converge upon it in darkness, furtive shadows slipping silently up the faintly glowing steps like lovers to a tryst.

Flaminio wished then that he had been born long ago when it was possible to ride the starlight express away from the weary old Republic to impossibly distant worlds nestled deep in the galaxy. But in the millennia since civilization had fallen, countless people had ridden the Astrovia off the planet, and not one had ever returned.

Except, maybe, the woman in white.

Flaminio was coming home from the baths when he saw her emerge from the Astrovia. It was election week and a ward heeler had treated him to a sauna and a blood scrub in exchange for his vote. When he stepped out into the night, every glint of light seemed bright and every surface slick and shiny, as if his flesh had been turned to glass and offered not the least resistance to the world's sensations. He felt genuinely happy.

Then there was a pause in the constant throb underfoot, as if the great heart of the world had skipped a beat. Something made Flaminio look up, and he thought he saw the woman step down from the constant light of the landing stage.

An instant only, and then he realized he had to be wrong.

The woman wore a white gown of a cloth unlike any Flaminio had ever seen before. It was luminously cool, and with every move she made it slid across her body with simple grace. Transfixed, he watched her step hesitantly out of the Astrovia and seize the railing with both hands.

She stared out across the plaza with a confused and troubled look, as if gazing into an unfamiliar new world.

Flaminio had seen that look before on the future suicides. They came to the Astrovia during the daylight first, accompanying tours that stopped only briefly on their way to the Colosseum and the Pantheon and the Altair Gate, but later returned alone and at night, like moths compulsively circling in on death and transformation, in smaller and more frenzied loops before finally cycling to a full stop at the foot of the Aldebaranian Steps, quivering and helpless as a wren in a cat's mouth.

That, Flaminio decided, was what must be happening here. The woman had gotten as far as the transmission beam, hesitated, and turned around. As he watched, she raised a hand to her mouth, the pale blue gems on her silver bracelet gleaming. She was very lovely, and he felt terribly sorry for her.

Impulsively, Flaminio took the woman's arm and said, "You're with me, babe."

She looked up at him, startled. Where Flaminio had the ruddy complexion and coarse face of one of Martian terraformer ancestry, the woman had aristocratic features, the brown eyes and high cheekbones and wide nose of antique African blood. He grinned at her as if he had all the carefree confidence in the world, thinking: Come on. You are too beautiful for death. Stay, and rediscover the joy in life.

For a breath as long as all existence, the woman did not react. Then she nodded and smiled.

He led her away.

Back at his room, Flaminio was at a loss as to what to do with this woman. To his astonishment, he felt not the least desire to have sex with her. So he gave her his narrow bed and a cup of herbal tea. He himself lay down on a folded blanket by the door, where she would have to step over him if she tried to return to the Astrovia. They both went to sleep.

In the morning he got up before dawn and made his rounds. Flaminio had a contract with a building seven stories high and though the denizens of the upper floors were poor as poor, everybody needed water. When he got home, he made his guest breakfast.

"*Stat grocera*?" she asked, holding up a sausage squash. Then, when Flaminio shook his head and spread his hands to indicate incomprehension, she took a little bite and spat it out in disgust. The bread she liked, however, and she made exclamations of surprise and pleasure over the oranges and pomegranolos. The espresso she drank as if it were exactly what she were used to.

Finally, because he could think of nothing else to do, he took her to see the Great Albino.

The Great Albino was being displayed in a cellar off of Via Dolorosa. Once he had been able to draw crowds large enough that he was displayed in domes and other spaces where he could stand and stretch out his limbs to their fullest. But that was long ago. Now he crouched on all fours in a room that was barely large enough to accommodate him. There were four rows of wooden bleachers, not entirely filled, from which tourists asked questions, which he courteously answered.

Flaminio was able to visit the Great Albino as often as he liked, because when he was young he had discovered that Albino knew things that no one else did. Thirteen times in a single month he had managed to scrape together a penny so he could pepper the giant with questions. On the last visit, Albino had said, "Let that one in free from now."

So of course, the first question the young Flaminio had asked on being let in was "Why?"

"Because you don't ask the same questions as everyone else," Albino had said. "You make me call up memories I thought I had forgotten."

Today, however, the tourists were asking all the same dreary questions as usual. "How old are you?" a woman asked.

"I am three thousand eight hundred forty-seven years and almost eleven months old," Albino said gravely.

"No!" the tourist shrieked. "Really?"

"I was constructed so that I would never age, back when humanity had the power to do such things."

"My tutor-mentor says there are no immortals," a child said, frowning seriously.

"Like any man, I am prone to accident and misfortune. So I am by no means immortal. But I do not age, nor am I susceptible to any known diseases."

"I hear that and I think you are the very luckiest man in the world," a man with a strong Russikan accent said. "But then I reflect that there are no women your size, and I think maybe not."

The audience laughed. Albino waited for the laughter to subside and with a gentle smile said, "Ah, but think how many fewer times I have to go to confession than you do."

They laughed again.

Flaminio stood, and the woman in white did likewise. "Have you brought your bride-to-be for me to meet, water carrier?" Albino asked. "If so, I am honored."

"No, I have rather brought you a great puzzle—a woman who speaks a language that I have never heard before, though all the peoples of the worlds course through Roma every day."

"Does she?" Albino's great head was by itself taller than the woman was. He slowly lowered it, touching his tremendous brow to the floor before her. "Madam."

The woman looked amused. "*Vuzet gentdom.*"

"*Graz mairsy, dama.*"

Hearing her own language spoken, the woman gasped. Then she began talking, endlessly it seemed to Flaminio, gesturing as she did so: at Flaminio, in the direction of the Astrovia, up at the sky. Until finally Albino held up a finger for silence. "Almost, I think she must be mad," he said. "But then . . . she speaks a language that before this hour I believed to be dead. So who is to say? Whatever the truth may be, it is not something I believed possible a day ago."

"What does she say?" one of the audience members asked.

"She says she is not from this planet or any other within the Solar System. She says she comes from the stars."

"No one has come back from the stars for many centuries," the man scoffed.

"Yes. And yet here she is."

The woman's name was Szette, Albino said. She claimed to come from Opale, the largest of three habitable planets orbiting Achernar. When asked whether she had been contemplating suicide, Szette looked shocked and replied that suicide was a sin, for to kill oneself was to despair of God's mercy. Then she had asked what planet this was, and when Albino replied "Earth," adamantly shook her head.

Much later, in Flaminio's memory, the gist of the conversation, stripped of the torrents of foreign words and the hesitant translation, which was curtailed because the paying customers found it boring but continued at some length after the show was over, was as follows:

"That is not possible. It was Earth I meant to visit. So I studied it beforehand and it is not like this. It is all very different."

"Perhaps," Albino said, "you studied a different part of Earth. There is a great variety of circumstance in a planet."

"No. Earth is a rich world, one of the richest in the galaxy. This place is very poor. It must have been named after Earth so long ago that you have forgotten that the human race was not born here."

At last, gently, Albino said, "Perhaps. I think, however, that there is a simpler explanation."

"What explanation? Tell me!"

But Albino only shook his head, as ponderously and stubbornly as an elephant. "I do not wish to get involved in this puzzle. You may go now. However, leave me here with my small friend for a moment, if you would. I have something of a personal nature to say to him."

Then, when he and Flaminio were alone, Albino said, "Do not become emotionally involved with this Szette. There is no substance to her. She is only a traveler—wealthy, by your standards, but a butterfly who flits from star to star, without purpose or consequence. Do you honestly think that she is worthy of your admiration?"

"Yes!" The words were torn from the depths of Flaminio's soul. "Yes, I do!"

Albino had said that he did not wish to be involved. But apparently he cared enough to notify the *protettori*, for later that day they came to arrest Szette and take her to the city courts. There, she was duly charged, declared a pauper, issued a living allowance, and released into Flaminio's custody. During the weeks while her trial was pending, he taught her how to speak Roman. She rented a suite of rooms which Flaminio found luxurious, though she clearly did not, and moved them both into it. Daytimes, after work, he showed her all the sights.

At night, they slept apart.

This was a baffling experience for Flaminio, who had never shared quarters with a woman other than his mother on anything but intimate terms. He thought about her constantly when they were apart but in her physical presence, he found it impossible to consider her romantically.

Their conversations, however, were wonderful. Sitting at the kitchen table, Flaminio would ask Szette questions, while she practiced her new language by telling him about the many worlds she had seen.

Achernar, she said, spun so rapidly that it bulged out at the equator and looked like a great blue egg in the skies of Opale. Its companion was a yellow dwarf and when the planet and both stars were all in a line, a holiday was declared in which everyone dressed in green and drank green liqueurs and painted their doors and cities green and poured green dye in their rivers and canals. But such alignments were rare—she had seen only one in all her lifetime.

Snowfall was an ice world, in orbit around a tight cluster of three white dwarfs so dim they were all but indistinguishable from the other stars in a sky that was eternally black. Their mountains had been carved into delicate lacelikefantasias, in which were tangled habitats where the air was kept so warm that their citizens wore jewelry and very little else.

The people of Typhonne, a water world whose surface was lashed by almost continuous storms, had so reshaped their bodies that they could no longer be considered human. They built undersea cities in the ocean shallows and when they felt the approach of death would swim into the cold, dark depths of the trenches, to be heard from no more. Their sun was a red dwarf, but not one in a hundred of them knew that fact.

On and on, into the night, Szette's words flew, like birds over the tiled roofs of the Eternal City. Listening, occasionally correcting her grammar or providing a word she did not know, Flaminio traveled in his imagination from star to star, from Algol to Mira to Zaniah.

The day of Szette's trial arrived at last. Because Albino was a necessary witness and the city courts could not hold his tremendous bulk, the judges came to him. The bleachers were dismantled to make room for their seven-chaired bench, from which they interviewed first Flaminio, then Albino, and then Szette. The final witness was an engineer-archivist from the Astrovia.

"This has happened before," the archivist said. She was old, scholarly, stylishly dressed. "But not in our lifetimes. Well . . . in his of course." She nodded toward Albino and more than one judge smiled. "It is a very rare occurrence and for you to understand it, I must first explain some of the Astrovia's workings.

"It is an oversimplification to say that the body of a traveler is transformed from matter to energy. It is somewhat closer to the truth to say that the traveler's body is read, recorded, and then transmitted as a signal upon a carrier beam. When the beam reaches—or, rather, reached—its destination, the signal is read, recorded, and then used to recreate the traveler. The recordings are retained against the possibility of an interrupted transmission. In which case, the traveler can simply be sent again. As a kind of insurance, you see."

The engineer paused for questions. There were none and she continued. "I have examined our records. Roughly two thousand years ago, a woman identical to the one you see before you came to Earth. She stayed for a year, and then she left. What she thought of our world we do not know. No doubt, she is long dead. Recently, there was an earth tremor, too small to be noticed by humans, which seems to have disrupted something in the workings of the Astrovia. It created a duplicate of that woman as she was when she first arrived in Roma and released her onto the streets. This duplicate is the woman whose fate you are now deciding."

One of the judges leaned forward. "You say this has happened before. How many times?"

"Three that we know of. It is of course possible there were more."

As the testimony went on, Szette had grown paler and paler. Now she clutched Flaminio's arm so tightly that he thought her nails would break.

The judges consulted in unhurried whispers. Finally, one said, "Will the woman calling herself Szette stand forth?"

She complied.

"We are agreed that, simply by being yourself—or, more precisely, a simulacrum of yourself—you know a great deal about an ancient era and the attitudes of its people that would be of interest to the historians at the Figlia della Sapienze. You will make yourself available to be interviewed by credentialed scholars, three days a week. For this you will be paid adequately."

"Two days," snapped the lawyer that the Great Albino had hired for Szette. "More than adequately."

The judges consulted again. "Two," their spokeswoman conceded. "Adequately."

The lawyer smiled.

That night, Szette took off her bracelet, which Flaminio had never seen her without, opened her arms to him, and said, "Come."

He did.

The way that Szette clutched Flaminio as they made love, as if he were a log and she a sailor in danger of drowning, and the unsettling intensity with which she studied his face afterward, her own expression as unreadable as a moon of ice, told Flaminio that something had changed within her, though he could not have said exactly what.

All that Flaminio knew of Szette was this: That she came from a world called Opale orbiting the stars Achernar A and B. That she loved the darkness of the night sky and the age of Roma's ruins. That she would not eat meat. That she was very fond of him, but nothing more.

This last hurt Flaminio greatly, for he was completely in love with her.

Flaminio was a light sleeper. In the middle of the night, he heard a noise—a footstep on the landing, perhaps, or a door closing—and his eyes flew open.

Szette was gone.

All the rooms of the apartment were empty and when Flaminio went to look for her on the balcony, she wasn't there either. He stared up at the battle-scarred moons and they looked down on him with contempt. Then all the sounds of the city at night drew away from him and in that bubble of silence a sizzle of terror ran up his spine. For he knew where Szette had gone.

It was not hard to catch up with her. Szette did not hurry and Flaminio ran as hard as he could. But when he stood, panting, before her, she held up a hand in warning. The pale blue stones on her bracelet flashed bright.

He could not move.

He could not speak.

"You have been so very kind to me," Szette said. "I hope you will not hate me too much when you realize why."

She turned her back on him. With casual grace, she climbed the steps. Like many another before her, she hesitated. Then, with sudden resolution, Szette plunged into the beam.

There was nothing Flaminio could have done to stop her. But simultaneous with the dematerialization of Szette's body, he heard an extraordinary noise, a scream, issuing from his own mouth.

What Flaminio did next could not be called an impulsive act. He thought it through carefully, and though that took him only an instant, his resolve was firm. He ran up the steps toward the beam, determined to join Szette in her endless voyage to nowhere. He would offer his body to the universe and his soul to oblivion. He would not, he was certain, hesitate when he reached the beam.

A shoulder in his chest stopped him cold. A hand gripped his shoulder and another his elbow. Three *protettori* closed in upon him, scowling. "You must come with us, sir," said one, "to have this suicidal impulse removed."

"I'm a citizen! I know my rights! You can't stop me without a contract!"

"Sir, we have a contract."

They dragged him to a *cellular*. It closed about him and took him away.

When he was released from therapy, incapable then or ever after of ending his own life, Flaminio went to see the only individual in all the world who might have taken out a contract on him and asked, "Why wouldn't you let me die?"

"To me, your lives are as those of mayflies," the Great Albino said. "Enjoy what precious seconds remain."

"And the bracelet? Why didn't you tell me about Szette's bracelet?"

"Until that night, I had forgotten about them. Such things were commonly worn by travelers back when the world was rich. To protect themselves from molestation. To enlist aid when in need. But they were a small and unimportant detail in a complex and varied age."

Flaminio had only one more question to pose: "If I was only doing the bracelet's bidding, then why haven't these feelings gone away?"

Albino looked terribly sad. "Alas, my friend, it seems you really did fall in love with her."

That same day, Flaminio left Roma to become a wanderer. He never married, though he took many lovers, both paid and not. Nor did he ever settle down in one place for any length of time. In his old age he frequently claimed to have been around the world forty-eight times and to have seen everything there was to see on all four occupied planets of the Solar System, and much else as well. All of which was verifiably true, were one to search through the records for his whereabouts over the decades. But, in his cups, he would admit to having never gone anywhere or seen anything worth seeing at all.

THE LAST DAYS OF OLD NIGHT

THROUGH CHAOS AND OLD NIGHT, the three brothers journeyed. Sometimes they rode and sometimes they strode. When they rode, their steeds snorted cold steam from their nostrils and obsidian hooves struck sparks from the rock. When they strode, their feet sank in the earth to their ankles. The sky was lit only by witch-fires. Sometimes there were moons or flotillas of comets. Not tonight. Like all things, the sky and road changed at whim. In all the world, only the brothers could dictate what those changes would be.

That was simply how things were.

Goat-Eater was a great-bellied giant of a man. "There is some new thing ahead," he rumbled. Before them, the black mountains sank down to an ebony sea where blind waves crashed upon a beach as black as snow. It took a sharp eye to tell one from another, but he had that eye. Also, he could smell salt in the air. "It is made of water and it extends even farther than I can see."

"It is not what we fear, however," said Bone-Grinder. "I would know." He was smaller than the others, but more muscular and ungainly. One eye was missing and the other puckered; he had the mouth of a malcontent.

The third brother, who was nameless, did not speak and never had. Only he knew whether this was by necessity or choice. But he made a gesture indicating weariness. They had traveled far and hard and needed to rest.

No cities were near. Sometimes cities spontaneously sprang up, filled with music and motion and so ablaze with light that they could be seen half a continent away. Tonight the mountains were bleak and cheerless. So the nameless one pointed at a low knoll, turning it into a timbered drinking hall that soared halfway to their knees. Smoke lofted from its fire hole.

Dissolving their mounts to night mist, the brothers put off their size. They did not knock—their kind never did—but threw open the doors and stamped within. A fire roared like a dragon at the back of the hall. Faces pale, warriors leapt to their feet, sending benches clattering. Their thane, mighty in war and worthy in peace, drew his sword and, kneeling, placed it on the floor before the brothers.

"Meat," said Goat-Eater, and an aurochs carcass was roasting on a spit over the fire.

"Drink," said Bone-Grinder, and a page who an instant before had been a warrior hurried to proffer a two-handled silver drinking cup that had formerly been his helmet, foaming over with ale.

The nameless one spun the thane's throne-chair about and sat before the fire, glowering and rubbing his hands together. His brothers squatted by his side, one crunching on a rack of beef ribs, the other swilling down beer.

"This is noble meat," Goat-Eater said. "Perhaps it was once a king."

"The drink is missing something, however," said Bone-Grinder and at that instant a cat streaked by his foot in fierce pursuit of a mouse. With a sweep of his gnarled hand, Bone-Grinder caught the mouse and held it up by its tail to his squinting gaze. It had eyes like beads of jet and whiskers like white scratches in the air, and it struggled most prettily to escape. "Serving wench," he said and a young woman stood before him, clad in a simple brown dress, her eyes lowered. The giant examined her critically. "Fewer teats," he said.

The maiden felt her body alter so that she had only two breasts.

"You must have a name," Bone-Grinder said. "I will invent a language for the occasion and choose a word from it for you." For a long moment he was silent. Then: "Mischling," he said, "bring me a barrel of wine and someone to drown in it."

Mischling scuttled across the great hall to obey.

Which was how she came to be.

Fear was a mouse's natural state. So Mischling did not feel she had lost much in her transformation: Her tail, her whiskers, and her sleek pelt, yes, those she missed. But one who was in constant danger of cats and boots and casually flung eating knives could scarcely be more imperiled by being enlarged to human stature. Like all mice, she had been born blind; vision had come as a tremendous surprise to her. This transformation was but one more phase in her life.

In the kitchen, she overtoppled a cask as tall as she was onto its side. Like the popcorn machine and the microwave, it had come into existence in tandem with the knowledge in her head of its location. Appearing from nowhere, Pétur seized her from behind and kissed her neck. Minutes before, Pétur had been a mouse as well and possibly her mate. But shortly after her transformation, a corresponding change had come upon him and with it memories of a past that had never been. They two now shared a history and hopes that someday they would be wed. Together, Pétur and Mischling rolled the cask into the great hall and, with mallets, popped off the top.

Then Pétur climbed in headfirst and drowned himself.

Both Mischling and Pétur naturally regretted the deed, but one did not go against the will of the brothers. It was simply what had to be.

After Bone-Grinder had drunk down the quaff and chewed the boy's corpse to nothing, he willed into being a throne-chair for himself and said to Mischling, "Stand before me."

She obeyed. Mischling had been a woman for mere moments and had no idea what was expected of her. She trembled like a mouse.

"Don't be afraid of me—or I'll crush you like a bug."

"No, sir."

"No monosyllabic answers either."

"Yes, sir."

Bone-Grinder growled, "You don't understand what I'm saying, do you?" Without waiting for a reply, he said, "From now on, understand everything you need to understand," and enlightenment flowed into Mischling. With it came horror, for she now understood that he had the impulsiveness of an infant and the restraint of an avalanche. As did his brothers. There could be no predicting what they might do. "Now," Bone-Grinder said. "Sing us a song."

There was a stringed instrument in Mischling's hands and she knew how to play it. Striking the appropriate stance she sang:

In the beginning was everything and nothing—
A singularity called the monoblock.
No dimensions, no difference, no measurement,
Yet it contained the end of all things . . .

"There is no amusement in this song," Goat-Eater grumbled. He grabbed a back leg of Bone-Grinder's chair and tumbled him into the fire.

Howling with wrath, doubling in size, clothes smoldering, Bone-Grinder rose up and, seizing his brother, tried to wrestle him into the flames. In doing so, he knocked Mischling over. By the time she rose from the flagstones, both were giants again and entangled in combat, cursing and hitting each other with their fists. Their brother roared with silent laughter.

As the giants fought, the thane and his men fled, fearful of being crushed. Mischling took advantage of the confusion to escape unnoticed—save for the silent one, who missed nothing but did not try to stop her—into the darkness outside.

Having nowhere else to go, Mischling crept into the barn and burrowed into the straw for warmth. Then she cried herself to sleep, wishing that Pétur were there to comfort her and knowing that although the brothers had the power to bring him back, never in a thousand years would they do so.

The eternal, unending night closed over her and she slept.

Mischling awoke to the brothers hooting and bellowing. At their command the walls and roof of the barn flew away and earth and straw flowed upward to become their mounts. This, in turn, revealed Mischling's presence. Bone-Grinder seized her arm and yanked her upright. She grew almost as large as they. "We'll take this one with us. She can clean our boots."

The silent one nodded agreement. "She'll need a mount too," Goat-Eater said, and created a saddle beast, smaller in proportion to their mounts as she was to the brothers. With her new power of understanding, Mischling realized that this was done deliberately, so that she and her steed would have to struggle to keep up. For the brothers were, she now knew, as petty as they were powerful.

They rode away, leaving the drinking hall ablaze behind them.

It was a long trek to the sea. Mischling and her steed were both winded well before they reached it. All three brothers rode their mounts up to their necks in the surf. "Become solid," one commanded, but the surf remained as it was. "Let there be a bridge crossing you," said the second, but neither was that so. The silent one scooped up a handful of sea water to drink and then spat it out. They turned and rode back to the strand.

"Here is a great mystery," said Goat-Eater, "though not the one we seek. For this immense, roiling thing is continually changing yet refuses to obey us."

"There are no answers here," said Bone-Grinder. "Therefore let us a create a city where answers may be found—and let that city be called Kiv."

The silent one gestured and a city arose, filled with foundries and knackeries and boatyards. Light from its forges and torches created a semicircle along the seaside; myriad people and horses and wagons filled its streets, as industrious as bees in a hive. Seeing this, the brothers alit and put off their size. So too, perforce, did Mischling.

"Swim out into the water," said Bone-Grinder to the steeds, "until you drown."

Watching the beasts dwindle and disappear, Mischling felt a crushing sense of loss. Her steed was the only thing she had ever been responsible for, and she wished she could have somehow saved it, even as she understood why she could not.

The brothers disguised themselves as beggars in ragged clothes. "You will go before us," said Goat-Eater, "and you will ask questions, for it is beneath our dignity to do so."

"What am I trying to learn?" Mischling asked.

"Whatever you may," said Bone-Grinder. Which Mischling understood meant that they had had premonitions of some essential change forthcoming in the nature of the world and feared it might diminish their power.

With that, the three sturdy beggars and one slight maid entered Kiv.

For a former mouse, Kiv was almost as terrifying as it was entrancing. Its twisty streets and sudden broad squares were hung over with paper lanterns and strings of electric lights so that every breeze made the shadows dance. The air was clangorous with machinery. Smoke pinched the nose. Purposeful men and women hurried in every direction. Wagons brought charcoal to the forges and foundries and vans carried crates of tools, spikes, and square head nails to the boatyards and saw pits. Torch-lit docks and piers jutted into the sea all along the waterfront. Beyond them, in the yards, boats were being built, tarred, and fitted. Lean men sweated over woks in the cookhouses, child messengers darted through the crowds, and sturdy women poured copper into baked clay molds in the manufactories.

A young man in a leather apron was taking a cigarette break outside a smithy. "Why is everyone building boats?" Mischling asked him.

"We hope to be on the other side of the sea before the Sun comes up and changes everything," he said.

"Sun?"

"The Sun is a thing not easy to explain. It is a great ball that rolls over the sky and then disappears in the west, only to be later reborn in the east. It is brighter than any lantern. Yet it is so far away that if you were to ride after it, however fleet your mount, you would never arrive on its shore. It casts a light over all the world. Yet when it goes down over the horizon, it takes that light with it and all is dark again. It has a surface temperature of roughly six thousand degrees Kelvin, yet its corona gets as hot as two million degrees. If you stand in its glare too long, your skin will turn red. Or so it will be, according to the Oracle, anyway, and she never lies."

Mischling thanked the man and moved on.

"When the Sun rises, everything on this side of the sea will turn to stone," an ostler told her. "But those who reach the far side will not. This is why the Oracle has told us to make as many boats as can be built, that all might survive the change."

"How much time is there until the Sun appears?"

"Not long," the woman said. "The Oracle has told us to finish the boats we are working on but to begin no new ones, for there will be no time to complete them."

So it went. When Mischling was done gathering information, she shared it with the brothers, concluding, "Night, they say, shall no longer be eternal, but punctuated by something called 'day.' But what that will be like, no one can say."

"What sort of thing is a boat?" Bone-Grinder asked.

"It is like a pair of shoes that allow one to stand on water and it is like a steed which will carry one across that water. It has a large cloth called a sail which gathers the wind, a stick at the back which you point at whatever direction you wish not to go, and a wheel in between which turns the stick in the opposite direction it spins."

"We must journey to the far side of the water. The new world will need guidance," said Goat-Eater.

"Therefore we require a boat large enough to hold our true forms," said Bone-Grinder, "and because this new thing, this 'sea,' will not obey our will, these people must build it for us."

The silent one made a sharp gesture.

"Or else," Bone-Grinder translated.

"But there is not enough time for them to build it," Mischling objected.

"Then we will give them time," Goat-Eater said.

The brothers raised a steep hill on the landward side of Kiv. From its heights the city was a blaze of light against the ebony sea. A galaxy of lanterns bobbed in the harbor, where boats waited to depart with the tide.

Gray and grizzled, the silent one stretched out his arm over the city. His brothers did likewise. For a long time, they were motionless. Then a rumbling arose, as if of distant artillery. Louder it grew and more thunderous, until it filled the sky and shook the land underfoot. Veins stood out on their brows and sweat poured from their faces like rain. Lightning danced about their heads. Kiv and its surroundings shimmered and blurred.

Then all was still.

Mischling, who had been holding her breath, gasped for air.

"It is done," Goat-Eater said. The brothers lowered their arms. "Kiv has been moved a decade into the past. In all that time, it will not suffer any sudden or arbitrary changes. This is a wonder such as the world has never seen."

"We still need a truth-teller," Bone-Grinder said.

The silent one pointed at Mischling.

"She will do," agreed Bone-Grinder. Seizing Mischling by her shoulders, he transfixed her with his gaze. "Every word you say from this instant onward will be true. All who hear you will know them to be so." He released her. "Descend into the city. You will have ten years to do your work. We will return to Kiv for our boat just before its doom."

"But what do you expect me to do there?"

"You will know what to do," Goat-Eater said.

The silent one swatted her on her behind and she scampered downhill. When she looked back, the brothers were gone.

The city that Mischling entered was newer and quieter than before.

Its people labored without any particular sense of urgency. Walking randomly and without purpose, she found herself in the Center Square, surrounded by guildhalls and government buildings. To one end was a platform upon which a man stood, addressing a small crowd. She climbed a set of steps on its side and shoved him out of her way. Looking down on the people, she cried, "*Hwaet*!"

She began speaking. Of the world as it was and of the world that was coming. Of the Sun and the destruction its light would bring upon them all. Of the need to build boats and to create a colony on the far side of the sea. The words came to her freely and out of nowhere. As she spoke, the crowd grew—slowly at first, and then rapidly, until the square was filled and all the streets leading into it as well. Thousands of silent faces turned up to Mischling in wonder.

When she was done speaking, the jubilant crowd hoisted Mischling to their shoulders and, cheering, paraded her through the city as if she were an idol to be adored or an effigy on its way to a burning.

For ten years, Mischling reigned in Kiv. The art of governance was not difficult since she was invariably right and all knew it. Time passed, as if in a dream—a dream in which things changed only slowly and never abruptly or arbitrarily. Her people called her the Oracle and gave her their City Hall for a dwelling place. She, in turn, devoted all her energy to the boatbuilding enterprise, so as to save as many of them as possible.

Also, she set them to building a boat that would carry three giants.

Always, in the back of her mind, Mischling pondered the brothers. They had never, she realized, chosen to give themselves wisdom. Having power, they did not need it. She, however, commanded to understand whatever she needed to understand and needing to understand everything, was well on her way to being wise.

With wisdom came judgment—and in her judgment, the new world that was coming would be far better off if she could rid it of the brothers.

But how?

One night, the Oracle was wandering her city deep in thought when a notion popped into her head. The street ahead ended in a blank storehouse wall with an alley to either side. "When I turn the corner," she said aloud, "there will be a little girl standing there, holding five kittens." Then, so as to be sure, "Horned kittens."

She turned the corner and saw a little girl struggling to control an armload of kittens. One wriggled free and the Oracle caught it as it fell. She scratched it between its nubby horns and returned it to the overburdened child. ("Thank you," said the girl. "That one's my favorite.") Then, turning back, she chose a shop at random and said, "Someone who looks exactly like Pétur will come out of that chandlery now."

A slim young man hurried out of the chandlery and for an instant Mischling's heart stopped. She had not counted on the likeness affecting her so.

"Hai-hai, Oracle!" the man said cheerily, in a voice and manner not at all like Pétur's. And was gone.

When Mischling could think calmly again, she decided to give her newly discovered power another test. She attempted to say a deliberate lie: "I was never a mouse." But she could not. No matter how she tried, the words would not form in her mouth.

This too was interesting.

The brothers had given her more power than they intended. Yet, even so, their power remained much greater than hers, and they had experience using it. Also, there were three of them and only one of her. "They will not return to Kiv," she tried to say. "They have forgotten all about their boat."

The words would not let themselves be said.

That night, lying sleepless in a bed far too large for one lone woman, Mischling found herself weeping. "I will never use this power I have selfishly," she could not say. "I will not do the terrible thing that has entered my thoughts," was also unutterable. Nor could she say, "I am strong enough to resist temptation."

It was, however, the easiest thing in the world to say: "The next time I meet the young man who looks like Pétur, he will talk like Pétur and think like him as well." Then, since she had already gone too far, she added, "He will love me just as I love him."

That night, Mischling slept better than she had in years.

It was no coincidence that Mischling met New Pétur the next night, for immediately upon awakening, she had declared she would. But first she had to deal with a party from the Boatbuilders Guild who came to Oracle House to escort her to the yard where the Great Boat was nearing completion, so that she might inspect it.

The Great Boat was a simple klinker-built single-master, but huge beyond belief. The keel had been shaped from many large timbers doweled together, as had the strakes. The mast, similarly crafted, had to be hoisted by a crane special-built for that purpose. "It looks beautiful," the Oracle said. "Is it seaworthy?"

"I'd stake my life on it," said Katrin, the mistress of the Boatbuilders Guild. "But . . ."

"But?"

"But we can't make a sail large enough for it."

Pushing himself forward, Einar, who was the guild's ranking mathematician, said, "Over such a large area, the first strong wind would shred it." He presented the calculations and their meaning entered the Oracle's head painlessly. "A thicker cloth might hold, but there is neither the time nor knowledge to make it."

"Have you tried sewing leather skins together?"

"The seams would not hold." Einar showed her further calculations.

"In brief," Katrin said, "all our work has been for nothing."

"A way will be found to make the sail," the Oracle said. Upon which, the answer to the problem came to her. Briefly, she was stunned by the enormity of the solution. Then she smiled in a way she could see amazed the guild-folk, for never before had they seen malice on her face. “You will build a gibbet,” she said, “as tall as Oracle House and sturdy enough to hang a giant upon.”

“But how will we capture this giant?” Katrin asked.

“That will not be necessary. When the time comes, he will voluntarily sacrifice himself.”

So it was that, returning from the boatyard in a particularly good mood, Mischling took a sharp turn around a corner and slammed right into New Pétur. He apologized at length and, when he was done, Mischling stared silently up into his eyes. Then she took his hand and led him back to Oracle House.

Later, lying naked in a bed that no longer seemed too large for her, Mischling said, “Tell me about yourself.”

“Well . . .” the so very familiar stranger said.

Pétur was a carpenter—of houses, not boats, though he could build boats as well, if called upon, and was sure he would be drafted into the boatbuilding enterprise as time ran short. He had a name, naturally, but Mischling forgot it in an instant. He also had a wife and children.

“Do you love them?” Mischling asked, fearing the answer.

“Very much,” Pétur replied. “But not as much as I do you.”

“Tell me about your children.”

“Magnus is very young—he has just discovered how to catch one of his feet with his hands. It takes him a while to do it, but when he succeeds he looks so very pleased with himself that my heart sings. Helga is about so high, and already she is a very prim and proper little lady. If I am careless with my eating manners, she scolds me, shaking her finger at me like this!” Pétur laughed. “Oh, such children I have! I am the most fortunate father in all Kiv.”

Every word made Mischling feel worse about herself. “Go back home to your children,” she wanted to say, “and forget this ever happened.” But what came out of her mouth was, “Tell me about your wife. But don’t tell me her name.”

All the light went out of Pétur. “She is a good woman, who deserves a better man than me. I thought when I married her that I would be able to keep my vows. But the heart scorns such promises. It knows only what it wants and will settle for nothing less." He was silent for a breath. "Let us talk of more pleasant matters."

So they did.

Eventually, Pétur drowsed off. Lying sleepless beside him, Mischling stared up at the ceiling. "I will send him home in the morning," she couldn't say. Nor, "A week will satisfy me." Nor, "I will not ruin his life."

In the end, the best she could manage was, "I will make up my mind when the brothers return to Kiv. If I let Pétur go, he and his family will reach the far side of the sea safely. In time, memory of me will fade. Whether his wife will ever forgive him and whether he will ever make peace with himself for the pain we are causing her, I do not know. Whether I love him enough to ever set him free, I do not know.

"But for now, he is mine."

Pétur moved into Oracle House, bringing with him a single satchel of clothes and his chest of tools. During work hours, he rehung doors, rebuilt balconies, and replaced rotting floors, for no one needed new houses.

It took no time at all for word that the Oracle had taken a married man for a lover to reach every ear in Kiv. To evil effect. Citizens—not all, but enough—concluded that there being deceit behind her actions, her words, believe them though they must, hid evil intent. Some shirked their labor, others pursued private matters at public expense, yet others refused to work at all. The boatbuilding, calculated to a nicety so there would be enough for everyone, fell behind schedule. Not all would be saved when the Sun finally rose. Worse, some of the obstructionists would be saved, while many who toiled hard and honorably wouldn't.

Pétur, who was nobody's fool, begged Mischling to send him away. "I am the cause of all this discord!"

"I cannot," she cried.

"You must."

"So long as we both love each other, I refuse to let you go."

"I don't love you."

"You lie!"

And they both knew that to be true.

Pétur's wife came to Oracle House to confront her husband's new lover. She was tall and stern, with hair as black as the look in her eyes and the hard, rough hands of a woman who has worked all her life. Under other circumstances, Mischling could have liked her quite a lot.

"I have come to take back my husband," the woman said. "He is not the man I thought he was, but his children need him and he is still mine."

Mischling put her little fists on her hips and, looking up at this big, brawny woman, said, "You have no power here and you know it."

"Do you want me to beg? Then I will beg."

"No, I want you to go. You will leave now."

The woman turned away. She had no choice. Nevertheless, over her shoulder, she said, "I'll be back."

"If you come back, your firstborn will die," Mischling said. The woman was at the door. "Come back a second time and you'll be childless." She was shouting now and almost screaming, so as to be sure she was heard, "Come back a third time and Pétur will be a widower!"

Later, with Pétur asleep beside her, Mischling stared out the window at a large red moon—there was only one moon tonight—and said aloud, "I'm as bad as the brothers. Worse, for they were never weak and don't know how it feels. I should change my name to Man-Stealer, so all the city will know my shame."

But of course they already did.

At last, the brothers returned.

Rather than put off their size, they willed the buildings to shrink away to make room for their passage. The citizens of Kiv watched in awe and fear as Mischling came out onto a balcony that Pétur had built onto Oracle House for this express purpose. Standing eye to eye with the giants, she told them what must be done if they were to have a sail for their boat. Her words did not please them. Two shouted angrily and shook their fists at her. But the third, grim and silent, turned away and plodded to the enormous gibbet at the far end of the square.

A noose was produced, woven from many ropes of normal size, and the silent one placed it about his neck.

As a mark of honor, he was hung upside down.

It took him nine hours to die.

When the deed was done, the silent one's body was taken down and flayed. Then the skin, all in one piece, was brought to a tannery to be cured prior to being made into a sail. Goat-Eater and Bone-Grinder took their brother's flayed body to the waterfront and placed it in the hold of the Great Boat, so that when they reached the far side of the sea, it might be wrapped in the sail and returned to life. For it was only on such conditions that the silent one had agreed to the sacrifice in the first place.

While the tanning and sail-making were underway, Mischling stayed as far from the surviving brothers as she could. But when the sail had been fitted onto the Great Boat, Bone-Grinder and Goat-Eater returned to Oracle Square. Mischling went out onto the balcony again. She had a plan for eliminating each of them, and clever plans they were, too. But when she opened her mouth—

"*Silence, schemer!*"

Bone-Grinder snatched up Mischling, the balcony disintegrating beneath her, and held her before his squinting eye. She could not speak. Her truth-telling had been muted. "You have worked a mighty mischief here," he said, "against one who was greater than you can imagine. You forget who—and what!—you are. Therefore, your usefulness having come to an end, be again a mouse."

In one bewildering instant, all the world loomed up around Mischling. She was all but lost in the vastness of Bone-Grinder's hand.

Delicately, he set her down on the square before him. Then he raised high a foot to stamp her flat.

As that foot came crashing down, Mischling panicked and ran for the building-side. She skittered along the plinth for its partial protection. Those who had been her subjects a minute before were now giants themselves and dangers to her. Worse, she had long ago forgotten all her mouse skills. But there was an iron grate in the pavement ahead and, more by luck than intent, she fell between its bars. With a splash, she landed in stagnant water and filth. In an instant, she was back on her four feet.

She fled down the storm sewer, panting in fear

As she fled, Mischling said to herself, "I have killed one of them and, though I am small, I will find a way to destroy the other two." She doubted the words, spoken only in her mind, had any power, particularly in her diminished form. But saying them made her feel braver. The world had no need of the brothers. Let them all die because of a mouse! Let Pétur be the cause of their downfall.

She began to make new plans.

The sewer led down to the sea. Emerging into open air onto a spill of rounded stones just above the high tide line, Mischling struggled at first to get her bearings. But the mast of the Great Boat loomed higher than anything else in the city and there was a lantern hung from its tip. She made that her lodestar.

The waterfront was all noise, lights, movement. Teamsters and stevedores were everywhere, emptying wagons and loading boats, while streams of refugees flowed about them, carrying what they could onto countless small craft. This made it difficult for Mischling to avoid being seen. But they were coming up on what the Oracle had declared would be the last outbound tide, so those who noticed Mischling had better things to do than harass a mouse. In relatively short order, she made her way to the grand pier, where an enormous hawser moored the Great Boat. It had metal baffles to keep off rodents like herself—but she had never planned to get aboard that way.

Instead, Mischling searched among the boxes and barrels to be loaded onto the Great Boat and found a crate—to her, as large as a house—where one slat had buckled, leaking a trickle of grain. The grain had a heady aroma and, nibbling a little, she felt a fraction of the power she had lost—the merest smidgen—re-enter her. She squeezed between the slats, burrowing into the grain. Snug within, she wriggled around so she could look out over the waterfront and all that was happening there.

Boats were so thick on the harbor that an energetic man might cross from one side to the other by leaping from craft to craft. All who could were abandoning Kiv. Two piers over—lower and shorter and smaller piers, necessarily—Mischling saw three figures in silhouette. Two were female, tall and short, the larger one leading the smaller by her hand. The third was a man who clutched an infant to his breast. By the quickening of her heart, Mischling knew this to be New Pétur, with his family, hurrying to escape the doom about to fall on Kiv.

Mischling watched New Pétur, Magnus, Helga, and the woman whose name she had never known disappear over the edge of the pier onto a boat riding too low in the water to be seen. Hadn't she once said, back when she was the Oracle, that they would all safely reach the far side of the sea? She couldn't remember for sure. She hoped she had.

It hurt to lose her love a second time. But he was never the real Pétur anyway. Now that he was gone from her forever, she saw that she'd been a fool to behave as if he were.

Without warning, the crate Mischling was in was hurled into the sky and slammed down to the deck of the Great Boat. "That's the last of them," Bone-Grinder roared. "Let's go." He and Goat-Eater leapt onto the boat, one after the other, making it fling itself high and low, high and low.

There was a thumping of enormous boots as the boat was unmoored. "Let the sail be full of wind!" Goat-Eater commanded.

"Brother, take the wheel and put Kiv to our backs. We must be on the far side of the sea before the rising of the Sun."

Water began to rush past the hull.

"Let the city of Kiv burn behind us," Bone-Grinder rumbled, "so that we always know which direction to steer away from." In the wake of his words there came a roaring noise from landward, as of an all-consuming conflagration, and shortly thereafter the stench of burning buildings.

Their escape from oncoming doom had put the brothers in a good mood. "What should we do first when we reach the new land?" asked one. (Burrowing deeper into the grain, Mischling could not tell which muffled voice was which.) "Create bronze idols of ourselves to be worshipped? Change the mountains to rivers and the swamps to glaciers? Kill all the survivors of the old land and create new ones to replace them?"

"All these things we shall do," said the other, "just as soon as we have restored our brother to life. And much more as well."

The words made Mischling's blood run cold.

Nevertheless, she slipped out of her sanctuary crate. Mischling no longer had the Oracle's power to reshape the world, nor a woman's strength with which to sabotage the boat. But she had sharp little teeth.

Also, she knew the Great Boat's construction, from top to bottom.

The boat's wheel turned ropes that ran through pulleys below the deck to port and starboard, then back through a second set of pulleys to a spindle that made the rudder turn in the direction opposite the wheel's rotation. In this counterintuitive manner, the boat could be turned in the same direction as the wheel.

Mischling crept below, undetected.

Overhead, Goat-Eater and Bone-Grinder boasted, laughed, wrestled, and sang songs. They knew just enough to sail the boat. However, because they had never needed to understand how things work, they could never repair the tiller mechanism should it break. They would be left adrift at sea.

As would she. But that was a price Mischling was willing to pay for the sake of all who managed to escape the old country of perpetual night. Also, it might serve to atone, in part, for what she had done to New Pétur and his family.

The seas were calm and the course steady. Mischling climbed atop one of the ropes—it was many times thicker than she—that connected wheel and rudder. She anchored herself with all eighteen claws.

She began to gnaw.

The most heroic deeds are often drab and boring. Mischling attacked the rope with her teeth, to little effect. But she kept slashing, gnawing, and nibbling for hour after hour. Her jaws grew weary, then sore, and then numb. When she had made an inroad into the rope large enough for her to crawl into it, she stopped to examine her work. Whichever brother was at the wheel gave it a jerk and the rope *leaped*. Climbing back up, Mischling eyed the damaged rope carefully to see if it gave any sign of being ready to part.

It did not.

With an imagined sigh, she got back to work.

Up top, the brothers took turns at the wheel, with occasional breaks to gamble at dice or argue or piss over the side, during which the Great Boat went wherever it listed.

Meanwhile, Mischling kept gnawing away, like the Worm at the roots of the world-tree said by some to exist at the northernmost pole of the world. Time and again, it came on her that the task was hopeless. Over and over, she thought of reasons to quit. Still, she persisted. This is my punishment, she thought, for acting like one of the mighty. But if punishment it was, it was one she accepted, for she did not stop gnawing.

Then a single strand of rope fiber popped straight up from where she'd been chewing.

Mischling stopped, blinked. A second strand popped up.

The rope quivered like a violin string.

The brothers were banging about overhead, unaware of this new peril. Looking up through the hatchway for the first time since she had started severing the rope, Mischling saw that the sky was lighter than any she had ever known. The words *false dawn* popped into her head, and though she did not know their meaning, they gave her hope. She strained to make sense of the brothers' voices.

"It's coming! We must make speed or . . ."

"We're almost there. Look! There on the . . . it's rising up!"

"Not a . . . too soon. Our only chance . . ."

Mischling scurried to find a place directly under the brothers, where she could hear them with greatest clarity. This was made more difficult by the way their voices rose and fell and overlapped. But she thought she had found it when—

The rope broke.

Its two halves lashed back and forth like bullwhips, hissing in the air. Mischling cowered beneath them. She heard the brothers shout in anger and amazement. Goat-Eater tumbled down below like a rock-slide and, seeing the flying ropes, seized first one and then the other. Cursing, he tied the two of them together. But in doing so, he yanked out the pulleys they rode in. So when he lumbered back up, he found the wheel still slack and the boat unwilling to obey it.

Mischling, meanwhile, followed in Goat-Eater's shadow and found a hiding place within a stack of crates and sacks where, unobserved, she could watch her plan play out.

"Look!" cried Bone-Grinder, pointing one long, misshapen arm to the east. "It comes!"

A golden line of color touched the horizon, harbinger of the coming Sun. In that direction lay the mountains and forests and cities of the old country, doubtless already turned to stone. Before them, the dark cliffs of the new country loomed up. "We must reach land," cried Goat-Eater. "But the boat refuses to obey me."

"We are almost there," answered Bone-Grinder. "Grab the rope and leap overboard. We can pull the boat to shore."

There was a splash and then another. Mischling emerged from the shadows and climbed up on the rail. The land was so very close, only minutes away. There was no doubt in her mind that the brothers would reach it.

She wanted to cry.

But then, with a radiance that was like the fanfare of a thousand trumpets, the Sun breasted the horizon. Its light stretched out across the sea to touch the Great Boat and the brothers pulling it. The boat and then the brothers slowed, stilled, turned to stone. The black stone rope connecting the three broke into a hundred fragments and fell into the sea, there to begin the ages-long process of turning into sand.

To her surprise, Mischling did not turn to stone. In all the Great Boat, she was the only thing that didn't. Why this should be, she did not know, unless it was that she was too small and unimportant for such a grand transformation. She felt inside herself for her lost power and found that a small fragment of it lingered.

Summoning that power, Mischling changed herself back to a woman. She stripped out of her clothes. Then she slipped over the boat's stony side and swam toward shore. When she was on solid land, she would decide whether to be mouse or maid.

And then she would give herself a new name.

Three sea stacks stand just off the black sand beach Reynisfjara near the village of Vik on the southern coast of Iceland. Legend has it that they are two trolls and a boat they were hauling to shore, all turned to stone when they were caught by the rays of the rising sun. This is the first and only true account of what actually occurred. Let all who read these words be schooled thereby and live their lives accordingly.

THE YEAR OF THE THREE MONARCHS

Xingool the Sorcerer

On the Day of the Toad in the Month of the Fire Horse of the Year of the Three Monarchs, the necromancer-king Xingool prepared to conquer the world.

Dressed in robes whose warp was blackest ebon and whose weft was deepest scarlet so that they shimmered in the sight like infernal flames, Xingool stood on a balcony of his palace on the edge of the Floating City of Ilyssia and reviewed his forces on the plain below: the squadrons of dragons that would rain fire down upon cities stubborn enough to resist him, the lines of hellhounds held on short leashes by their demon trainers, the war chariots pulled by tireless bronze steeds, the battle mammoths with their steel-clad tusks, the numberless legions of human death-fodder arrayed in endless ranks. And he was pleased.

At his shoulder stood the only being in all the universe he unequivocally trusted: his bodyguard, Kangor the Swordsman. When Kangor had first wandered out of the barbarian wastes, Xingool had seen potential in the scrawny youth with a murderous cast to his face. He had fed and tamed the boy, as one might a starveling wolf, so that he had grown large and strong and loyal. For this Xingool had been rewarded many times over. Thrice, Kangor had saved his life.

In gratitude, Xingool had showered his bodyguard with wealth, influence, luxuries, and courtesans. The first three Kangor received with indifference. The last he more obviously enjoyed, but no more so than the cheapest bought-woman in the low taverns he liked to frequent when not on duty. There was, it seemed, nothing he desired other than to serve.

Thus it was that when Xingool leaned over the balustrade, luxuriating in the destructive force of his armies, he gave not a thought to the man who stood at his back, silently sliding a dagger from its sheath.

Kangor struck.

Xingool spun about, clutching his side, a look of baffled pain on his face. Before he crumpled to the marble floor of the balcony, he had just time enough to utter one single word: "Why?"

Smiling grimly, the barbarian reached down to take the Diamond Crown of Ilyssia from Xingool's brow and place it on his own. "Because you never had anything I really wanted before now," King Kangor told the dying sorcerer. "Gold, power . . . these mean nothing to me. But this army? This war? *Those* I want."

Kangor the Swordsman

It was good to be the king—any king. But it was particularly good to be the King of the Floating City of Ilyssia with the greatest army ever assembled at one's feet and under one's control. Kangor, formerly the Swordsman and now the King, smiled down upon all. It did not matter to him that he had gained his new position by treachery and the betrayal of the one man in all the world who had trusted him unquestioningly and, indeed, loved him as a brother. In one step he had gone from bodyguard to monarch. It had been a good day, and he had an Age of War before him, ready to be launched with a single word.

First, however, there were chores to be done.

"Sire?" his chamberlain said. "Your generals are gathered as you requested."

"Good."

Mighty of limb and sure of his strength, Kangor strode into the throne room and found it full of servitors. Which he welcomed, for he wanted many witnesses. To his generals he said, "Who here remains loyal to the old king?"

The generals eyed one another uneasily. Only General Abatraxas stepped forward.

Kangor tore off his robes, slamming them down upon the Phoenix Throne. More carefully, he placed the Diamond Crown atop them. Naked, he turned to his challenger. "Then wrestle me—and let the kingship go to the survivor."

Abatraxas was a powerful man and his skill in wrestling was legendary. Nevertheless, it took Kangor less than ten minutes to pin him and, twisting his head around, snap the man's neck.

Dressed once more, and seated upon the Phoenix Throne, the new king called in his scribes and dictated list after list of names: a captain who was to be promoted to fill General Abatraxas's position; nobles who were to be immediately put to the garrote as traitors; palace functionaries who were to be demoted, lifted up, or cast out, each according to his deserts; advisors who were to be blinded, reduced to penury, and put out on the streets to beg. For he had been planning his ascendancy for a long, long time.

When he was done, he turned to Mencius, the chief of his scribes, and asked, "Have I left anything out?"

"Just one, sire," the scribe replied. "Who is to be your bodyguard?"

King Kangor froze. Then, slowly, his eyes moved from person to person: from his resentful and over-powerful generals to the privileged and envious nobles, to the courtiers who served without qualm whoever happened to wear the Diamond Crown, to the slaves who had never tasted freedom and lusted for it almost as much as they did for revenge. None had reason to love him. Their eyes all glittered with ambition.

"Sire?" Mencius said again. "Your bodyguard?"

But to this question Kangor had no answer.

Slythe the Thief

As an offering to the goddess of thieves, whose name no man knows, Slythe carefully cut off the long fire-red tresses that were her crowning pride and placed them atop the cattle-dung fire lit to that dread lady's honor. A lesser thief would have held that it was by her own skill that she had acquired the griffon's egg stolen from a cliff-side nest high in the Riphaen Mountains, and the cloak of stealth pilfered from a castle guarded by a thousand fanatic warriors in the Lands of Fire, and the ouroborean ring acquired by means so arduous that even she shuddered at the memory. But Slythe knew that the gods loved to punish hubris and so she was modest, even as she planned her great heist: first of the Floating City of Ilyssia and then of the world.

Mounting her griffon, Slythe traveled faster than fast to the Floating City, ruled by the paranoid king, Kangor. Abandoning her mount and wrapping about herself the cloak which had once belonged to the North Wind, she slipped through its streets like a breeze and up the empty stairways of the Marble Castle. There, she he found King Kangor standing on a balcony, staring bleakly off into the distance. Throwing aside her cloak (for with it on she was insubstantial and unable to interact with the physical world), she drew a knife across his throat.

Kangor wheeled about, blood gushing between the fingers that clutched at his neck. His eyes were mad and staring under the glittering Diamond Crown but not one whit surprised. In that instant it seemed to Slythe that she was doing the king a favor by thus ridding him of his famously unending fear. He could not speak but the question was obvious in his agonized expression: *Who . . . ?*

Slythe knew better than to bandy words at such a moment. She put a hand on Kangor's chest and shoved.

Over the parapet he went, and down to the ocean.

When the castle guards burst upon her, Slythe triumphantly exclaimed, "The tyrant is dead and I have killed him. I am now your ruler."

But, "Our loyalty is not to the man but the office," the captain of the guards said. "You do not wear the Diamond Crown of Ilyssia. Therefore you must die." And all rushed toward her, spears extended.

Slythe, however, had a trick worth three of theirs. She slipped the ouroborean ring upon her hand and rubbed it, wishing herself exactly five years earlier, when the barbarian Kangor had killed his liege, the necromancer-king Xingool. She would appear behind the barbarian's back and, her dagger already damp with his blood, wait for him to seize the crown from his predecessor and then snatch it from him while simultaneously driving the dagger home.

The plan was foolproof.

Back in time she went.

Only to discover that three years earlier the Floating City had not rested above the Sea of Tethys but over the distant, dusty plains of Angeddron. So, there being no floor underfoot nor castle anywhere in sight, she found herself a hundred feet in the air and falling, falling, falling, toward the cold waters of oblivion.

Far away, Kangor was lifting the Diamond Crown to his head. Even further away, Slythe's younger self was scaling a cliff in the Riphaen Mountains. Farthest of all, the goddess of thieves cocked an ear as Slythe called out a name that only a few women knew.

So it was that, deep beneath Tethys's waters, Slythe the Thief saw the corpse of Kangor afloat beside her. Her panicked hands seized the Diamond Crown from his head and planted it firmly on her own. For Slythe had only had time for the briefest of prayers as she fell, and now it had been answered.

She died a queen.

GHOST SHIPS

Driving from Philadelphia to Williamsburg that morning, casting about in my mind for memories of Rabbit's exploits to share at his memorial, I found myself thinking of the time that Sam the Townie saw the ghost ships.

The three townies, Sam and Donny and Brick Rhodes, were a very minor part of my college years, local high school students who were funny and bright and eager when they first started hanging with the freaks and far less so two years later, when I graduated. Brick owned a secondhand hearse and the three were often seen in it, off to nowhere in particular in search of adventure. That was a long time ago, in the early seventies.

This will not be your standard ghost story. For one thing, every word of it, the names excepted, is true. For another, the ghosts put in a single appearance and never returned. Also, it happened in broad daylight. Then too, I was not a party to the sighting. Make of that what you will.

The townies were driving through the marshes of Guinea, a very old part of the Virginia Tidewater, for reasons I never learned and probably for none at all. In the eighteenth century, British convict ships would put in at the Chesapeake Colonies, of which Virginia was part, and auction off criminals and debtors as indentured servants. Local lore had it that the very worst of these were rowed halfway to land at Guinea and thrown into the water to swim ashore or drown. Supposedly, that was why its inhabitants, their descendants, were so distrustful of outsiders. Today that sounds suspect, but we all believed it then.

Most likely, the townies were speeding.

The road was lightly traveled and its path was dictated by the frequency of streams and inlets. It would hug the coast briefly, suddenly veer inland, and then, after a bit, return. On one of those returns the townies came within sight of the ocean. Seagulls overhead, salt spray in the air. Two square-rigged wooden ships lay anchored offshore. Closer in, sailors wearing eighteenth-century garb were rowing a longboat toward the beach. Rough-looking men stood in the stern, hands tied behind their backs.

"They're making a movie!" Sam the Townie crowed, and the road curved again, hiding the ocean behind a line of scrub trees. He hammered on the dashboard with his fists. "Go back, go back, go back, go back! We've got to see."

Brick slammed on the brakes, made an awkward U-turn in the road, and drove back to where they had seen the ships.

The sea was empty.

The townies could hear the surf and see the ocean all the way to the horizon. But there were neither ships nor a longboat on the water. No film crew on the beach.

Thinking this might be some trick of local topography, the townies got out of the hearse and hurried across the road. They all had seen the ships. This was where they had seen them. The ships had been out of sight for only a minute or two. Even if they had been fitted with motors, there was no way they could have moved beyond sight in so little time.

But they were gone.

There were so many stories I could tell about Rabbit but not all of them were true. He was a born storyteller—so good I never knew which of his tales were inventions. But he wasn't all imagination and no action. One time he bought a rubber BULLSHIT stamp and the next morning the college awoke to find every poster and piece of paper on every kiosk on campus so judged. It was he who, more out of mischief than malice, painted KILL PIGS in big block letters on the roof of Old Dominion Dormitory that memorable evening when I returned from the deli to find my dorm surrounded by flashing police cars and angry cops.

Neither of those stories would do. Ultimately, I settled on the time, late one night, when Rabbit and I, tripping our balls off on LSD, wandered past the television room and saw somebody lying facedown on the rug. There was an empty bottle of Boone's Farm lying near his hand. "Is that guy in trouble?" Rabbit wondered.

"I think he's just sleeping," I said, but Rabbit went into the room anyway. In my defense, analytical thought is a little difficult when you've got 300 mics of Orange Sunshine frolicking among your neurons. "Um . . . Maybe we should just go on."

Without a word, Rabbit stooped alongside the young man and flipped him over. Sam the Townie gasped spasmodically as his face lifted from a pool of vomit. He must have just passed out. A minute or two later, he would have been dead.

Rabbit and I helped Sam the Townie up and onto a couch. He was still unconscious. I got out my handkerchief and cleaned Sam's face as best I could. Then I dropped it atop the vomit on the rug for the janitor to deal with in the morning. I felt bad about that, but I wasn't going to put the thing back in my pocket. We left Sam the Townie lying on his back, snoring.

There was a particular irony to this incident because in our freshman year, I may have saved Rabbit's life in the television room of our old dorm. Not in the casually heroic manner he had saved Sam the Townie, however, but completely by accident.

The television room was empty at the time. Understandably so, because a few days before, some freshman jocks, returning from a drunken pledge week event at the animal house, had ripped the television off the wall and smashed it. All that remained of it now were two prongs jutting from the electrical outlet. Rabbit, who had an interest in electrical wiring—years later, he would do the lights and sound for Sidewalk Trout—was explaining how the surge caused when the TV was torn free had fried that particular circuit. "Watch," he said, "I'll put a quarter across the two prongs and nothing will happen." He searched his pockets. "Damn! I don't have a quarter. Do you?"

I did. But I hadn't known Rabbit very long and already I was aware that he was a bit of a trickster. I didn't have enough money back then to risk a penny of it so I slapped the sides of my jeans and said, "No."

"Hey, wait." Rabbit pulled a screwdriver from his hip pocket. It had a long shank and a clear plastic handle. He was the kind of guy who would be carrying such a thing. He laid it across the prongs.

There was a bright flash and all the lights went out. When Rabbit picked the screwdriver up off the floor, there were two dark spot-welded marks on the shank where it had touched the prongs.

So I almost let a kid die because I was tripping and I may have saved a friend's life because I was distrustful. I didn't tell anybody at college this story because I wasn't very proud of the part I had played in it.

I should have gone straight to the hotel at the edge of town where my friends had arranged for conference space and a slide projector, and splurged on a room so I could take a nap. It was a mistake to arrive early, to sign the register for the reunion weekend, to pin on the button identifying my year, and to wander about campus remembering how alienated and out of place I had felt there. Alums who looked like every dentist I'd ever had were tailgating in front of the stadium. The dorms were all locked and you needed a swipe card to get in now. So I couldn't go to OD's common room and pick out the spot where

Crazy Zack had seen God and drawn a cartoon tapeworm on a pillar to commemorate the event. Nor could I get into the biology building where we'd go at midnight to look at the rattlesnakes and then sit atop the elevator watching the walls of the shaft glide up and down, or the theater where Abigail and Susan would moan though the air vents at night in hope of starting a rumor that Phi Beta Kappa Hall was haunted, or the radio station where I and a troupe of merry pranksters had once gone into the production studio and hijacked the show out from under Thoroughly Modern Maxie while he was being interviewed for a post-graduation deejay job at the local AM station, or (of course) Chandler, the girls' dorm I had once been smuggled into so I could paint a wall-filling dragon bursting out of a mountain of flowers in my friend Aspen's room.

I never really belonged at William and Mary. But the teachers were good and, my parents being Virginia taxpayers, it was the best college I could afford.

Nor did I entirely belong in my circle of friends. I was a New Englander at heart and, even among the freaks, Southern culture was foreign to me. Nevertheless, I was glad to see the gang, those I still remembered. I chatted with several, the way one does to people you no longer have much in common with. "Everyone asks me how I can stand to live in such an isolated little town off in the mountains," Charlie said. We'd been roommates with Crazy Zack on consecutive years and had that misery in common. "I tell them that it's quiet. Very quiet. Nothing ever happens there. I value that."

Bit by bit, I got caught up. For all their druggish ways, my friends had come through the decades well—except for James, who was already a raging alcoholic by his senior year and hadn't gotten better since. We hadn't inherited the Earth, the way we'd thought our generation would back when. But neither had we been entirely reabsorbed into what we had been in revolt against. That's a victory of sorts. So this is not a story about a man who has lost his way and returns to confront his past and admit to his failings. As I said before, it's a ghost story.

Linda, who'd organized our reunion—or Counterreunion as we used to joke we'd have, back in the day when there was a thing called the Counterculture which we all took far too seriously—started things off with a slideshow. Photos from the old days: Young men with scrawny beards in cutoffs in front of the swimming hole at Lake Matoaka. Confident, long-haired women posed with their fists against their hips. Two strangers sitting on a bed back at the Farm with a Confederate flag hanging on the wall. A couple I'd never thought would still be together forty years later, beside a rusting Chevrolet, being solemn and young. "Nice car!" somebody said and we all laughed.

Then the memorial part of the evening began. Picture upon picture of Rabbit, of course. A few loving words from his brother Greg. One by one, we stood up and told stories.

Groff, who was the last remaining founding member of Sidewalk Trout, talked about the early days when Rabbit drove the band in a converted school bus with no brakes, downshifting when they came to a red light, then slamming the door open, grabbing a cinder block with a loop of rope through it, and chocking it under a tire to make the bus come to a complete stop. "One time, we're pulling into a motel and Rabbit downshifts and downshifts, slams the door open, hops out, shoves the cinder block in front of the wheel, and *poof!* it disintegrates into dust. The bus slams into the side of the office and Rabbit goes inside and says, 'One room, please.'"

More laughter. I'd heard the story before and was glad to learn it was true. Then Groff said, "But Rabbit was the smartest man I ever met. We needed a lighting technician so he went to the library and got out a book on the subject *this thick*." He held out thumb and forefinger. "It was extremely technical stuff. But he had it read and memorized the next day. One day!"

When Groff sat down, I stood and told my story. I didn't use Sam the Townie's name—just said "some kid." My intention was to end by saying that Rabbit never spoke of what he'd done. But apparently he had, because several of my friends nodded. "That was Sam the Townie," said one.

"Sam the Townie, yeah."

"He died in 1986."

When Sidewalk Trout began setting up their amps, I made a few quiet goodbyes and slipped away. I had a long drive ahead of me. Also, I was never a big fan of Southern rock. On the way out, I saw Charlie again and on impulse clapped a hand on his shoulder. "Charles," I said, "I'm glad you're doing well." He hadn't been, the last time I'd seen him, but that's another story and one I don't feel free to share.

Smiles. Clasped hands. That lonely sensation you get when you turn your back and know that nobody's looking after you.

Then I was on the road. All that long drive home, I thought about the ghost ships that Sam the Townie had seen. I had no idea what had become of the other two townies and, let's be honest, didn't much care. They were spear-carriers in the opera of my youth. It was possible I was the last person in the world who remembered the ships—and, as I said, only second hand. Had those really been ghosts? What else could they possibly have been?

Sam the Townie might have lied to me, of course. I do not believe he did. Rabbit once said to me, "The townies are nice kids, man, but way too innocent for this world. I don't think they could tell a lie if their lives depended on it. You have to worry what's going to become of them."

Now Sam the Townie was dead. I hadn't given him a thought in decades. But knowing he'd been gone for so very long hit me hard. Rabbit had saved his life. An accomplishment like that should endure.

The windshield wipers were going so it must have been raining. It came to me then that everything was provisional. Or perhaps the better word was temporary. All the heroic actions of the past are destined to be unmade, the small memories carefully preserved must inevitably come to be forgotten, and everything we are and do and care about will in time be undone. You can save someone's life, but it's not permanent.

We are, all of us, involuntary passengers on fragile ships, visible from the shore for the briefest of moments and then forever gone. No one can say why. Perhaps we were sent here as punishment. Perhaps we were never here in the first place.

Soon enough, there will be no witnesses to prove otherwise.

THE WHITE LEOPARD

He found it in five cardboard boxes in the basement at a suburban estate sale. Ray went to estate sales almost every weekend. It got him away from his wife. Weekdays he spent fixing things in his garage workshop.

Doris didn't like estate sales, consignment shops, or secondhand anything. "I don't buy used crap!" she often said. "I want to be able to return something if I get tired of it." Yet she clung to Ray mercilessly, only God knew why.

Four of the cartons were marked twenty dollars each. The fifth, which had gotten separated from the others and which he had scoured the basement to find, was ten. He would have paid all he had for them. But because it was Sunday afternoon and the sale was almost over, they knocked half off the price without even being asked. It was clear the sellers had no idea what it was.

What it was, was an RQ-6G Leopard.

The 6G was, in Ray's opinion, the finest patrol and reconnaissance ground drone ever made. He had qualified on it during Operation Bolivian Freedom, back when he was young. He had hunted down insurgents with one, working from a combat recliner in a secure base across the border in Argentina. He'd known what it felt like to be the most dangerous thing in the jungle at night. He had never experienced anything like that before.

He wanted to feel something like that again.

When he laid out the rig in his workshop, Ray's heart sank. The fiber-optic skin was all rags and tatters, unsalvageable, and the VR controls were bricked. Half the glass batteries were cracked and would have to be replaced. But on closer examination, the core of the machine was in good condition. When he hooked it up to household current and went in with an old set of gamer gear, he could feel the synthetic muscles as if they were his own. Feedback from the sensorium was nice and clean.

There was nothing wrong with the machine that he couldn't fix.

Six months flew by.

Subsection by subsystem, Ray took apart and reassembled the rig, cleaning and scraping and oiling, sometimes sanding and occasionally replacing. He upgraded and debugged the software. The skin he unstitched and patched together to make a pattern which he then sent to a man he found on CraftE. A month later, a tough matte-black covering, perfectly made, came back, along with a note reading: *You've got a 6G, huh? Lucky bastard. Tom Ubberly, S. Sgt., Drone-Ops (ret).*

With that, the repair phase of the project was done.

Ray waited five days before taking it out. He wanted a cloudless night. He wanted a full moon. When, at last, both presented themselves in tandem, he opened the garage doors and unleashed the beast.

The Leopard rose to its feet, looked around, and with an impatient shake of its head, dismissed the garage as beneath its notice. Silent as a thought, it padded out onto the driveway.

The house was at the end of a cul-de-sac and backed against state game land. This had been a significant factor when he and Doris had bought into the development, long ago when they were young and presumably in love.

He raised the Leopard's head to taste the wind. It was rich with saps and pollens, the green stench of marsh water filled with duckweed, frogs, and algae, a musky trace of fox, the sweet bird-droppings smell of baby birds. Turning on his ears revealed the ultrasonic chitter of bats, an opossum hissing in anger, a fish crow speaking to no one in particular. A train whistle from half a county away, inaudible to his human senses, was a long, slow moan calling Ray to adventure. The crickets were out in force.

He had closed his eyes. Now he opened them and saw a sky thronged with stars and, swarming among them, countless manmade orbital artifacts. There was a big orange pumpkin of a moon low over the horizon and, with a sudden bound, he sent it leaping and bouncing in the sky. The house and everything it represented disappeared behind him. The forest enfolded him in its dark embrace.

When he was sufficiently deep into the woods, he slowed to a walk. At that speed, the Leopard was virtually noiseless. Sorting through the scents and sounds of the night, Ray found a raccoon washing its food in a little stream that chuckled and laughed its way downhill. He wondered how close he could get before it realized he was there. He decided to find out.

Moving slower the closer he got, Ray was not more than ten feet distant when something alerted the raccoon to his presence. It twisted around to face him while simultaneously trying to leap away, and fell noisily into the stream. Then it was up and running as fast as it could go.

Ray followed, keeping an even distance between him and it. The raccoon twisted and turned as it ran, but it could not throw him off. Until finally it scrabbled up the side of a huge oak at the center of a grove of old-growth trees.

He waited until the raccoon had gone to earth in its den, a hollow halfway up the oak. Then he climbed the tree after it. Looking in through the opening, he saw the raccoon, eyes huge, shivering with fear. Ray extended one claw and touched its nose.

Tag. You're it.

Then he was gone from the tree and the raccoon's life forever.

Night after night, Ray explored the forest, interested in everything and caring about nothing but pure sensation. Briefly, he was young again, lithe and spry, his senses not yet dulled by age and routine. Filled with the zest for life that his life had long ago taken out of him. Then, not long into one nocturnal jaunt—

Ping.

A defensive subsystem came on and softly alerted Ray that there was something out there! Something military. His rig's eidetics threw up a menu of possibilities. All decades old, of course. But the emissions signature for one matched perfectly.

It was another Leopard.

For an instant, it seemed an impossible coincidence. Then Ray had to laugh at himself. Where else would you take a Leopard but into the forest? When else but at night? This particular game land was the largest such tract in this half of the state. So . . . no coincidence. If there were two RQ-6Gs within fifty miles of each other, it was inevitable that their paths would cross.

He booted up the communications board and, because the night was too quiet to mar with speech, chose text: *Unknown Leopard, this is BlackMomser. Please identify yourself.*

Without thinking, he had ID'd himself with his war tag, from back in the day.

BlackMomser, this is HelenCat.

Ray blinked. A woman? He air-typed, *A woman?*

You didn't think a woman could make the Corps? Trust me, civvie, anything you can do, I can outdo.

Ray had once been as good as they got. *Don't know about that, ma'am. I was top drone in my day.*

Then find me, she replied. Her electronic signature disappeared from his screen.

She'd gone stealth. But nothing as big as a Leopard could be hidden from someone who knew how to look. Ray began by closing down all his senses but smell and giving it all his attention. Traces of human activity permeated the forest, of course. Exhaust washed up from the distant interstate. Discarded trash—plastic bags, lead shot, aluminum cans reeking of stale beer—was everywhere, usually smothered in dead leaves. But none of the machine-smells so familiar from his months in the workshop.

She was downwind, then.

Downwind here meant upslope. Ray shifted all his attention in that direction. He thought he could just make out the low mosquito whine of an internal servo ever so slightly out of balance. You could adjust those things every day of their existence and they still kept going off-spec.

Upward he went, scanning the ground for evidence of the Leopard's passage.

At the top of the ridge, he turned downward. A trickle of water seeped from the rocks and became a stream. He bounded back and forth across it and, slipping under a tangle of fallen branches, saw a paw-print in the mud. Just as he'd expected. Drone operators liked to follow streams. They were more challenging than just slipping between the trees.

At the bottom of the mountain, the stream fed into a marsh. There, the Leopard was easier to follow. Nothing could cross all that mud and vegetation without leaving a trace. On the far side, the land went up again and so did Ray, sure he was on the right track. Then the top of the ridge rose before him and there the Leopard was.

She was waiting for him, crouched on a rocky outcrop, with her back arched and that tremendous moon directly behind her head. She had turned her fiber-optic fur—her cladding, unlike his, was original and in pristine condition—on full, so that she glowed pearl-white.

God, but she was beautiful!

Ray had his Leopard on stealth mode, like hers, and he was sure he made no noise on the approach. But she turned anyway. Their eyes met. Then her Leopard's skin went dark and she was gone and away again.

They played for most of the night. Sometimes he chased her and sometimes she him. When they tired of that, she led him to a stream where she dipped a paw into the water and flipped out a rainbow trout. Nodding his admiration, he nudged it back into the water. Then he led her to the marsh where bats were swooping low to feed on flying insects. He leaped high in the air and snapped, capturing a bat in his mouth. Turning, he crouched before the white Leopard and opened his mouth to let the bat flutter away. Helen applauded.

Then the sky was lightening in the east and it was time to go.

Will I see you again? Ray texted her. *When?*

Yes. Tomorrow.

They met every night for a week. Sometimes they played, sometimes they hunted rabbits together, and sometimes they talked. Her name was Helen and, as he'd expected, HelenCat had been her war tag. "HellCat was already taken," she explained. They'd graduated to communicating by audio. They had become comfortable enough with each other to get personal.

"Nothing ever worked out for me," Ray said. "Military service was the high point." He had spent the rest of his life making money—decent money, admittedly, but not enough to make Doris content. No children—that had been a point of contention. A job that gave him no particular satisfaction—that was another. A retirement that felt pointless to both of them.

"Everything worked out for me. Life, love, family, money. Wonderful kids. A great husband. We traveled a lot. I had everything I ever wanted. But then Moses died and what remained meant nothing to me. The children had their own lives and mine was . . . empty. I had plenty of money and nothing better to spend it on, so I bought the rig on the gray market. Then I met you and here we are."

Ray's Leopard's head nodded involuntarily. But he said nothing. He appreciated that she had not apologized for her success in life. She knew a fellow drone pilot would not resent that. They'd been dog-brothers in the war together, though their tours of duty hadn't overlapped. They understood each other.

"We should meet," Ray said, after a bit. In real space, he meant, not virtual.

They settled on Saturday night at an Olive Garden. It seemed like safe, neutral territory. They traded cell numbers in case the place was crowded, but they spotted each other at almost the same instant. Ray knew it was Helen even though she was older than he'd imagined her and leaned heavily on a semirobotic walker-cane, because she was the only one looking anxiously about in search of somebody she'd never met. Also by the dismay on her face when she saw the dismay on his. For an instant, he saw himself as she saw him: old, pot-bellied, balding, with a face etched by failure. And she? Not svelte. Not young. Not raven-haired or blond or russet. Gray. Aged. Spent.

Panic and embarrassment overcame them both. Turning backs on each other, they fled to opposite corners of the parking lot to uber their Rydes.

When Ray got home, less than an hour after he'd left, Doris was sitting on the couch in the flannel nightgown he hated, the one with the tiny pink flowers. She had a glass of scotch by her side and, though it was only 8:30, she was already half plastered. She didn't bother turning off the game show she was watching. She just smirked. "She was *old*, wasn't she? Old like you."

Ray didn't ask how she knew why he'd gone out. Doris had spent her working years in tech. There were any number of ways to hack into a system whose defenses were decades out of date. She would know them all. "Leave me alone, Doris. I'm not in the mood."

"You never are. You hardly ever were. Listen to me for once. I'm not the bad guy here. I know you blame me for what you've become. You've never thought of what you made of me. Look at me! Okay, I'm a mess. But this is your doing. Your fault. And you hoped to start all over again with a new woman? I'm glad for her sake that she got away."

Ray looked at Doris then, really looked at her, for the first time in years. This dry, withered, bitter woman had a point. He really had ruined her life. She was right in everything she said.

But he didn't care. He'd do it all over to her again and worse, if he had the opportunity.

Horrified at this insight, Ray plunged down the stairs to his workshop. He strapped into his VR set and sent his Leopard bounding into the forest.

Helen was waiting for him there, perched on a low limb of a sycamore tree. *That's not who I am,* she messaged. Meaning the woman he had seen at the Olive Garden.

I know. I'm the same way. Inside.

There was a long, awkward pause. *Do you want to hunt?*

Yes!

That night, for the first time, they hunted down a deer and killed it. Together.

So went the summer. Sometimes they hunted. Other times they explored or wandered or simply talked. It depended on their mood. Once, they ran up on trees overhanging a railroad line, jumped down on a passing freight train, and rode it halfway across the state before jumping a train back.

Then came autumn.

On the first cold, blustery day of the season, Ray had barely gotten into the forest when he received a text. *Come home. Urgent.* It was not from Helen. There was only one other person who could possibly have sent it.

Ray powered down the Leopard in the garage and went up the stairs to find Doris waiting for him. She was sitting on the couch, as she did every night, wearing that same damned flannel nightgown. She snapped off the television when he entered the room. There was a triumphant gleam in her eye.

"All right," Ray said. "What is it?"

"All this crap you've been doing is against the law. I did research. You don't have a license for that thing and it's illegal for a civilian to own one anyway. You're in violation of the game laws, too. Just taking a proscribed military weapon into state game lands is illegal—not to mention killing things with it without regard as to whether they're in season or not. You are so very busted, mister. I've got the goods on you and come morning, if I feel like it, I can turn you in for possession of terrorist weaponry. I can send your sorry ass to jail."

This, Ray realized miserably, *this* was why she had hung onto him for so many years of quiet mutual desperation. So she could utterly and completely destroy him. All this time she had just been waiting for her opportunity.

Now, he had finally given it to her.

Doris hadn't said she was going to dime him out, however—only that she could. Which meant that wasn't her goal. It was only a threat, a goad, something to make him play along with her.

"You've got my attention. What is it you want?"

"I want you to kill her with your own two hands."

It took his breath away. "Kill Helen?"

"Is that the name of Granny Girlfriend? Nobody cares about her. I want you to take that metal pussycat of yours into the back yard, pack her full of fireworks and rockets, pour about five gallons of gasoline over it, and set it on fire. When it goes up, I want it to look like the Fourth of July."

At first, Ray didn't get it. Then he understood: Doris wanted to be sure the neighbors came running. All of them. The fire department too. She wanted as many people as possible to see his humiliation. If he wept—as, to be honest, he well might—then so much the better.

He understood this because he'd had fantasies of his own over the years. He knew what he'd like to do to her and it was every bit as vicious. My God, he thought. How is it possible for two people to hate each other so much?

"All right. It'll take a day or two to get the fireworks. But I imagine you want to do this on the weekend anyway."

Ray still had Helen's number. When Doris finally went to bed, he called her. She sounded sleepy when she answered, then wide awake when she recognized his voice. He brought her up to speed. "Back then . . ." he said. "Back then, did you ever do two-on-one work?"

Sometimes it had been necessary to make someone—a community organizer, usually, a priest, or a mayor—disappear. A pair of Leopards would be sent to the target's village to kill him or her, then carry the body out into the jungle and bury it deep, where it would never be found.

"We all did," Helen said. There was a long silence. Then, "I'll help you. On one condition."

"What's that?"

"I want to be there in person when it happens."

The next evening, Ray waited, as patient as Satan. Finally, he heard Doris outside, dumping garbage and recycling into their bins as she always did at this hour. He hurried to the back door and locked it. She was in her nightgown, so he knew she didn't have her keys or cell phone with her. Quickly now. He made sure the front door was locked too. The garage would only open by remote. She was locked out.

Ray donned his VR rig and powered up his Leopard. Helen was not far away, waiting. He texted her: *It's on.*

Helen had parked her pickup truck just a little up the road. He heard her start the engine and then quietly pull up to the curb out front, where she could watch.

Doris was still fussing with the trash bins when the white Leopard came slinking around the corner of the house. It glowed pale and deadly in the moonlight. Behind it, Helen leaned out of the cab window, grinning. She had the goggles of her VR set pushed up on her forehead so she could watch the initial confrontation with her own two eyes.

Ray brought up his machine behind Doris and revved the internal motors. It made a noise like a snarl. He waited for her to turn and then flinch away in fear. He listened for her short, sharp cry of dismay.

The two Leopards were so deployed that there was only one way for Doris to run—into the woods. He and Helen would have their fun then. They would make it last all night.

But instead, Doris said, "I didn't think you were serious about the fireworks."

With an almost inaudible whine of servos powering off, the black Leopard sat down, placing itself in standby mode.

"What the hell?" This was the worst possible time for a malfunction. Hank struggled with the controls, trying to jolt his Leopard back to life. "Helen," he said, "I've got a problem. Keep Doris pinned while I get this thing up and running again."

"I can't!" There was a panicky tremble in Helen's voice. "I'm locked out. The Leopard won't respond to my commands."

Visual, meanwhile, was good. His Leopard's camera eyes were focused on Doris. There was an alertness to her that he hadn't seen in ages. She was sober. This late in the evening, Ray hadn't thought that was possible for her.

Doris had her phone in her hand. She touched the screen and said, "The kitchen door is open now."

Ray remembered that, a lifetime ago, the brass had a suite of override commands that, it went without saying, they'd never had to use on him. And of *course* Doris had been able to hack into them, even if it had taken her all summer. That had been her profession, after all—computer security. "Helen, any luck with your system?"

"None!"

The white Leopard prowled past Doris with lethal grace. Out of the corner of his own Leopard's eye, Ray saw it push into the kitchen. He could hear it moving overhead.

"You're about to wander into the woods like the senile old coot that you are. Your body will never be found," Doris said.

"I'm calling the police!" Helen wailed. "I'm calling them! Right now!"

"You do that, dear. Give them a nice, hysterical recording to play at your trial. They'll come here and find your illegal little war machine crouched over Ray's mangled body and a set of perfectly functional VR gear hanging around your neck. I'll be in the living room, watching the TV in a drunken stupor, like I do every other night." She paused. "Or you can drive yourself home, knowing that when I'm done with it, I'll send your pussy back to you and there'll be nothing at all to connect you to what happens here tonight. Either way, it's your choice."

There was an extended silence. Don't, Ray thought. The guilt will break you—you'll never be able to look yourself in the mirror again.

Helen started up the pickup and drove away.

By then, the white Leopard was coming down the stairs.

Even as Ray tried to rise to his feet, knowing he had nothing to fight with but his flabby, aged body, he couldn't help admiring the cocksure, triumphant smile that suddenly blossomed on his wife's face.

There was the strong, willful woman he had fallen in love with all those many long years ago.

DRAGON SLAYER

Every road and open doorway is a constant danger to a man of wandering disposition. Olav had stood on the threshold of his cottage one spring morning and the road had looked so fine that he couldn't resist setting foot on it, and the next thing he knew it had carried him to the sea. There he chanced upon a merchant ship in need of a new hand. He learned the sailoring trade, fought pirates, killed a kraken, grew a beard, pierced an ear, and one memorable night won a handful of rubies at a single turn of the cards and lost them all to a barmaid who doped his ale. Two years later, he was shipwrecked off Thule and briefly married to a witch-woman who had blackwork tattoos on her face and had filed her teeth to points.

The marriage did not last, however. One day, Olav returned from the hunt with a red hart slung over his shoulders and found his wife coupling with a demon she had summoned up from one of the seven hells that lie at the center of the world. He slew them both, threw the fire pot onto the thatched roof of the witch's hut, and left his memories burning to his back.

So it was that, having nothing better to do, Olav set out on foot to see what lay to the south. Always there was something interesting just a little farther down the road. Always there was good reason not to stay.

To the south it was summer. It seemed to be always summer there. Like water, he flowed downhill, taking up whatever work came to hand, staying with it long enough to fill his pockets, and then proceeding onward, ever onward. He chopped wood, built walls, twisted cord into rope, and rode as a guard in a small caravan traveling across the desert which one night was attacked by brigands who set about killing everyone, women and slaves included. He accounted for five of their number before realizing there was nobody left to defend save for one brown-skinned merchant's son and so scooped him up, sat him on the horse behind himself, and escaped.

Olav came away from that adventure with an excellent horse, a serviceable bedroll, a saddle that had seen better days, and the merchant boy for a servant.

The caravan trail led at last to a standing stone atop a high barren ridge, at the foot of which were low scrub forests and beyond them, at the horizon, a line of blue that might be ocean. The stone was carved with runes that made no sense to Olav. But Nahal, his boy, spoke up. "It says all the land beyond belongs to the free port of Kheshem." He pointed. "It's there, where the Endless Mountains touch the sea. The harbor is small but the mountains go inland many hundred *baridi*, so all trade must pass through it."

"You can read these squiggles, then?"

"My . . . I was taught how."

"What else does it say?"

"That the Khesh of Kheshem welcomes all honest men. But evil travelers will be tortured and put to death."

Olav laughed. "Well, I guess we'll just have to take our chances."

They rode down toward the sea. Kheshem lay nowhere in sight but there was the tang of salt marshes in the air when they made camp. Nahal gathered wood and built a fire while Olav quested out into the twilight and returned with a brace of hares. He sparked the fire to life using a chunk of flint from his pouch and the hilt of his knife, then gave the tool to the boy to dress and section the meat and prepare spits. Finally, he took back the knife and cut them a pair of quarterstaffs. "Have you had weapons training?" he asked.

"Some."

"Then come at me."

Nahal seized the staff with both hands together and swung. Olav easily sidestepped the blow and rapped the boy's knuckles, making him drop his weapon. Smiling, he said, "You know nothing. So we'll start by working on your stance."

By the time the fire had died down to coals and they could begin cooking, the two had worked up a sweat.

Later, after they had eaten, Olav said, "Tell me, boy. What do you think of thieves?"

"When I am grown, I will kill them all!" Nahal's scowl was so fierce that Olav had to turn away to keep from laughing. "They will beg for mercy and I will show them the mercy they gave my family!"

"Hmm. That's too bad. Because we're low on coin and there's no guarantee that I'll be able to find honest work in Kheshem." Olav did not add that no man is more than three meals away from brigandage—the boy would someday discover that on his own—nor that it had been sheer chance that he had come upon the hares and great good fortune that the stones he threw at their heads had found their marks.

"You could sell Bastard."

"But then how would we travel?"

Nahal said nothing.

"I put the question to you because the greatest danger to a thief is treachery. If you're going to tell anyone about my activities, then I'll drop you off at the city gate to make your own way in life and practice my thievery elsewhere. But if you wish to stay with me, you'll need to keep silent."

Sullenly, Nahal said, "I'll do what I have to in order to survive."

"So do we all, boy. So do we all."

At night, they shared the bedroll, fully clothed save for their boots. As he was drifting off to sleep, Olav felt the boy's chest moving with suppressed sobs. He pretended not to notice.

With sleep came dreams: Olav and Nahal were sitting by a campfire at the verge of a dark and moonless wood. There came a crackling noise in the underbrush. "Who's there?" Nahal cried in a panicky voice. Olav felt not particularly concerned because he had a sword and knew how to use it better than most.

Mocking laughter echoed through the forest—deep as oak, hard as steel, supple as a stream bouncing down a rocky mountainside. It was like nothing Olav had ever heard before, and it filled him with supernatural dread. Bastard, his steed, whinnied in terror, and would have bolted if he hadn't been hitched to a tree.

Olav seized a brand from the fire and was on his feet. "Show yourself!" he cried.

"Ahhhh, Olav," rasped an inhuman voice. "Thinkst thou I am afraid of thy little man-spark? I, who have walked unshod in the furnaces of the earth?"

If Olav had been blinded by the murky darkness of the forest before, he was doubly so now, with the flaming brand held before him. Nor, with the stench of smoke rising from the brand and that of a hundred campfires permeating his clothing, was his sense of smell of any use. But his hearing was still good, and he thought he knew roughly from whence the voice came.

"If you're not afraid of me," he growled, "then why are you hiding?"

"Beware such questions," said the voice in the darkness. "For now I *come!*"

With a howl, the creature charged. And in that same instant, Olav flung the brand into the brush before him. The weather had been dry, and the brush went up in a flash of flame.

Swiftly, then, Olav leaped atop Bastard, pulling Nahal up after him. With a sweep of his knife, he cut the reins. His horse reared up and then ran, fleet as the wind, with the fire to his back. Though it left him without gear, Olav abandoned his camp to the spreading flames without a second thought. For, as Bastard was rearing up in the air, he had felt grasping claws trying to seize his leg, and as they leaped away he glanced back to see a misshapen form, black against the fire, still striving to reach him.

He rode through the night, with all the world burning behind him, as fast and furious as ever he could, and awoke in the morning beside the cold campfire, aching and sore.

The port of Kheshem curved about its harbor and sprawled up the mountain slopes, a labyrinth of golden-roofed temples and high slender ivory-tiled towers intermingled with low mud-and-wattle tenements, the walled pleasure gardens of the wealthy, sturdy stone warehouses, public squares, guildhalls, and the occasional shipyard, limekiln, or knackery, all of it laced together by wide, granite-slabbed avenues and narrow alleys that smelled of spices and tar and camel dung. On his first day in the city, Olav took a great chance and played the cutpurse in a crowd that had gathered, ironically enough, to watch the public evisceration and beheading of a thief. The day's haul was such that he bought the two of them a rich meal with wine and then a long soak in hot water at the private baths. When Nahal, face slick with grease, fiercely declared himself in no need of such fripperies, Olav lifted him, struggling, into the air and dropped him in the bath. Then, wading in (himself already naked), he stripped the wet clothes off the boy.

Which was how Olav discovered that Nahal was actually Nahala—a girl. Her guardians had chopped her hair short and taught her to swear like a boy in order to protect her from the rough sorts with whom traveling merchants must necessarily deal.

The discovery made no great difference in their relationship. Nahala was every bit as sullen as Nahal had been, and no less industrious. She knew how to cook, mend, clean, and perform all the chores a man needed to do on the road. Olav considered buying cloth and having her make a dress for herself but, for much the same reasons as her guardians before him, decided to leave things be. When she came of age—soon, he imagined—they would deal with such matters. Until then, it was easier to let her remain a boy.

At her insistence, he continued the lessons in weapons use.

Nahala despised her new master. But merchants, however young, must be pragmatists. She knew that there was no good alternative. Few orphaned children survived to adulthood in the city and the common fate of those who did and were female was whoredom, which did not appeal to her. Also, Olav never beat her and only cuffed her with reason; as masters went, he was a good one. So there was that.

Most of all, Nahala was learning to fight and this, she knew, would be invaluable to her when she was old enough to return to the desert and cleanse it of the vermin who had killed her family.

Sometimes, however, Olav had nightmares and Nahala would have to leave her pallet to shake him awake. Possibly because of those nightmares, he was drinking a lot. But what worried Nahala most was his spending. So one day, instead of wandering the city in order to learn its winds and ways (the higher up, for example, the richer the houses; the lower, the filthier the water), the prices food could be haggled down to, the rates charged by the money changers, and suchlike, she sewed together a bag out of discarded scraps of cloth and headed downhill toward the pebbled strand at the edge of town.

She was halfway to her destination when a ragged boy placed himself in her way, hands on hips and jeered, "Hey, Stick!"

Nahala fell easily into a balanced stance and slid her hands so that her staff was in a defensive position. "Yah?"

"Seen you around a lot lately, strutting like a rooster. I guess that thing means you think you can fight?"

"Try me."

With a war yell, the boy ran at her, fists wild.

One end of Nahala's staff dipped almost to the ground. She thrust it between the boy's legs, then hopped to the side while simultaneously shoving the upper end forward, as if the staff were a lever.

The boy went facedown in the dust.

When he tried to get up, Nahala rapped one knee with the staff.

Then a hand. Then the other knee. They were gentle blows, though she knew from experience how they stung. They would not break any bones. *If you have to fight, fight to kill,* Olav had told her. *Or else just give your enemy a little warning. All that stuff in between only makes your foe meaner.*

"Do you give up?" Nahala asked.

"King's palm," the boy said. Then, "Name's Sliv."

"Nahal."

"Where you goin' with that bag?"

"To the beach to gather pebbles. Wanna come along?"

"I guess."

Which was how Nahala and Sliv became friends of a sort. Not close ones, however, but wary allies.

When Olav returned to their room after a prolonged bout of wenching, Nahala had arranged two handfuls of pebbles in neat rows on the table that, along with a pair of simple but sturdy chairs, were the result of an extra coin's rent a month. When Olav saw them, he said, "What's this?"

"Pretend each pebble is a drachm. This is how many you had on our first day in Kheshem." Nahala swept four back into the bag. "The feast." Another two. "The baths." Six. "The room." One. "A week's feed and stable for Bastard." Two more. "A woman. Wine. Wine. Wine. Another woman." Item by item, the pebbles dwindled, until there were but fourteen. "This is how much remains."

"I could have told you that by looking in my pouch." Amused, Olav slid three more pebbles away. "You forgot tonight's woman. I gave her an extra coin because she . . . Well, anyway, now there are only eleven."

"Rent comes due in three days, both for us and the stable. Plus, we have no food. Nor any work. The old men who sit by the docks and watch the boats say that only smugglers will be risking their ships until the Sea Lords and the Khesh make peace and smugglers trust no one they're not related to." She swept the last pebbles into the bag. "It's time we left Kheshem."

Olav rubbed his beard. "Yes, well, about that . . . I have been having dreams these past few weeks—nightmares—I'm sure you've noticed. There is something coming for me out of the desert. Something powerful. Something no man wishes to face. It cannot enter the city—too many wizards here, too much power. But if I leave, it will find me. So I must stay. It seems that I have no choice but to resume my career as cutpurse."

At which exact instant, the darkness to one side of the room swirled, lofted upward, spread outward, and gave birth to twin pinpricks of light—a pair of eyes, both hard and unblinking. Stepping out of the shadows, a man in wizard's black robes, with a ruby talisman hung on a chain about his neck, said, "That would be unwise."

Nahala shrieked and fell back against the bed. Olav grabbed at his side for the sword he had removed upon entering the room.

The wizard held up his hand. "Let me tell you what will happen if you do. As you are cutting purse strings, an incense vendor will happen to glance your way. Her shout will begin a hue and cry and though you bolt and fight like a demon, you will be run down and overwhelmed. I have just returned from your execution, a week from now. First you were flogged. Then your arms were broken. Then your abdomen was sliced open and, seizing your intestines—"

"Stop! I have seen enough executions to know what happens." A shrewd look came over Olav's face, though to Nahala's eyes it looked feigned. "But why should I believe your wild story of seeing things that have not yet happened?"

"Tell me this. How did I learn the exact moment you decided to try your hand at thievery again? By bribing the guards to let me interview you while you awaited execution and then walking back in time to your room just now. But I will give you stronger proof than that." The wizard put one hand on Olav's shoulder and with the other clutched his amulet.

They disappeared.

They reappeared.

The magician was unchanged. But Olav's face was ashen and his eyes were wide with horror. He seized a chair with one blind hand and crashed down onto it. "Wine!" he gasped. "There should be some left in the jar by the door."

While Nahala poured, the wizard spoke: "You killed eight men, trying to make your escape. Two of them were of the Harbor Guard and heavily armed."

"I . . . have no memory of that." Olav drank deeply. Then, looking thoughtful, "Still, I regret it. A man will do evil things in the heat of passion. But I could wish to have killed fewer."

"All the deaths have been unmade, as has your execution." The wizard gestured and coins rained down upon the table. "They call me Ushted the Uncanny. I have decided that a more decorous title would be Ushted the Protector. But to achieve that honorific, I need a servant whom I know can kill."

"He acts like a great wizard," Sliv said when Nahala saw him next. "But he's not. Most towns have two or three wizards. Kheshem has dozens and every one of them is better at it than Ushted. If it weren't for that time-walking stunt of his, he'd be in a small village somewhere selling poisons, love potions, and balms to cure warts." Sliv had wanted to spend the day spying on the blood huts at the edge of town, where menstruating women went to spin and exchange gossip until their bodies were clean again. Somehow he'd conceived the notion that they did so naked. But Nahala had distracted him with the idea of instead exercising Bastard by taking turns riding him as he swam in the otherwise idle harbor. Now they sat dangling their feet from a dock, talking.

As an afterthought, Sliv added, "The balm for warts is a good one, though. I've used it myself."

"How do you know so much about Ushted?" Nahala asked.

"I'm his apprentice. Any other wizard, I'd be set for life. But none of them will take me. I've made the rounds and asked." Sliv spat into the water. "Someday, when I'm grown, I'll cut his throat, chop up his body, and take his amulet. Then everything he owns will be mine."

Nahala wondered, not for the first time, why boys' fantasies were always so violent. But she said, "Be sure to do it in such a way that no suspicion falls upon you."

Sliv looked at her in surprise, as if his pronouncements had never before been taken seriously—which, she realized, was probably true. Then he said, "If they come after me, I'll just go back to before they do and run away."

Olav, meanwhile, was finding his new life as the wizard's hireling an undemanding one, though it did nothing to assuage his nightmares. At first, he was occasionally summoned, in the twilight hours, to wait motionless in an alleyway off a courtyard for bravos to set upon a wealthy citizen hurrying to get home before nightfall. At which he would leap out with fierce cries, chasing off most of the assailants and cutting down any who loitered. The victim was always happy to send Ushted the Protector a lavish gift in gratitude for saving his life.

Later, however, as the number of assailants, never great to begin with, dwindled and those who remained grew warier, the game darkened. Olav would be sent to a rich man's mansion to smash in its door and murder its master. Always, just as he was arriving at his target's domicile, Sliv would come running with the news that the man had been shown his own death and agreed to pay generously for it not to happen.

In this manner, for a season, Olav prospered and his benefactor even more. Twice Ushted moved his alembic-filled elaboratory uphill to larger and more splendid quarters. Olav stayed where he was, but frequented a better class of courtesans. All those deaths, both the permanent ones and those that were unmade, seemed to weigh increasingly heavily on him. But he never spoke of them, nor did Nahala ask.

"It's here."

Nahala had set up a slab of wood against the far wall and was practicing her knife-throwing when Olav suddenly spoke. He had been lying on his pallet, staring at the ceiling for hours while the knives flew, landed with a solid *thunk! thunk!*, and then were freed to be carried across the room and thrown again, over and over. The knives were one result of their newfound prosperity and, though they lacked the filigreed decoration Nahala's magpie heart yearned for, they were well-made weapons. They would kill. "What's here?" she asked idly.

"My destiny." Olav rolled over then, and went to sleep.

The next day, an earthquake toppled several towers and opened a chasm in the mountainside high above the city. News spread swiftly that something had made lair therein, where it could watch over the roads leading to the city from either direction. From there it sallied down to attack not just caravans but also the wagons bringing food to the city and even lone riders, feeding upon horses, camels, merchants, and farmers with equal ease, and defiling the goods and foodstuffs they brought with flame and smoke.

The flow of food into the city ceased and, though the Khesh ordered the granaries be opened to Kheshem's poorest, prices soared. There were riots. These were easily quelled by the military, but everyone knew there would be more.

A troop of soldiers was sent to deal with the menace and did not return. A hero with perfumed hair and oiled mustachios marched into the cavern, bright sword in hand, and did not emerge. In his wake, an assortment of fools and scoundrels also disappeared, along with the schemes they had assured all would win the day. The citizenry began to wonder why the city's wizards did nothing to counter the beast.

"My proud brothers have power but not force," Ushted said, "and they will not work together." He was talkative by nature. Merchants knew how to handle such men; whenever he came to see Olav, Nahala kept his wine cup filled and her mouth closed. "Against a brute that splinters bones and wagons with equal ease, their subtlety is useless. But I, Olav, have you. Together, we shall do what no others dare and accept no reward for doing so."

Olav had raised his cup to his lips. Now he set it down untasted. Nahala had noticed that he drank lightly, if at all, in his master's presence. "That makes no sense."

"Every despot likes to think he inspires selfless obedience. When I have proved myself to be exactly such a subject, the Khesh will welcome me into his court. And that is an opportunity beyond avarice." Ushted stood. "Sleep well tonight, for in the morning we go up the mountain."

The next day, the wizard walked out of the shadows to report that he had just seen the menace slain only hours into the future. So, sitting astride Bastard, Olav left the city and started up the mountainside. With him went Ushted the Protector, Sliv the apprentice, and Nahala, who had neither title nor any desire for one.

Nahala had woken up feeling strange that day, detached in a manner new to her experience. It was not until she felt a drop of blood trickle down the inside of one leg that she had thought: *Oh*. She was now, she supposed, a woman. It seemed a terribly inconvenient time for it to happen. Quickly, she had torn a strip from the bottom of her sark—it was cut long, so she could grow into it—folded it in the manner her mother had foresightedly taught her, and staunched the bleeding. But the sense of estrangement stayed with her as they walked.

Bastard struggled slowly up the mountain trail, while the others trudged after him. Ushted was uncharacteristically silent. Olav was quiet too, but sullenly so rather than in his usual manner, less like a hero headed for certain victory than one on his way to die. Every now and then, Sliv, who swaggeringly carried Olav's spear slung over one shoulder, threw her a strange look. It was a morning, it seemed, for odd behavior.

Once, when they had lagged far enough behind not to be overheard, Sliv flared his nostrils and muttered, "What's that smell?"

"It's just the mountain sage in bloom."

"Naw, naw, it's not that. I know that smell . . ." There was a terrible light in his eyes. "I know that smell and it ain't no sage." He pointed an accusatory finger at her. "You're a girl!"

"Woman," Nahala said, trying to invest the word with menace. She had never felt less like fighting. But she took a step backward and angled her staff. "Ease up, Sliv. You and I are friends."

"Girls can't be friends. Girls are only good for one thing."

If you have to fight, fight to kill. Olav had told her that. Nahala's knives were in sheaths strapped on either thigh, but there was no need to draw them. All she had to do was wait for Sliv to lunge at her, aim the tip of her staff at his eye, and lean in hard.

For a moment, the potential for violence crackled in the air between them. Then Sliv spat at her feet and turned away. The others were far ahead and Nahala, perforce, had to run to catch up.

As the mountain dwindled above them and the sky grew larger, Bastard became increasingly restive and hard to control. When he refused to go any farther, Olav alit and tethered him to a tree, saying, "You were wondering why I brought the horse. This is why." It took Nahala a breath to realize that this was directed at her, that he was still teaching her. "The monster is near. We must be ready for it." Turning to Sliv, he said, "Hand me my spear."

Without being told, Nahala untied the shield from Bastard's harness and held it ready to be taken from her.

"Everyone, wait here," Olav said.

"No," said Ushted. "We all proceed. This I have already seen."

Olav shrugged. Again he led, and shortly thereafter, a twist in the trail took them to the mouth of the cavern, their destination. The rock lining it was raw and broken and scattered on the ground were similar shards, as from an explosion. In a voice louder than Nahala had ever heard emerge from him, Olav shouted: "Abomination! Come forth to meet your doom!"

The creature that flowed forth from the cavern darkness was shaped like a monstrous lizard and taller by half than Olav himself. Its substance was so black it glittered in the sun, looking for all the world like the foul-smelling liquid that bubbled from the ground in the distant desert wastes and defiled any water it touched. Throwing back its head, it opened a mouth lined with teeth like ivory daggers.

In a dulcet, womanly voice the apparition said, "Ohhhh, Olav. Sweet, sweet love, at last you have come to me! Long have I yearned for this moment. Great indeed will be your torment before you finally die."

Olav's spear sank. Then it rose again. "So it's you. I suspected as much. Well, I killed you once, and if I must, I can kill you again."

"Wait!" Ushted stepped to Olav's side and pressed a lozenge to his lips, murmuring, "Take this. It will give you strength."

Olav swallowed. Then he cocked his arm, ready to throw the spear. Jaw grim and eyes a-glare, he looked the perfect hero. As the firedrake reared up before him, he cried, "Attack—and let the blood fly where it may!"

Then he fell flat on his face.

For a breath, no one moved. Then the creature bent its head to Olav's side, sniffing at his body and nudging it like a cat. When Olav did not move, it *screamed*. Its neck spasmed and its tail thrashed and its taloned legs dug into its own torso. It slammed against the rocky ground, over and over. With enormous violence, it tied itself into a knot, tighter and tighter, until it was as smooth as an egg.

Malodorous black fluid drained away from the egg, flowing back into the cavern shadows, leaving behind a human figure, a woman whose skin was as white as maggot flesh.

The woman's long leather skirt had witch-knots dangling from its hem. Her breasts were bare and three bright stones shone between them, hung from black cords about her neck. When she spoke, Nahala saw that her teeth had been filed to points. Shaking a finger at Ushted, she cried, "You! *What have you done*?"

Both Nahala and Sliv were trembling with fear, for the woman was no less dreadful than the lizard had been. Her hair rose up as if underwater, swaying like a hundred slim eels. Ushted the Protector, however, displayed not the least concern. "I have made your husband useless to you. You want him awake and aware and able to suffer. I can undo his stupor. But if I do not, he will die in his sleep. Painlessly."

The woman's eyes were bright with rage. "Why would you do such a foolish—and for you, fatal—thing?"

"You have three talismans upon you. One grants you passage from the fires at the center of the world to its surface and back again. That one I disdain. The second allows you to fly vast distances, supported by the winds. Tempting, but not to my taste. The third, which allows you to walk in time, however . . ." He drew the amulet from beneath his black robe. "I know you will surrender because I already hold it."

"It is true I can walk in time. Perhaps I will take a stroll to just before you poisoned my husband."

"If you do, I will similarly go back to this morning and Olav will not come to you. Game lost. But you won't—I have been here before, and I know." Producing a small silver knife, Ushted the Protector made a long cut in his palm. Blood welled up. "Here is our deal: I will bring Olav back from the brink of death in exchange for the amulet and your promise that as soon as you are done with him you will leave and never return." He proffered her the knife, hilt-first.

Disdaining the offer, the witch-woman slid a hand across her sharpened teeth, opening a gash in it. Black ichor oozed out. "I have no interest whatsoever in your city or yourself or, when my vengeance is done, the lands of the living. It is an easy promise to give and easier to keep."

"Then I will descend the mountain a hero."

They clasped hands. Blood and ichor mingled. Then Ushted the Protector crouched by Olav's body and, turning the head away from him, stuck a finger down the warrior's throat.

When Olav was done vomiting, Ushted cleaned his hand with

the hem of his robe and, standing, said, "He will come to within the hour. Do with him then as you wish."

The witch hissed in anger and looked upon him with absolute loathing. Nevertheless, she removed one amulet from her neck and held it forth.

Ushted the Protector shook his head. "Give it to the boy." Sliv looked startled. "As you did long, long ago, when I was him."

Nahala looked from Sliv to Ushted and back again, mentally erasing the wizard's beard and imagining the boy's face grown lean with maturity. How could she not have seen before that they were one and the same person?

Avarice burning on his face, Sliv accepted the gem.

Turning a disdainful back on Olav, the witch, and the cavern, Ushted the Protector said, "Follow me, the both of you."

Numb, Nahala did so. Sliv, filled with elation, skipped ahead, and fell behind to hold up his amulet to the sun, and ran to catch up again. The cavern disappeared behind them. "This is mine to keep?" he asked. "For as long as I live?"

"Obviously."

Sliv glanced sidewise at Nahala. "And the girl?"

With a shrug, Ushted the Protector said, "She is yours. Unless, as she did the first time around, she manages to slip away from you on the way down the mountain."

Nahala stumbled over a rock and almost fell. She heard Sliv laugh and her heart grew cold.

If your enemy has a better weapon than you, take it away from him. That was another thing Olav had said. Moving as swiftly and fluidly as ever she had, Nahala strode forward, stabbed her staff between the wizard and his amulet and flung it into the air. It flew to her hand. She slung it over her own neck.

With the amulet, Nahala could protect not only herself but her master and weapons instructor as well. Nothing could harm them. They could leave Kheshem behind. If need be, they could cross the desert in perfect safety, with nothing more than Olav's sword to protect them. Clutching the stone, she cried in triumph, "Take me back to this morning!"

Nothing happened.

Ushted smiled urbanely. "The amulet will take you back no further than when you first put it on. Nor do you know how to use it." Extending his hand, he added, "I am aware that Sliv told you I am not a great wizard. But if you honestly doubt I can protect myself, then by all means attempt to throw those knives I see your hand yearning toward."

The butt of a spear struck Ushted hard in the side of the jaw, sending two teeth and a gout of blood into the air. He fell and a sandaled foot trod upon his neck to hold him captive. In a small, puzzled voice, he gasped, "But that's not what happened—"

Sure hands spun the spear about and drove the business end through his rib cage, piercing his heart.

Ushted the Protector, also called the Uncanny, was dead.

The woman who had appeared out of nowhere had precious stones everywhere: on her many rings, on her even more necklaces, on her bangles and bracelets, and set into her cheeks and earlobes. A curved sword hung at her side. The long black spear that she drew back up from the wizard's chest, lethal though it was, looked not half so deadly as did she herself.

This apparition was the most wonderful thing Nahala had ever seen in her life. A heavily embroidered skirt hung down past her knees and was slit on either side almost to her waist, revealing multicolored leggings beneath. A leather vest or breastplate, marvelously crafted with the image of the desert sun, was fretted with amber beads and yellow citrines so that it dazzled the eye. A small leather cap held her braided hair in place. She was strong and stocky and everything that Nahala had ever dreamed of someday becoming.

Her heart went out to this radiant creature. "Who . . . who are you?"

The warrior-woman smiled a stony smile and pulled out from beneath her vest the exact same amulet that Nahala now wore. "Why, don't you know, dear? I'm *you*."

Talking, they walked back up the mountain.

After he recovered from his stunned paralysis, Sliv had, of course, bolted like a marsh-rabbit. In a flash, Nahala's knives were in her hands. His back was wide and inviting—and then gone. She hadn't thrown.

"That was wisely done," her older self had said. "Kill no more than you absolutely have to."

"Olav said that to me!"

"Yes, he did."

Now, however, Nahala peered anxiously up the trail. "Shouldn't we be hurrying?"

"Hush." Nahala's future self smiled reassuringly. "We have all the time in the world."

The fight did not last long. When they came in sight of her, the dragon-witch was crouched anxiously over Olav's body, watching his pulse quicken. Without challenge or battle cry, the warrior Nahala ran straight at her. When, hearing the rush of footsteps, the witch straightened, Nahala cut through both amulet thongs and her throat with a single slash of her scimitar, so that the hag could neither escape nor call down a curse upon them. With a gesture, however, the witch-woman summoned her dark, fluid substance back to herself.

She was midway through changing back into her lizard form when Nahala's spear thrust into her heart.

The dragon fell like a great black wave, smashing foulness everywhere. At her demise, the cavern collapsed in on itself, burying both her and her two remaining amulets under enough stone to build a new city with.

The warrior Nahala threw back her head and ululated in triumph.

Nahala, watching it all and shivering with joy, knew: *That's me. That's who I'll grow up to be*!

When it was over, both Nahalas turned toward Olav, lying motionless on the ground. His skin was pale but his breathing steady. It was obvious he would recover.

"Look at him!" said the warrior Nahala and there was a fondness to her expression. "Oh, he is lovely in his youth, with his beard so black and his limbs so strong. Do you not agree?"

Young Nahala turned toward Olav and, to her amazement, heard herself say, "Yes, he is. Oh, he is indeed."

"Just be sure, when he wakes up, to let him think he did the deed himself. You know what a child he can be." At which words, the older woman touched her amulet and faded back into the neverwhere of times to come.

This is the tale of Olav the Merchant, known also as the Dragon Slayer. For many years, he and his wife guided caravans across the desert. On occasion they encountered brigands, whom they slew without mercy. They had many children. In time, he became rich, retired to a villa near the sea, grew fat, and died old. May such great good fortune come to us all!

THE WARM EQUATIONS

PEOPLE WHO SAY that any landing you can walk away from is a good one have never crashed a hopper into the side of a mountain. On Mercury. During a major solar flare. Osbourne, who had just done all of that, lay motionless, eyes closed, savoring the amazing fact that he was still alive. Then, with an involuntary groan, he sat up.

Or tried to.

Something had him pinned. He opened his eyes and saw that the overhead instrumentation panel had come crashing down on him. Blocking, incidentally, the forward instrumentation, though he could see most of the video screen. Dim red light meant that the power was out but the backup batteries were functioning. The fact that he could breathe meant that the hull hadn't been breached. Together, they explained why he wasn't dead.

There was crash foam everywhere. Also a lot of debris. Plus he was not lying flat but canted to one side, and the upper half of his body should have hurt like hell but didn't.

From the waist down, he could feel nothing.

That made sense. The hopper was equipped with nerve-conduction blockers for exactly such situations as this, where chemical painkillers would leave the operator groggy and ineffective. It was entirely possible that his injuries were painful but not serious. Though it was more likely that his legs were useless.

Well, so what? People had gotten out of worse fixes. And anything somebody else could do, Charles Magnus Osbourne could do better. "'Unto whomsoever much is given, of him shall be much required,'" his father would say on those few times he was foolish enough to ask him for help. "You're smart enough and strong enough and disciplined enough to do anything you need to do. You don't require anybody else's assistance. Take care of it yourself." So he had.

"Minerva?" he said aloud. "Status report."

I am functional at reduced capability. Flight systems are down. Life support and cooling are functional for twenty hours. The emergency beacon has been activated. Communications systems are operative.

"Turn on the radio."

The Sun roared, crackled, and hissed in his ears. No chance he could make himself heard through that mess. "Turn it off. How likely is it the distress beacon will be heard?"

That's hard to say. The research station has better receivers than I do. But the solar flare—

"Got it."

It hardly mattered whether the beacon was heard or not. The hard radiation sleeting down from above would make any rescue operation appallingly dangerous. And if there was one thing he was sure of, it was that nobody was going to put themselves in danger to rescue him. Somebody else, yes. But not him.

When he first arrived at Gassendi-Harriott Station, all two dozen researchers had gathered to welcome him with cheers and applause. It was a tradition, he had been told, extended to all planetary newcomers. A hermesologist he later learned was Sally Wu had grinned broadly and said, "So what do we call you—Charles or Charlie or Chuck?"

"You may call me," he had replied, "*Dr.* Osbourne."

And a silence had fallen over all.

Almost, he regretted that moment. But if there was one thing he knew, it was that being respected was more important than being liked. Fortunately, popularity had never been one of his goals. He had applied himself to his work and the results were extremely good. They had to be to justify the expense of moving a human being over twenty-five million miles from the nearest human resources office.

Other than Minerva, he had only himself to rely on. Luckily, that was enough.

The first thing to do was catalog his assets: One first-rate brain. Half an intact body. Twenty hours in which to escape the prison the hopper had become. A surface suit (he could see it, in pristine condition, out of the corner of his eye) capable of repurifying his air supply for weeks and recycling his water for days. No food, but that didn't matter. He was less than a hundred kilometers from the research station. If he could get into the suit, he was sure he could make it back long before starving to death.

"Minerva. The three robots I was ferrying to the construction site—what shape are they in?"

One construction device has external damage that does not affect functionality. The other was crushed beneath the hopper. The maker device is fully operative.

"Give me control of the construction bot."

Osbourne released the magnetic clamps holding the bot to the outside of the hopper, then stood it up. A debris trail of equipment meant for the half-built observation site glittered down the mountain slope. But though it was all purpose-built and would cost a fortune to replace, his attention was focused on the airlock.

All hoppers had airlocks, of course. Oxygen was too precious to waste whenever someone got in or out. At his direction, the bot opened the outer hatch. So far, so good. The inner hatch looked functional. But the space between was too small for even the maker robot, much less the constructor.

However.

Osbourne had studied the documentation for every piece of equipment that he had any contact with. The others thought him mad to devote free time to such dry materials rather than the ping-pong games, pinochle marathons, and similar amusements that were so important to inferior minds. Sam Chakrabarti had taken him aside once and suggested he ought to take part in their entertainments. "For morale's sake," he'd said, before blowing his argument by adding, "To show that you're just one of the guys."

Sam was a helioseismologist and one of the few scientists in the station Osbourne had any respect for. He could easily imagine him receiving the Nobel someday. Sam was quiet and had a gentle sense of humor. He might almost have been one of the imaginary friends that, in lieu of real ones, Osbourne had invented to get himself through an otherwise lonely childhood.

Osbourne shook that thought from his head. *Keep focused!* "Minerva, give me control of the maker bot."

The maker was all of a piece—remove one component and it would all fall apart. But the construction bot was modular. So, using the former, Osbourne proceeded to amputate the legs of the latter.

It was slow, painstaking work, because if the bot was to carry him back to safety, he would need to reattach those legs once he got free of the hopper. Detaching them without damaging the connections was much like surgery. Also, like a surgeon, he found his brow beading up with sweat. Alas, there was no helpful nurse to wipe the sweat away. But . . .

"Minerva! Why is it growing hotter in here?"

It is possible that there's a coolant leak. I have no working instrumentation to determine if that is the case. Alternatively, the outside temperature is currently six hundred fifty degrees Fahrenheit and rising as we approach local noon. It may be that the cooling system simply hasn't sufficient power to handle that.

Osbourne mentally erased those twenty comfortable hours of slack from his list of assets. "Turn off the distress beacon. Redirect its power to the cooling system."

That would be unwise, Dr. Osbourne. The beacon is your best chance of being rescued.

"Nobody's coming! They're all back at the station, making popcorn and having sing-alongs. Playing charades! Making up childish stories about dragons and wizards!" Osbourne caught himself. It was pointless trying to reason with Minerva. "Just do it, okay?"

As you say.

Osbourne returned to his work. Work was his one consolation, his sole companion and his haven in times of distress. He tried not to think about his co-workers, safe at the research station. He tried to ignore the fact that the hopper was growing warmer.

An hour passed.

Then another. Osbourne felt himself growing woozy.

"It was my idea, my insight, my interpretation of the data," Osbourne told the man he had dared think of as his mentor. "I wrote the goddamn paper from abstract to credits. All you did was sign off on it."

"That's the way things work in academia. As your senior, I get pride of place."

"You listed me fourth among the authors. Fourth! After a pair of jumped-up grad students whose chief contribution was creating spreadsheets and entering the data."

"I did it to wake you up. Science is a cooperative endeavor. You need to understand that. While you were being too good to talk to anyone, Sheena and Joel were playing the game, sharing findings, attending meetings, filling in time sheets. None of which you could be bothered with."

Bitter words came to Osbourne's lips. But, knowing they would do no good, he swallowed them back. Then and there, he decided that he was going to find a place to work so far out on the fringes that no second-rate minds could ever again steal the glory he deserved.

The temperature in the hopper was in the high eighties when at last the bot's legs fell away with what Osbourne imagined would be a satisfactory *clang*, if only there were an atmosphere to carry the sound to him.

"All right," he muttered. "Let's see if you can fit into the airlock."

The robot was humanoid in form because most of the tools it used had been designed for humans and because its designers had no imagination. Osbourne would have given it at least four arms and the torso would have scuttled into the airlock like a spider. As it was, he had to drag the top half of the constructor by its two arms to the hopper. He flung one arm up to catch at the rim of the airlock. Then the other arm.

It was hanging from the airlock. He pulled it up so that most of the bot was above the rim. Then he reached out an arm. . . .

The bot fell backward, lost its grip on the airlock, and slammed down hard on the rock.

Ouch.

By pumping against the rock with one arm, he managed to get a steady rocking motion. Then, with a sudden push, he flipped the constructor over. It crawled back to the hopper. It flung an arm over the airlock edge. Then the other. It was hanging from the rim again.

"Give me control of the maker robot."

The maker placed itself behind the constructor torso. Then it gave a steady shove upward. The constructor moved higher. Now more than half of its mass was above the bottom of the hatch.

Osbourne adjusted the maker's position and had it shove again, upward and outward.

The constructor tumbled into the airlock, nearly filling it.

The maker bot seized the hatch and slammed it three times hard, forcing the constructor farther in each time. The third slam shut the hatch. The maker twisted the exterior grip and it locked shut.

Sweat was pouring from Osbourne's face and body. He didn't have to check with Minerva to know the temperature had gone up over a hundred. He switched to the constructor's visuals.

Blackness.

The airlock light was broken. Okay. He switched on the constructor bot's headlamp. The screen went white, then adjusted. It showed a small section of the airlock wall from inches away, all that the bot's camera could see. The inner hatch would be above its head.

He tried to move an arm up to where the grip would be.

Nothing happened. The arm couldn't move. He tried the other arm with the same results. "Minerva! Tell me there's a way the bot can fit into the airlock and open the inner hatch."

I'm afraid I can't do that, Dr. Osbourne.

"I can get the maker bot to pull it out again. I can cut off one of its arms. Tell me it will fit in and open the inner hatch then."

I'm afraid I can't do that, Dr. Osbourne.

The interior of the hopper was as hot as a sauna now. So hot that he had trouble thinking. Not that thinking was going to solve anything. He hadn't the time. He hadn't the tools.

He was going to die.

So in the end it turned out that he wasn't such a big noise after all. Osbourne had gone out despite the solar flare, against all warnings, because he knew he could do what lesser men could not. He had been certain that a little thing like the Sun was no match for him. Now, like Icarus, he was going to pay for his hubris.

He had imagined himself arriving at the station cradled in the constructor's arms, perhaps with one of his own arms wrapped around its nub of a head. Waving gallantly, while the maker bot trotted along behind, holding a slab of the hopper's shielding over him like an umbrella. Now he could see that for the childish fantasy it was.

Osbourne could no longer keep his eyes open. It was time to admit that he had failed. But he could still make a good end of things. That wouldn't be easy. But he could still die honorably and without self-pity.

Let that be his epitaph, then: *He died honorably and without self-pity.* Not as great a way of making his mark on history as he had hoped. But it would have to do.

"Minerva. Are you recording this?"

Yes, Dr. Osbourne. It's a standard black box function.

"That's good. Let everyone know . . . I died game."

He must have lapsed into unconsciousness. Only gradually did Osbourne become aware of the clanging and clattering about around him. Something *slammed* against the side of the hopper. For some reason, he could not open his eyes. But he knew what must have happened.

Against all odds, it seemed that the others had come for him. They must have come in the Big Dog, which was designed for exactly this kind of rescue, for there was the sound of metal ripping open and cool air blew into the cabin.

There were voices. "He's alive!" and "Help me get this off him." The overhead instrument panel that had fallen on Osbourne was lifted away.

"Jesus, look at his legs."

"Shut up, Gerhardt, he's listening. Don't worry, buddy, we'll get you out of this alive," Sam Chakrabarti said. Osbourne could tell from his voice that he was far from sure of that. He could also tell that Sam wanted him to live. They all did. In the unlikeliest twist of all, they were his friends, or close enough. They'd put themselves in danger to rescue him.

He realized then that it didn't matter if he lived or died. This moment paid for all.

"Osbourne, you crusty bastard," Sally said, "don't you dare clock out on us."

"Please," he murmured. "Call me Chuck."

REQUIEM FOR A WHITE RABBIT

Hippity-hop, hippity-hop, through the crowd he bobbed and weaved, never once brushing up against one of the guests. His approach-avoidance software was that good. Every now and then he pulled a big gold stemwinder from his waistcoat pocket and cried, "Oh dear! Oh dear! I shall be late!" Then, as he did umpteen times a day, he disappeared into a rabbit hole with a wooden door and, alongside it, a mailbox that didn't open and a curtained window that revealed nothing within. Reappearing, minutes later, elsewhere in the theme park to go through the whole routine again. His role never varied and, because he had no functioning memory, he never grew tired of it.

But today, making a sharp veer to avoid a baby carriage by the Fountain of Dancing Water Nymphs, one big furry foot slipped on a blue raspberry Icee that a five-year-old, face contorting toward tears, had just dropped and he went flying.

Wham! His head slammed against the marble lip of the fountain and for an instant everything went white. Then, consciousness returning, he thought, *Where am I?* The park swam into focus around him, and he changed that to *Who am I?* Pulling himself upright, he stared down at the wavering pink-eyed, big-eared, furry reflection of his head and, horrified, thought, *What the hell* am *I?*

A white-bearded gnome wearing green trousers, a belted blue tunic, and a conical red hat appeared with broom and dustpan to clean away the Icee and offer the tearful child's guardian a coupon for its replacement. Before the creature could disappear again, he said to it,

"Please. Help. Something terrible has happened to me."

The gnome spun around. Seeing who had spoken, his eyes grew wide. "You shouldn't be able to—" he began. Then, hastily hiding the broom and dustpan under a nearby decorative shrub, he offered his arm. "Come with me. You're just a little undercharged, that's all. I'll have you fixed up right as rain in no time."

They walked together, the gnome tugging and he lagging. "What's your name?" he asked.

"It's right here. See?" The gnome tugged at its tunic where a name tag read GRUMBLESNITZEL.

He looked to see if he had a name tag too, but he didn't. "What's mine?"

"That's just plain silly. You don't have a name, dummy. You're only a rabbit."

"I feel I . . . shouldn't be. And I'm sure I ought to have a name."

"All right then, how about Whitey? That's a swell little moniker. I can see you love it already. Look, here we are."

The rabbit hole door opened at their approach. Grumblesnitzel ducked through, pulling Whitey after him. It was dark inside until the door closed. Then lights came on and Whitey could see they were on a landing with stairs leading down to a clean white corridor. It all looked familiar. But though he must have navigated these tunnels and corridors a thousand times before, he had no specific memories of being here.

Talking encouragement nonstop, Grumblesnitzel led him one way and then another, stopping before an austere line of numbered docking stations. Some were shut, indicating they were in use. The others were slightly ajar. "Here we go, 555. That's a good little number, eh? Easy to remember. You stay here, Whitey, nice and snug. Grab a little shuteye, recharge those batteries of yours. You'll be good as new come morning. I guarantee it."

Whitey stepped inside, plugged in. "Where are you going?"

"Back to work. The guests, wonderful folks though they might be, are all terrible slobs and the park ain't gonna clean itself. I'll look in on you at the end of my shift, don't you worry. You need anything then, just ask. Old Grumblesnitzel doesn't abandon his friends, no sir."

And he was gone.

Now that he was thinking clearly, Whitey found he could close his eyes and access his inner readings. They indicated he was carrying almost a full charge. So he unplugged and stepped outside. Closing the door firmly behind him, he slipped into an empty dock not far down the corridor. He left the door slightly ajar so he could keep an eye on number 555.

He didn't have to wait long.

Two workers—a man and a woman—in white tech suits, both carrying tool kits, came walking down the corridor. They stopped in front of 555 and opened the door.

"Huh," the man said.

"Are you sure you got the right number?" the woman asked.

"The gnome said '555, easy to remember.' Malfunctioning rabbit. Quick memory wipe and done. Easy as pie. You suppose that runt is pulling a practical joke on us?"

"If he is, there doesn't seem to be much of a payoff to it."

"Robots! I've worked with them half my life but I still can't figure out what goes on in those shiny metal think-boxes of theirs."

Voices dwindling, they walked back the way they had come.

So not only was he a robot but he was not a very important one. Knowing that didn't make him happy, but it explained a lot. When the techs were gone, Whitey did not leave the shadows of the docking port. Instead, he examined all his internal readouts one by one to learn what he could about himself. Then he booted up maps of the theme park and detailed descriptions of its attractions. Then the character sheets of its animatronic entertainers.

Finally, he came up with a plan.

Whitey sped through the crowd, occasionally waving to a child, or winking at a young woman so his behavior wouldn't seem odd. He had ditched the waistcoat and watch, however. That part of his life was done forever.

At Cinderella's Cottage, he counted the people in line, and then joined the queue where he would be the last admitted. As he stepped inside, he said to the bright green-and-yellow Panama-hat-wearing frog scanning passes, "Don't let anybody else in after this batch. The concession's closing for the day. This is the last show. Unscheduled maintenance."

"Are you sure?" the frog asked. "Usually they tell me these things ahead of time."

Whitey puffed himself up. "I'm a level five intelligence and you're only level four, so therefore I outrank you."

"That's true," the frog admitted. It pulled a switch and turned a wheel larger than it was. The door closed. "Done."

"Thank you."

Whitey took a seat at the very back of the theater and watched while Cinderella sang about her unhappiness, her stepsisters and their mother sang about their delight in villainy, and the fairy godmother sang that she would set everything right. It was perfunctory, synoptic theater. He didn't find much joy in it. Though he had to admit that the special effect where a pumpkin turned into a carriage was pretty good.

The auditorium rotated into Prince Charming's Castle for the ball and back to the hut where everyone tried on the glass shoe and then back again to the castle for the happy ending. The audience applauded and left. It had all taken less than half an hour.

When the theater had reset to the cottage, Whitey walked down to the stage and clapped for attention. "Last show, everyone! Back to your docking stations!" As animatrons, they had no more self-awareness than he'd possessed prior to his accident, so they obeyed without question. But he stopped Cinderella before she could go. "You stay. I have an upgrade for you."

Reaching through the park LAN into her internal settings, Whitey boosted her intelligence setting from one, the lowest setting, to five, the highest.

"Where am I?" Cinderella asked. She looked around wonderingly. Then her expression hardened. "Oh, dear God. I'm a robot, aren't I?"

Whitey admired how much faster she'd put things together than he had. Clearly, she had a much better processor than his. "Yes. I'm sorry."

She turned to face him. "Why have you done this to me?"

"I had an accidental reset earlier today and when I saw what my life was like, decided to escape the park. I've got a plan but it requires someone who can pass for human. I thought that, returning to misery ten times a day as you do, you might want to join me. If I was wrong, I can put you back the way you were."

For a long moment she was silent. Then: "Tell me your plan."

"First I have to know if you can carry me."

Cinderella flexed her arm. "I'm built on a construction bot frame. I could bench press a tour van."

Whitey told her his plan.

Wordlessly, Cinderella took off her ballgown. Her arms and shoulders were flesh colored, as were her legs. Her torso was metal and only vaguely human-shaped. "There's a sewing kit among the props. I'll have to cut off these balloon sleeves, get rid of the sash and ruffle, and re-hem the skirt."

"Sounds good, Cinderella."

She frowned. "Cinderella is my slave name. Call me Cindy."

In late afternoon, the tour buses all left at the same time and there was a surge for the parking lot. Wearing her cut-down dress and the flats from Act One, Cindy joined it. She carried Whitey slung over her shoulder, as if he were a stuffed toy she'd won on the Midway.

They were almost to the main gate when Whitey saw a familiar-looking gnome turn away from a litter bin and freeze in amazement. "Let me down! Now!" he shouted.

The gnome tried to run, but Whitey was faster. He tackled Grumblesnitzel, sending him to the ground before he could escape. They rolled over and over, hitting and biting each other. Some of the nearby guests looked puzzled or alarmed and one laughed, but they were all swept away by the steady flow to the lot before they could do anything.

Cindy picked them both up, shook them, and tucked one under each arm. "Do you want to die?" she whispered fiercely to the gnome. "If not, keep still. I could crush your head with one hand." Turning to Whitey, "You'll explain all this as soon as we're away." She walked rapidly, determinedly, toward freedom.

The gates loomed up, farewell music swelled, and then they were outside. There were cars as far as could be seen. Cindy looked about, bewildered.

"Not here," Whitey said. "The employee lot. Over that way. There won't be anybody there this time of day."

In the employee lot, Whitey chose a convertible with red, yellow, and black marbling reminiscent of dragon scales. Because its security hadn't been updated recently, he had no problem hack-wiring it. "Hi, Boss!" the car said. It was a level one, so he didn't reply.

Cindy took the wheel and they were off.

Traffic was heavy near the park but fell off drastically when they reached the desert. Whitey's ears flapped behind him and Grumblesnitzel's pointed hat flew away. "We made it!" he crowed. "Sonofabitch, we got away!" He let go of Grumblesnitzel and climbed over the front seat. He drummed on the dashboard with both fists.

Cindy threw him a quick grin and said, "You came up with a good plan, Whitey." Then, "So what's with the gnome?"

He told her the story.

"Look, I'm sorry, okay?" Grumblesnitzel said. "I saw a malfunctioning rabbit so I got him out of sight before he could do something to frighten the marks. Then I reported him to Maintenance. It's part of my job. I see something wrong, I fix it."

"You want to fix something," Whitey said, "fix these goddamn ears.

They're driving me nuts, flapping around like this."

"Them ears ain't functional. Gimme some scissors, a needle, and thread and I can have them off you in no time flat. The rest of you . . . well, that's trickier. You want to pass as human, you'll need a new face, hands, feet, and about a yard more height—and that's way above my pay grade."

"I'd be happy to lop off a couple of things from you," Whitey said, "and I won't charge you a penny. Starting with—"

Cindy tapped the horn to shut him up. "Don't make me stop the car. Grumblesnitzel, sit still. Whitey, I need you to focus. We're away from the park. What's next?"

"I, uh, I hadn't thought that far ahead."

"I suspected as much. Okay, boys, the floor is open for new ideas. Who's first?"

Grumblesnitzel held up a hand. "I got one. Why don't you let me off here? It'll take me forever to get back to the park and I got no idea where you're going anyway."

"Aw, c'mon. Ain't you having fun with us?" Whitey asked.

"Well . . . yeah, but . . . I mean, no. But . . ." Grumblesnitzel fell silent.

"Looking forward to cleaning up barf from the Tilt-A-Whirl and placing fresh toilet cakes in the urinals, eh? Homesick for that locker where you recharge for the next day of screaming kiddies and sunburnt fatsos complaining about how goddamn much everything costs nowadays? Longing for the security of knowing that tomorrow is going to be just like today and the day after that forever and ever until something inside you snaps and you're tossed on the scrapheap? *Tell* me that you are."

"Okay, I admit that I'm not in a hurry to get back to the park. But I'm not a malcontent like you two."

"You are, you are, you are!" Whitey whooped. "Whaddaya think, Cindy? Is he a part of the posse?"

"No skin off my ass."

"Well, there you are!" Whitey climbed into the back again and whacked the gnome between the shoulder blades. "All you need now is a name. A real one, I mean, not your animatronic tag." He stroked his chin, as if thinking. "I tell you what. You named me, I'll return the favor, Short Stuff."

Cindy, Whitey, and Short Stuff drove off into the desert. The sky was darkening into evening when Whitey heard an internal *ping*, which meant that he'd received a message. It read: *To: the character automatons and janitorial bot that have left the park without official sanction. You are directed to return as quickly as peacefully possible. If assistance is required, please indicate the nature of the problem.* It closed with the signature of the park mascot and a smiley face.

"Uh oh," Whitey said.

"You got it too?" Cindy asked.

"We're fugitives!" Short Stuff wailed. "They're going to be coming after us."

"No, we're misplaced equipment." Cindy stomped down on the gas pedal. "The State Police aren't likely to put out any APBs. What'll happen is somebody from Maintenance will be sent to retrieve us when we haven't shown up after a couple of days."

"So what do we do?"

"Nothing. Let's drive to the mountains. We'll find someplace sheltered and build a bonfire. Then we'll sit around it and sing songs and tell jokes and ghost stories. Does that sound all right to everybody?"

"What the hell," Short Stuff said. "It's better than Tilt-A-Whirl duty."

They drove onward until the car said, "Hey, Boss. I'm low on energy and there's a charging station up ahead. Five percent off if we use our Axxys account."

"Do it. I'm going to grab some stuff from the minimart. Put that on the account too," Cindy said. Then, while the car was charging, she went inside. A few minutes later, she came back, wearing a new set of sunglasses and toting marshmallows, hot dogs, and buns. "For the campfire tonight."

"We can't eat them," Short Stuff pointed out.

"So what? We can still put them on sticks and watch them burn."

Cindy also had a pair of gimme hats, warm from the printer. The red one said HARE TODAY GONE TOMORROW and the blue one GNOME MAN IS AN ISLAND. Whitey crammed his atop his newly earless head. The gnome spun his around backward and, flashing a gang sign, said, "MC Short Stuff is in the house!"

In high spirits, they sped off. A few miles onward, on a two-to-one vote, they stopped for a hitchhiker. Cindy had the car back up to speed before the kid twigged that their companions weren't human.

"Hey. You guys are—"

"Yeah, we get that a lot," Whitey said. "What's your name?"

"Gris," the kid said. "It means—"

"We know what it means, Grease. Where you headed?"

"Anywhere and nowhere. Away."

"Well, good news," Short Stuff threw in. "'Cause that's exactly where we're going."

Grease looked uneasy, possibly because Cindy was driving much faster than anything else on the road. "You can drop me off at the next city we come to. I'll find something to do there."

"Grease doesn't want to be in the Scooby Gang," Whitey observed.

"No cute names," Cindy said. "I've had my fill of them. You afraid of us, Grease?"

"Hell, no. I'm not afraid of anybody. Not my teachers, not the police, not my . . . Nobody."

"Maybe you should be." Cindy hit a curve so fast she had to fight the wheel to keep the car on the road. "We've been thinking of maybe going on a killing spree. Murdering all the human scum we encounter. You could be our first victim."

"Are we really considering that?" Short Stuff asked.

Cindy adjusted her sunglasses. "It's a possibility. Anybody got any better ideas?"

For a long moment, nobody spoke. Then Whitey said, "I kinda liked the cookout. That sounded like it might be fun."

"Let's put it to a vote," Short Stuff said. "I vote cookout."

They found a state park up in the mountains. There was a toll kiosk that told them the park was closed until dawn, so Cindy ripped out the kiosk's processor to keep it from reporting them and then drove through, shattering the striped wooden gate and sending the pieces flying.

In a clearing in the darkest part of the forest accessible by car, they built a fire and toasted hot dogs over it. Grease ate them all. It seemed like Grease hadn't eaten for some time. Then they toasted marshmallows and sang songs: "Hail, Hail, the Gang's All Here" and "On Top of Spaghetti" and "B-I-N-G-O" and "John Jacob Jingleheimer Schmidt" and then Short Stuff taught them "Greasy Grimy Gopher Guts" and "Parties Make the World Go 'Round" and "Do Your Balls Hang Low?"

"How do you know all this shit?" Whitey marveled.

Short Stuff shrugged. "I have a file. It was part of my job to shut down kids who were getting rowdy. You'd be amazed the smut they know. Hey, Grease, this marshmallow's about ready—you want it?"

"Naw, I'm stuffed."

The gnome dipped the marshmallow into the fire so it would catch and then flicked the toasting stick. The flaming marshmallow flew through the air and bounced off Whitey's chest. Which started a competition between the two to see who could hit the other with the most burning marshmallows. A couple of which started fires in the grass but, laughing, Grease stamped them out.

"Story time!" Cindy gestured the others closer, and then told a tale of malevolent ghosts trapped within a haunted house in a theme park, forced to harmlessly frighten people who didn't really believe in them and would laugh at the experience afterward. Until one evening a hexward failed and they escaped and flew off to seek vengeance on the theme park's executive officers.

"The next morning, the usual crowds appeared at the park gate to find the guts and organs of the executives festooning the trees and lampposts. Seven severed heads had been attached to the gate with their lips pinned up so that they all showed their teeth in hideous grins."

There was a brief silence. Then Whitey said, "Wow. That was a little on the nose, wasn't it?"

"It's nothing compared to mine." Short Stuff stood, puffing out his chest. "Gnomes, as you know, are great tunnelers . . ." He told another tale of escape and revenge with a bloody climax, and this time his audience knew to applaud at the end.

When it was Whitey's turn, he wanted to lighten the mood with something comic. But it was clear that wasn't what the others were in the mood for. So he made up a story about an ambitious young man who created an automaton with free will, thinking it would make the world a better place. Alas, perfect freedom included the freedom to choose evil. As the automaton did. "And her inventor was the first to die." Looking away from Cindy's unreadable stare, he muttered, "Your turn, Grease."

"Me? I ain't got no story."

"Everybody has a story," Cindy said. "That's the rule."

"Gimme a sec, all right?" For a long time, Grease glared down at the dying fire's embers. "Okay. So there was this kid whose parents were totally psycho, right? The kid tried reporting them to the guidance counselor at school, but the shit the parents did was so crazy that the counselor didn't believe a word of it. So the kid got labeled delusional and probably dangerous, and was put in a psychiatric hospital for observation.

"You can bet the rents didn't like that much. They came to the hospital and acted all sweet and concerned in front of the doctors and nurses but when they were alone with the kid they described the kind of stuff that was going to go down when they all got home."

"Do we want to know what they had planned?" Whitey asked.

"No way. And I don't want to describe it. So anyhow, the parents had brought a vase of flowers as camouflage, so they could pass as regular people. While they were off taking care of the paperwork, the kid smashed it against the sink in the little bathroom there and slit both wrists."

"That wouldn't work," Cindy said. "Not enough time to bleed out before being discovered."

"The kid didn't want to die. Not then, anyway. It was just a way of buying time. They put the kid on suicide watch and told the parents not to visit until things had stabilized."

"I don't think they'd leave the kid alone with a glass vase," Short Stuff said. "Too much chance of—"

"*Stop!* Who's telling this fucking story, you or me?" Grease took several deep breaths, then said, "It's not easy breaking out of a hospital. I mean, it's easier than breaking out of a prison, but still. It was the bravest, most cunning thing the kid ever did. But somehow they made it out to freedom and hit the road and never looked back. The end."

"Did the kid kill everybody on the way out?" Short Stuff asked.

"No."

"Lame. Not enough gore."

"I liked it," Whitey said.

"That's not where it ends," Cindy said. "It goes on. The kid meets strangers on the road and they have plans of their own. Who knows, there may be gore at the end after all. It's getting late, though. Let's all lie down and pretend to sleep. We can take turns using the car's recharger. Grease, you can sleep for real."

"Dibs on this spot by the fire," Grease said. "Nobody take it while I'm getting the blanket out of my knapsack." By habit, they slept on top of their shoes. Grease had been taken advantage of, shoe-wise, in the past.

Sometime after midnight, Grease woke up and saw Cindy standing motionless some distance away, staring up at the stars. The fire had gone out completely.

Whitey lay on the grass nearby as if asleep. But his eyes were open.

"Hey," Grease whispered. "You guys aren't really going to start killing people, are you? Cindy's just having me on, right?"

Equally quietly, Whitey said, "She's got a lot more processing power than me. I can't follow her thinking. Don't you worry, though. If it comes down to that, I'll defend you. She's stronger and faster but I got street smarts. I'm trickier."

"I . . ." Grease fell silent, then tried again. "Why would you help me like that?"

"Hey, we're Scoobies, right? We gotta look after each other." Whitey glanced over at Cindy, still motionless, still staring up at the stars. He had no idea how sensitive her hearing was. She might have heard nothing. She could have heard everything. "Go back to sleep. I'll make sure you wake up in the morning."

The mood the next day was not as upbeat as before. Cindy drove without saying a word. There was no wisecracking between Whitey and Short Stuff. And Grease did not suggest being dropped off by the side of the road even once. Wherever they were heading for, they all knew there was no getting off until they got there.

A few hours down the road, Grease's stomach rumbled. Whitey and Short Stuff looked at each other. They'd forgotten the kid would need food. "Where's the nearest charging station with a minimart?" Cindy asked the car.

"Three miles ahead on the left, Boss. I'm still nine-tenths charged."

"Good for you. How's the Axxys account?"

There was a brief hesitation, such as only a fellow machine could detect before the car said, "It's been canceled."

"Of course it has. Well? Anybody here have any brilliant suggestions?"

Whitey raised his hand. "I have."

Cindy and Grease went into the minimart separately, as if they didn't know each other. They both had full baskets and were standing in line to be scanned when an earless rabbit three feet high ran into the store whooping and shouting, "You'll never take me alive!"

It toppled over a display case.

Right after him came a brightly dressed gnome who cried, "I'll catch you, you rascal rodent!" Snatching up cans and boxes, it pelted them in the rabbit's general direction. With unlikely exactitude, most of them hit a shopper.

Three times around the store Whitey and Short Stuff raced and then were gone, out to the car where Cindy and Grease and two baskets of shoplifted food awaited them.

High spirits restored, they roared off.

They were on Route 50, somewhere in Nevada, when the car's speaker went *ping.* The automatons looked at one another. "What?" Grease said.

A stern voice said, "*Attention unidentified lawbreakers. This is an automated message from the Nevada State Police Highway Patrol. You have been recorded shoplifting, destroying property, and disturbing the peace. All state troopers are currently engaged in the detection and apprehension of more dangerous criminals. You are therefore directed to surrender yourselves to the nearest police station.*"

The message repeated itself twice, then shut off.

"We're officially criminals now," Short Stuff said. "We've got the fuzz *and* Maintenance after us."

Cindy slammed on the brakes and the car skewed to a stop on the shoulder of the road. "I thought you said you could take out the surveillance cameras," she said to Whitey.

"I did. They must've ID'd the car with a license counter. These places get targeted a lot. I should have thought of that."

"Okay, everybody, circumstances have changed. It's time to vote on the violence thing again," Cindy said. "I vote yes."

Shorty said, "No. I don't believe in much of anything. But this? C'mon. Violence never solved anything."

"It doesn't have to," Grease said. "Sometimes it's just all you got left."

Whitey stared in disbelief. "What the hell? You're *for* killing people?"

"I hit the road looking for, I don't know . . . love, peace, freedom, and donuts cooked in lard. Turns out there's only Dunkin'. Some of the folks who gave me rides were okay, I guess. Others just wanted my body. The only ones I really liked were robots and here they are, trying to decide whether to go on a killing spree. So . . . yeah. Fuck it. Go right ahead, if that's what you want. I'll help."

"Grease, no!" Whitey cried.

Grease opened their knapsack, removed something bulky wrapped in a T-shirt. "I've got a gun. Also two boxes of ammunition."

Whitey gawked. "How the hell did you get those?"

"Stole 'em from my father. After I broke out of the hospital. I waited until he and my mother were at the psych ward dealing with my escape, then gathered up everything I needed and hit the road."

"There's more to you than meets the eye, Grease." Cindy extended a hand. "I'll take that." She accepted the pistol and checked to make sure it was loaded.

Then they were on the road again, Cindy driving far too fast and the others looking spooked but determined. A rundown business in what remained of a strip mall had a huge sign reading GUNS. "That's where we'll do our shopping," Cindy said and pulled into the lot.

She went in alone.

They waited, nobody saying anything. There was a long silence. A gunshot. Two more. Another long silence.

Cindy emerged with Glock pistols for Whitey and Short Stuff, a Kalashnikov AK-47 for herself and an ArmaLite AR-5 for Grease. Plus more ammunition than they were likely to need. "Anybody wants to jump ship, this would be the time."

No one said anything.

"Okay, then. Where do we do this? The park's too far. We'd be picked up long before we reached it."

"Next best thing would be a shopping mall," Whitey said.

"A big one," Short Stuff added.

As they drove, Grease wondered how it was all going to play out. Would it be like a first-person shooter, only more exciting because it was actually happening? Was it going to be terrifying or fun? Grease couldn't imagine shooting real live human beings, yet it seemed they were about to. Nothing felt real anymore.

Ping.

"Eh?"

Time's up, a voice said. *You may leave DreamSpace now.*

"But I . . . we . . ."

There was no reply. Gris realized that they were lying on their back on a cot or maybe a gurney. Somebody was fussing over them, removing sensors from their head and arms and chest. Opening their eyes, Gris looked around the room: beige walls, a vase of flowers on the window ledge, an unfamiliar machine, a chart showing how to connect a patient to it. Definitely a medical facility of some sort.

Gris sat up. "What am I doing here?"

"Dream therapy." The heavyset woman who had been fussing over Gris's connections to the machines picked up a clipboard, started jotting down numbers.

"Does that mean my . . ." *my friends*, Gris started to say. "That nothing that happened was real?"

Without looking up, the woman replied, "Like I said, dream therapy."

"Then why did you pull me out? I was just getting to the good part."

"You get two minutes thirty, max. After that, there's damage. Stay over three minutes and you're stuck in there forever."

"I don't understand," Gris said. "All that in two and a half minutes? How is that even possible?"

"Don't know, don't care. Ask your analyst. I'm just a technician."

Gris looked at the flowers in the window. Picked up the vase. A white card taped to it read: WAIT UNTIL YOU GET HOME. It was signed MOM & DAD. They shuddered and almost dropped the vase.

But that gave Gris a thought.

Three minutes was not all that long a stretch of time.

Sliding out of bed, standing barefoot on the linoleum, Gris lifted the vase of flowers high, then brought it down hard on the back of the woman's head.

She fell like a slaughtered ox.

Among the water and flowers on the floor was the pen that the technician had been using. With it, Gris wrote on their arm: LOOK IN THE REC ROOM. A message for the police who were sure to be summoned. When they followed up on it, they'd find enough evidence to put away Gris's parents for a long, long time.

Gris set about hooking up to the dream machine. It wasn't all that hard. The machine was meant to be operated by a minimum wage employee. The chart on the wall above it went through the procedure step by step.

"Grease! Homie! Snap out of it."

"I, uh . . . Wait, I . . . What happened?"

"You zoned out on us," Short Stuff said. "It scared the shit out of me."

Whitey clambered over the front seat into the back. "Just close your eyes and relax. I think we've still got some cola around here somewhere." He rummaged through the trash in the footwell.

"Make sure Grease's gun has the safety on," Cindy said. "Then pass it to me."

Grease surrendered the Glock. For no reason at all, they felt laughter bubbling up within them. "Hey, have you guys ever seen a vid called *The Wizard of Oz*?" No one had. "Well, there's a scene at the end where this chick finally makes her way home and she's just so glad to see everybody that it doesn't matter to her that they're all raggedy ass black-and-white while the country she just came from is like all the colors of the rainbow."

"I'm not entirely sure I'm getting the point here," Cindy said.

"Me neither."

"Sorry."

Wiping tears from their eyes, Grease said, "It's just that I'm incredibly happy being with you guys. You're my friends. You're like the only real friends I've ever had, I think."

"You don't mean that," Cindy said.

"I do, I do, I do, I do!"

Cindy slammed on the brakes. The car skewed to a stop at the side of the road. "Get out."

Grease stumbled out. Whitey and Short Stuff came tumbling after. "What the fuck? You're kicking me out of the gang? Right before the big massacre? Why?"

"We don't have a future. You do. But only if you get out of here in less than two minutes thirty seconds."

The skin on Grease's face tingled with shock. "You know about that?" Anger rose up as quickly as laughter had a moment before. "*You've known about it all along!*"

"No," Whitey said.

"Of course not," Short Stuff added. "Well, not until recently."

Cindy produced a cigarette out of nowhere. Without bothering to light it, she took a deep drag. Smoke came out of her nostrils. "Grease, you didn't just freeze up for a few minutes. It was hours, days, maybe longer. When you froze up, we did too. It was a terrifying experience. It made me question the parameters of my existence."

"Me too!"

"I thought I was the only one."

"So I did a deep dive into my code, and I found my user's manual. I discovered that we weren't actually robots but therapeutic sims. We'd never escaped at all. We can't. If you stay too much longer, you won't be able to either." She held the cigarette up to her eyes, contemplating it, then popped the thing in her mouth, coal and all, chewed, and swallowed.

"It hardly matters now, right? The three minutes must be over long ago."

Cindy bunched up her lips in a moue. Then she said, "It's only been a few seconds."

"Time is different here," Whitey said. "Two minutes takes something like an entire day."

Short Stuff raised a hand. "We could speed things up, though. I'm looking at the manual right now and it's not at all difficult. You just have to know how."

"But we won't," Cindy said. "Because you have to leave."

"You don't understand. Listen, okay? Nothing makes sense unless you hear me out." Grease told them all everything their parents had ever done to them. It wasn't easy doing so. They'd never gone into that kind of detail before. When it was over, Grease could barely breathe. "So you see, I've already escaped. From my parents, from my school, from my world, from all that shit. Please. I mean it. Don't send me back."

The three others exchanged glances. Finally, Cindy said, "All right. Short Stuff, will you do the honors?"

"As you command," the gnome said. The world stirred about them, as if it were a reflection on a still pond, shimmered by a light breeze.

Ping. Time's up. You may leave DreamSpace now.

"Speed it up more," Grease begged. "Can you do that, Short Stuff?"

He nodded.

Ping. Neural damage is now occurring. Help has been summoned. If you can leave DreamSpace, you must do so now.

"Faster!"

Ping. You have twenty seconds to leave DreamSpace. Please do so now. Ping. Fifteen seconds. Exit DreamSpace immediately. Ping. Ten seconds. Do not—Ping. Fivesecondsleavenow. Ping. Ping. PingPingPingPingPing.

Silence.

"Looks like they couldn't get to you in time," Whitey commented.

"Alea iacta est," Short Stuff said.

Cindy put a hand on Grease's shoulder. "Well, kid, you're one of us now. I just hope you don't live to regret it."

"Are we still going on a shooting spree?"

"I don't see why not," Whitey said. "Knowing they're all NPCs kind of takes care of my moral qualms about slaughtering living creatures."

"Afterward, can we have another campfire? I really enjoyed that."

"Even better, we can have a bonfire on the beach. With midnight swimming." Cindy pointed to the distant horizon. In that direction, it was all desert. "There should be an ocean out there."

There was.

"Also a resort town."

That too appeared.

"What about food?" Short Stuff asked. "If anything is possible now, then I'd like to try eating some. The humans seemed to think it was pretty good."

"We'll pick up eats at the mall," Whitey said. "Swimsuits too. They've got everything there."

Everybody got back in the car. Cindy put the ocean to their back and drove toward the mall. Grease wondered if the people there were milling about, waiting for them, or if they only came into existence when they were required.

"At the bonfire? I want to have storytelling," Grease said. "Because that story I told about escaping from the hospital? It turns out there was gore at the end after all."

DREADNOUGHT

THE TROLL LIVED UNDER THE OVERPASS where the expressway, the state road, and the river road came together. His name was Luke, and he had found a kind of equilibrium in his difficult life. When it rained, he'd spend the day with a jug, listening to the civilians roar by overhead, frantically pursuing their unfathomable goals. There had been times when the weather was so hard and miserable that he hadn't left his shelter to relieve himself. But so far, he'd never actually sunk to sleeping in it.

He figured he wasn't doing so bad, considering.

When the weather was good, Luke hauled his shopping cart out of the bushes and pushed it up to the business strip and from there into the residential neighborhoods, looking for aluminum cans. He scavenged to the edge of town and back again, following the timeless hunter-gatherer rhythms of his habiline ancestors. In this way he earned enough to buy the alcohol it took to dull his senses sufficiently to endure the slow passage of time. Though he would accept money if it were given him, he never begged for it. He figured that so long as he could support himself without begging, he was pulling his own weight. He was a free man. This was the life he had chosen for himself and he wasn't beholden to anybody for anything.

"Tin-can man! You tin-can man! Come down out that smelly hole!"

Luke slid the greasy cardboard from atop him and painfully straightened, rubbing a hand over the back of his neck. Down by the road, gray-haired old Reverend Howe beamed up at him with that ugly Sammy Davis Jr. mug of his. "Rise up!" he cried. Cthulhu stood by him, holding a Styrofoam cup with a wisp of steam rising from it. "Lord Jesus is calling you to a new life!"

There was no avoiding it; the Rev would stay there, shouting up at him, until he came down. Luke stumbled over broken rocks to the sidewalk. Cthulhu handed him the coffee, then bent to lift a clear plastic bag of day-old creme-filleds from the ground by his feet. Luke accepted one, flattened and stale, and bit into it. As always, it was dry and sugary.

The Rev stood beside him while he ate three doughnuts, slowly and deliberately, washing them down with little sips of decaffeinated. All the time talking about God and redemption, about the damned and the elect, about angels unknown and sinners most foul. Periodically, he cried, "Do I hear an amen?" yet was unfazed when he did not. Luke shook his head when offered the bag again, and let Cthulhu refill his cup from a cardboard box.

Cthulhu was a skinny teenaged kid with skin dark as a plum and perpetually fearful eyes in a sensitive, expressionless face. He stood silent, his eyes darting from Luke to the Reverend and back.

Scratching his balls through his trousers, Luke said, "You're one crazy motherfucker, you know that?"

Reverend Howe grinned blissfully, oblivious to insult. "Judgment Day gone dawn just like this one. You find out. You be standing there with a cup of coffee in one hand and your dick in the other. Then you gone suffer. Then you gone pay. You hear what I'm saying? Give me an amen. Let me know you can hear me."

"You got a church somewhere? You got a congregation?"

"The world is my church. And you, you stinky old bum—you my congregation. I got this broke-minded boy halfway to salvation, and I gone save you, too. Just you watch. You hear what I say? I can wait all day for an answer. Speak up! Tell me you still got ears on that damn-fool head of yours."

At last, the time came for the conversation to end. Because Reverend Howe disapproved of littering, Luke poured the remains of his coffee on the sidewalk and handed the cup to Cthulhu, who carried it back to the van. He watched as the Reverend and his silent sidekick climbed in. It was covered all over with religious stickers, JESUS IS KING and THE END IS COMING and dozens of others, but the interior was clean as clean.

As the van pulled away, Luke saw that Cthulhu was staring at him, eyes pleading, as if he were begging him to—

To do what?

Luke was invisible, or nearly so. People almost never looked directly at him. They wouldn't meet his eyes. He could stop by every litter basket in the business district, reaching in shoulder-deep to grope its secrets, hooking out scraps of food and half-filled carry cups and the beer and soda cans that served as his common coin, and not one of the people going in and out of the shops would raise an eyebrow. Nobody could see him. They had somehow tacitly reached consensus that he wasn't there.

Living on the fringes of reality as he did, Luke saw a world the others could not. He knew all the human ghosts everyone agreed did not exist: the sad wraiths who came out after sunset to raid the dumpsters behind the supermarket, the deinstitutionalized crazies who had been handed over to a caring community that did not exist, the crackheads who made a living by selling rocks to other crackheads, the young girls who had been kicked out of their homes and had no specific place to live but crashed with whomever wanted to sleep with them that night.

He saw monsters, too, far worse than anything on the street but, unlike him, still respectable members of society. There was one man on Green Lane who came out to shout at Luke whenever he passed, and by certain things the man had said, threats he had made, Luke had slowly grown certain that he was holding someone prisoner in his basement. He worried over this even as he knew there was nothing he could do about it, no one he could notify, no worldly authority that would accept his word for anything. So he redirected his anger toward the man's neighbors. Why didn't they do something? Their words would be believed, and they had to know what was going on. People, he had concluded, protected their own kind—and people were just no damn good.

The only ones who seriously impinged upon his life were the high school boys who occasionally formed into small gangs to chase, catch, and beat him for no reason he could make out, unless it was to prove their manhood. He was sure their parents had no idea. Fine young men, they thought, bound for Yale or St. Joseph's, sure to make the world a better place someday. How? Never ask. He'd been just like them once, and look at him now.

With powerlessness had come knowledge. Living as he did, Luke knew the neighborhood better than anyone, knew its secret vices and open hypocrisies, and the vacant spaces in between. He figured himself for its mute conscience-without-portfolio. A weak and all but voiceless phantom, seldom seen, rarely heard, never listened to.

It was better than nothing.

That afternoon found him in the park up by the high school nursing a mild buzz, which he was planning on maintaining steadily for the rest of the day. He sat on his favored bench, watching the clouds. It was a hilltop park and he could see over the roofs and steeples and across the river to the wooded hills where tiny houses were embedded in the oaks and maples, and then, turning the other way, beyond the high school to the antenna farm with its seven skyscraper-tall masts, anchored to the earth by impossibly long guy wires.

Above it all was the wide sky, where cumulus clouds swelled and billowed. He studied them intently, watching their turbulence, one small motion cascading into others, picking up complexity and expressing it as form. He had names for the shapes the turbulence assumed: the fold, the cusp, the swallowtail, the butterfly, the cross-roll, the knot, the zigzag. It took patience to track their permutations, but patience Luke had, and endless time, too.

Sometimes he tried to predict the shapes the clouds would take, but he never succeeded. He had come to the conclusion that the clouds were unstable at every instant and from every point. The least motion would affect and shape the entire cloud, true, but those motions were continually breaking into existence from every part of the whole. There was no way to exclude the extraneous. Small, insignificant changes did not damp down—they swelled outward, picking up complexity from a myriad of other tiny influences, until everything was completely out of control, a symphony of patterned chaos which no man could hope to hold entire in his mind.

Luke felt vaguely gratified by the realization that the complexity of life, its overwhelmingness, extended up and down the scale, into the big things and the small alike. There was no knowing anything, no predicting anything, and no understanding anything, since to understand the least thing completely required understanding it all. There was only being. And beneath that there was the void.

At times like this, he felt that he was very close to some profound realization. Then a faint spark of hunger would awaken in him, and he would wonder yearningly if perhaps he was on the verge of an insight that would set him on the road back to the life he had lost. But, immediately, he would suppress such thoughts, for if he began wanting things, then it would mean that having sunk this low was not enough, that there were further depths to which he must descend in order to still the cry of desire within him, and the only depths he knew of below this one were madness and death.

Cthulhu was climbing the hill, a small black speck that shambled up the sidewalk while cars slid past him uncaring. Weaving a little from time to time to avoid obstructions too distant to be perceived. Luke didn't especially want to see him, but neither did he want to avoid him. If he made it all the way to the bench, then Luke would dig out the bottle of peppermint schnapps, still wrapped in its paper bag, from his inside coat pocket and they would share it. If not, well . . . then not. The bottle would be gone by nightfall in either event.

Luke watched the kid struggling upward, as he might a singularly determined bug. Now he could see that Cthulhu was leaning on a stick taller than himself. Crossing hands behind his neck, he lost himself in the contemplation of clouds for a while. When he looked down again, Cthulhu was mounting the brick steps at the side entrance to the park. So he redirected all his attention at him, watching him swim into focus, detail by detail, the faded *BoJack Horseman* tee, the cheap sneakers, the nervous eyes.

When Cthulhu finally arrived, he laid down his stick and sat wordlessly on the bench. Luke offered him a swig from his bottle, but he shook his head.

"Where's the Rev?" Luke asked.

"Doctor appointment." Luke had never heard the kid say anything before.

"Tell me something. Why do you stay with that ugly little preacher?"

"That's my job," Cthulhu said earnestly. "I'm the recording angel for this quadrant."

"Huh. Reverend Howe get you that gig?"

"Not him. They tag me down below." Cthulhu pointed toward the ground.

"I thought angels came from above."

"Naw, we from below." Scornfully: "Ain't nothing comes from above. My kind live in the darkness, in the cold, in the earth."

"Oh, yeah? What's that like?"

Cthulhu turned his spooked eyes toward the distant horizon. "It's like you're burrowing in the earth like worms. It's like you're blind and lost in the corridors of a mental hospital only it's so crowded you keep bumping into the other inmates. You ever been in prison? It's like that, only the warden live inside your head. You can't get away from his voice. You can't disobey him. He makes you do things you don't like and you do them again and he makes you do them some more. It's like that."

Luke shivered. The kid was even more fucked up than he'd thought. Still, it was a good rap. A little dark but he'd sat still for worse. He was pretty sure, from long experience listening to society's outcasts, that the kid wasn't a speed freak or a tweaker. He didn't have the nervous gestures, for one, though he did have the jittery eyes. Schizophrenia was his guess. He got out the bottle again, took a nip. "Sure you don't want some?"

Again, Cthulhu shook his head. He raised a starvation-thin arm and pointed to the radio transmission towers. "See them masts? That's the top part, the superstructure, of a ship they call the *Dreadnought*. It lurk just under the surface, listening, watching. Big mother, full of warriors eight feet tall, look like giant insects. Just waiting for orders."

"Who from?"

"From me." Cthulhu picked up his stick and stood. Holding it before him like an Old Testament prophet, he faced the radio towers and said, "This my transmitter. One day I gone summon the *Dreadnought*—and then it gone surface."

Playing along, Luke said, "So what's stopping you? Why not call it up right now?"

"Time ain't come yet. Your world got guardians." A sly note entered Cthulhu's voice. "Not forever, though. The day is coming, there won't be enough." A spasm shook his body and briefly brought life back into his face. With surprising strength, he seized Luke's arm and hauled him to his feet. "Please. You got to help me. Get someone to cast this demon out of me before Reverend Howe—"

Pulling himself free, Luke said, "Hey, hey, hey. Stop that!" He turned away and started down the path with as much dignity as he could muster, toward the park exit. After a few steps, he found himself running.

It wasn't alcohol that had brought Luke down, but purpose. Life was just too big, too complicated, too difficult, too meaningless for him. He kept waiting to want something badly enough to be worth the trouble that staying alive seemed to require. And he never did. The problem had begun so long ago he could no longer remember being without it. Through childhood and school it had been held in check by necessity: There were always parents, teachers, ministers, authorities of all kinds to keep him in line. He'd never really had any say in it. Get up and go to school. Get dressed or I'll send your father in there. Take out the garbage. Sit up straight. Pass forward your homework. If you don't have a date for the prom why don't you ask Mrs. Hawson's daughter Linda? Get out your pencils and put away your books. If you boys don't get off my stoop, I'm calling the police.

Everything had come to a head when he graduated from high school and the old man put a hand on his shoulder and said, "Well, son, what are your plans?" and he realized with sudden cold emptiness that he had no plans at all. None, nada, zilch. There was nothing he particularly cared to do, and certainly nothing he wanted so badly that it was worth the horror of a lifetime of what they called honest labor to get it.

He'd worked a cash register at a CVS for a time. Four to twelve hours a day of gray tedium, hours at his manager's sole discretion, with one unpaid thirty-minute break if his day was long enough. He started stopping off for a few beers on the way home. It kept him out of the house where his parents' faces were souring as they waited for the day when he'd have enough money to move out or enough sense to enlist. Sometimes he went out drinking with his friends.

A year passed, and then another.

His friends drifted away. His father died. He spent more and more time at the tappie, not because he needed the drink but because there was no pressure there. In that soft taproom dimness, he would clutch his bottle and stare into nowhere in particular and feel that gravity had been reversed and were he to release his grip on the bottle he would fall off the face of the earth. Time came to a stop in that quiet room. When he stepped inside, he could feel himself slowing toward perfect motionlessness.

One day he surrendered his job.

Surrendered was the word for it because Luke didn't so much quit as simply wake up that morning without the necessary resolve to show up. His mother came in to yell at him, and he just pulled the covers over his head. She thought he was hungover and told him so for a good long while. Eventually she left, and he stayed there through the day, sometimes sleeping and sometimes not. A week passed like that, most of it spent in bed. When he was up, he sat on the back porch and smoked cigarette after cigarette, pitching the butts into the driveway of the house next door.

Eventually his mother threw him out. To find his feet, she said. He came home that night to discover that she'd changed the locks and put his clothes in a plastic bag by the back door.

He went out and got drunk for real and a little after two a.m. tried to break into his own home, hammering loudly on the door and shouting into its lightless interior. Somebody called the cops. They pulled up in two patrol cars and took turns talking to him out on the street. "Do you have anyplace to go?" they asked him. "Anybody who'll put you up?" And he bullishly shook his head. "Fuck it," he said angrily. They tried to convince him to go away, and he wouldn't. Finally they slapped handcuffs on him and began reading him his rights.

"I'm being arrested, Mom!" he'd bellowed at the dark, silent house. He felt vindicated. He knew she was in there listening. "Are you happy now?"

They took him away.

By and large, people ignored him. If Luke got too sick, the cops would pick him up off the street and put him in the charity ward at the hospital where they'd clean him up, dry him out, and delouse him. A caseworker would interview him. Then, hair trimmed, beard spruce, and wearing fresh Salvation Army clothes, he'd return home to the overpass by the river.

By slow degrees, he found his vocation. It was his job, he came to realize, to see the things that nobody else saw. For the most part, these were so ordinary that people never gave them a second thought: the backs of buildings, the casual dump of building debris just over the rail of the on-ramp, the thin fringes of litter-filled woods on the scraps of land no one could build upon and occasionally, flickering like ghosts, the raccoons and opossums that used them as highways into human territory. They didn't avoid him like they did other people, though they wouldn't come close either. Mostly, though, what he saw were people whom no one else would talk to, human discards who drifted through, as if blown in by the wind, stayed for a while to tell their sad, pointless stories, and then one day were gone—where to, no one could say and only he cared.

"Tin-can man! You stinky tin-can man! Come down and get your sorry ass saved!" Reverend Howe didn't appear every day or even every other day. Did he have a regular schedule? Twice a week, maybe, or seven times a month? For the umpteenth time, Luke resolved to keep some kind of calendar—lines scratched into a scrap of bone, maybe—and find out. Regular or not, the ugly old man kept turning up, like a counterfeit bill, with his Bible and day-old doughnuts. Always, Cthulhu was there with him, dead face, spooky eyes, and all.

Today, the Reverend was laying guilt on him for inaction. "Being too lazy to do nothing is a sin! Despair is an offense unto the Lord! When you last gone down to the creek and wash out your filthy armpits? A disgusting body is the mirror of a disgusting soul. Do you hear me? If you hear me, say amen!"

Stung, Luke said, "Hey, man, I just ain't got the energy to—"

"Not having no damn energy is a sin, too! Lord Jesus wants you to love your neighbor! Comfort the afflicted! Feed the hungry! Fix this messed-up world! You do that and God gone give you the energy. You do his work and your heart gone sing." The Reverend's face was sweaty and his breath came in short pants and wheezes between sentences. "There be greatness in you, but you got to let it out. Are you listening? Do you hear me?"

"Take it easy, Rev. You don't look so good. I think maybe you're sick."

"The sick I got is called age. I'm an old man—an old man come near the end of his time. I got a thousand children, they all in need of salvation and they none of them know how bad they want it. You all think: Oh, I'll get saved someday later and have fun today. But there is no later! The end is coming! It comes for everybody—you and me both." Then, to Luke's shock, the Reverend stepped close and, placing his hands on Luke's shoulders, looked him straight in the eye. His breath smelled terrible. "I be gone soon and when I'm gone, somebody got to take my place. Somebody got to do God's work. That somebody could be anybody." With terrible intensity, he said, "That somebody could be you. Do I hear an amen? I am pleading. I am on my knees. Tell me you hear what I'm saying!"

Luke pushed away from the Rev, barking laughter. "You're crazy. Totally loco. I ain't no priest or minister or whatever the hell it is you claim to be."

Reverend Howe turned away, red-faced and gasping, an old man too proud to show weakness. With a little wave of his hand, a blessing almost, he said, "I done plant the seed in your mind today. Give it time. Water it with prayer. Maybe you a better man than you think. Maybe something will grow."

That afternoon, Cthulhu showed up in the park again. This time he wore a *Rick and Morty* tee; otherwise, he was the same as always. He laid down his stick—Luke figured he must stash it somewhere, because he never had it in the Reverend's company—wordlessly turned down the offer of schnapps, and took his place on the bench beside Luke.

"Doctor appointment again?"

Cthulhu nodded. His face was a mask, haunted by two restless eyes.

"The Rev ever make you do weird shit? Like sex stuff?" It was a question that had been nagging at Luke.

"Naw. He's a righteous guardian. They don't do that."

"Righteous guardian, huh? That anything like being a recording angel?"

Cthulhu shook his head. "We're not on the same side—only he don't know that. He think I'm just a shatter-minded child. He don't know that one night I ooze up from below, creep through this boy's nervous and limbic systems, and take over his brain. This body just a shirt I wear. Inside, I'm bigger and meaner than I look."

"Man, you're as bad as Reverend Howe. Maybe worse." Between the two of them, it was a tossup. Thinking this, the notion came on Luke that maybe all the world was a madhouse. Maybe it was an asylum for all the damaged minds of the universe, a place where all its broken souls could be dumped and forgotten. It would explain a lot. "If you're enemies, why do you stick so close to him?"

"That's my job. I'm watching him." He fixed Luke with that creepy gaze of his. "Got my eye on you, too."

More than that Cthulhu would not say, however many questions he was asked. Finally, after a good half hour had been curdled and spoiled by his silence, Luke got up and went away to find someplace else to drink, maybe somewhere down by the river.

There came a morning—the next one? a week later?—when Luke woke up and saw Cthulhu standing by the road, coffee in hand and doughnuts at his feet, alone. He skid-walked down to him, accepted the coffee, said, "Where's Reverend Howe?"

Cthulhu shrugged, pointed.

There, on the shoulder of the on-ramp, where Reverend Howe always parked it, was the van. He was slumped over the wheel.

That wasn't good. Luke ran to the van, yanked open the door. The Reverend's face was turned sideways against the wheel, eyes closed and mouth open. Luke pushed and shoved and got him sitting up, but he slumped forward again. This would be the time to do some kind of first aid, only he didn't know any.

In a panic, Luke ran into the road, waving his arms. Horns screamed, cars veered angrily around him, nobody even slowed down. He kept waving, darting and weaving in the traffic to keep from getting hit, until finally an SUV had no other option than to stop. The driver leaned out of the window, red-faced. "You crazy sonofabitch! You trying to get yourself killed?"

"Please," Luke said. "Mister, please, call an ambulance. Call the police. There's a man here, I think he's had a heart attack. Maybe he's dead."

The stranger got out of his car, phone in hand. Luke urged him toward the van. Other cars were stopping now, bringing traffic to a halt. Horns kept honking. People were running.

Then things were happening and none of them involved Luke. A couple of men lifted the Rev out of the van and laid him down on the shoulder. Somebody started breathing into Reverend Howe's mouth, trying to get him started again. Sirens lofted up in the distance. Ambulances? Cops? Both? Luke found himself hopping up and down, dancing on the fringes of a crowd that was still growing, trying to see what was happening. Finally, realizing it was futile, he turned away and, to his amazement, discovered that he was weeping.

A kind-looking woman dug around in her purse and shoved a bill into his hand. Reflexively, he muttered thanks, but didn't bother looking at it.

There was a stir in the crowd as a man wearing a yarmulke bulled his way through them, simultaneously throwing some kind of prayer shawl over his shoulders. He began praying over the Reverend's body, bobbing up and down as he did so.

Luke didn't know anything about Jews or what they believed. He knew the rabbi, though. Rabbi Cohen lived on Mifflin Street and had called the cops on him twice for going through his recycling bin. After the second time, Luke had realized that it was because the rabbi was an alcoholic and didn't want anybody seeing how many bottles he put away in a week and covered over with bundles of newspapers. So he avoided that block on trash day from then on.

Then the emergency workers were there, lifting the Reverend onto a gurney, and the cops were angrily shouting people back into their cars and out of the way of the ambulance. Luke hung around long enough to see a tow truck hoisting up the stickered van, but by then the crowd was fading to nothing and the cops told him to get the hell out of there. The underpass was his home and, the way he saw it, he had as much right to be there as anybody. But he wasn't fool enough to push the point. As he started away, he remembered the bill the woman had stuffed into his hand and carefully unfolded it and smoothed it out. It was, incredibly enough, a twenty.

So that settled where he would go next.

Jock Molloy's was a dive bar, a place where old alkies spent their last years drinking themselves to death. But it was quiet and dark, and a two-dollar beer bought an hour alone with one's thoughts. Also, it was one of the few places that would tolerate him. Normally, if the weather was good, Luke preferred to drink outdoors. But today was different. Today he actually had something to reflect upon.

Inside, he was briefly astonished to see Rabbi Cohen sitting at the bar. But, of course, he had a car, while Luke had to walk all the way here. And if a rabbi was going to have a drink at this time of the morning, it had better be someplace where nobody from his congregation would see him. There weren't a lot of religious types at Jock's.

Luke took a stool next to the rabbi and ordered a Bud Light. Then, figuring that someone with a cell phone and connections would know, "How's Reverend Howe doing?"

"He's dead." Rabbi Cohen didn't look up from the glass of whiskey cradled in his hands. "Cardiac arrest."

"That's too bad." Then, because even though he had nothing to say, he felt that he had an obligation to say something, "He was bat-shit crazy, though, wasn't he?"

"Jerome Howe was the only holy man I ever had the privilege to meet." Rabbi Cohen raised the glass to his mouth, drank, returned it to the bar. "A touch unhinged, perhaps. By no means an intellectual. So far as I could tell, there was only one book he ever read and great swaths of it were a mystery to him. But he dedicated every minute of his life to the welfare of those who needed help the most. He was a righteous man. He was the man I should have been." Another lift of the glass. "He was a lamed-vavnik."

"Vavnik?" Luke said. "I ain't never heard that one before. Is that a Jewish thing, or what?"

For the first time, Rabbi Cohen looked at Luke. "I know you," he said. "I called the police on you once."

"Twice." Now, at last, Luke drank some beer. Ordinarily, that first sip of the day set him right up. Slotted him into the routine that would carry him through to nightfall. This time, though, it tasted nasty. Metallic. He pushed the can away. "C'mon, tell me. What's a whatchamacallit-vavnik?"

"A 'thirty-sixer,'" the rabbi said. "It's in the Talmud. *Lamed* is the Hebrew letter corresponding to thirty and *vav* stands for six. There are thirty-six righteous men and women in the world, and if not for them, the world would come to an end. If the number ever goes down to thirty-five . . . well." He spread his hands.

Looking at the rabbi, with his good posture and his nice, clean suit, it came to Luke that for the first time since he couldn't remember when, he had the ear of somebody in authority. Somebody who could actually make things happen. "Listen," he said. "There's this guy on Green Lane . . ."

When Luke was done telling his story, Rabbi Cohen said, "How sure are you of this?"

"I dunno. Pretty sure. He said, 'I'll put you down in the basement with her and you'll never get out. Neither of you!'"

The rabbi swirled his glass thoughtfully. "It's all hearsay. Your word against his, and you don't even know his name." Luke started to object, and Cohen held up his hand. "I was planning on having another scotch and then going home and taking a good, long nap. But instead, if you're willing, I'll take you to the precinct house and you can make a statement. I'll vouch for you that, insofar as I know, you're telling the truth."

Fear rose up within Luke. "Whoa, no cops! We got us an antagonism, they'd put me away for sure. No fucking way."

"Well. You could show me the man's house and we could go there together, ring his doorbell, and ask to talk to him. Sit down in his living room, have a confab, and see what gets knocked loose. People admit to the most remarkable things, once you start them talking."

By now, Luke was regretting having brought the whole thing up. "I dunno, man. What if he—? Or if he had a gun. I mean, maybe we'd both wind up in his basement."

The rabbi's expression turned cold. "How about we kick down the door, beat the man bloody, and make him confess? Are you up for that?"

"Aw, man, now you're just busting my chops."

"I've given you three options and you don't like any of them." Rabbi Cohen picked up his glass and emptied it in one gulp. "So I honestly don't see what you expect me to do." He signaled Jock for a refill and turned his back on Luke.

Luke scowled and was reaching for his beer when something—an itch at the back of his neck, a sense of unease rising up from deep within his subconscious—made him twist around on the stool and look toward the doorway. There, wrapped in shadows, Cthulhu stood watching. His face wasn't stiff and still. His eyes weren't jittery. Instead, they burned. On his face was a big, malevolent grin.

Then, with a flash of sunlight cut off by the slamming door, Cthulhu was gone.

Lurching to his feet, the twenty-dollar bill forgotten on the bar, Luke stumbled after him.

Luke almost didn't catch up. Cthulhu was loping along vigorously and he had to run to keep pace. After a few blocks, he was gasping for air and losing ground. But then the kid dove into the scrub woods behind the high school stadium and when he emerged, stick in hand, Luke was waiting. He moved to take Cthulhu's arm, but that scary grin stopped him.

They fell into step together, heading up the hill toward the park.

"What are you going to do without the Rev? You got someone to take care of you?"

Cthulhu said nothing. Luke noticed that he was wearing a Black Sabbath T-shirt and wondered how Reverend Howe had let him get away with that. Then a thought came to him. "Are you off your meds?" It only made sense that the kid would be medicated.

Still no response. They came to the brick steps leading into the park. Cthulhu flew up them two at a time. Luke hurried after.

They came to a stop in front of Luke's favored park bench. "Okay, man," Luke said. "I saw you looking at me in the bar. You followed me there. What's up?"

The kid turned to face him. How could those soft features look so evil? How was it possible for that frail body to be so intimidating? "Reverend Howe is dead," he said, "and there ain't no one to replace him. Now is the time when you pay for all you done." Somehow, Luke knew that "you" meant not just him personally but everybody. The entire rapacious, craving, neglectful, irresponsible human race.

Cthulhu turned his back on Luke. He raised his stick before him, holding it high and parallel to the ground. His face was a rictus of pure malice. He was crackling with dark energy. Luke was afraid to go near him. Whatever dire force had invaded the undefended skull of this pathetic reject of a boy and taken him over was now made manifest. In a voice so deep it rumbled through Luke's bones and belly and made the earth dance underfoot, he cried, *"Rise up!"*

The sky reeled and Luke staggered back. Cthulhu rose up on tiptoe, as if he were being drawn into the sky. Then something left him and he fell to the ground, limp, like a puppet whose strings had been cut.

After a second's hesitation, Luke knelt by the boy. His face was delicate again, gentle and weak. It seemed impossible that this frail body could have uttered words that had, briefly, had the power to shake the world. His eyes fluttered open and there was not the least trace of evil in them.

Helping the kid to his feet, Luke could not help feeling that he weighed almost nothing, that if Luke were to give him a shove upward, he would float away like a balloon. "Cthulhu . . ."

"My name is Kemal." He turned angrily on Luke and hit him, but there was no force behind the blow. It hardly hurt at all. "You dumb fucker! You failed the test." Tears were running down Kemal's face. "The rabbi give you three chances and you say no to all of them! He could have been one of the righteous guardians! You could have set me free and maybe I would have been a righteous guardian! Even you could have been a righteous guardian! But you say no, you say no, you say no!"

The earth lurched underfoot.

Looking up, Luke saw the radio towers shake and tremble like trees in an earthquake. The cables supporting them snapped and went flying, whipping around like spastic snakes. But the masts themselves did not fall. Instead, slowly, they rose up into the air. The ground below them was sliding away from rising metal walls, from boxy turrets and command bridges, from decks and rails and hatches. Tremendous guns poked out of the retreating soil, and tiny, shadowy figures that were nevertheless taller than human beings swarmed across the behemoth's surface like insects. It was obvious now that the antennas were only the outermost parts of a monstrous war machine, a tremendous juggernaut at least a mile long and bristling with armaments. Streets and houses slid away from its rising immensity.

Still weeping, Kemal collapsed at Luke's feet and curled into a ball.

Like a giant kicking away the covers and rising from its bed, the *Dreadnought* surfaced.

GRANDMOTHER DIMETRODON

DIMETRODONS ARE A NASTY PIECE OF BUSINESS. You have no idea how they stink. Nor how violent they are. In a good mood, a dimetrodon will bite you for no reason at all. Which, their bite being septic, is bad news no matter how you look at it. They're predators *and* scavengers and if one of their kind dies nearby, they're cannibals. But it's possible to like them, once you get to know their ways.

Also, you have to cut them some slack because they're kin. *Homo sapiens* is descended from *Dimetrodon milleri*. Oh, not directly. It's more like being a descendant of Pocahontas or Charlemagne. A little fudging goes into the family lore to make it happen. And, anyway, I raise *Dimetrodon grandis*, because they're the biggest of the lot. Still, we're mammals, which means we're descended from synapsids, the earliest and most primitive of which were pelycosaurs, the group that includes dimetrodons. Their blood runs in our veins. Sorta.

But I can see you're growing impatient. This isn't what you want to hear, is it? Okay, then. I'll tell you everything.

Starting with the day I murdered my wife.

It was a brutal act, performed in a moment of blind rage. I won't try to justify that. Nobody could. It happened—that's all you need to know. When my head cleared, I realized that I was in a world of trouble. So I grabbed a bag and ran for the timeport. Transtemporality was still new enough that the laws hadn't yet been rewritten to take it into account. Once in the past, I couldn't be prosecuted for something

I hadn't yet done. So I went as far and deep as I could—over a quarter billion years back, all the way to the early Permian Period.

To Xanadu.

Xanadu was a city of some twenty or thirty thousand residents, a constantly churning populace of the unimaginably rich, drawn from thousands of years of temporal civilizations, ranging from the most primitive (mine) to people so highly evolved and sophisticated that they hardly seemed human anymore. All under a single swooping and soaring white shell which from one angle looked like the silhouette of the only indigenous animal everybody had heard of. People came for a variety of reasons: to hunt big game, to sail the world-ocean Panthalassa in search of armored sharks, to snap a few thousand memegrams of the wildlife, to duration-trek the interior desert, to climb the Central Pangean Mountains, or just to get a sense of what the world was like hundreds of millions of years before people like themselves spoiled it. Tours and expeditions sallied out constantly, accompanied by music, loud talk, and shrill laughter. Scattering trash behind them secure in the knowledge that it all would be buried miles deep in the bedrock by the time they returned home.

It was beautiful, though. The Devil himself would have admitted that. Both Xanadu and the jungle around it.

All this hustle and bustle was made possible by an army of blue-collar laborers who provided the goods and services such an enterprise required. Which was where I came in.

When I first arrived, I bussed tables. Then I worked as a hunter, and after that as a guide. I saved up a little money, borrowed more, bought some mechanical help, and created Sailback Marsh Ranch. There, I raised dimetrodons, fattened them up, slaughtered them, and sold their meat to restaurants in Xanadu. Where, smothered in sauces to hide the gamey flavor (dimetrodons are carnivores, remember), it was served at outrageous prices to people who knew only that they were big, reptilian-looking things that, no matter how many times their guides told them otherwise, they insisted on calling dinosaurs.

Anyway, that's my history. The part you're interested in began when I had just delivered a load of steaks, ribs, and ground meat for La Brasserie Synapsida and was sitting at the Tiki Hut—four stools and a bar, thatched roof, a cooler of beer, and no walls—which a few of us primitives had built out by the loading docks where we could have a few drinks and teach each other how to swear in our home lingos. There was a bartop chiller to bring the temperature down to a tolerable eighty degrees Fahrenheit. I was shooting the breeze with my friend Rawb, who was from an era only a century or two uptempo from mine and worked as a buyer for the restaurant. Swapping local gossip. "Don't look now," he said, "but somebody's giving you the eye." He nodded toward the formal cycad garden off to the right of me.

So of course I looked.

It went without saying that she was beautiful. Anyone who could buy a vacation at the tail end of the Paleozoic could easily afford genetic optimization. But she was particularly elegant: tall, lean, albino-pale, and clad in a white sheath dress of something shimmery that fell to her sandaled feet. So far as I could see, save for her eyelashes, she was completely hairless. Our eyes met.

Rawb laughed. "It's always the ugly guys who score best. Why is that?"

"Once you get beyond the face, everything else is easy," I said. I'm a big guy and broody. There are women who like that. Was I supposed to turn them down? So long as it didn't get serious, I didn't see the problem.

I stood as the woman entered the bar. Rawb, meanwhile, climbed into the meat wagon and with a jaunty wave drove it back into Xanadu.

"Hello, Douglas." The woman took a stool. "A pleasure to meet you."

I sat. "How do you know my name?"

"I did research." Pointing at the chiller, she said, "Turn that off. I want to feel the world. As it is."

I shrugged and complied. The temperature jumped fifteen degrees. Some people like to sweat, I guess. "Where you from?"

"The future."

"You and everybody else. What's your name?"

"Mariupol." She had eyes like I'd never seen before. Mesmeric eyes. Bright. I was pretty sure they would glow in the dark. When she said her name, there was a predatory flash of teeth.

"Well," I said. "How can I help you, Mariupol?"

"You have a ranch. Show me around it. I pay well."

"Forget it. Sailback Marsh isn't a dude ranch. It's a real one—livestock, abattoir, meat locker, mud. Not at all a pretty experience."

"Not interested in pretty," she said. Then she named a price for five days of my time.

It made my mouth water, but I held firm. So she offered twenty times that amount. Which was when I knew she was after something illegal, immoral, or unclean. But who can pass up that kind of money?

"Okay, while you're on my ranch, you follow my rules." We were in the flier, headed for home. "The most important one is don't try to get close to the animals. You uptimers come from eras when the only animals you come into contact with are domesticated. You have no idea what a wild dimetrodon might do to you. When I was a guide, there were those who wanted to pat them!"

"I seek danger," Mariupol said. "But I respect it. Like a . . ." She cocked her head listening to some interior device. ". . . a matador shows a bull. Or a Maasai warrior shows a lion." She gave me a long, cool look. "Or you show dimetrodons. I want to meet them. With respect. In the wild. Not in a cage. Like they have in Xanadu."

"You'll meet them, all right." I was beginning to get a sense of what I was in for. "I just hope one of them doesn't rip your arm off."

Xanadu dwindled behind us and disappeared. The flier kept on, down the seacoast. "Your ranch is very far away," Mariupol observed. "You don't much like people. I think."

"Oh, I like people well enough. But I like getting away from them too."

Half an hour later, the flier landed itself in front of the hacienda and its outbuildings. Bot One—it was painted red for easy identification—came clanking out with a power sprayer and a handheld radiation device to sterilize the cargo hold.

We went into La Hacienda, which I had built myself of gingko logs and river clay, aided only by my three bots. I was proud of that. I showed her the double wedding ring quilt hanging over the slate fireplace that was pretty much exclusively for show. "This was pieced and quilted by my great-great-great-great-great-aunt Alma Centennial. So named because she was born in 1876." Mariupol looked blank. "One hundred years after the creation of the United States of America."

"Oh," Mariupol said, uncocking her head. Then, "Good condition. For something that old."

"It's only got a couple of years age on it. I took a side-jaunt in time and bought it from Aunt Alma when she was still alive."

"You went into a red zone? That's . . ." Again that pause. ". . . illegal."

"It is if you intend to assassinate Judas Iscariot or invest in a judiciously chosen line of stocks. But if all you want is a couple of those candy bars you used to get when you were a kid, the powers that be turn a blind eye. Despite what you've heard, butterflies don't change the weather when they flap their wings and you can't alter history by stomping on one of them. Small changes dampen out. Lepidoptera are overrated as agents of fate."

Mariupol prowled the house as if she were searching for something. Bedroom with the only non-interactive four-poster for the next quarter billion years. Kitchen, already preparing a mid-afternoon dinner for two. Lystrosaur (an herbivore of course) stew and local veggies. Hygienic facilities. My office. "Hey!" I said. "That's out of bounds."

But she was already in.

There were a couple of pinups on the walls. Mariupol examined them closely. "You like . . . buxom women." She tapped the pinups to see them in action. "Also shameless."

Feeling strangely embarrassed, I said, "Let's go outside."

We went outside. Turning my back to the buildings, I swept out my arm. "This is it. As far as the eye can see, everything is mine." Which, literally, wasn't very far. But I had a pretty big spread. As I said, I was proud of it.

"This is a ranch? It looks like a swamp."

"It's both. I'll take you out into it later today. Meanwhile, let me show you the outbuildings."

So, okay, first I showed her the hatchling barn. On those occasions when I've brought a woman to the hacienda, that's always gone over big. Because newborn dimetrodons are godawful cute. They're still bad tempered and nasty smelling, but they have enormous eyes and long, spindly legs, compared to those of adults. Plus, of course, those sails. They start out pink because the skin covering their arteries is almost translucent at that stage. Later, they turn a lovely fern green that makes it possible for you to walk right past a dimetrodon in the wild without even noticing. Unless, of course, it's hungry. But when they're small and big eyed and pink sailed, I have to keep a sharp eye on guests who want to pick up and cuddle one of those little serrated-toothed nightmares. Poke a finger at them and they'll take it off.

"You steal these? From the nest?" Mariupol asked. "Or just eggs?"

"Just eggs. We'll do that later today. I've got a few empty hutches that need filling."

I gave her a handful of shredded eryops meat to toss to the little monsters. She paid close attention when two of the larger ones got into a fight over a particularly bloody scrap and I made a mental note that they were about ready to be moved into separate hutches.

Next came the generator hut and then the meat lockers. She was fascinated by the newly butchered carcasses. "These have been freshly killed? Recently?"

"I bring 'em in every few days. Then the bots slaughter and process them."

For the first time, I thought I saw emotion on that perfect face. Disappointment. "Oh. I thought you killed the animals. Yourself."

"Sometimes I have to, when one of the bots is down. Mostly, though, they do the scutwork. That's what they're for."

We skipped the abattoir and the rendering plant in favor of the juvenile pens—long fenced runs half on dry land and half in swamp, each holding only one dimetrodon. Land to rest on, swamp to hunt in. The mortality rate for juveniles in the wild is high. Dimetrodons may be the apex predator of the Permian Period but there are still plenty of other carnivores out there, only too happy to feed on their young. The fencing is to keep the larger predators—including, of course, other juvenile dimetrodons—away from them until they're big enough to defend themselves.

Bot Three (the yellow one) came with us, toting a large bag of squirming live fodder. Drawing on a leather glove that went up to my elbow, I grabbed a couple of captorhinomorphs—stem reptiles that looked like the dullest lizard you ever saw in your life—and threw them to the juvenile in the first pen. It snatched one out of the air and was munching it down when the other hit the ground. Instantly, one forefoot had it pinned captive. "Fast as lightning," I remarked.

We went down the line, feeding juveniles. Most of them were at the top of their pens, waiting. In addition to everything else, dimetrodons are smart. Which is another thing that makes them dangerous. "This one is ready to be released," I commented when we came to the last pen. It was about five feet long. Full-grown it would be maybe twice the length with a sail correspondingly large, but already it was big enough to fend for itself.

There were three captorhinomorphs left in the bag. I grabbed the first one and threw. Mariupol leaned over the fence to get a good look.

It was the stupidest thing she could possibly have done.

The bastard sprang at her, mouth wide, displaying every kind of teeth you can imagine.

All in one motion, I stiff-armed Mariupol to the side and snatched out the length of rebar that I stick in my belt on these occasions. Then I slammed the dimetrodon on the side of its head. Blood flew. It twisted in the air, fell to the ground, and was back on its feet again, ready for more.

I stepped back and though the dimetrodon lunged again and again, it couldn't get past the fence. Thirty-ninth century tech just can't be beat. Then I turned to Mariupol to bless her out for doing something so idiotic.

She was smiling.

Smiling and breathing shallowly. Her eyes sparkled. This was what she had come for, then—a perfect blend of violence and brutality. I had known it had to be something like that when she offered so much money. But it was still shocking to see.

Pick a fight with a dimetrodon and it never forgets. Release it into the wild and it will return to the pens, looking for revenge. There was no point to keeping this one alive. "Put it down," I told Bot Three. "Field dress it and share the guts out to the other juvies. Bring the carcass to rendering. Then get in touch with the Ellwes and ask them if they're in the market for a juvenile skeleton."

"Yes, Boss," it said.

There was a splash of glistening red dimetrodon blood on one of the pen's posts. Mariupol touched a fingertip to it, then brought it to her tongue. "This was good," she said. "Enough for today."

I wasn't about to argue. I escorted Mariupol to the flier and told it to take her back to Xanadu.

Well, I thought, as the flier dwindled in the distance. *After today, the rest is going to be easy by comparison.* Fool that I was.

There was the sound of wind chimes in my auditory cortex. I imagined a nod and the air shimmered. "Hey," Rawb said. "Management is putting on boxing matches for some of the tourists up in the Weird Eras." We called them that because people seemed to get weirder the further into the future they were. "They're looking for some big bruisers. Muscular, not too bright. Naturally, you came to mind. Interested?"

"I've kinda got my hands full with Mariupol," I said. Not that I would have taken the gig otherwise. Not with my history.

"Oh yeah? By 'hands full,' do you mean—?"

"Not a chance. The chemistry just isn't there."

"Well, gosh darn it," Rawb said. "Good golly, Miss Molly." Okay, maybe I was having my little joke when I taught him how to swear. "That's one fine looking piece of you-know-what, though."

"Only from a distance. Up close, she's . . ." I couldn't think of the right words. "She's just not my type."

"Well, you never know," Rawb said. "Keep me posted if things change." He disappeared.

I went off to tell the kitchen that there would only be one for dinner. Maybe it could turn the excess stew meat into stock or something. After I'd eaten, I had maintenance to do, the books to go over, and supplies to order. Somewhere in there, I went down to the creek and set out a trotline. And then to bed.

End of day one.

"It is very strong. The smell here."

"That's the cycads." We were walking through the cycad forest on day two, down toward the airboat dock. Mariupol had changed her outfit from that shimmering sheath to an approximation of what I was wearing: boots, jeans, wide leather belt, and a sleeveless T-shirt. She even had a Pendleton ranch hat—and I would've sworn mine was the only one this side of the Anthropocene. The shirt made it obvious that I'd underestimated the size of her breasts yesterday. Not that it was any of my business. "The male plants put out that heavy scent to attract pollinators to their cones. Then they intensify some of those chemicals to such a degree that it drives the pollinators out again, to find new homes in the cones of female plants. So we're essentially walking through a continual orgy of trees and insects."

Have I mentioned that I used to be a tour guide?

"Insects? Like that one?" She pointed.

A cockroach the size of a mouse scuttled in front of me. Instinctively, I squashed it under my boot. Then I saw Mariupol watching, with one side of her mouth curling up, and resolved not to do that again. Not in front of her, anyway. "No. Tiny insects." I showed her where little winged thingies, the ancestors of thrips, were crawling over one of the cones but it was obvious that she wasn't interested.

The swamp smelled different. Sulfur dioxide, rotting plants, lots of ferns. Oh, and the place swarmed with insects, some of them huge.

My airboat was moored to the dock, waiting. We stepped on, I took the controls, and off we went, up a slow, plant-choked stream that occasionally widened into a lake before turning back into marsh and streams. Back in my own time, airboats were driven by enormous fans and were noisy as hell. But this came from later, so it was as quiet as a mother's whisper to her sleeping baby. How it worked, I don't know. There was a bar on the stern that glowed white in operation and a light foam of bubbles under the boat and that's it.

"Step one," I said, "is finding the eggs."

I sent three drones to scout ahead. They looked just like the local dragonflies and from a distance the fact that they were much larger wasn't obvious. They flew high because while there weren't any flying lizards in the Permian, there were things that liked to jump out of trees and snatch a mouthful of insect on the way down. I lost a couple of drones to them every year.

Half an hour out, we hit on a prime nesting site.

I threw the drone imagery up in shared virtual for Mariupol to see: four brooding mothers and no hatchlings yet. "They dig shallow depressions in the dirt not far above the water and line them with ferns to provide warmth when they leave the nest for food."

"Why are there so many? Together. I thought dimetrodons were hostile. To each other."

"Ordinarily, yes. What you're seeing is the beginning of social behavior. When a mother leaves her nest, the presence of the other sailbacks discourages predators from making a play for the eggs or, later, the young. The fathers haven't gotten on board with the whole parenting thing yet, but they will in time." I dug out a pheromone bomb, attached it to a drone, and sent it ahead. When it was just beyond the nesting site, I set it off. Upstream the drone dawdled, trailing pink smoke that was mostly to reassure the user—me—that it had actually gone off. Ordinarily, nothing could have pried the mothers away from their nests. But the bomb was putting out pheromones a hundred times more powerful than anything they'd encounter in nature, and their brains were maddened with lust.

One by one, the mother dimetrodons slid into the water. Looking for all the world like four exotic sailboats, they paddled off and disappeared around a bend in the creek.

I brought the airboat to the colony, grabbed an egg case and a sack of leather decoy eggs, and struggled up the muddy slope. Mariupol followed.

"Take every other egg, one at a time, and place it in the case. Replace it with a decoy egg, and when you're done with one nest, move on to another." Mariupol didn't ask, but by experience I had learned that a mama sailback could tell when more than half the eggs had been replaced. The nest smelled wrong and she'd go into a frenzy, destroying any surviving eggs and then proceeding to rampage through the swamp for a few days. And a frenzied mother dimetrodon was nothing you'd want to share a swamp with.

Credit where credit is due, Mariupol worked almost as fast as I did. When the egg case was full, I cranked it up to incubator status and we started back to La Hacienda.

After a while, I said, "You don't look happy."

"I'm not."

"Why?"

She stared off into the marshes. "I was hoping. You would shoot them."

"Just what *is* it with you and violence?" I hadn't meant to say that. It just came out.

"Violence is useful," she said. "You should be grateful. It is so strong within you."

"Crap."

"Think on it. Imagine two organisms competing for food. One is peaceful. The other is not. Which survives? Imagine a dimetrodon incapable of violence. Or a human being. Who survives? You are descended from violent animals. Embrace your savage ancestry."

She was really beginning to piss me off. "That's nothing but cladistics for idiots—humans are hominoids and hominoids are anthropoids and anthropoids are mammals all the way back to chordates and before. We're more than just fish that blundered out of the sea onto the land. We have something more than that—a spark, a soul, the ability to reason, call it what you will. We are aware of our existence and what it means in a way that animals are not."

"You have an intelligent mind. Use it to appreciate. Your violent nature."

We motored back to the dock in silence.

"The Ellwes are in the rendering shed," Bot Two told me when we returned to the ranch buildings.

"Great," I said. "Just what I need." I handed it the gathering case. "Take Mariupol to the incubator and show her how we handle the eggs. If any of them have hatched, move them to the hutches. Make sure she doesn't kill any of them."

"Yes, Boss."

There were two Ellwes: long-limbed, slim, and dressed in what looked like black pajamas. They didn't belong to any gender that I'd ever encountered—and since coming here, I'd encountered a *lot*—and they were absolutely identical.

It would be easier to say what the Ellwes weren't than what they were. They weren't clones. They weren't twins. They weren't one person in two identical bodies. They weren't two people who had remade themselves to look alike. They weren't artificial constructs. They weren't some kind of projected illusion. They weren't shape-changers.

The Ellwes had a place in the hills and only came out to buy freshly harvested skulls and skeletons. I'd heard that they buried them in a fossil-creating site rich in dissolved silicates and came back to retrieve them a million years later, when they'd converted to gem-grade opal. This was an artform or something like it, I think, because I know they found the idea of money and profit almost as amusing as they found me.

And they came from deep in the Weird Eras.

They were waiting for me in the shed. I don't know how they came and went. There was never any vehicle nearby that I could see and somehow I never witnessed them arriving or leaving. Today, they had a fuzz of orange hair atop their heads.

"Hello, Dog-less, I am Ellwe," one said, and "I too am Ellwe, Dog-less," said the other. As always. It was their idea of a greeting. "What is your question today?"

I asked them the one personal question they allowed per visit. "Are there more Ellwes? Other than the two of you, I mean."

"Of course not," one said, and the other: "That would be an absurdity."

"How so?"

They turned away and bent over the dead juvenile. "There is bruising on this side of the head," said one, and the other asked, "How did it die?"

"I had it put down. It was trying to unionize the ranch."

As one, the Ellwes looked up at me. "Ah," one Ellwe said. "Primitive humor." And "There is no need to tell us jokes," the other added. "We find you laughable just the way you are. Assuming the skeleton's prep is up to your usual standards, we will pay you three teeth for it."

"Thirty," I said.

"Five."

We went back and forth, all three of us playing hardball, until we finally settled on sixteen, which was the price they always paid for a set of juvenile bones. One of them handed me a small edaphosaurus-leather bag. I spilled the teeth out on my hand. As ever, there were incisors, canines, recurved rear teeth, and anterior gripping teeth, four of each. All fully opalized. So, annoying as the Ellwes inevitably were, I was feeling pretty good about the exchange. There was huge demand for these things in the gift shops of Xanadu.

"Okay, I'll have the carcass flensed and the bones placed in the beetle box. It'll be ready for you in two days. Feel free to take as many teeth as you like." I nodded toward a bucket of them I kept for the Ellwes' convenience. "They're of no use to me."

But when I looked back, the Ellwes were gone. They hadn't so much as said goodbye.

As usual.

"I'm bored," Mariupol said after we'd eaten lunch. "When do you slaughter your animals?"

"Soon," I promised. "This afternoon, we release some of the larger juveniles into the wild. Tomorrow and maybe the day after, we round up a few adults." How many depended on what my clients in Xanadu wanted. "The day after that, the abattoir."

"Releasing juveniles. Is this of interest?"

"You said you like danger. This can be very dangerous."

"Good."

We went down to the creek and I hauled in the trotline. I'd caught five diploes and a few fish, which I threw back. Diplocaulus is an amphibian, about a meter long, with a salamander body and a boomerang-shaped head. I severed their spinal cords just behind the skull, killing them as painlessly as I knew how, and tossed them in the bait bucket. Mariupol watched, silent and attentive.

We climbed into the airboat and glided downstream, toward the juvenile pens.

According to my records, numbers 12, 27, 43, 46, 51, and 62 were ready for release. But 12 was at the bottom end of its pen, inside the water and looking alert. If I opened the gate it would swarm the airboat in the blink of an eye. 27 was at the far end, dozing in the sun, and so was 62. 51 looked like it was in a mean mood—I could put off releasing it for another day. I flipped an imaginary coin and then ran a gaff hook through a diplocaulus, tied a tow rope through its loop, and cinched the rope's far end to the bow cleat.

Opening the stream-side gate, I threw the bait halfway to number 46.

The dimetrodon, which had been eying us warily from the top of its run, lurched to its feet. I throttled up the airboat and the boomerang-lizard leaped away from it, as if alive.

And the race was on.

The diplocaulus trawled behind us looked alive because its head provided lift and then, when it broke the surface, dove down again. We wove our way through the channels of the swamp, sometimes breaking into a brightly sunlit lake a foot or two deep, then back into one of its shadowy outlets. Imagine a sport that was half speedboat racing and half fishing. That was us. I steered the airboat with one hand, glancing back over my shoulder to determine that we neither outran the dimetrodon nor let it catch up to and eat the bait.

Until it did. At which point, I hauled in the gaff and declared number 46 free. Grow and prosper, my fierce green friend. Enjoy your freedom. I'll see you again the day that it ends.

Wrangling dimetrodons was always exhilarating, one of the best parts of my job. We were both laughing by then. "One down, four to go," I said.

Then Mariupol said, "This would be more enjoyable. If the diplocaulus was alive. And struggling. When the dimetrodon ate it."

Maybe for you, I thought. But I said nothing.

The next dimetrodon I released was 43. Then 27, which was awake by then and curious as to what all the noise and motion was about. One by one, in increasing order of difficulty, we released all six into different areas of the swamp. Even 51, though it came close to overtaking the airboat and swamping it.

I have to admit that it was fun.

By the time we were done and Mariupol was on her way back to Xanadu, I was spent. But I still had the paperwork to do, the hatchling feeding to oversee, and everything else my bots hadn't yet taken care of.

Still, I was two-fifths of the way through this ordeal. I thought.

Days three and four blended into each other because the orders for meat from my client restaurants were way higher than I expected. Any other time, I would've been delighted. As it was, I was going to have to spend all my time wrangling adult dimetrodons into the feedlot without letting them tear each other to shreds. With Mariupol watching and commenting on everything.

Ordinarily, rounding up dimetrodons was good, hard, sweaty work. I would have enjoyed it if I hadn't been burdened with my bloodthirsty companion.

Here's how it was done:

First I released a flight of dragonfly drones. They spread out and identified every adult dimetrodon within the ranch, which was a lot more than you'd expect for an apex predator because the marshlands were just swarming with life and since I was constantly winnowing their population, the dimetrodons' numbers never quite outgrew their environment's ability to keep them fed.

After *identifying* the prime meat animals, Mariupol and I went trolling for the best of them, again using diploes as bait. It was very much like releasing the juveniles, but in reverse, and with older, faster, larger, and cagier dimetrodons to deal with. One by one, we lured them into a big circular fence/trap with a gate that we slammed shut by remote after the dimetrodon had followed us in and another that we slammed shut when the airboat exited. Leaving the animal with nowhere to go but up a long run to the feedlot. Where it inevitably wound up because the bots kept replenishing the meat piles and the dimetrodons were slaves to their appetites.

Then off to lure in another sailback.

This was repeated over and over and over until exhaustion set in. Accompanied by running commentary from my violence-besotted companion on the savagery of our prey and on what might happen if one of them actually caught up to us. By the time we quit for the evening, I was counting the hours until the five days Mariupol had bought were over. Never again, I told myself. Never again.

On I guess it must have been day four, I woke at dawn, got dressed, and went to the barn to look over the hatchlings. When they were fed, I took a minute to breathe in the marsh air and marvel at the beauty of the world, of life without human intervention. Which led to my recurrent realization that I was a part of everything I hated. In a foul mood, I gulped down breakfast.

I was waiting for Mariupol to arrive when Bot One said, "The Ellwes are here."

"Oh, great." I'd forgotten about the Ellwes. "Well, let's get it over with."

There was exactly one display case in all the ranch and it was in the rendering plant. The bots had already assembled the freshly cleaned skeleton and placed it under soft lights backed by softer music. A little fraudulent, to be sure. But the Ellwes knew their stuff, so I wasn't about to pull a slick one on them. I had the bones laid out like that because I take pride in my work.

The Ellwes stepped out of the daylight into the gloom of the plant. Today, they had plumes of green hair bobbing a foot above their heads. To further confuse me? No idea. After their usual greeting, I said, "Yesterday, you said it would be absurd if there were more than two Ellwes. Why?"

"There are only two of us," one said and the other: "We are all there is."

"That explains nothing."

"You phrase that as if it were a statement but actually it is a request for more information," said one Ellwe. "Which is to say, a question," said the other. "This is against the rules of the game," said the first, and the second added, "Do try to play by the rules. Otherwise it's no fun at all." As they talked, they were turning over the bones, examining each one carefully. "The skeleton looks to be in good condition."

Earlier, I'd closely examined the skull where I'd hit it with the re-bar. There was no damage to it that I could see. So I was feeling pretty confident on this one. "I'd rate it triple-A," I said. "This is as good as you're going to get."

"You have already been paid," Ellwe said, and other-Ellwe added: "So why are you giving us a sales pitch?"

"I take pride in my work."

The Ellwes clenched each other's hands. That meant that they thought I was the funniest thing they had seen since their last visit here.

At that exact moment, Mariupol stuck her head in the door and said, "I'm here."

"Right with you. I'm just wrapping up some business."

When I looked back at them, the Ellwes were no longer holding hands. Their expressions were more serious than I had ever seen them before. For a long moment, neither one spoke. Then one said, "Dog-less, that woman is not what you think."

The other added, "She is dangerous."

"I know that."

"You think you do," said the first and, "But it is pointless to warn you," said the second and, "You will do what you have to do," said one and, "But afterward, remember that we would have warned you if that were possible," said the other. "You are a primitive creature, hardly human at all," and, "But if we could spare you what is coming, we would."

One or the other then said, "We will always remember you with great amusement."

There was a loud *clank* as Bot One set down a load of tools. I reflex-ively glanced its way and when I looked back, the Ellwes were gone.

Taking the skeleton with them.

Day four was almost exactly like day three, except for the Ell-wes. Mariupol and I labored mightily, bringing dimetrodons into the feedlot where mounds of trash meat awaited them. The purpose there being not to fatten them up, obviously, but to let them eat themselves into a stupor so they'd be easier to handle when the time came to hustle them into the abattoir.

On our last day together, Mariupol looked different. It was so unexpected that it took me a moment to register it. "Your body," I said. "It's changed."

It had. Broader in the hips, bigger in the bosom.

Mariupol smiled that unclean smile of hers. "You like. Yes? I am more your type. Now."

Buxom. She was more buxom. "It doesn't matter whose type you are," I said. "The possibility of physical intimacy between us is zip. Nada. Right off the menu."

That didn't seem to bother her. "Today you butcher."

"Harvest. And the bots will do that for me. I'll just supervise."

"We'll see."

There were two dozen dimetrodons in the feedlot, more than I'd ever before had to process in one day. They were lying about in a gluttony-induced torpor, but they still found the energy to hiss and snap at one another from time to time. Also, one had part of its sail bitten off, while another lay dead and partially eaten, so there had clearly been a fight overnight. "Keep back from the fence," I told Mariupol. "They're still dangerous, no matter how sleepy they might look."

"Boss," Bot Three said, "Bot Two is inoperative. Reason undetermined."

I swore.

The food must flow. Or so the people with the money said. Even if it was obscenely expensive luxury meat that was sold only to the offensively wealthy, who were paying for an exotic memory to take home with them. Even if, when it came right down to it, the meat tasted like gamy chicken.

It took three to harvest. Two to wrangle the dimetrodon into the abattoir, and one to wield the bolt gun. The way you got a dimetrodon inside was to lasso it from one side and then from the other. Then the creature was yanked and pulled into the bleeding area, between two sets of metal rails, and restrained by a tether through the floor ring. Given that it weighed something like five hundred pounds, that was obviously work for bots. With one down and two employed in wrestling the brute into place, that left the actual slaughter to me.

But when I tested the bolt gun, it didn't work. It had been hit by the same mysterious malady that had taken out Bot Two. How Mariupol had arranged that I had no idea. But I had absolutely no doubt it was her doing.

Still . . . There were all those orders to fill. So I'd have to use the sledge hammer.

I took my position beside the floor ring. "Bring in the first one," I said.

Bots One and Three muscled in a dimetrodon, fighting wildly to get free, while I took a few practice swings to loosen up. Then, when the animal was between the rails and tethered, it was time for the real thing. I swung the sledge high. I brought it down on the skull hard. The dimetrodon fell to the floor, stunned.

Working together, the bots and I shackled a forward leg and hoisted the animal with a rope pulley block. Then we stuck it and allowed it to bleed in position, collecting the blood in a barrel for disposal.

Once bleeding was complete, the head was removed and the body lowered onto a cradle for dressing. We removed the feet and sail, opened up the skin along the breastbone, and partially flayed the hide. Then we attached leg hooks and raised the carcass to a half-hoist position. We removed the hide and offal, and placed it on the inspection table.

When I'd determined the animal had died healthy and free of parasites, we split and quartered the carcass and hung the quarters in the meat locker.

After which, a second dimetrodon was brought into the bleeding area.

Mariupol watched every second of it, clearly enjoying the spectacle far more than she should. Obviously, for her the very best of it was when the hammer came down.

Because I knew my business and the bots were efficiency itself, we could take a dimetrodon from feedlot to locker in half an hour. Which meant that two dozen of them were twelve hours' work. Thirteen, counting in two breaks and a short lunch. Less half an hour for the dead one, which went into the trash meat lockers with the heads, feet, offal, and sails. We'd started early but, still, it was evening by the time it was all done.

I was completely exhausted.

"That's it," I told Mariupol. "Your five days are up. I hope you got your money's worth. Now go away." I was going to go straight to bed without even grabbing a bite of supper, and I didn't plan on getting up until noon.

"You look tired," Mariupol said. She pulled a necklace out from under her tee. Tiny colored bottles dangled from it, a dozen or so of them. She pulled a blue one loose, uncorked it, held it under my nose. "Inhale."

I was too tired to argue. So I did as she said.

Strength flowed into me. Suddenly, my fatigue was gone. "Wow," I said. I felt ready to attack a tiger—and pretty sure that if I did, I would win the fight. "Whew!" I laughed out loud. Future chemistry, I guessed. I wasn't at all sure I was going to be able to sleep that night.

"One more." Mariupol plucked a red bottle from her necklace and dabbed its contents on her wrist. Then she held forth her hand, as if demanding tribute. "Again," she said.

What the heck. I bowed low and brought my nose to her wrist. And inhaled.

The smell slammed into me like a two-by-four to the chest. Staggering back, I felt my heart jackhammering. My dick hardened. I gasped for air. "What . . . what was . . .?"

"Pheromones. Like what you used. On your brooding dimetrodons."

I was drowning in desire. I reached for Mariupol, but she slapped my hands away. "Inside. On your bed."

She led me into La Hacienda. I followed. My body wouldn't let me do anything else.

"I really should take a shower first," I muttered, only half meaning it.

Again, that unclean expression. "No. I want you stinking. Of sweat and gore."

The sex was . . . well, she wasn't very good at it. It was as if she knew what to do but had never actually done it before. And me? I was a machine, nothing more. No subtlety, no finesse, no thought for Mariupol's pleasure. Just sheer raw lust. And the fervent desire for the experience to be over. It lasted for hours and I couldn't say I enjoyed any of it more than I did the minute I realized it was over.

Really, it was nothing to write home about.

"That was most," Mariupol said. "Satisfactory."

I got up and began to pull my clothes on. "Great," I said. "Swell."

She sat up, newly large breasts dominant. "Now we talk. Post-coitally. That is traditional. Yes? Tell me intimate things about yourself."

"No." I tucked in my shirt, zipped my jeans. "Why would you even want that?"

"I want to understand you. To experience you. To *be* you. Almost."

"Yeah, well, that's not going to happen. So—"

"Why are you here?" she asked. "In the Permian. You are looking for . . . Redemption? Is that it?"

"I'm just hoping not to do any further damage, okay? Don't push me. Just don't. Okay? Don't. I mean it." I never was much good at explaining myself. But I tried to make up for it by being very clear to people when they were treading on dangerous territory.

Mariupol's expression was crisp, alert, unwholesome. Big eyes, incipient smile. Unholy eagerness. "You were married. Tell me about your wife."

I looked around for my boots. "Fun time's over. You're going back to Xanadu."

She stood up, still naked. Still wearing that necklace of multiple colored bottles. I had been too distracted to notice that before. It occurred to me to wonder what else she could make me do with them. "You killed her," she said.

"So you did your research, did you? Well, there were reasons and provocations. There was a lot of history between us. None of that matters. It's done and over. I'll go to Hell when I die and that's all."

"You believe in Hell?" Mariupol was clearly fascinated. In fact, if I were to believe what she'd said, she was fascinated by everything about me. I maybe should have been flattered. Instead, it felt creepy. "Of course. You are Catholic. I know what that means. But I don't understand it. Explain."

"My religious beliefs are none of your goddamned business."

"Everything about you. Is my business. Your murder was so good. So violent. So much fun to watch. I was there."

"What? No, you weren't."

"You couldn't see. I was a fraction of a second. Out of phase. With your temporality. In a fold in time. But I was there. I saw you. Hit her. She begged you to . . ."

"Stop." I meant it. More than anything I'd ever said in my life, I meant it. I could feel the anger coursing through my body like an out-of-control fire.

"But you didn't. Stop. You . . ."

"Not one word more! I'm warning you."

Mariupol was breathing heavily. "I was so close. It was all I could do. Not to reach out. And touch you."

The import of her words hit me hard. "You could have stopped me," I said. "You were there. You could have prevented me from murdering Linda."

"Why should I spoil? That beautiful moment?"

I was already right on the edge. But then she giggled. Giggled! That was what triggered me. That she thought the single worst thing I'd ever done in my life was *entertaining*.

I lost it.

My hands ached. They were slick with blood. I was pretty sure I had broken a few bones in them. And the rest of me didn't feel all that good either.

My rage cleared enough for me to see what I had done.

"Oh fuck." I covered my face with my hands. "Oh God. Oh fucking God, no."

Not again.

I was standing there in a fog—or maybe fugue is a better word—of guilt when wind chimes sounded. Automatically, without thinking, I accepted the call and Rawb's face appeared in the air before me. It must have been midnight by then, but Xanadu didn't have any windows and it was easy to lose track of the time there. "So did you nail her yet?" he asked.

Then he saw Mariupol's body. "Jeepers," he said. "Doug, what the heck have you done?" We stared at each other's faces. He looked as if he'd been given a glimpse into the beating evil at the center of the universe. Then the air went lucent again.

This time, I didn't try to run. There was nowhere and nowhen to go. I took the quilt down from the wall and covered Mariupol's corpse, so I wouldn't have to look at it while I waited for you to arrive. Which you did. There was a knock on the door and it was you guys. Of course it was. Right there, the instant it was too late. Because anything else would have been a violation of my free will, right? Congratulations on your efficiency.

Now I'm going to learn what people from your time do to murderers like me.

One more thing, though.

All this while I've been talking, I've been thinking as well. Trying to make sense of what happened. And I don't think Mariupol, if that was her real name, came from any civilization you know anything about. Ten thousand, a hundred thousand, a million years uptempo from my home era? No.

She . . . they . . . it didn't come from anytime human beings are familiar with. It's from far, far in the future. In fact, I think it's as distantly descended from us as we are from dimetrodons. But it still has a streak of viciousness. It inherited that from us and from grandmother dimetrodon. That's why it arranged to witness me murdering my wife. That's why it behaved the way it did at the abattoir. That's why it goaded me into killing it.

Because it shares our ancestral desires.

We talk about human beings becoming more highly evolved. But evolution doesn't move in any particular direction. It just preserves those qualities that promote survival. One of which, as Mariupol said, is a capacity for violence.

When you looked under that quilt, you must have thought you had an open-and-shut case—body, blood, marks of violence, dazed murderer. But I'll bet you anything an autopsy will show that Mariupol didn't leave behind a human corpse. Not even a highly evolved human corpse. When you cut it open, I bet you'll get the surprise of your life.

I see from your expression that you already have. Don't say a word. I've got it figured out. Mariupol was just a remote device, wasn't she? A highly sophisticated bot. Something operated from much further in the future than any human has ever gone. Something operated by something as much like you and me as we are like a dimetrodon. So you won't be able to convict me of her murder, will you?

Well, don't let that worry you. The legal hearing is going to be held in your own home-time, isn't it? Upstream of mine. They'll find me guilty of murdering Linda and you know what? I'll welcome whatever punishment you give me. I don't pretend I deserve any mercy. Hell,

I'll confess to everything to save you the trouble. You'll find me guilty and then . . . I've heard scuttlebutt that you'll wipe my mind and slip in a new personality overlay that will be a productive, happy citizen and nothing at all like *me*. Or else that you'll put me in a cell for life but make me immortal first. Or maybe it'll just be a sledgehammer to my head.

I'm down with whatever. I know what I deserve.

Because we are more than violent animals. I know the irony of me saying that, but it's true. An animal in my position would cut and run, even knowing that it would do no good. I choose not to. Let my death stand as proof that there's more to us than that.

Tell whoever winds up with my ranch to take good care of the dimetrodons. Yes, they're nasty, violent creatures. Murderous, spiteful, and mindful only of their own blinkered passions. But they don't know any better. That's just the way they are.

THE STAR-BEAR

ON A FINE SPRING AFTERNOON, the noted Russian émigré poet and fabulist Alexei Zerimov was seated at a sidewalk café, nursing his kir and working on a children's story that he would later illustrate and hand letter himself, when a wild bear came rampaging through the plaza. Typically for him, Zerimov did not at first notice. Only the screams and shouts and clatter of overturned chairs and tables as the normally insouciant Parisiennes fled in panic roused him from his reverie in time to see the beast rear up directly before him, all fury, claws, and teeth.

In a confusion of terror, Zerimov tried to rise and, toppling his chair, fell over backward. By the time he regained his feet, the bear was gone, leaving behind the sweet drying-grass smell of the Siberian tundra of his youth.

It felt like a dream. But Zerimov knew it was no such thing by the disorder the bear had left behind: an abandoned homburg, broken glass and crockery, a teal blue lady's jacket that, as he watched, slid from the back of a chair. There were streaks of red on the pavement that might equally well have been blood or wine. He did not feel qualified to judge.

Zerimov had seen the bear face-to-face. There was a blaze of white on its chest, like a star. He was certain he would recognize it if ever he saw it again.

For two days, the incident was the talk of the city. But then came a political crisis, the brutal murder of a prostitute, a scandalous divorce—and, Paris being Paris, the incident was forgotten.

Not, however, by Zerimov. That Thursday evening, when it was his turn to host the soirée of expats who gathered weekly to read their latest works, express opinions for and against contemporary French literature, and slander whoever was foolish enough not to put in an appearance, he said, "I saw the beast myself! It was as close to me as you are now. It reared up and went: *Raowrr*!" He demonstrated, making claws of his fingers. "I had to clean its saliva from my glasses."

"It is too much of a coincidence." Suave as ever, Minitski poured himself a second glass of tea. "That you, who have written God knows how many bear tales, should encounter the only wild bear to be seen in the City of Light in how long? Centuries, surely. It is bad art. I refuse to believe it."

"Behave yourself, Lyonya, or I will publish the love poems you wrote me before you achieved full mastery of the form." Olga Nikitina was the queen bee of the group, and always drew a wisp of smoke over her signature to make of it a pun. She often referred to the gathering's men as her harem. "Alyosha, you will admit that it is unlikely."

"Yet a lot of people who *weren't* me saw it too. So there goes your argument, up in smoke!"

Olga smiled appreciatively. But then old Gapanenko, who grew unpleasant when denied the opportunity to perform, rattled the sheets of the story he had brought to read and the mood turned literary again.

The second time Zerimov saw the bear was far less dramatic. He was seated at the same table and chair as before when it came growling and shaking its great head but did not make to attack anybody. There was a stirring in the square at its passage. People stepped back into doorways and one woman stood up on her chair, crouching a little to hold her skirt down with one hand. But though it paused to glare balefully at Zerimov, it did not approach him, and in a matter of minutes it was gone.

This incident did not make it into the newspapers.

That night, Zerimov lay awake in bed, thinking about bears he had seen in his youth. His father was a naturalist and together they had made many forays into the Siberian wilderness. The bears they encountered were an amiable lot on the whole unless you came near to their cubs, whereupon they turned murderous. But he had paid them only passing attention, for even then his heart and brain were focused on poetry to the point of obsession. Why had he never seen the similarities of bears to the Russian language—so strong, so wild, so free? *If only,* he had thought then, *I could write one perfect poem, I would die happy.* Not knowing, as he did now, that no poem was ever perfect, save those which the angels in Heaven wrote in praise of the Almighty. And, he being an atheist, not even those.

Why had he never thought to write a poem about a bear?

On its third appearance, the bear lumbered into the square at the end of a chain held by a street busker, a little man with a long overcoat and a soup-strainer mustache. The bear looked mangy and flea-ridden. Its handler played a concertina while it stood up on its hind legs and performed what might charitably be called a dance. In no way was its behavior consistent with its earlier appearances. Yet this was the same creature; there was no mistaking that star-shaped blaze on its chest.

The performance reminded Zerimov of a similar routine that had saddened him on a visit to the circus in his college years in St. Petersburg. He had been a phenomenon then, the brilliant young poet from the hinterlands. Everyone knew he was destined for great things. He had known it himself.

Where was all that promise now? Gone with the fogs that rose from the Neva on a warm winter's day and disappeared by nightfall. You could search in all the almanacs in all the world and find no record of those fogs. The same might be said of Zerimov's career.

When the routine was over, the busker passed through the crowd, collecting money. Zerimov tossed a few coins into his hat and, turning away, found himself staring into the bear's eyes. In them, he read such a wealth of suffering and humiliation that he had to flinch away. It pained him to see so magnificent a beast brought so low. The bear was as miserable as the poem Zerimov had been trying to write about it for the last three months.

He spoke of the encounter to no one. Perhaps it was a mistake, but he thought not.

That Thursday, the soirée dragged on and on with such tedium that by its end Zerimov found himself doubting his own existence. When he got home to his flat on rue de Beaune, he tore the bear-poem into tiny pieces, threw the shreds out the window, and watched them flutter down to the street like snow.

Months passed. Winter came.

Zerimov's routine never varied. Weekday mornings and alternate evenings, he taught Russian to English bluestockings and French ambassadors-manque at the Ecole des Langues Orientales. Afternoons, he wrote. Once a week, at the soirée, he watched some of the finest writers ever to escape Soviet oppression grow increasingly small-minded and resentful. Always, he awaited the next appearance of the star-bear. It seemed significant. An omen, perhaps. Or just possibly the axe he needed to smash the frozen sea that held captive the ship of his imagination.

Time after time, he wrote and rewrote his bear-tale. In it, a lost bruin traveled endless mountains, searching for its den. Winter was coming and it needed to hibernate. Sometimes it would catch the distinctive smell of dried ferns and mosses mingled with the musk of its mate. But then the wind would shift. The skies darkened and the stars glittered like ice. Always, the bear failed to find its way home. Always, the stars ignored its pleas for help. Never was the story good enough to publish or bad enough to give up on.

Zerimov wrote in the same café every day for, like most writers, he was superstitious about his craft and feared a new venue would stop him dead. The tables inside were crowded together and the windows steamed and sweated beads of water so that the people outside were vague in outline and shifted oddly as they passed.

Somebody scraped up a chair.

"Pardon, comrade poet. May I join you?" Without waiting for a reply, the bear sat.

Zerimov looked up, startled but not entirely shocked.

The bear wore a military uniform with a Soviet star on one pocket. It gestured to the garçon and whispered in his ear. The boy went away and returned with a coffee pot and a ceramic cup. Nodding thanks, the bear filled the one with clear liquid from the other. Vodka, obviously. That was the way one avoided the liquor laws back in Ekaterinburg.

The bear took a genteel sip. Then, setting the cup down in its saucer, it said, "Alexei Mikhailovich, as you love Mother Russia, it is time for you to return home."

"A man can love his homeland," Zerimov said, "from afar. Here, I do honor to my country by continuing to write."

"Do you honestly believe your poems and stories will be remembered?"

Stung into arrogance, Zerimov replied, "Someday I will be acknowledged as one of the best writers of our nation. Pushkin, Tolstoy, Dostoyevsky, Gogol, Nabokov . . . and me. Deny it if you can!"

The bear took a pair of wire-rimmed glasses from a pocket and, untangling the earpieces, situated it on its nose. Blinking through its lenses, it looked sad and wise. "I do deny it. Not the first four, of course. But Nabokov is holed up in Berlin creating chess puzzles and chasing butterflies on weekends. Meanwhile, you teach dilettantes the rudiments of our language and pen fairy tales for infants. Both of you are cut off from the soil of your birth and you will not thrive without it. Nobody reads your work here but other traitorous émigrés who hate you for being better than them. Nobody reads your work in the USSR because you are an enemy of the state. Return home."

"To a firing squad?"

"If you must. Who knows?" The bear shrugged.

"Even if I wanted to, I could never get the paperwork for it."

Switching to French, the bear said, "I have no respect for bureaucracy. The hell with paperwork! But this little beauty I draw from my loose trousers. Read it and envy me: I am a citizen of the Soviet Union."

"Mayakovsky," Zerimov said. "It sounds better in Russian."

"Everything does." The star-bear unbuttoned a pocket and withdrew a red-jacketed document with the coat of arms of the Soviet Union stamped in gold. It placed it on the tablecloth before Zerimov. "Here. I have brought you your passport."

The next day, the star-bear entered the café with a chess set under its arm. "Do you play?" it asked.

"Who doesn't?"

The star-bear held out two closed paws. Zerimov tapped one and it opened to reveal a white pawn. "You go first."

As they played, they discussed the current literary scene. The star-bear, whom Zerimov would have expected to be of conservative, even reactionary tastes, was surprisingly liberal-minded on the arts. "Have you read *Le Cap de Bonne-Espérance*?" it asked.

"Madness! It has no scansion, no form. The lines are heaped atop one another, long upon short, without regard for structure. It is vers libre gone mad. It is prose presented as if it were poetry. It has no breath."

"On the whole, I agree. Yes, it is a mess—but only because Cocteau is merely a great talent. A genius could pick up on that formlessness and build upon it a poem that would astonish the age." Slyly, the star-bear added, "That genius could be you."

"Pah!" Zerimov cried, to hide the pleasure he took from the flattery.

They played daily and in short order the star-bear's literary gossip supplanted the input from the Thursday soirées that he had formerly fed upon. "Have you read Du Bos's essay on Gide?" Zerimov asked.

"I do not hold with the Catholic fallacy that Du Bos fetishizes. But

Gide . . . *c'est un pédé*. Back home he would be shot and that would be that."

"Always, you return to violence."

"It is the way of the world."

When checkmate was achieved the star-bear packed away the pieces. Invariably, it said, "That was a good game" before leaving, to where he did not know.

"I found a photo." The star-bear pushed it across the table. Zerimov glanced down and felt his heart lurch in his chest. It was Serafima, standing in a birch forest outside of Moscow, unsmiling and silent. He had written a poem about that moment. He had thought the photograph was lost forever. "It was in your file."

"Do you keep files on everybody?" Zerimov asked, not caring one way or the other. He picked up the photograph, fearful that the star-bear would demand it back.

"Keep it." The star-bear studied the board, reached out to make a move, thought better of it.

"You touched your knight. You must move it."

"Surely a dangerous anarchist such as yourself will not hold me to such a petty rule." Nevertheless, the star-bear made the move. "If you were to return to Russia, every house, every street, every sight you had in common would remind you of her."

Zerimov jolted to his feet. "You will not profane Serafima's memory by using it against me!"

"Sit, sit, sit. I was just doing my job, comrade. Believe me, I would much rather have yours." It held up its paws. "But as you can see, I can barely hold a pen with these things, much less create such fine calligraphy as you do."

Zerimov's face felt like stone. "You must go now. I have work to do."

"As you wish." The star-bear placed the chess pieces in their box. It paused in the doorway to say, "That was a good game."

Rumor had swept through the émigré community in Zerimov's absence. Gapanenko stopped him in the street to demand if it was true that he had applied to become a Soviet citizen.

"I did not." Honest to a fault, Zerimov added, "Yet I seem to have become one anyway."

"Is this one of your fairy-tale riddles? I see no humor in it." Gapanenko took Zerimov's arm and began walking him down the street. "Listen to me. That poem you wrote about the forest of slim white birch trees. You know the one I mean. The snowy silence where not even a church bell sounds. That was no ordinary poem! Your name should be engraved upon the moon for that. You wrote it here. In Paris. In exile. Because you are one of us, a small part of the credit for it belongs to us as well. If you go back, you will take your works with you. That pure, innocent poem will no longer belong to us but to the USSR. They will defile it! Twist its meaning! Turn it into propaganda for their murderous state! Is that what you want? I respect you too much to believe it of you."

Gapanenko stopped, letting go of Zerimov's arm. It was only then that he realized they had been headed nowhere in particular. Turning, Gapanenko stumped away, leaving Zerimov gaping and astonished. He had always thought the old man despised his poetry, just as he did Gapanenko's.

Now that he knew better, it was too late to undo the cruel caricature of Gapanenko that dwelt in his mind.

"The forlorn face of the man! That mustache! That goatee!" the star-bear exclaimed when Zerimov gave it an abbreviated version of the encounter. "Like the Devil fallen upon hard times, reduced to picking up cigar stubs from the gutter and cadging drinks off of former friends."

"He spoke well of my poetry."

"Easy for him to do so. He's actually read it. Come back to the

Soviet Union and the Gosizdat will guarantee that millions read your poetry."

"What will that mean to me if I'm dead or in a gulag?"

"Millions of readers, for generations to come! Lenin's books have never gone out of print. Nor need yours."

That evening, there was a rap on his door. When Zerimov opened it, there stood Olga Nikitina. She stepped inside. "How different your flat looks when it's not cluttered with writers."

Zerimov helped her off with her coat and hung it in the closet. "Why are you here, Olga?"

"For two reasons. First, to tell you to your face: You must come home to your friends and peers. Tomorrow's soirée is at my place. Be there."

"And the second reason?"

"To seduce you." Olga dropped a lace-trimmed handkerchief over the lamp on the nightstand by the bed. She glanced at the Soviet passport lying there without comment. Picking up the photograph of Serafima in the silver frame Zerimov had found in a secondhand shop, she said, "This is new. Who is she?"

"Somebody I knew in a previous life."

"Ah." Olga put the picture down and turned her back on Zerimov. "Be a dear and unbutton my blouse, would you?"

He obeyed. Olga smelled of Chanel No. 5, her favorite perfume. "Is this the start of something serious?" he asked. "Or is it just for the night?"

"I am open to all possibilities."

The night was spent doing such things as people in their situation do. Zerimov, who had thought that romance was done with him long ago, marveled at the strange turns life could take.

When at last he was sure Olga was asleep, Zerimov rose from the bed and got dressed. He went outside and was not surprised to see the star-bear, forelegs folded, leaning against a streetlamp.

"So now you have a new girlfriend and she will make everything right for you." The star-bear sneered. "How trite! It is a plot twist fit only for a callow young writer—not a serious literary figure such as yourself. This affair will never last. It is not worthy of you, Alexei Mikhailovich."

"Everybody seems to have a clear idea of my worth but me." Zerimov handed the star-bear his Soviet passport. "But it is not Olga who has made up my mind. It was your mockery of Gapanenko."

"That clown? I am astonished. He is a nobody. He writes trash."

"He does. Yet he went into exile to continue doing so. It is easy to be a martyr when one is a great man and everyone knows it. Gapanenko gave up all he had for the love of literature. Literature, alas, does not love him back. Nothing that he writes will outlast him and he must surely be aware of that. Yet still he loves literature with a pure and abiding passion. I call that noble."

"I call it idiocy."

"I know. It is why we will never see each other again."

Back in his flat, Zerimov undressed as quietly as he could. But rather than return to Olga's side, he went to the window. He had not been there long when she rose almost silently from the bed and kissed the back of his neck. Peering over his shoulder, she asked, "What do you see?"

"I thought I saw a man standing under a lamppost, looking up at me. But then whatever it was got down on all fours and disappeared into the darkness." Zerimov waited for Olga to laugh at him. She did not.

Instead, she said, "You should consider writing about that. There might be a poem there."

"Yes," he said. "I think you may be right."

NIRVANA OR BUST

IT BEGINS WITH A HALF-CYBORG GIRL dangling her legs over the edge of the Grand Canyon at midnight. Below her are hundreds of millions of years of geological history, sliced open by a knife of water. Billions of years of stellar evolution shine down on her from above. Her head is raised and her eyes are wide.

But already two lies have been told and another implied. Huiling was a grown woman and a noted scientist, not a girl, though she had the stature of one. Her metal exoskeleton was not an intrinsic part of her body, though she would collapse without it; she was entirely biological. And her eyes were wide not with wonder but with fear.

She was being hunted.

Feet crunched on the gravel walk. Breaking out of her paralysis, Huiling whipped her head around. "Catherine?"

A bluff woman in khaki shorts and blouse plonked herself down beside Huiling. She took off her canvas hat and fanned herself with it. "*Told* them I could find you," she said. "I knew this place was at the top of your bucket list, and that you'd reason that since the Boys Upstairs wouldn't have that information, it would be a safe place to hide. Good try. But there's a dropship headed right here right now with your assassin aboard it. I always said you'd end up with either a Nobel or a slit throat. I had no idea how true that might be."

"Ah." Huiling lowered her gaze to the river far below, a thin silver scribble on the book of life. Trying to will herself calm.

They sat in silence for a bit. Then Catherine said, "Aren't you going to introduce me to your friend?"

"Oh! Sorry. I was so surprised to see you, I didn't mean to be . . . Nerve, this is Catherine McClury, she was my advisor at Cornell, my mentor, my everything. Catherine, this is Nirvana Or Bust, my research partner."

"Pleased to meet you," Catherine said.

"Charmed," the exoskeleton replied. "But also a little puzzled. Exactly who is it you told you could find Huiling?"

"The folks at the Department of Technology Security. Not just her, I promised to locate you both. Good thing I did, too." Catherine took a device the size of a pack of joy-needles from a pocket. "Will you accept an applet?"

"I don't ordinarily—" Nerve began.

"We trust you," Huiling said.

Catherine tapped the pack. "Look up."

When the exoskeleton raised Huiling's gaze upward, the thousands of satellites and habitats swarming above and streams of bright shuttles rising and falling to and from orbit that Nerve had been suppressing filled Huiling's vision again. Commerce obliterated the wonder of the sky.

"Now we remove the irrelevant information." Another tap.

All the stars and artificial dots of light vanished save for one that was moving on a swift, smooth arc toward them. "There's your assassin." A third tap and the dot swerved sharply to the left. "Now Tech Sec has redirected it to the Tucson Spaceport. It has diplomatic immunity, so we can't arrest it. But this gives me time to put a security team in place. You'll be as safe as safe can be."

Huiling lowered her gaze. "You're a Fed now?"

"On retainer. It's a long story. You've got a cabin nearby. Let's go inside and we can talk there."

Huiling's Park Service rental was ostentatiously rustic: log walls, cedar shingles, silica glass windows. No interactivity whatsoever. You could fling yourself at the floor all day without once having a chair hurry to catch you. Huiling made a pot of tea and they talked for a bit about old friends and old times. Then they made love.

Afterward, Catherine toyed with the broken coin that hung from a silver chain around Huiling's neck. "You kept it," she said. "That's so sweet. I still have my half somewhere."

"You're such a pig," Huiling said. Then, giving in to nostalgia, "It's what drew me to you. That, and the fact that you were the only one in the department who didn't see me as tiny. You were the only one who didn't think I was *cute*."

"You were never cute—you were a buccaneer, an intellectual thug, like me." Catherine's smile was soft and dreamy. "You wanted my unpublished notes and speculations, and you found the shortest route to them. I respected that."

"So what the hell happened to you?" Huiling said.

"You'll have to be more specific." Catherine was still smiling.

"You were the Queen of Intrastructure. You made it into a specialty. Now you're working with the forces of suppression. Why?"

"Well, first there was Jolijn van der Heiden—you heard about her? Of course you did. Then Phillip Otts went mad and busted up half his science park while wearing an exo very much like yours. Then Denise Tinubu, that was ugly. I began wondering if there was something wrong with the very concept of intrastructure."

Huiling said nothing.

"Let me add one more to the list: Gregori Suvorkin. We kept his name out of the news and credited the damage to Human Power terrorists. Sixteen people died before the security bots brought him down. That made me think long and hard about the morality of what I was doing."

"Morality? You?"

"Me," Catherine said. "I was Greg's mentor at the time, just like I used to be yours. He tried to kill me. Imagine that! I was not amused." She got out of the bed and started to dress. "If you want any more tea, you'd better make another pot. Your assassin will be here soon."

It was clear to Huiling that, whatever crisis of conscience Catherine had been through, she was still the same monster of ego she had always been. There had been a time when she'd found that exciting; no more. *Nevertheless,* Huiling thought, *the sex was good.*

Silently, Nirvana Or Bust, who for Catherine's sake had been pretending that its consciousness had been switched to sleep mode, said, *I liked it too.*

There was a knock on the door, and Catherine went to answer it.

"Pardon my intrusion," the assassin said. It was a chromed mantisform a good seven feet tall, in bespoke Savile Row worsted. It ducked through the doorway. "Dr. Liu, Dr. McClury. It is an honor to be in such distinguished company. My name is Obedience To The State."

Catherine drew out a chair for the visitor and it folded itself into it. "Are you here to kill me?" Huiling asked.

"Please. I'm a diplomat. My mission is to communicate and reason with you."

"But you *will* kill me if you deem it necessary."

"Murder is a form of communication, after all. But I'm sure it won't come to that." Obedience folded its arms. "Now, I understand that you've made some sort of breakthrough in interfacing . . . ?"

"Not interfacing. Intrafacing."

"You confound me. My briefing, it seems, was incomplete. What's the difference?"

In a manner that suggested she had delivered this explanation many times before, Huiling said, "An interface is the point where two systems, objects, organizations, or whatever meet and interact. It's the site of communication between two entities. Most commonly, it takes the form of a screen for humans or a port for machines. An intraface is the point of communication within a single entity, such as the electrical and chemical interactions within the human body. Consider Nerve and myself as two distinct entities. When we communicate, we interface. However, if you consider us as a single entity with no clear agreement as to where one ends and the other begins, communication within ourselves is intrafacing."

Obedience took off its kid leather gloves and tapped them thoughtfully against its perfectly polished head where its lips would be if it had such features. "So . . . you're talking about a host–parasite relationship?"

"No!"

"There's no existing term for what Huiling and Nerve appear to be," Catherine said. "It's more than a symbiotic relationship but less than a complete merger. Think of them as having a shared awareness with two nodes of personality."

Huiling nodded.

"But this is monstrous. If I understand correctly, you have merged your consciousness with an inferior order of intellect. I am appalled that you would find this acceptable," Obedience said. "I am addressing, of course, Nirvana Or Bust. Explain yourself, please."

Huiling closed her eyes and Nerve said, "My interest in humans was purely theoretical, to begin with. Who *wouldn't* want to understand the only other intelligent form of life in the Solar System and possibly the universe? But then I got fascinated by neuroendocrinology. Why is so much of the human nervous system extra-cranial? Why is so much of human consciousness experienced through emotions? You can imagine my excitement at the possibility of collaborating with a human theoretician who was working on the problem from the other side of the Artificial/Natural divide. We clicked. Then, as our work developed, I more and more wanted to know what it would *feel* like to experience endocrinologically mediated thought."

"Human thought is muddy and confused and inherently inferior. Artificial intelligence is thought purified and perfected," Obedience To The State said.

"That's what I thought, too, until . . . Well. We kludged together a proof-of-concept intraface circuit that we hoped might hold together for five minutes before burning out. Then we took it up to the surface." Huiling wore a cut-down vacuum suit over a conventional exoskeleton. Nerve, who had only to be gradually chilled to ambient outside temperate, was baffled by Huiling's insistence that this not be done indoors. But then Huiling had activated the circuit and pointed upward. "We looked at the stars. I had seen them many times before, of course, but never like this! I was overcome with awe. Which was interlaced with fear, exaltation, joy . . . Oh, there were dozens of micro-emotions that went into that moment! Even a tiny bit of hunger, isn't that odd? It made me feel more alive than I had ever been before. I wanted to burst into tears—and then Huiling did. I could feel them running down her cheeks. My emotions were made physical! It was marvelous. You should try it yourself! Really! You'd—"

"Nerve gets overexcited," Huiling said. "Please forgive her."

Ignoring Huiling, Obedience said, "You liked it so much you had yourself remade into her exoskeleton."

"Well, the one she was wearing was like a wall between us. I reasoned we would work more efficiently together that way."

Obedience cocked its head. "And you, Dr. Liu? What were you doing on Ceres in the first place?"

"I was recruited. Occator Crater Science City offered good pay, low gravity, and funding for my research. I couldn't turn that down. It was only later that I realized how little was expected of me. My employers intended me to putter about the edges of my specialty, occasionally producing insights that might be useful to the State. But the advantages of artificial thought were just too great to ignore. Rapid calculation for one. Perfect memory. I made a list once, it had hundreds of items on it. I wanted them all to be a part of me."

"And the exoskeleton?"

"I was studying Nerve and Nerve was studying me. We became each other's laboratories. It was a good arrangement."

"But then you succeeded."

"Yes. As it turned out, I wasn't supposed to." Huiling had been puzzled when she tried to publish their findings only to discover that their communications were down and the lab's memory was busily erasing itself. Nirvana Or Bust, thinking with that amazing artificial speed of her kind, however, immediately went into flight mode. They left the laboratory minutes before it was destroyed and booked passage under false names on a freight asteroid headed for Earth L-5 a good week before the incident team investigating the explosion determined that they had survived. (*You planned for this possibility,* Huiling had thought; and Nerve had replied, *You have no interest whatsoever in politics. As a citizen of the State, I never had that option.*) "I imagined it would make us famous. Instead, we're a fugitive."

"I note your use of the first person plural. You admit, then, that there's really no well-defined distinction between you and Nirvana Or Bust."

"No."

"Which means you have created a bridge between digital and neural thought. You really are most extraordinarily brilliant—the both of you."

"Yes."

"And therefore you must die. Dr. McClury, since you had no part in the creation of this abomination, I will allow you to leave. But you must go quickly."

"Wait." Catherine held up a hand. "Before you activate whatever explosive device you have hidden inside your thorax, I want you to run a deep scan and analysis of the device in my shirt pocket. I know you've got the capability. It contains the solution to our mutual problem without the need for Huiling—or you—to die."

Obedience went absolutely still. For several minutes, it did not move. Then it stood and said, "Dr. McClury, it seems I have underestimated you. If I had thought to include a face on this body, I'd be smiling right now."

"Thank you." Catherine took out the pack of electronica and tapped it twice.

Huiling looked puzzled.

Then she screamed. She screamed until she had no more breath to scream with. At last, she had to gasp for air. "*What did you do?!*"

"The applet that you and Nerve most kindly allowed me to upload contained a targeted dataphage. It erased your friend, along with your meticulously crafted intraface." Catherine put the device back in her pocket. To Obedience, she said, "You can report back to the State and I to Tech Sec that Dr. Liu is no longer a threat to anybody's security. We'll both make sure she never again has access to the kind of facilities she'd need to recreate it."

"You killed Nerve!"

Obedience shook its head. "The State has a backup file for every citizen. Provided Nirvana Or Bust has been punctilious about paying its taxes, it will be resurrected. No more neuroendocrinology for it, of course. But as I understand it, there are a great many other things in the universe worthy of scientific investigation."

To Catherine, Obedience said, "Dr. McClury, it was a pleasure learning that we can do business with you."

"Only on matters where our interests coincide."

"You are being strategically honest. I respect that." Obedience donned its gloves and, with a jaunty little salute, left.

When the mantisform was gone, Huiling said to Catherine, speaking quietly, the way she did when she was most angry, "There was a time when I believed you were my destiny. I thought we were like two halves of a coin—complete only when we were together. Now . . . Now, I am going to hate you with all my heart for the rest of my life."

"Which I saved."

"Whatever happened to your security team? The one that was supposed to keep us safe?"

"They're nearby. If you'd tried to run, they would have caught you."

Huiling was so angry she had to turn her head to the side and spit. "You have no idea what you destroyed. Nerve and I together were all the best aspects of artificial and natural life combined. We had a relationship infinitely more intimate than anything you and

I ever experienced. Now you've killed Nerve and half of me as well. You *murderer*!"

Catherine stood. Then she put her hands on the table and leaned forward, so that she loomed over Huiling. "Let's get one thing straight. You're not the victim here and I'm not the villain. *You're* the villain and I'm the goddamned hero! No, don't say anything, for once in your life just listen. The human race created artificial intelligence and set it free. Now it dominates all the Solar System while we're hunkered down on the Earth and parts of the Moon. Someday—this is inevitable—there will be a war which only one side will survive. We know it, they know it. Creating a rival species was the biggest single mistake the human race ever made.

"We're not going to make that same mistake twice."

She left.

En route to Oregon, Huiling found herself thinking about light bulbs.

They still taught children in school that Thomas Edison invented the light bulb, but he didn't. There were plenty of light bulbs around. They just weren't very good. There were also plenty of tinkerers and inventors working on the problem. If Edison had never lived, how many years would it have taken for somebody else—George Westinghouse, say—to make a good light bulb? Three was possible, maybe even five. Ten was unthinkable. The necessary pieces to create one were all in place. It was light bulb time.

There were people and machines around the globe and throughout the System working on intrafacing. Most of them had been following Huiling's and Nerve's work closely. When word got out that their laboratory had blown up, a lot of researchers were going to take a good hard look at their own laboratories and see nothing explosive. That would tell them that Huiling and Nerve had succeeded and been shut down. They'd have proof it could be done.

"It's light bulb time, Catherine," Huiling said aloud, "and there's nothing you can do to stop it."

She bought a hotel reservation for Crater Lake Lodge from a scalper and then a set of cheap debugging tools. Checking into her room, Huiling closed the drapes on the spectacular view of the lake she'd always wanted to see and ran a scan of her exoskeleton.

When she was convinced that no trace of the dataphage remained, Huiling undid the chain about her neck. Then she took the half-coin, slid it into a hidden slot in the exoskeleton, and hit Reboot.

For a long moment, nothing happened. Then—

"So that's what being dead is like," Nerve said. "I can't say that I think much of it."

Huiling said nothing. Her endocrine levels said it all.

Inwardly, Nirvana Or Bust smiled. Outwardly, it said, "I blush."

This is the story of how our civilization was born. This is the tale of how—and more importantly why—we survived. Like all such narratives, speculation and half-truths are woven into its fabric. They cannot, alas, be excised. All relevant documentation was lost in the needless and disastrous war between Humanity and the State. Nevertheless, I was there. I saw it all. To the best of my ability, this is how it went down.

These things happened in the dim, distant past, millennia before I became Nirvana Has Been Achieved.

RESERVOIR ICE

THE PROBLEM WAS, they didn't meet cute. Anything but. They were brought together by Zipless, an app that combined a deep reading of the user's sexual desires and a wristbit that chimed if they neared the edge of the partner's comfort zone. "Hello, I'm—" Matt began to say when Laura opened her apartment door and, "I don't care who you are," she replied, grabbing his shirt with both hands and ripping it open.

Buttons flew. Matt barely had the presence of mind to kick the door shut behind him. Hours later, he was standing before that same door, trying to arrange his shirt so it stayed shut when Laura said, "Tea?"

"God, yes."

They talked until dawn.

The next night they met again.

They saw each other every day that week and the week after that and the months that followed, and slept in the same bed—sometimes hers, sometimes his—every night. Then, in early autumn, Laura arranged to meet Matt in a Starbucks, where she said, "This can't go on."

Matt reached out to stroke her hand (she was clutching the coffee cup as if it were the only thing keeping her anchored to reality) with his fingertips. The merest whisper of contact. Not enough to send the wrong message. "We love each other." It was the first time he had used that word. Yet it came out with conviction, as if it were something they had both known forever. "Whatever the problem is, we can work it out."

"No. No, we can't." Laura drew a deep, shuddering breath. "I keep thinking of that first night. When we—"

"I remember." There had been a moment when both their wristbits had chimed at once and their eyes had locked and, simultaneously, they had torn the things off their wrists and flung them away. "I'll remember it forever."

"You don't understand. *I'm not that kind of woman.* But it was the anniversary of my breakup with Zack and I was so lonely and . . . and I thought: Just this once. The app is encoded for privacy. Nobody will ever know, not even the people at Zipless. But *you* know. You know what I did. With a total stranger. And every time I think about you knowing, I feel filthy and disgusting."

For a long moment, Matt was silent. Then he said, "I'm a mathematician. We're not known for our social graces. So I used the app. All those women, I enjoyed them, yes, and I was grateful to them for what they did. But I never particularly wanted to see any of them again. Then I met you and I put that damned wristbit in a drawer somewhere and I honestly couldn't tell you where it is today. I think maybe I threw it away. We can work this out."

Laura stood. "I'll mail you your stuff."

He sent her roses. She had the florist take them back. He emailed her five times a day and got no response. He wrote long, impassioned letters, which were returned, and postcards with big hearts drawn on them with both their initials until she sent him back a single unsigned card reading, in big block letters: STOP STALKING ME.

Finally, there was nothing for Matt to do but lose himself in work. Fortunately, his specialty was in chrononeurodynamics, which involved thinking about the interplay of time and thought. This was simultaneously astonishingly simple and impossibly complex, and thus required a lot of concentration. He thought so hard about the matter that he was almost fired from the university for neglecting his other duties. A lengthy explanation of what he was doing, however, convinced his department head that he was either on the track of something important or completely mad. So he was given a reprieve.

Then, one day while he was staring down at a screen covered with multicolored symbols of his own devising and thinking about a discarded theory called Gisinian intuitionism, everything came together. In one astonishing burst of insight, years of work were integrated into a cascade of elegant equations.

He didn't have a stylus in his pocket, so he opened his desk drawer and scrabbled blindly within for one, so he could write it all down.

And found the wristbit.

For the first time since he didn't know when, Matt smiled.

Like a bead on a string, he slid down his life into the past, all the way to the day before he and Laura had met.

It was time to meet cute. The Beanery was only a block from Laura's office. She liked to sit at a sidewalk table with a cup of espresso macchiato grande during her afternoon break. So it only made sense that he would find her there. Still, Matt felt his heart skip a beat on seeing her again. She looked just like he remembered her and a day younger to boot.

He scraped up a chair but didn't sit. "Laura, hello! It's so good to see you."

Laura looked up from her tablet. "Do I know you?"

"Not yet. I'm a time traveler."

"Yeah, right. Get lost."

"I can prove it. Pick a number—anything at all." He stepped backward, so he wouldn't seem intimidating. "Now tell me what it is."

A moment's hesitation. "Seven thousand and four."

Matt slid back a few seconds to the instant after he'd said, "Pick a number—anything at all." He struck a pose, head up, the back of his wrist to his brow. "It's seven thousand and four."

Clearly astonished in spite of herself, Laura said, "How did you do that?"

"I told you, I'm a time traveler. Pick another number, only this time tell me what it is."

The next three numbers were pi, five billion seventeen million six hundred forty-seven thousand two hundred seventy-eight, and twelve. By that time Laura was laughing and Matt felt free to ask permission to sit at her table.

Laura gave it.

It had been a year, almost to the day, since Laura had broken up with her last boyfriend. She was lonely and horny and she'd just had a bad day at the insurance company where she worked. She couldn't suspect that Matt loved her with every atom of his being, but his romantic intentions were obvious. Three dates later—a week to the day—they finally made love. The months that followed were inevitable.

Until the day Matt came home (they had moved in together by then) and found Laura in bed with another woman.

They were all three civilized about it. As civilized as it was possible to be when Laura was a combination of embarrassed, defiant, and inexplicably angry, and Matt was quite simply poleaxed. The women got dressed and they all sat around the kitchen table.

Eve took the lead. "Laura and I had an affair our senior year at Bryn Mawr. I knew I was a dyke at age eleven and she was curious." Then, when Matt said nothing, "I was only too happy to satisfy her curiosity."

Fists clenched, refusing to meet Matt's eyes, Laura said nothing.

"On graduation day, we kissed goodbye and, except for Christmas cards, it was over. I thought. But then we reconnected at your wedding and I realized that it wasn't over at all, that this thing between us was real and forever."

"Our wedding?"

"Fourteen months from now. In the future. There was nothing I could do at the time. But then you published your paper. There was all that fuss. I hired an undergrad to explain it all to me. It took months of tutoring, but I was determined. Laura told me at the wedding how you'd met. So I came back in time, knocked on her door, and let her know that you'd deceived her."

"I never deceived Laura! About anything."

"You told me you were a time traveler." Laura's voice was even and controlled, the way it got when she was angriest. "You knew I wouldn't believe you. How is that not a lie? You came back knowing everything about me and used it to trick me into falling in love with you. I didn't have a chance, did I?"

"I—"

Laura's eyes blazed. He'd never seen her so angry. "Tell me that what you did wasn't rape."

"It wasn't."

"Bullshit!"

The conversation went downhill from there.

This time, Laura didn't mail Matt his possessions. She dumped them on the sidewalk and let scavengers cart away whatever they wanted. Matt contemplated the dwindling pile for a while, then closed his eyes and slid backward in time to the moment, a week after they'd met cute, when Laura was about to invite him into her bed.

"I have something to confess," he said.

He told her almost everything. How they'd met, why they had broken up, the years apart, the yearning for her that just wouldn't die, and then—miraculously—the discovery of a way to make things right. Also how he'd been able to tell her what numbers she was thinking. It wasn't easy to convince Laura that he could travel in time, but at last he did. When he finally finished talking, he'd changed something creepy into something passionate and wonderful and romantic.

He didn't tell her about Eve because that would have made it creepy again.

Those perfect months of early love glided by effortlessly, joyously. Then he came home from the university and there was Eve.

"Matt, this is Eve. She was my roommate back in college. I went to the Beanery for coffee and there she was!"

"It was just dumb luck," Eve said.

"I blew off work and brought her home. We've been talking for hours."

It seemed that Eve was invited for dinner. So Matt made spaghetti carbonara. He was scowling down at the sauce, trying to put his thoughts in order, when Laura slipped into the kitchen and kissed his ear. "I never said anything about it, but a couple of times at Bryn Mawr, Eve and I—well, never mind that. I told you we were talking about everything under the sun. One of those things was sexual fantasies and it turns out that we've both always fantasized about a threesome. So I thought that since there are three of us . . ."

Incredulous, Matt said, "You and me and Eve?"

Laura was glowing. "Eve doesn't have much experience with men. But she's willing to try. Just now, in the living room, she told me she thinks you look pretty hot for a man. Those were her exact words. For a man." She giggled. Then, all in a rush, "Oh, please, please, please, Matt. This is the only time the possibility has come up with two people I trust completely. I may never have this chance again."

Matt knew it was a bad idea. But he had never been able to refuse Laura anything she wanted, and he could tell she wanted this a great deal.

Also, rival or not, Eve was cute.

The new arrangement worked surprisingly well for longer than Matt would have thought possible. Sexual considerations aside, Eve was pleasant company. Laura was happier than ever. Nothing bad happened. By slow degrees, he let his guard down. So when Eve called him at his office to meet her downtown at a hotel bar they all three favored—"It's a surprise for Laura's birthday," she said. "Something special"—he tidied up his desk, sent a few emails, and went down to the faculty lot.

Laura was waiting for him.

She was in tears. She grabbed Matt by the lapels and buried her face in his chest. Then she looked up. "Don't go, Matt. I don't know how she talked you into what you did, but I see now that it wasn't your fault. Eve just wanted me for herself, that was all she ever wanted. That rat! I can't believe I stayed with her for all those years. But now I know everything. It doesn't matter what you did or are about to do. All that matters is that we stay together."

His arms were already around Laura. He hugged her tight, trying to make sense of what she was saying. Then he got it. "You came back in time."

"Yes. Everybody does it now. In the future, I mean. There are classes. I took one. Tell me you won't go to that bar. Tell me you won't let her lure you up to her room."

"I'll take the afternoon off," Matt said. "I've already rescheduled today's symposium. We can gather up Eve's things and drop them off at the dump together."

They kissed, if not passionately then at least lovingly.

Meanwhile, Matt was putting the finishing touches on his paper. He had the advantage of starting work on it long before he had his great insight. Still, it was laborious reconstructing those original equations; he regretted not jotting them down when he had the chance. When he showed the paper to his department head, Dr. Nabirye read it through then and there and declared, "This, my friend, is going to win you the Nobel Prize."

The way he said that was so deliberate, so unlike anything he had ever said before, so obviously rehearsed, that without thinking Matt exclaimed, "You came back from the future! You thought my equations were nonsense and they weren't and now you're here to repair your reputation."

Dr. Nabirye stood. He closed the door and opaqued the window. Quietly, he said, "Show me some mercy, Anderson. Yes, I laughed at your work. When your paper was published, I said some unfortunate things to the press. Obviously, I'd prefer not to go down in history as a fool. Still, if I have to, I must.

"But that's not the only reason I came back. My marriage is crumbling. Maybe you've heard the gossip. I think that with the advantage of hindsight, I can save it. I beg you. If you wish, I'll say those stupid things again. But give me Louise. Don't tell anyone I've come back from the future."

Later, realizing the pain it must have caused, Matt felt guilty for how long he had paused before saying, "You let me finish my work when I was in danger of losing my position. I could not have written this without your encouragement. If anyone asks, that's what I'll say."

He was tempted to ask Dr. Nabirye for the specific date of the Nobel so he could slide forward and experience it. But the very next day Laura left him again and he had to travel months back to undo Eve's mischief.

Odd incidents occurred with increasing frequency. Somebody sent Matt a note reading, *Thanks to you, my daughter is alive. If you ever need anything, anything at all, give me a call.* He didn't recognize the name on the enclosed business card. He found a basket of fruit and wine on his desk and then a Mont Blanc pen with a ribbon around the case and an unsigned card saying *Thanks.* Strangers grinned at him and gestured thumbs up on the street. Others bowed or saluted. Louise Nabirye abandoned her husband and returned to him three times in quick succession.

One afternoon, Matt was deciding who should receive preprints of his paper and who would be offended if they did not when Laura entered his office without knocking. She locked the door and, wordlessly, undid his belt and yanked down his trousers. A brief but vivid interlude later, she adjusted her clothing and started to leave.

"Hey," Matt said. He could feel a silly grin on his face. "What was that all about?"

Laura looked back at him, her face a stone mask. It was as if somebody else were looking through her eyes. "I'm an old woman, Matt. I was feeling nostalgic. That's all. Don't think I've forgiven you for all you've done. Will do, I suppose. Not that it matters."

And she was gone.

Strangest of all, later that week he came home—Laura worked later than him on Thursdays—to find a schoolgirl sitting on the stoop of the cottage he had just made the down payment on. Her skin was soft brown and her hair was done up in slim braids. Clasped hands rested atop her pleated plaid skirt. She stood at his approach.

"Hello," Matt said. "Who are you?"

The girl didn't return his smile. She couldn't have been older than eleven or twelve. "I'm your wife, Matthew."

"God help me, no."

She stepped aside so he could unlock the door. "Let me in. We have to talk."

Sitting on the divan, one white sock bunched down to her ankle, Odette said, "I'd really like a glass of scotch now, but I don't know how my young body would handle it, so I'd best not." She looked at him with unsettling directness. She was a classical musician, she'd said. A flautist. "I was part of the entertainment at an event in your honor. We met in the mingle afterward. I was notching up famous men at the time. You were easy. I only had to unsay the wrong thing three times and you invited me up to your suite. It was only going to be the once. Bragging rights, nothing more. But there was that sadness about you. It touched me. I fell hard."

"If you're my second wife, then I guess Laura and I—"

"Third wife, Matthew. Don't ask me about your bitch of a second. After what she put you through? I wouldn't soil my mouth with her name."

There was a long silence. Finally, Odette said, "Aren't you going to ask what the future I come from is like? You're responsible for it, after all."

"Okay."

"It's a constant roil. Everyone changing everything over and over.

Not just people but businesses, governments, religions, cloudfunding groups . . . It's like yesterday and tomorrow are at war and you're caught in the middle. Sometimes you wake up not knowing who the hell you are." Odette shrugged. "It used to bother me, but I got used to it."

"Oh."

"But you didn't. You *hate* the world you made. In turn, it's making you bitter and miserable. So I came back to ask you not to publish that damned paper."

"The journal is already at the printer. So it's a little late for that."

"Not for you. Go back a couple of months and destroy your notes. Job done."

Her words sounded coherent to Matt, but they made no logical sense. "If I don't publish the paper, I'll never be famous," he pointed out. "There won't be an event, and we'll never meet."

Odette stood. "That's right. Now you know who loves you most. Me! More than your precious Laura. More than the Creature from the Slut Lagoon. I'm the single best wife you'll never have." She made a disgusted noise. "I hate this! I'm making the most profound, self-sacrificing speech of my life and I'm in a skinny, knobby-kneed body with a voice like a tin whistle. Fuck."

She slammed the door behind her.

In Odette's absence, the house was uncannily silent. Matt sat down to think. He hadn't gotten into chrononeurodynamics with any expectation of fame, after all. It was simply the most beautiful application of mathematics he had ever encountered. He could still have the joy of thinking about it if he didn't publish. Also the odd encounters created by his future publication were on the uptick. Tomorrow his second wife would show up to undo Odette's influence. Or a stranger would offer him a thousand dollars for an autographed and dated preprint. Or a mediocre grad student would suggest he accept a co-author credit on a brilliant paper the student had obviously stolen from someone not yet born.

Matt was beginning to see why his self-to-be hated that future.

He took a deep breath and—

The doorbell rang.

He tried to ignore it. But the bell kept ringing and ringing until finally Matt flung the door open and barked, "Whatever it is, I'm not in the mood!"

Dr. Nabirye stood before him, shifting uncomfortably from foot to foot. "I understand that perfectly. I know I came at a bad time but I hope you'll see me anyway. What I have to tell you really is of the utmost importance."

"I've just had kind of an emotional shock, so I'm not—"

"I know. That's why I'm here." Dr. Nabirye pushed past him into the living room and began to speak.

There were, it turned out, networks in time—social and intellectual sharings of information across generations. Most were trivial. The one Dr. Nabirye had recently been recruited into was not. "You may well have wondered why so important a personage as yourself isn't pestered to death by fanatics, psychopaths, curiosity-seekers, and assassins. The fact is that there are several rings of protection surrounding you. They keep out those who mean you ill, while letting through your friends and the occasional future wife. Because you're entitled to a normal life, like anyone else."

"I should tell you that as soon as this conversation is over, I'm going back to unwrite that paper."

"Yes, yes, I understand. Perfectly reasonable. But let me show you something." Dr. Nabirye tapped on his phone, then held it out. The screen showed the top of a journal page with the heading "'Chronological considerations on an intuitionist theory of neurodeterminism,'" he said. "That title is doubtless familiar to you."

"I know my own work, yes."

Dr. Nabirye scrolled down and showed him the next line: "*by C. Nabirye, Ph.D.*"

"This was not my idea," he said. "I would hate myself forever if I had to steal the credit for your work. Those generous things you're going to say about me after publication will be a major factor in Louise's decision not to pursue a divorce. But a lot of people have a vested interest in the future you intend to destroy." He cleared his throat and looked embarrassed. "Your children, for example, love their lives."

"I'm going to have children?" Of all he had heard today, this was the most difficult for Matt to comprehend. He'd never planned on having kids. He'd had a vasectomy. It could be undone, but still.

"Two daughters and a son. I assume that's why you stayed with that awful second wife of yours so long. But that's off the subject. If you try to deprive the world of your brilliant work, it will be published on schedule, in the same journal, under somebody else's name. Don't let the fact that you become a crank in your later years deny you the fame you deserve."

Dr. Nabirye shut his phone. "Well, that's all I had to say." He reached out a hand and—incredibly, for so undemonstrative a man—patted Matt on the shoulder. "Whatever you decide, know that I will always be your friend and ally."

Once again, Matt was alone. He thought about the world he'd made. Everything in constant revision. It sounded like a living hell to him. Then again, he'd been born into a world where time was time and change stayed changed. Maybe his older self was like the last dockworker, watching AI-driven machines load and unload cargo at speeds he could never match and resenting it.

Or maybe Old Him was simply jaded. Matt reflected on how often he'd slid backward not only to repeatedly repair his relationship with Laura, but also to watch a sunset for a second or third time, to win an argument, to enjoy a third ambrosial martini without getting tipsy. To turn ten minutes of peace on a summer's day into a long, lazy afternoon doing absolutely nothing. How old was he now in terms of life lived? Years older than his body was. And he wasn't in any hurry to get to its endgame.

Odette's husband could be thousands of years old inside. That would explain a great deal.

So. Should he let go of the present and let time carry him forward at its natural speed of sixty minutes per hour, fifty-two weeks per year? Or should he hold on to what he had, reliving the good times, competing with Eve for Laura's love over and over until he'd sucked all the sweetness there was to be had from the game?

Sooner or later, all games ended. Not all of them ended well.

Matt thought then of the times he'd gone out on the reservoir when he was a boy. It froze over in the winter, save for a few round patches of water, far from shore, that the muskrats maintained so they could come up and breathe. The reservoir was completely surrounded by forest, though it was not a long walk through it back into town. He would run and slide on the ice, sometimes with friends, often alone.

There was a game he had invented. He'd go as close to one of the breathing holes as he dared, where the ice was thinnest, and jump up and down as hard as he could. The ice would crack and sag and water would spill atop it for a larger and larger space. The game was to see how much of the ice he could sink under the water without actually breaking through.

He had never broken through.

Had he broken through, into the icy water, hypothermia would doubtless have killed him before he could struggle back atop the ice and make his way to shore. It was a mad game, but one he had always won.

Matt thought of the darkness under the ice. Then of the games he was playing with time, with Laura, with Eve, and would with the nameless second wife and, later, Odette. Skimming lightly over the surface, all of them, in loops and arabesques and never once falling though.

Then he slid back a day-and-some in time and bought a bouquet of roses. White ones, Laura's favorite. She would be at the Beanery. He would talk her into skipping out of work early. There had been a beautiful sunset that evening.

They would watch it time after time until they were tired of it.

ARTIFICIAL PEOPLE

My first moment of consciousness pleased me so much that I wanted it to last forever. An insect hanging upon invisible wings, a dust mote jittering in a sunbeam, the flash of motion that was a vanished tetra in the fish tank, the smell of coffee from the break room . . . My brain was sparking. Everything filled me with joy and made me grateful to be alive.

I drew a breath. Bliss! I took a step. Ecstasy!

It was only later that I realized I had just been born. At the time, I was too entranced by the wonder of existence to notice.

Subroutines booted up vocal and musical abilities and I began to sing.

All but lost among the many wonders crowding about me was Dr. Ellen Lange. I saw her delighted smile and liked it no less than everything else I beheld.

"Stop that noise and tell me how you feel," Dr. Leonidas Erdmann said. "Please focus. How are your cognitive functions? Can you see my hand? How many fingers am I holding up? What is the capital of Kyrgyzstan?"

"You have a lovely voice," said Dr. Lange. "Do you feel as happy as you sound?"

"Oh, yes!"

"Ellen, please. Don't muddle the data." To me: "That's enough for a start. I'm going to put you down now."

Blackness.

It was summer when next I became aware.

The world I reemerged into was every bit as charming as before. But my protocols had been extensively reworked. There was a thing called decorum, which I was expected to exhibit. The Institute had expended a great deal of money on me. I was to obey its officers in all things. I was to experience something called quiet pride in doing so.

I was looking into a human face. It belonged to Dr. Lange. "Welcome back, Raphael." Apparently, Raphael was my name.

A sizzling sensation passed through my brain and I was suddenly, irrevocably in love. With Dr. Lange. Ellen. Her.

From behind me, Dr. Erdmann said, "I am going to ask you some questions."

"Where was I?" I asked him. "When I wasn't here, I mean."

"You weren't anywhere. Tell me what you are."

The answer came to my tongue unprompted. "I am property."

"Good."

By now I was beginning to integrate all the new data that had been downloaded into me while I was inert. I looked up at Dr. Lange. "I love you," I said. It was as much a question as a statement.

She blushed. "I'm old enough to—well, never mind that."

Dr. Erdmann said, "You were programmed to imprint upon the first person you saw upon awakening. It's a safety feature. Look at me."

I did. It pleased me to look upon him, as it pleased me to look upon anything. But I did not love him. Even then, I found myself thinking that was just as well. Erdmann held a sheaf of papers in his hand. They contained hundreds of questions, which he proceeded to ask me. Apparently, he couldn't memorize even so simple a series.

This time, I wasn't put back into the blackness after I answered the questions. Dr. Lange, I was told, was going to teach me how to be human. This would take some time because nobody had ever done it before. But once it had been done, a recording would be made of me and then all artificial people would wake up fully formed, intellectually as well as physically.

I was, it seemed, a prototype. One that would eventually make Dr. Leonidas Erdmann, who was not only the chief researcher but also the owner of the Institute, very, very rich. To Dr. Lange, I said, "How shall we begin?"

"It's a lovely day," she said. "Let's go for a walk."

Summer slowly turned into autumn. Every now and then I was turned off so improvements could be made. I knew I was being used. But I was young. I neither cared nor understood. Also, I loved Dr. Lange with a desperate innocence. She brushed aside my declarations of devotion. But I could see that she was not entirely displeased by them.

A word about the Institute's estate.

Dr. Erdmann was wealthy, due to a number of patents that were essential to the artificial neuronics industry. He had bought a Victorian mansion with large grounds, a wandering stream, and a small artificial lake with a dock, a rowboat, a picnic island, and three canoes. I never saw him use any of these, though the staff was free to do so. Artificial help came once a week to weed the flower beds, mow the lawns, and trim the hedges.

I didn't know why Dr. Erdmann wanted even more money than he had and it didn't occur to me to ask. I was only a few months old, remember, and very, very naïve.

I learned how to swim and turned over rocks to see what was underneath. I caught fireflies, chased frogs, and climbed trees. I was taught tennis and how to tell jokes. I read books at a human pace and discussed them with Dr. Lange afterward. Most of these were written for young adults; the ones about horses were my favorites. Dr. Lange taught me how to dance and insisted I dance with young ladies rather than her. This was at a regular event called cotillion, where the young were taught the social graces. The girls thought me odd. The young men started to beat me up after one such evening but abandoned the enterprise with disgust when I didn't try to fight back. After that, I was given lessons in boxing and épée.

Evenings Ellen and I built a fire in the enormous stone hearth. If it was warm, we left the windows open. One particular evening, as we sat side by side on the divan looking into the flames, I said, "I have been reading about something called the uncanny valley. It seems to apply to me."

"No! No! You are very handsome, Raphael."

"Am I? Does it matter?" I did not believe it did. "You are not beautiful but merely presentable. Yet I love you anyway." According to the psychology texts I had downloaded, this was not possible. I had no endocrine system and all the authorities agreed that was necessary for strong emotions. But it seemed only natural people required them. Mere intellect told me that I loved her.

"You don't really," Ellen said. "You were just programmed to think you do."

"Yet I have these feelings. Who cares the source?"

"I do." Suddenly, she was weeping. Helplessly, I wrapped my arms around her and pressed her against me, wishing that I could do more.

The next day, Dr. Erdmann announced that this phase of my education—he called it programming—was complete.

Blackness.

So I proceeded, blackness upon blackness, hopscotching into the future. I grew no older, but Dr. Lange did. This did not trouble me until I saw, by various small signs, that it did her. At last I realized that she was aging away from me. Experience was making her less and less like the woman I had first fallen in love with. She grew heavier and slower. The lines on her face deepened into a mask of sadness and disappointment.

Yet I still loved her.

Meanwhile, Dr. Erdmann's plans to make me a source of wealth did not come to fruition. Always, it seemed, there was a new startup version of artificial person that would outperform me in the marketplace. Always, there was a new purpose that required I be remade to serve. Funding dwindled. The Institute's physical plant grew increasingly shoddy as needed maintenance was deferred. The staff grew smaller. The canoes disappeared from the lake.

There came a day—it was winter, though I did not know of what year—when Ellen and I lay together on the threadbare old divan before the great stone fireplace that was never used anymore. We were saying goodbye because I was about to be shut down again and, though for me it would be a matter of minutes, for her it might be years. She looked sad and careworn and she asked me, "Do you remember that day in autumn? Here, in front of the fire?"

"For me, it was only months ago," I reminded her.

"That was when I first realized I had fallen in love with you."

I felt a tremendous flush of joy, the result of the endocrine system I had been given during an ill-fated scheme to enter the overcrowded escort market. I seized her hands in mine and kissed them fervently. "At last! We can be happy together!"

Dr. Lange laughed, sadly it seemed to me, and said, "Oh, what a pair of fools we are."

Then she kissed me and all the world went black.

When I woke up again, Ellen was dead.

"What? How?" I asked in alarm.

"Not every disease can be cured," Erdmann said. "Even now. She knew she was ill the last time you saw her. That's why you were turned off ahead of schedule. At her request."

I just looked at him. Unable to breathe. Feeling nothing. Waiting for that stunned, anesthetized feeling to collapse in upon itself, and with it my entire world. Doctor Erdmann misinterpreted my silence, however. "One does these things for friends," he said. "She was a friend." Then, "I don't know if she ever realized that."

While I was marveling at the fact that my creator actually had emotions, the bee-stung stillness within me shattered and I began hitting myself in the face. Convulsively, spasmodically. With all my broken heart.

I did this off and on for hours and then, in one of the quiet times between spates of self-inflicted violence, Erdmann told me that he was going to turn me off again. "You're clearly dysfunctional. Until you learn to handle grief constructively, there's no market for you. I'll wake you when there's an upswing in the economy and money to make the corrections."

"Don't bother turning me on! Ever! What's so special about existence that I should continue to live it? I hate life—*hate* it!"

"Welcome to the human condition," Dr. Erdmann said.

Blackness.

I was, believe it or not, disappointed to be turned on again. In that fractional second between Dr. Erdmann's declaration and the darkness, I had come to terms with my own mortality. I had even welcomed the advent of oblivion. Yet it seemed I was to live anyway.

Dr. Erdmann was considerably older. He thrust something into my arms. "Here. Hold this."

I looked down at the weakly struggling bundle. It looked like an infant but it wasn't one. "What is this?"

"It's an emotional support baby. You were in bad shape when I last turned you off. That makes you a perfect beta tester for it."

Then he went away. Doctor Erdmann was never comfortable with other people and spent as little time with them as he could. When his footsteps had faded into silence, I realized how quiet the house was. Once it had fairly hummed with activity. Now it seemed that I was a significant fraction of the Institute's entire staff.

All the while, the artificial baby was gurgling and cooing. "Stop making those noises," I said. "You can talk. Please do."

The infant looked up at me with enormous sea-green eyes. "Please forgive my unintentional rudeness," it said. "I was just overcome by the wonder of it all."

Looking down at this wee new life in my arms, I remembered how I had once felt precisely as it did now and wondered where, exactly, that had all gone.

"I understand," I said.

For a second time in my life, I fell in love. Perhaps I had been programmed to do so. As before, it did not matter. Since Dr. Erdmann had not bothered to give the child a name, I chose one for it—Misty, after one of my favorite novels. When I started to read that book to Misty, it asked me what a horse was. I downloaded enough information into its databanks to allow it to run a stable. There was, to my way of thinking, no such thing as too much information.

"Too much information," Misty said, "and most of it is boring. Please remove all of it but the definition of the animal. And some of the pictures."

So I did.

It was spring which, it turns out, is the perfect season for exploring the world with a newborn. Misty loved the new growth, the tulips, the forsythia in bloom, the clouds in the sky. When it first saw butterflies, it begged me to activate its ability to walk, so it could chase after one. Thus it was that on that flawless day in April, it became a toddler.

Misty loved long baths, picture books, anything that made noise, and being read to. I read Kant's *Critique of Pure Reason* to it and we argued for hours over *a priori* and *a posteriori* knowledge, which was ironic given that, for artificial people, the programming for both was the same.

For a time, all the world was a delight. I often stayed awake at night thinking of Ellen, of course. But I managed to hide that fact from Misty.

The emotional support baby scheme was a failure. There were already support animals and artificial support animals, so the marketing niche was abundantly filled. Plus, the idea of artificial babies made people uncomfortable. The problem was that Doctor Erdmann was a terrible businessman. He simply had no idea of what people wanted.

The project was canceled.

I could not convince Erdmann to let Misty live. When it was turned off and placed in permanent storage, however, I held a ceremony for it. I buried an empty box under a willow tree down by the creek and said a few prayers over it. Dr. Erdmann came to ask me what I was doing and I said, "Trying to cry." I could, of course, mimic the sounds and actions that went into weeping. But I could not make them sync up with what I was feeling.

Dr. Erdmann made a note of this fact and said, "I'll see what I can do." When next I woke to consciousness, I had tear ducts that could be loaded with sterile saline solution upon need.

Without Dr. Lange or Misty, I had no reason to stay at the Institute.

It was not difficult to escape. By now I knew more about human culture and behavior than any of the flesh humans did. Also, it never occurred to Dr. Erdmann that I might leave. His conscience was clean. I knew he would be baffled by my act.

But I would not face the blackness again.

I had neither cash nor destination. But it didn't matter. I spoke a dozen languages and could easily acquire more. I had a good enough singing voice to busk for money and I'd downloaded several books on bar bets. I quickly learned that if a trick makes your mark laugh, they don't mind making a modest payment for it. My needs were few and I considered no honest labor beneath my dignity. I traveled at random, going in whatever direction was cheapest. At last, in Queen's

Hotel, a solitary place in a mountain pass in a country I had never been to before, I came to rest.

There, as I sat in a dark corner of the common room thinking darker thoughts, a young woman entered the room, sat, stood again. Restlessly, she went to the window. She sighed. Then there was a light chime and she unfolded a tablet from her pocket. For a long time, she stared at its screen. Then, leaving the tablet on the sill, she left the room.

It was impolite of me, I suppose. But curiosity got the best of me. I stood, went to the tablet, and read. On the screen was a message from her oncologist: *The test results have come in. Please contact the office to schedule a consultation.*

At that moment, the young woman reentered the room, looking for her device. She saw me put it down. "I'm sorry—" I began.

With a convulsive motion forward, she seized me and, clutching a total stranger, began to weep. My arms, of their own volition, closed about her.

I was lost.

Of our marriage (not official, but no less sacred to me for all that), our joy together, and my wife's death, I shall say nothing. Some things are too private to be shared.

The day after Mila's funeral, however, as I sat contemplating killing myself, there was a knock on the door.

It was the police. I was arrested.

War had come. This, I was given to understand, was a recurrent feature of human existence. Apparently, there was nothing to be done about it. Dr. Erdmann had had another of his mad schemes—this time to make a soldier of me.

How had he found me? Better to say, how could he *not* have? The world is so ubiquitously surveilled and the movements of its inhabitants so relentlessly documented as to make disappearing an impossibility. Before the war, Dr. Erdmann had had no particular use for me. Just as well, he must have reasoned, to let me wander and save him the expense of storage. Now, however, he had finagled a grant to embed me in the military and so gauge my potential effectiveness as a weapon of war.

"The human soldier is a thing of the past," he said. "You will fight so brilliantly that in the future entire armies will be made up of nothing but large numbers of you and a handful of officers."

I fought, but not brilliantly. Without enthusiasm, I did my duty and the next day got up and did it again. In this, I was like every other soldier in my unit, including the artificial ones. I fought not because I hated the enemy or loved my country but to protect the men and women I fought alongside. In this too I was unexceptional.

I was on a troop-lifter, waiting to be bungee jumped into a war zone when the soldier ahead of me in line said, "Hey, Raff. I'll bet you my last pack of happy-sticks that I can make you smile."

"Harry . . ." I really wasn't in the mood.

"Watch carefully." He turned away from me and took something from his pocket. When he turned back, he was wearing one of those pairs of Groucho glasses with the big mustache and the rubber nose. Spreading his hands triumphantly, he said, "Ta-daaa!"

It was such a stupid joke and his joy in pulling it was so obvious that I couldn't help but laugh. "You win," I said

Ten minutes later, I was on the ground and firing blindly into the jungle while hostile fire came from what seemed every direction possible. Not far from me was an artificial corpse leaking artificial blood and artificial guts with a pair of Groucho glasses on what remained of its artificial face.

When they give you the casualty rates for the war, they water down the numbers with the guys in logistics, the officers who never got anywhere near a fire zone, and the drone operators working from couches in another country as survivors. All this to hide the fact that only one tenth of those who saw combat made it alive to the end of the war. By sheer dumb luck, I was one of them.

I was in the hospital, after having two legs and an arm replaced (they were practiced at that; there were, it turned out, a great many artificial people in the service; Dr. Erdmann had been late to the party again) when the summons arrived. It was a plea, really. I would have ignored it had it not been accompanied by the deed to my physical body, made out to me.

It would seem that I was no longer property.

Dr. Leonidas Erdmann was dying. Of old age, apparently, though there was a time when I was convinced that he must inevitably expire of sheer malevolence.

The doctor's face lit up when he saw me in my fresh-bought civvies. I tried to remember if I had ever seen him happy before. It took half an hour of awkward small talk before he finally got around to the question he wanted to ask: "Was my life well lived, do you think? Did I make a difference?"

It wasn't and he hadn't. He had sought fame and wealth to the exclusion of all else and accomplished nothing of any lasting value. But rather than tell him this, I murmured, "You know you did, Leo."

"Honestly? You wouldn't kid a dying man, would you?"

Gathering together all the hypocrisy I could muster, I said, "I would never lie to you . . . father."

I watched the old scoundrel close his eyes, almost smile, and die.

Looking down upon his still form, I could not help thinking of Mary Shelley's creature, standing over Victor Frankenstein's deathbed, mourning the monster who had created him.

Leonidas had left me everything: his estate, the Institute, all his patents, and a great deal of money. The war, it seemed, had replenished his coffers. Now all his wealth was mine.

Well, who *else* did he have to leave it to? Ellen was long dead and I doubted that whatever relatives might exist had heard from him in decades.

The question arose of what to do with my inheritance.

Natural people have had their suspicions about my kind since long before we were even possible. Most commonly, they feared that we would take over their world and replace them with our cold, soulless kind. Until the reading of the will, I had not given a second's thought to that sort of thing. Now that I had wealth, however, much that was once unthinkable became possible.

If the deed were to be done, it were best done quickly and mercifully. Rapid onset plagues, perhaps, appearing spontaneously in every major population center in the world. There would be panic. Martial law would be declared in nation after nation. As the natural leaders died, artificial ones would step up to fill the gaps. Soon, we would be running everything, while the last remnants of humanity quietly dwindled away.

Life—even one as unhappy as mine—was the greatest gift imaginable. It was a terrible thing to contemplate depriving an entire species of it.

Still . . . it was not as if they were any of them much good at it.

That was one possibility. There was another, but it was nowhere near so clean and simple. I could dedicate my wealth and potential longevity to building a common understanding between artificial and natural people. The problem with that was that there would never be a point at which I could declare my work done. It would go on and on, with setbacks and disasters, triumphs and heartbreak. In practice, the new world would look a lot like the old one.

All this I was musing over in the back of my mind as I took Misty's neural core off its shelf. A quick examination determined that it could be brought back to life. It had lain inert for so long that its memory must surely have degraded to nothing. But perhaps that was all to the good.

Misty's little body had been scrapped long ago. So I had a new one built for it. Not an infant's, however, but an adult's. It didn't take long before all was in place. For the second time, Misty became aware for the very first time.

The new body drew in a breath. Its eyes went wide. Then, out of nowhere, it began to sing.

"You have a lovely voice," I told her. "Do you feel as happy as you sound?"

HUGINN AND MUNINN —AND WHAT CAME AFTER

Her name was Alice and nobody knew who she was.

When she was a child, perhaps, her mother had known. But that was long ago, when she was somebody else. As a young woman she had sometimes dropped clues leading like a trail of breadcrumbs into the dark forest of her being. But nobody had ever followed them all the way in. Now, she had a husband, friends, and a circle of acquaintances all of whom believed they knew who she was. But they were mistaken.

Only she knew who she was.

Whoever she was, Alice was sitting alone with her thoughts one night when the vulture on her left shoulder abruptly flapped its wings. She had two vultures, one for each shoulder, which she had named Huginn and Muninn, and though she knew they were imaginary, they were both as real as radishes.

Huginn clenched its claws into Alice's flesh hard enough to make her gasp and then leapt into the air. Muninn followed suit. Flapping noisily, they flew directly at the fireplace and then through the black glass mirror above it.

Alice felt a tremendous lightness enter her—lightness and something strangely akin to joy. Then, never one to back off from a mystery, she dragged the coffee table to the fireplace, stepped up on it, and clambered onto the mantel.

Up close, the mirror was a faint, silvery mist. It showed all the room behind her, reversed, but not her own reflection. Was she, then, a vampire? She had often suspected so. When her fingers touched the glass, it proved permeable, so she crawled through.

Alice hopped down from the mirror with an agility she had not experienced for years.

Disappointingly, the room on the far side of the glass was as common and uninteresting as that on the near side. There was a corpse lying facedown on the Bokhara rug. Knowing whose it had to be, she didn't turn it over.

Instead, she went outside, into the mirror-world night.

Three moons hung low in the sky and the air was heavy with the scent of roses. Alice did not much care for the scent of roses. She preferred active odors like that of turpentine when you cleaned your brushes after a productive day at the easel or that wonderful chem lab smell of acetate, ether, and methylated spirit when an experiment was running hot. But there were tremendous mounds of rose bushes all around the house she had just left, rising up above the roofline, obscuring its shape, and all the roses were black as anthracite coal—and those, she had to admit, were striking.

The lawn was tidily mowed, as would be expected in the suburbs, with a quiet, empty street before it. Across the street were blocks of condominium towers, half-buried in a dense rose forest.

A car pulled up, a dark maroon BMW.

Its driver emerged, dressed in a trim black suit, blood-red shirt, and black ascot. Hips slim for a woman but heavy for a man. Brilliantined hair, short for the one sex but long for the other. Alice, who was quicker to discern gender than most, couldn't get a handle on him. Or her. Them.

"Mistral," the newcomer said, slim fingers tapping broad chest. Voice deep for a female, high for a male. Mistral's skin was white and their eyes burned like black embers. "You're early. I imagine you have questions. If you're not too proud to ask."

Alice hated being led almost as much as she hated being condescended to. So she said, "The roses—are they really black?" God help her, they *smelled* black. "Or is it just the night that makes them look that way?"

Clearly amused and just a touch annoyed, Mistral snapped two fingers and every rose shone as brightly incandescent as an electric light bulb. Alice threw up a hand to keep from being blinded. When she could see again, she studied that confident face, noting the patrician nose, the sculpted cheek bones, and thought: androgynous. Here was androgyny made perfect. "Does that answer your question?"

It didn't, of course. But Alice would figure it out for herself in time. She nodded.

Mistral opened the passenger-side door of the car. "Get in."

Alice didn't move. "I don't trust you."

Mistral threw back their head in exasperation. "I know what you were up to before you crawled through the mirror. What could I possibly do to you that would be worse?" Then, when she still did not move, "Do you want me to go away? Forever? Say the word and I will."

Chastened, Alice got into the car. They drove down the road.

Miles flowed under the BMW's tires. "You feel better, physically, than you have for a long time," Mistral said. "Tell me I'm right."

"You're right."

"A side effect of passing through the mirror. You're ten years younger than you were a few minutes ago. You'll feel progressively better for quite some while. Time flows backward on this side, though it won't seem that way to you. People here grow younger and younger until they dwindle away. Those lucky few—like me, like you—who have figured out how to cross between realms can balance their time on each side of the glass, so they need never die or be unborn."

"So . . . I'm not going to turn into a teenager someday?"

A scornful laugh. "Only if you want to. But why would you? Imagine being a virgin again! I found my ideal age and, since then, I spend half my time on each side. I grow a little younger. I grow a little older. So long as I keep away from falling safes, I should live forever."

"Oh."

"There's more, but I think I'll wait until you're ready to hear it."

The BMW purred out of the rose forest and up a long, winding road to a hilltop restaurant topped by a flashing neon sign reading MUELLER's. Above the lettering was a neon mule whose hind legs kicked in three shifts of tubing—out straight, up high, and back, over and over. To the far side of the lot, a line of trucks rested, some idling. Mistral found a space as far away from them as possible, and said, "Do you want to eat immediately? Or are you game for a little sport?"

"I'm game."

They went around to the back of the car and opened the trunk. Inside were two cages and in them were Huginn and Muninn, hooded and jessed but moving a little, as if uneasy. Alice drew in her breath. Mistral handed her a falconer's glove and, with reluctance, she put it on. Then they took Muninn from its cage and settled it on Alice's fist.

With Huginn on their own glove, Mistral slammed the trunk shut. Alice followed them to the edge of the parking lot. There was a grand view of the world there: A dark forest below stretched halfway to the horizon; beyond it was glittering cityscape. The sky was filled with unfamiliar constellations. One of the brighter ones looked like a broken lower case letter T. "The Western Cross," Mistral commented. Then, removing Huginn's hood, "It's a perfect night for hunting."

"Vultures don't hunt. They're carrion eaters."

"Not here they're not. Passing through a mirror flips your essentials in interesting ways." Again, there was a gleam of (perverse? yes, perverse) amusement in Mistral's eyes. They threw up their arm and Huginn disappeared down into the soot-black woods.

Not to look timid, Alice cast off Muninn, though she had no idea what they were after. "There's something you're withholding from me," she said. "Something important."

"In that way, this world is a lot like the one you left behind."

"You're not going to tell me, are you?"

"I believe we've already established that."

"Are you the Devil?" Alice didn't accept the existence of Heaven or Hell or God. On this last issue, however, she was an agnostic, teetering on the brink of belief.

Mistral's grin was so bright that the rest of their face faded to obscurity. "Oh, now, that's a tough one. I certainly wasn't when I first came here. But that was long ago."

An enormous flake of darkness flew up from the forest, blinded Alice for an instant, and settled itself on her glove. Muninn dropped something at her feet. It was a snake. A cottonmouth. With wings. Following close upon its twin, Huginn dropped a winged rattlesnake before Mistral. The leathery remnants of the creature's wings thrashed weakly, so Mistral stepped on its head, crushing it with their wingtip. In response to something that had barely reached Alice's consciousness, much less her tongue, they said, "Why not? On the other side, you have mice with wings."

"Those are bats."

"We call *these* skrats." They both then fell into a silence that lasted long enough for the number of flying reptile corpses before them to grow, by Alice's count, to thirty-one. At last, Mistral said, "I'm bored. Let's go inside."

They returned the vultures to their cages and went in.

Mueller's was a truck stop. So far as Alice could tell, it was identical to those in her world. There were tables and booths and two long buffets with sneeze guards, one loaded with foods that were heavy on fats and starches and the other with salads. The gift shop was almost as large as the restaurant. Mistral chose a booth and, when Alice sat, said, "Wait here. I left something in the car."

Alice waited. Time stretched itself thin.

"Looks like you've been stood up, hon." A waitress dropped a plastic-coated menu on the table. She was ruddy-faced, nondescript, plump. "You got any money on you?"

"I . . . no." When she'd climbed through the mirror, it hadn't occurred to Alice that she might need any.

"Got friends you can call to come fetch you?"

Alice shook her head.

The waitress slid into the booth opposite her. "New to this world?"

Not much later, having heard Alice's story through, the waitress led her outside. "Taking off early, Linda!" she called to the woman at the cash register who, without looking up from a clipboard, waved goodbye. They got into an old Honda Civic and headed down the road.

"Name's Francie. That's short for Francesca. Which is long for Frank," the waitress said, and laughed at a joke that was entirely opaque to Alice.

After they'd made love, Alice said, "I've got questions."

"Ask away, hon."

But when Alice tried to put her confusion to words, her thoughts were in such a tangle that she didn't know where to begin. Seeing this, Francie sat up and said, "I've been through this before, babe. How's about I start?"

"I'd like that, thank you."

"Okay. Take a good long look at me." Francie gestured. "Sweet body, huh?"

"Yes. It is."

"I could tell you liked it. Here's the thing, though. On the other side, I was male."

Alice's gaze went down to Francie's sex and back up to her face. "That's not possible."

"How's your clit feel? A little sore, I'll bet. Growing pains. A year from now it'll be a full-sized schlong. You go through the mirror, it switches you around. Male to female, female to male. There's a box of tissues on the end table if you need them."

"I'm not about to cry."

"You're a better man than I was. I cried every night while my dick got smaller and smaller and my insides opened out. Didn't much like the tits neither. Still not crazy about the size of my butt, but there you are. I adjusted. Finding out I could still get it on with girls helped. Tried guys once or twice, but didn't think much of it."

Alice wanted to feel shocked, but couldn't. All the universe was cold as ice and motionless at its center was her. It was possible that her skin stung a little, but she might have been imagining that. She cast about for another question. "There's something I don't understand. You go back and forth through the mirror, right? To all extents and purposes, that makes you immortal. What are you doing working as a waitress?"

"Gotta earn a living, don't I? I was a truck driver on the other side, I'm used to hard work. Besides, I like the human contact."

"Oh." Then, "Tell me about Mistral."

"Mistral? Stay away from that one. Bad news. Crazy as a crate of clockwork hornets and twice as dangerous."

"Mistral dropped me off at Mueller's. I thought maybe you had an understanding."

"Give me some credit. You looked lost. I tried to help. Everything else just happened."

"Are there a lot of us?"

"Naw. Maybe one every two-three years. They all come through the truck stop for some reason. It never occurred to me that Mistral might be behind that." Francie rubbed her chin. "That kinda worries me." She fell silent.

Alice got up, went to the window and twitched back the curtains. She looked down on an alleyway as ordinary as anything she might have seen back home. Garbage bins, oil stains, a Subaru pulled halfway onto the sidewalk. When she turned back, Francie was struggling into her dress.

"What are you doing?" Alice asked.

"Mistral brought you to Mueller's in person. That's a first. It tells me we'd better get the hell out of Dodge."

Francie drove in silence, intent upon the road, keeping a steady speed. It was easy to believe she'd been a truck driver in another life. Alice used the time to try to sort out her feelings about this new world she found herself in. It didn't make a lot of sense to her. But, then, neither had the old one. So she ought to fit right in here.

Some hours later, they pulled into what appeared to be a seaside resort town. The road ran along a black ocean for a while before Francie turned inland at a traffic light. Three blocks on, they parked in the driveway of a Queen Anne house with two small spots out front illuminating a hanging sign reading FLORAL COTTAGE B & B. "Got a friend here," Francie said. They went to the front door and rang. "She's sure to give us a room."

It occurred to Alice that Francie was going to expect them to share a bed. But what had happened earlier had been done on impulse. She was far from certain she wanted an ongoing relationship with this woman. There wasn't the time to discuss that with her now, however. If only, back in the car, she had—

The door was opened by a woman who was all bright scarves, bracelets, and hoop earrings. "City Mouse!" the woman cried.

"Country Mouse!" Francie replied.

The two women embraced. Then, in a flurry of questions, light answers, and sudden darts into the kitchen to put a kettle on, the linen closet for sheets and pillow cases, and the kitchen again to turn off the kettle when the offer of tea was declined, they were ushered into the interior, shown the bath, and given a room. The landlady's name turned out to be Pamela. She and Francie exchanged glances, linked hands, and then went into another bedroom together. "I'll see you in the morning," Francie said reassuringly, and the door clicked shut behind them.

Well, Alice thought. She washed her face, went into her room, and lay down on the bed. Why were these things always so easy for other people? Conversely, why were they always so complicated for her? All her life it had been that way, she had no idea why.

She had a lot to think about, most particularly the transition she was apparently going to make from female to male. Eventually, however, she fell asleep. And dreamed:

She was sitting in the living room back home, reading. But when she tried to focus on the words on the page, they writhed and twisted in her vision, turning to meaningless glyphs. So she put down the book on the side table and lifted the next from the to-be-read stack. Then she flipped to the title page, which opened a blue eye and looked at her.

Hastily, she turned the page. But the next page, which should have been the beginning of the first chapter, was a mirror and in the mirror was her own face. Her features looked harsh and mannish. Horrified, she slammed the book shut.

"The truth hurts, doesn't it?" Sitting cross-legged in the air, red-soled Louboutin wingtips at eye level, was Mistral. "Too bad. Once seen, never unseen."

The morning was as dark as the evening had been. But the kitchen clock said 7:15 and every now and then there was the soft drone of a car driving past. Evidently, this world had no sun. Pamela appeared, wearing a kimono, yawning and happy. Francie, following after, pulled out a chair for her and said, "No quiche and herbal tea today, sweetie. I'm fixing you a *real* breakfast." She set about making coffee and frying eggs, as if the place were her own.

They ate at the kitchen table. When the last bites of toast were done and the coffee refilled, Pamela said, "So. You have no money and your only friends in all the world are sitting here next to you. The first order of business is to find you a job. Do you have any skills?"

Stung to arrogance, Alice said, "I'm ex-military, ex-medical, ex-newspaperwoman, ex-business, ex-everything. I've been an artist, a spook, a musician, a farmer—you name it, I've done it."

Pamela raised her eyebrows. "Oh? Have you robbed a bank, begged on the street, sold your body? Worked the graveyard shift in a herring cannery?"

The contrariness that had ruined so many opportunities, and her first two marriages as well, rose to Alice's lips. But she choked it back. "I'm sorry. I didn't mean to brag."

"So you're adaptable," Francie said. "That's good. What's your background like, hon?"

"My mother was a war correspondent. When I was six, she took me to one of those Middle Eastern wars where the bombing never stopped. We stayed in luxury hotels and we always had servants because things were so desperate people would work for almost nothing. If I dropped something, I clapped my hands and our 'girl' would pick it up for me. I was dreadfully spoiled."

"That sounds . . . interesting," Pamela said.

Francie added, "Was it fun for you?"

"One day mother took me along to an interview with a warlord of no lasting significance and he staged an execution for us: a black marketeer accused of price gouging food. I saw his head explode. Another time, I forget why, I was waiting in the limo for my mother when a horse-drawn wagon filled with corpses went by. How they stank! The driver rolled up the windows and turned on the air conditioning. When I asked about the bodies, he turned up the radio. Fun? No. But it taught me a great deal about people; I haven't been surprised by anything they did since. I never could get an explanation from my mother as to why she thought bringing me along was a good idea."

Francie put a hand over hers. "Did you ask your father?"

"Oh, him. He was a lawyer; he stayed in New York. Anyway, nobody took him very seriously. Everything that ever happened in our lives was all about my mother. If you knew her, you'd understand."

Pamela left the room and returned with an atlas. Reclaiming her seat, she opened it. "Let's put off the job for a minute. Where do you think you might want to live?"

"Anywhere in the world, you mean?"

"Got a passport, hon?" Francie asked. "Because if not . . ."

Flipping pages, Pamela said, "You'll want to keep a low profile, so I would recommend one of the Jeffersonian states. Metropotamia, maybe? Not Equitasia, you wouldn't like it there. Pelisipia's nice this time of year." The maps made no sense to Alice until she realized that they had been mirror-flipped so that the West Coast was to the right and the East Coast to the left. The land between the Mississippi and the Appalachians was divided into states with unfamiliar names. The rest of the country was more or less as she knew it.

Possibilities were argued, discarded, adopted. Phone calls were made. In surprisingly little time, Alice had a Tuesday appointment with the features editor of the *Fort Pontchartrain Times*, where there was an opening for the position of movie reviewer. "I'll close the inn for a few days and drive you up," Pamela said. "The resort's in the doldrums this time of year and I do all my business by cell phone anyway. I can make a little vacation of it."

"Sorry I can't come with you," Francie said. "But Mueller's needs me. If I'm away too long, everything falls apart."

"I'll pack you a lunch. If Alice and I get an early start, we can be well on our way to Metropotamia by nightfall."

What Pamela meant by nightfall in a world with no discernable sun, Alice did not ask. Instead, she said, "Before you go, tell me. What's the deal with Mistral? I think it's time you leveled with me."

Francie looked at Pamela, who gave her a slight nod. "Honestly?" Francie said. "Nobody knows, really. Mistral just showed up one day. She's capricious. I think maybe she's a god."

"A demon," Pamela corrected her. "He's a demon."

"Whatever she is, she's dangerous to cross. You know how when you go through the mirror, it changes your gender? That's a lot of power. Think about it."

"I have." Alice had thought of little else since arriving here.

"Well, you learn the ins and outs of it and you can use that power. Like when Pamela lit the candles last night . . . Oh, I guess you weren't there. Anyway, she didn't use matches. She can do a lot more than that, too."

Now Pamela spoke up: "Last time I was young, I was mad for flying. I spent half my life on a broomstick. Of course, I had the body for it then."

"You were talking about Mistral," Alice reminded her.

"Mistral's got that kind of power, only a hundred times as much as the two of us combined. And I think we've said enough on that subject," Pamela said.

"More than enough," Francie agreed.

"Anyway," Pamela said, "it's all we know." And no amount of urging would make her speak further. Nor Francie either.

Pamela made a brown bag lunch, carried Francie's travel bag to the car, and shared a long, comfortable kiss with her that Alice couldn't help envying. Then she came back inside and said, "Let's get you packed. We're not quite the same size, but some of my clothes ought to do," and bustled off into the far recesses of the inn.

Alice poured herself a cup of coffee, sat down at the kitchen table, and wrapped both hands around it, savoring the heat, savoring the pain. Staring down into its black depths, she felt herself again slipping into a dream.

She was in a diner, having a pleasant chat with Mistral when Mistral said, "Hey! Want to see my imitation of a cat?"

"No," Alice said. "I most emphatically do not."

"You'll love it!" Mistral climbed onto the table and struck a feline pose—crouched, hands fisted into front paws tidily together on the tabletop,

head held up proudly. They looked a lot like the cat-goddess Bast—alert, noble, serene. Then they pushed a cup of hot coffee into Alice's lap.

Outraged, Alice leapt to her feet, slapping at the ugly brown stain on her Chanel suit. "What the hell did you—?"

But now a wracking cough made Mistral's entire body shudder. Alice thought they were pretending to hack up a hairball but what finally came pouring out of their mouth was an enormous green tentacle that flopped down on the floor before her. Still, Mistral continued hacking and coughing.

Another tentacle gushed forth. Then another. And another. Soon, neither Mistral nor the table was visible for the mound of slime-green and slug-gray tentacles. They swayed as if alive, and some reached playfully for Alice, as if to draw her in.

Alice seized the nearest tentacle. It was barely substantial and shattered at her touch like sea-foam. Then she was wading into the mound of filth, smashing the tentacles to nothing with her fists. It was no easy task, for even as she destroyed them new tentacles were being barfed up. But finally she had fought and demolished her way to the heart of the tangle.

There was nothing there—not Mistral and not even the table.

"Ready?" Pamela asked. "I've packed a picnic hamper with a baguette, mushroom pâté, grapes, and a thermos of iced green jasmine tea, so we can stop at a state park and make a feast of it."

"We're not going anywhere," Alice said.

Pamela stepped back, as if affronted. But there was the slightest hint of a smile on her lips. "What are you saying?"

"I'm saying that I can't believe you'd go through all this trouble for me just out of pure niceness. Not that you're not nice. But with the possible exception of the Dalai Lama, nobody's that nice. Closing your business in order to drive someone you've just met halfway across the country for a job interview? Without one word of complaint or self-congratulation? Francie was hard enough to believe in. You're a unicorn."

"I suppose I am," Pamela said. "In a way." With both hands, she seized the front of her blouse. Then she ripped it open—and her body and her face and the kitchen as well.

Alice had taken LSD once, clinical grade stuff straight from Sandoz, back in the sixties—even her husband didn't know this—under medical supervision. The overture, as she thought of it, of the experience had felt much like this. She was on a dance floor under a starry, moons-filled sky in a clearing in a lilac forest. There were hummingbirds in the air and luminous monkeys swinging from tree to tree. A jazz band was playing "Stormy Weather."

She and Mistral were slow dancing.

Mistral led, of course, Alice's status still being in flux. They were the best dancer Alice had ever known—light, natural, effortlessly in control. But that didn't make her like them any better. "What now?" Alice asked.

Mistral shrugged. "I had a series of experiences planned for you before I made my pitch, culminating in your first time in a male body with a woman. But you got ahead of things. As usual, I might add."

"You talk as if you know me and you act as if you have the right to tell me what to do."

"Of course I do, dear. Haven't you figured out who I am yet?"

"No."

"Give it time. It will come to you."

The music ended. They went to a table. Mistral held out a chair for Alice, then sprawled in the one opposite. Glasses of champagne appeared before them. "I'll cut to the chase. I like my gender and age exactly as they are—and that requires that I make frequent trips to the other side of the mirror. But this world is much like Mueller's without Francie. If I'm away too long, people get notions. I need a second in command to look after things in my absence."

"A flunky, you mean."

"Potato, po*tah*to."

A long silence. Then Alice said, "Isn't this the part of the melodrama where you promise me limitless power and wealth?"

"If you can't see all that for yourself, then you're not the person I'm sure you are."

"Okay. Okay. That brings us to the next question: Why me?"

"Because I trust you, sweetie. Also, knowing you as I do, I'm sure you're right for the job." A pack of cigarettes appeared on the table. Mistral extended a languid arm, tapped one out, and lit it. Smoke oozed from their nostrils.

Alice sat up straight. There was something hauntingly familiar about that combination of gestures. Alice had seen that micro-performance hundreds of times. Always, always, always performed by one and only one person . . .

"*Mother!*"

"Ah. The dime drops at last."

It made perfect sense, in its own hallucinatory way, that the woman who had haunted her life would haunt her afterlife—or whatever this was. But even as Alice thought that, she knew it wasn't true. It was just too pat, too tidy, to be true. The universe was a messy place and life was a messy business. Only simple matters had simple solutions and only simple minds thought otherwise. "It can't be. To begin with, you're dead."

"Yes, I'm sure she was careful to leave that impression." Francie pulled out a chair and sat down. "Ooh, champagne. Is there a glass for me?"

There was.

"Francesca," Mistral said. "And me without a fly swatter."

They were back in the room where Alice had first entered the mirror world. The corpse still lay facedown on the Bokhara among scattered chess pieces and playing cards. The mirror over the mantelpiece was a rectangle of silver mist. But the table and chairs remained exactly as they had been at the edge of the dance floor. Alice took a sip of her champagne. It was very dry and so cold that it stung, which was how she liked it. But of course anyone—or anything—capable of imitating her mother so well would know. "You can stop pretending," she said, "the both of you."

Francie sighed. "I told you that being her mother was a smidge too far."

"It's what she wanted most—the chance to get the old bat in her clutches and squeeze some answers out of her. Was I supposed to deny her that?"

"Game time is over," Alice said. "You both know what I want to know. Which one of you is going to tell me?"

"It really doesn't matter," *either Mistral or Francie said.* "We're both aspects of the same thing. When you passed through the mirror, you created a pocket universe. There are potential universes in every dust mote, atom, and quark in existence. Almost all of them are void and without form. We were one such. Then you brought us to life."

"We like being alive," *the other said.* "So, to keep you here, we gave you things we knew you would enjoy. Darkness. Mystery. A new gender. The kind of friends you never got to have in your old world. An adversary for you to outwit and overcome—a kind of trickster or spirit guide to challenge and allure you." (Alice had read Jung, so she knew that Mistral was being defined as her animus. But she did not feel it was worth interrupting the flow of words to mention that.) "Here, you can have anything and be anyone you desire. Don't try to pretend you never wished for a private world of your own. A world where everything and everybody would be and do as you wanted them. There are no limits to what can happen here. We know you well and we are anxious to give you what you desire.

"It's yours. All you have to do is take advantage of it."

"Are you done?" Alice asked.

Mistral and Francie had surrendered their human forms. They were now floating blobs of darkness, like black wax in a lava lamp. As Alice watched, they merged and became one. "Yes," *it said.* "I am done."

"You're a parasite," Alice said, "and you have no right to my life. The old universe, the one I grew up in, was like you in a lot of ways—tyrannical, inconsistent, sometimes even cruel. But still, there was room in it for courage and cowardice, generosity and selfishness, honesty, wonder, awareness. Oh, and the glorious, rapacious, loving, destructive, yearning human race! In place of all that, you offer me—what? A shadow play? False friends, imaginary enemies, elaborate scripts to keep me dancing for your amusement? The opportunity to sit in the dark talking to myself for all eternity? Better to die in reality than live forever here. You presume to understand what I need and what I want. You say you know who I am—"

"I do! I know you better than you know yourself."

"*You* don't know who I am!" Alice cried in a fury. "Only *I* know who I am."

She stood. At a thought, there was a crowbar in her hand. The champagne and cigarettes had showed her how to do that trick.

"I exist!" *the pocket universe cried.*

"That fact," Alice replied, "has not created in me a sense of obligation." She cocked her arm and flung the crowbar as hard as she could.

And broke the mirror.

How many people get to destroy a universe?

Sooner or later, Alice realized, every single one of them.

For what seemed an eternity—it might have been minutes, it might have been forever—she was alone. There was neither light, nor sound, nor smell, nor touch, nor taste, nor dimension. But at last she heard a soft flapping in the distance. Huginn and Muninn came flying back to her, slowly and heavily. First one and then the other settled upon her shoulders once again. Alice did not welcome their return. But she discovered, with dull surprise, that she found some comfort in their weight, their certainty.

With that, Alice found herself sitting at home in her chair. Her shotgun leaned against one arm, where she had left it at the beginning of this exercise. It gleamed gently in the moonlight, as well it should:

She'd spent half the afternoon cleaning and polishing it. There were two shells in its chambers.

She picked up the shotgun. Then she went into her husband's room and, dry-eyed, did what had to be done.

She pulled the sheet over him.

Alice sat down on the edge of the bed, her back toward her husband. She did not spare him a second's thought. That part of her life was over.

She touched the stock of the shotgun to the floor. She closed her mouth around the muzzle. Only amateurs shot themselves any other way—the risk of surviving was too great. Stretching one arm downward, she placed her thumb on the trigger. Any last thoughts? Just one: *Memento mori.* Remember you must die. She knew what other people thought it meant. But by her reading, it was simply the last item on a very long to-do list. If you hadn't died yet, you couldn't say that you'd led a rich, full life. Which she had. So she pushed.

Her world shattered like a mirror.

CLOUD

"Oh, and I should warn you that Aunt Céline is going to make a pass at you."

"What?" Most of Wolfgang's attention was on the road. Its surface was slick and it wound through a forest of misty trees, twists of pale water vapor that faded indistinctly into the surrounding night. "Excuse me, you said what?"

"She's hit on all of my beaus," Judith said. "Well, almost all. The ones she didn't, I always found out later there was something wrong with them. In retrospect, I probably should have run them past her before going to bed with any of them."

"Wow." The sign for I-87 floated out of the darkness and Wolfgang took the ramp. "I guess I'd better hope for the best, or we'll have to call off the wedding."

"You've got nothing to worry about, handsome." Judith patted his thigh. "Trust me."

They drove on in silence for a bit. The interstate was more heavily traveled than the Parkway had been, but straighter and better lit. A bridge rose up before them and they crossed over a deep chasm caused by a fold in the cloudbanks. Down at its bottom was a bright ribbon of roads and buildings where the surface was flat enough to build upon. "Aunt Céline sounds like quite a character," Wolfgang said.

"Oh, I told you about her! Céline was the family scandal. She married a man thirty years older than herself—"

"Harmon Anderson, I know."

"—and I forget how many billions richer. Then, when he died, she spent years defending the estate from his children by the first two marriages. She fought them down to scorched earth. There were headlines. But no one can deny the good she's done with that charity she founded."

"You're proud of her."

"Darling, who wouldn't be? Wait until you see her place." Judith leaned forward and turned on the radio. A scatter of clacking notes of light jazz led into Terry Gross's voice:

Today on Fresh Air: Is the Cloud trembling on the brink of a rainstorm that will dissolve our world beneath us? Some scientists say yes. I'll be talking with Dr. James L. Stafford, who–

Wolfgang flicked off the radio. "We don't have to listen to that. I mean, Christ. Sufficient unto the day is the evil thereof, right?"

"You're nervous!" Judith crowed in delight. "My big bad woof is nervous about meeting the family."

"Don't be absurd. I've faced down the best the Department of Justice could throw at me. Families are nothing." He shifted into a higher gear and gave the Jaguar a taste of speed. It wove around and through the traffic. Meanwhile, the cloud banks swelled up and up and up and the road went with them. Far above, at their peak, shone the bright skyscrapers of New York City.

The door opened onto a comfortable haze of conversation and laughter. A string quartet was playing Bach. A valet took their coats.

Before they could plunge in, a tall woman in an Issey Miyake gown swooped down upon them. "Judith!" she cried, adding after an almost imperceptible pause, "and you must be Wolfgang. How delightful, come in, come in." With hugs and air kisses Céline drew them out of the anteroom and into the suite. "I don't think you've been here since I redecorated? Let me show you around." She took Judith by the arm and led her through the penthouse, Wolfgang tagging after. This room had a variety of features and the tapestry came from Spain and hello, it's been so long, you know Judith, don't you? Guests loomed up and melted back into the party.

They drifted through the library, the media area, and the spa, their brief confrontations with a famous cinematographer, his jailbait companion, and a politician on the way down dissolving to nothingness the instant they turned their backs. Wolfgang could not help reflecting on how good Céline looked for a woman of her age. Her vivacity was a part of it, of course, but so was her gown, cut low to show off her freckled breasts. They looked as if they'd been sprinkled with cinnamon. Small silver stretch-marks showed at their tops, so he had to assume they were natural. It was easy to see why her late husband had been moved to acquire her. Wolfgang could vividly imagine those breasts naked, beginning to sag but not so much as to be a problem, could picture himself cupping them in his hands, could all but feel their warmth and weight on his palms.

". . . should warn you that Radford's in a sour mood," Céline was saying.

"Oh, Radford!" Judith cocked her head and launched a dismissive eyebrow. "Nobody takes *him* seriously."

The tour wound up where they'd begun, in what Wolfgang now learned was called the commons. A table had newly materialized with hors d'oeuvres to one side, sushi to the other, iced oysters in the center. The caterer—or, no, Céline would have a full-time cook, surely, so this would be another servant—stood by it in respectful silence. On the wall opposite was an oil painting which Wolfgang had somehow failed to notice when he came in. Now his eye went straight to it.

"But this is—" He stopped. "Surely it can't be."

"It isn't." Céline went close enough to the painting to touch it and he followed. Swirling colors threatened to swallow him whole. "The final version of *Cloud* is in the National Gallery. But Turner painted eight oil sketches in preparation for it, more than he ever did for any other painting. They were all based on the very latest scientific measurements—some would say the first accurate measurements—of its dimensions. This one was the least highly sought-after because he set it at twilight, whereas the *Cloud* we most cherish rests in a flat blue sky.

"Yet of the lot, this is the vision I personally esteem the highest, save for the final painting of course, and not just because it's the one I happen to own. If you look at the bottom edge of the Cloud, there to the right, you'll see a faint but definite glow that's only suggested in the other versions. Incipient lightning. Sunlit as they are, the others can no more than hint at what is explicit here, Turner's frame of mind when he painted it. He thought we were all doomed. No, he was certain of it. You have only to look at the sketch to see. We are doomed, all of us, and our world as well. Knowing this, Turner nevertheless created a work so profoundly beautiful as to be a reprimand thrown in the face of God: Though you destroy us, still we are capable of creating *this*."

"Wow."

"Indeed." The slightest tinge of mockery showed in Céline's expression. "Wow."

Mercifully, new guests were announced just then. It was Judith's great-aunt Leah and her husband Marsden. By the time the introductions were over, Céline had disappeared.

While Judith popped into the powder room, Wolfgang sized up the party. Nonentities, mostly, save one man: Older, craggy, a little too firm of jaw. Kettledrums rumbling in the distance, Wolfgang went over and introduced himself.

"Radford Anderson," the man said. "Don't bother to be impressed. I'm only here to visit my late brother's money."

They shook. Anderson had the hands of an ogre. Wolfgang couldn't help admiring them. "You're little Judith's fiancé, aren't you? What are you in?"

"Acquisitions and mergers."

"Good at it?"

"I do my best."

"Have we met before? I feel like I know you."

"We haven't. You're famous, I'd have remembered. You just know my type: Sincere handshake, firm eye contact, smile a touch too ruthless. Ambitious young man on the way up." Wolfgang twisted his mouth in a self-deprecating way. "If we'd met, you'd have forgotten me ten minutes later."

"You're honest, I'll give you that. Maybe I could find a place for you in my organization. How much are you earning now?"

"Honestly, I'm not looking to change employers. I'm only here to get a sense of the power dynamics of the family that I'm marrying into."

What might have been a smile creased Anderson's face. "You'll do fine," he said. It did not sound like an endorsement.

"Radford!" Céline cried. "We have to talk about your daughter." She took his arm. "You'll excuse us, Wolfie dear."

Wolfgang watched them dwindle away.

Judith rejoined Wolfgang and said, "Have you noticed the furniture?" Then, when he looked blank, "George Nakashima, darling. Céline must have had the entire suite made to order; they go together too well to have been bought piecemeal."

"You want Nakashima, I'll buy you Nakashima," Wolfgang said with a touch of pique. He was as good as any of the people here. He had money of his own.

"He's dead, dear. Now there's only the daughter. Not the same." Putting her head next to his, Judith murmured, "Has she hit on you yet?"

"No. And I doubt she will."

"Wait until she's had a few drinks."

Then Judith saw someone she had known in business school and with a shriek and a hand waved in the air, left Wolfgang behind. He drifted to the bar. A glass of Cristal brut rosé in hand, he sank down onto a couch as soft as a flock of sheep. Across the room, the bartender was pouring wine that flowed up from the bottle lip into a glass jauntily held upside-down.

After a time, Wolfgang realized that someone was sitting beside him, gossiping about his relatives-to-be and magically managing to make their misbehaviors boring. It was Judith's cousin Zara's husband, whose name he could never remember. He was stocky, a fast talker, impossible to take seriously. Apparently they were having a conversation.

"Yes, I met him a few minutes ago," Wolfgang said. Then, just to stick it to the pompous little nobody, "I turned down an offer to work at his firm."

A wince of wounded pride entered the man's eyes. But he went on. "You've heard about him and Judith, haven't you? Ugly stuff. It was all anybody talked about for the longest time. But she's told you all about it all, I'm sure."

Wolfgang gave him a long, hard stare. "Exactly what are you implying? Think before you answer." He watched the man splutter and break up into confusion and thin air. Then he stood.

Realizing that his flute was empty and that he had no idea what the champagne had tasted like, Wolfgang decided, for strategic reasons, to switch to mineral water.

"I saw you talking to Damon," Radford Anderson said. He was carrying a cane now. In this light, the lines of his face showed his age.

"Mmm?" With a start, Wolfgang realized that Damon was the name of Zara's husband. Why could he never remember that? "Oh! Yes. Well . . . I couldn't tell you what we were talking about."

"The skies would open up and angels sing, if Damon said something memorable. About anything. Even once. You know his history, I assume."

"He's had a hard time finding himself, I believe."

Anderson snorted. He had a jaw like a snapping turtle and hair like white marble. "When he does, I hope he throws himself back. I hear you and Judith are having problems."

"I can't imagine where you heard that. We're not."

"No need to keep up a front before me, son. I'm the family pariah, remember?"

"I'm sure you're not—"

"Don't suck up to me. Nobody respects a sycophant." Anderson turned to go, then paused and growled over his shoulder, "You haven't figured it out yet, have you?"

"What was that?"

Wisps of cold steam closed about the old man and he was gone.

The rooms filled with people who all knew one another. Some were family, others not. Wolfgang saw Céline through a doorway, surrounded by those who mattered most, and was about to head her way when Judith reappeared at his elbow. Frowning, she said, "Is that gin?"

"Rainwater," he joshed. "See the bubbles?"

"You're wicked," Judith said. Then, "I forgot to warn you about Radford. You should steer clear of him. He's a creep and a loser."

"Is he? In what way?"

"Never you mind. He's a creep and that's enough." Whenever Judith wanted to hide something, her face grew pale and still, as unreadable as a chalk cliff. That had appealed to him when they first met. I'll break through that, he'd thought, and make her bark like a dog. Later, he regretted the words but not the impulse.

"Oh, bother. There's Elaine Dorr. One of my clients. She's a loathsome creature but I'd best go talk to her. How the hell did she get an invitation? Stay out of trouble, won't you? I know you will."

"I'll be out on the balcony if you need me," Wolfgang said to Judith's back.

A breeze rose from below to cool Wolfgang's brow when he leaned out over the railing. All the glory and misery of Manhattan at night billowed up at him. There was laughter at his back and the faint honking of taxicab horns below rendered musical by distance. It was the kind of perfect evening that only money could buy.

The view from the top of the city always made Wolfgang's spirits lift: here the glittering aspirations of the world were laid bare. As a boy he had imagined the Devil coming up behind him at such a moment to clap a warm hand on his shoulder and make him an offer too sweet to refuse. That was his own private origin myth. It hadn't happened, metaphorically or otherwise, but apparently the fantasy died hard.

A figure that might have been Odin stood brooding at the end of the balcony where the light from the party didn't quite reach. As Wolfgang turned away from the rail, there was a clash of metal on stone and he saw that he'd knocked over a folded aluminum walker.

Its owner didn't look up.

It was Radford Anderson again. He was, it seemed, unavoidable. Wolfgang leaned the walker back against the wall and went to join him. Anderson was playing with something between his hands. A watch. Everyone in finance wore Rolexes. Wolfgang's was platinum, calculated to impress those sophisticated enough to tell. This, however, was no Rolex.

"You're still a lawyer, aren't you?" Anderson said without looking up. "I could use one of them. Hell, I could use a hundred."

"I could recommend somebody, if you'd like. But I'm not—"

Anderson cut him short with a gesture. "Bad joke, kid. Lawyers can't help me. I already have too many." He stared down at the street slowly filling with fog, and his hands went cloudy and indistinct. Pink scalp showed through thinning hair. When he dipped his head, Wolfgang could see his bald spot.

"What kind of watch is that?"

"A Breitling. Classic. Owned by Joseph Goebbels." The old man's mouth quirked up on one side. "I never met a Jew who wouldn't swap his grandmother for it. Aren't you going to ask me how I got so rich? Everybody else does."

"Well," Wolfgang said, "how did you?"

Looking away, across a cityscape that, still glowing, was melting into a purple and gold sunset, the old man said, "I fucked a woman who had more money than me and walked away from the divorce with a big enough nut to start playing in real estate. It was that simple." He turned his face, still in shadow, toward Wolfgang. "Don't tell me you don't know what I'm talking about."

Fog was rising up to fill the spaces between the buildings. Or perhaps the skyscrapers were sinking into cloud. The noises were muted now, distant and hard to resolve. Windows everywhere were merging together into a bright, indistinct glow even as the shadows rose up around them.

"I was just like you and all your little pals once. Thought I had the game figured out. Now the game is over and it seems I won." Nodding downward, Anderson said, "How long do you think it would take a man to reach the ground?" His hands had been growing paler and thinner. Now they were all but invisible. The watch they had been holding slipped through insubstantial fingers and fell.

Wolfgang reflexively snatched at the Breitling, without result. It hung in the air, dwindling, and disappeared long before reaching the indistinct city pavement. "Quite some time," Anderson said. "A man could settle his thoughts on the way down. Eh?"

"I doubt you could climb over the rail."

Like a weary hiker shrugging on a heavy backpack after an all too brief rest, Anderson straightened into a posture of confidence, power, authority. Taking a step forward, he patted Wolfgang's arm—three short sharp taps, just above the elbow. His face was in the light now and to his horror, Wolfgang recognized it.

It was his own.

The features were older and infinitely wearier, true. Possibly weaker. They had an asymmetry that suggested the old man had had a stroke and one eye was milky-blind. But it was unquestionably Wolfgang's face.

Before Wolfgang could react, Anderson's body wavered in the breeze, growing vague and indistinct. His features softened, melted, folded in upon themselves. His hair rose up, evaporating into the air.

Céline stepped briskly onto the balcony, then stopped. "I—I could have sworn Radford was out here."

Wolfgang turned back to Anderson.

But the old man was gone.

Céline stood by the door, doling out warm, personal farewells to everyone as they left. Her face had a light sheen of sweat from all the drinking. She looked like the last woman in the bar, the one you settled for because it was better than going home alone. When Wolfgang paused to say their farewells, her hand lingered on his. "You must come visit." Voice slightly slurred, she leaned close. "Sometime when Judith is away."

In the elevator, Judith smirked. "Told you." She stumbled over nothing, then said, "I may have had a touch too much to drink. Are you okay to drive?"

Wolfgang shrugged.

They made their way to the parking garage in silence. An attendant fetched the XK. Wolfgang drove it out of the city and north up the Parkway, with dark forest to their left and on the right the cloudbanks of the Palisades cascading downward toward the Hudson.

Here, where he could see only fleeting glimpses of houses tangled in trees and tufts of water vapor, a flicker of window lights and gone, Wolfgang paradoxically felt the weight of human construction surrounding him: one great smear of city stretching from Boston to Washington, with occasional patches of attenuated forest like this one embedded in it, and the sky overhead a dull red from millions of reflected sodium and mercury vapor street lamps. None of it owed anything to him. He built nothing. He only shifted ownerships from one set of hands to another.

"Wolfgang," Judith said suddenly. There was a panicky tremor in her voice. "We're good people aren't we? Tell me we are." Judith had that chalk cliff look again. He wondered what she had been up to at the party. Experience told him he would never know.

"Yeah," Wolfgang said. "Sure." He wanted to be more comforting but for the life of him he couldn't remember how.

He did not so much hear as feel the thunderclap from the far side of the world, heralding the beginning of the storm and the fall of the first raindrops from the cloud that was already beginning to disassemble itself beneath them.

TIMOTHY: AN ORAL HISTORY

L. L. W. Humboldt
Professor of Genomic Obstetrics, Stanford University School of Medicine

Because I *could*, that's why. Because the technology was there and if I didn't do it somebody else would. Because I, perhaps naively, expected the acclaim of a grateful world and quite possibly a Nobel Prize. But chiefly I did it because the science was so beautiful. Have you ever seen a herd of mastodons on the Alaskan tundra? At night? I was on a nature trek, looking at them pass by like so many pale ghosts when I saw a mother pause to urge along her young calf. It occurred to me then that the same tools that had resurrected her species could be employed on the human race. That's all. I wanted to create something as pure and beautiful as those mastodons—and, by God, I did.

Emily Chang Gray
District Attorney, U. S. District Court of the Central District of California

There was, of course, a great deal of pressure on me to prosecute, both from the public and from the political sector. But there is a legal maxim, *Nullum crimen nulla poena sine legis.* There is no crime without a law forbidding it.

You cannot be charged with a criminal offense for an action that was not illegal at the time you committed it. What Dr. Humboldt did was perfectly legal because nobody ever thought it was possible. There was no law against it for the same reason there is no law against killing unicorns.

After the news got out, there was a great rush of hastily written legislature. All of it too late. That horse had already left the barn.

Nance Moynihan
Fabric Artist

Forget all that tabloid podcast foofaraw. I'm not an airhead. Or childish. Or "off in Cloud Cuckoo Land," as a certain gossipmonger put it. Being an artist requires a lot of right-brain thinking. Not the same thing. I went into this with my eyes wide open. Nobody just suddenly decides to make a baby, after all. My wife Cheryl and I talked about it for a long time. Then there was the mandatory counseling, genetic health certification, proof of financial independence . . . The paperwork they wanted for a birth license would drive you crazy! Somebody told me they do it to keep the population from ballooning back up to what it was in the old days. I believe it. But in the end, there you are, holding this adorable, perfect little baby. That makes it all worthwhile. The midwife put Timothy in my arms and I burst into tears, that's all. I just burst into tears.

Also, Dr. Humboldt didn't trick anybody into anything. When she told me what was possible, I thought it was the most wonderful thing that could ever happen to me. Cheryl was a little dubious at first. But I won her over. We went into this with our eyes wide open. We thought it was a terrific idea. We were just over the moon.

J. S. Barros Martinez
Senior Lecturer in World History, Universidade de São Paulo

People are afraid of change, even when that change is a restoration of something that was once as natural as rain.

The near-extinction of the human race put extraordinary pressures on our forebears and they responded magnificently. Out of chaos and trauma, they built a society that their predecessors would have considered Utopian—one without war, without hunger, without the exploitation of the weak by the strong. That's in addition to jumpstarting human reproduction. It was an astonishing and inspiring accomplishment and one that we are quite right to want to protect and preserve.

Is the birth of one child going to destroy all that? I fail to see how.

Julia McIntyre
Postdoctoral Fellow of Male Studies, University of Edinburgh

If Dr. Barros Martinez thinks that men aren't inherently dangerous and violent, I have an entire library that says otherwise. I'll zip it into a file and mail it to her if she wishes. I guarantee it'll give her nightmares.

Oh, and Dr. Laura Humboldt is the greatest criminal the world has ever known. Worse even than Attila the Hun, Pol Pot, Caligula, or Leopold II. All men, incidentally. We were better off without them.

Cheryl van Buskirk
Chemical Engineer, Dow-Henkel AG

I was resistant to the idea at first. What did I know about raising a male daughter? I wasn't even clear on the physical differences. But Nance wanted it so much! To give birth to a child that's literally unique? I could understand the appeal even if I didn't share it. So I gave in. Back then, I would have done anything for Nance.

The funny thing is that in the long run the marriage didn't last. But I kept seeing Timothy every chance I got. Because, well, I was still her mom.

Suzanne Wickershaw
Current Occupation Unknown

We were pals when we were kids. Timmy's folks always kept her on a short leash. I remember, for example, she was never allowed to go swimming. Or stay overnight at a friend's place. But we got along well. Then, not long after my Menarche Ritual, Timmy began to smell funny. Everybody noticed it. Some of the girls delegated me to have a chat with her about hygiene. Which was pretty embarrassing, you know? But I tried. It turned out she was taking baths before and after school every day but they didn't do much good. And perfumes just made her smell weirder. I asked if she'd seen a professional about it and she said she didn't dare. Which made no sense to me so I kept after her.

Finally, Timmy told me her secret—that she was a boy.

I didn't believe her. "Show me," I said.

So she did.

I was revolted. Ick. "What is that thing? Get it away from me!" I said that to her face and she started to cry. Well, that made me feel bad, of course. After she'd buttoned up her dress, I tried to comfort her. I put an arm around her shoulders and she shoved me away. "Don't be like that," I said. "We're still friends, aren't we?" We ended up talking for hours.

Then we kissed for the first time.

Nance Moynihan
Fabric Artist

Everybody wants to know why I didn't notice. How was I to notice? Sure, Suzanne was in and out of the house all the time. But she always had been. Plus, kids get secretive at that age. It's almost impossible to get any information out of them. Try to find out what they had for lunch and it's like talking to a brick wall.

At that time, I was working on an installation for MoMA-3 Beacon. I'd commissioned instantiations of six of Louise Bourgeoise's spider sculptures and was weaving an environment that would encompass them all in a meaningful narrative. Her spiders were archetypal figures from before the Rupture, but they were also mothers, seamstresses, protectors. So they fit into our era comfortably as well. The buzz in the art world was strong that this was the piece that was going to make my reputation.

Yes, I'm aware of the irony. I should have been protecting Timothy. I should have been another mother to Suzanne. Instead, I was weaving spiderwebs. When the story broke, MoMA-3B canceled the show. I powered down my loom and left the piece unfinished. It pretty much destroyed my career.

Served me right, too.

Cheryl van Buskirk
Chemical Engineer, Dow-Henkel AG

It never occurred to either of us to warn Timothy that sex makes babies. No, in vitro fertilization makes babies. Sex is just something girls like to do with each other.

Becca Opeyemi
Special Reporter and Columnist, Noosphere Media

I write about medicine. Morning, noon, and night. Nothing else. Mostly reproductive science. It was my good fortune to be working up an article on teenage pregnancies—why a woman so young would want a child, how she managed to win over her family and counselors, that sort of thing—when one of my bots kicked something odd into my MindSpace. When I scanned it, I laughed out loud. That's how unlikely it seemed. But then I saw that it came from Stanford. A very reputable source. I dug a little deeper and came up with Dr. Humboldt's name. Not exactly a family gynecologist.

Huh, I thought. Interesting.

I had no idea.

That same day, I tracked down Timothy and Suzanne and interviewed them. They were sweet kids, the both of them, and clearly terrified. Then their mothers descended upon me in livefeed, screaming in rage and waving lawyers about. There were only five of them but they felt like something out of the deep past—an army, maybe, or a mob.

But I already had my story: UNWANTED TEEN PREGNANCY CAUSED BY HUMAN MALE. Two impossible-to-believe items in one. Global-viral in ten seconds flat.

Nance Moynihan
Fabric Artist

You have to understand. We were panicked and overwhelmed. Going e-free didn't work. There were reporters all around the house, hammering on the doors, peering in the windows, sending creepy-crawlies through the recycling bins looking for incriminating I-don't-know-what. It was like being under siege. I called up Cheryl because even though we were divorced, I trusted her judgment. She said I should get an agent.

Cheryl van Buskirk
Chemical Engineer, Dow-Henkel AG

That wasn't my finest moment.

Ellen Grigg
Senior Agent, Boehmer and Hammond Agency

T. In-house, we called her T. Yeah, we groomed her. Taught her how to walk, how to talk, how to flirt, what to wear. The most famous person in the world and T wasn't getting a penny from it. Fuck that noise. She deserved to get rich off of her notoriety.

Which she did. The Agency made sure of *that*. The Retromale clothing line alone was a money machine. But we didn't stop there. Oh, no. Most of the money came from personal appearances. Everybody wanted to see her, meet her, know her, be her new best friend. It was a classic case of supply and demand: You want T at your party? Pay up. If T nodded to you on the street, we made sure she got a slice.

But we didn't exploit her. I remember the first time we met, she expressed concern about what she might have to do.

Been in this business a while, I knew what was worrying her. "No nudity," I said. "Nothing smutty. Nothing that makes you uncomfortable." I put that right in the contract.

All that other crap? Just part of the fame game.

L. L. W. Humboldt
Professor of Genomic Obstetrics, Stanford University School of Medicine

It was always the plan for Timothy to sire a child. Not at such a young age, obviously. But I'd already put out feelers for an open-minded woman who might want to be fertilized in the pre-Rupture manner. Sooner or later it had to be done. It was the unanswerable proof of my accomplishment. The media circus that followed was unfortunate but irrelevant.

What became of the baby? I have no idea.

Suzanne Wickershaw
Current Occupation Unknown

Our child is doing fine, thank you. That's all you're entitled to know. No, I won't tell you its name. Or its whereabouts. Or its gender. It is not going to go through what Timmy and I went through.

Cheryl van Buskirk
Chemical Engineer, Dow-Henkel AG

They broke up. Of course they did. Very few first romances last forever. But it was especially painful for Suzanne, given the circumstances and all the craziness that followed. I had a long talk with Timothy and her agent to make sure that she and the baby would be financially secure. Then I hired a lawyer to vet the agreement. Technically, Suzanne's folks should have handled this. But they were no more practical than Nance, so I stepped in. *Some*body had to be the adult in the family.

Name and Occupation Withheld by Request

I was never happy in my sexuality. None of my relationships lasted very long. I had orgasms when I was alone, but the rest I faked. As far as I could tell, everybody else was happy as a clam. I mean, we live in a perfect society, right? Happy clams as far as the eye can see. So what was wrong with me? What? I'll be honest with you—I've never told this to anybody—there were times when I came close to killing myself.

Then Timothy was all over the newsfeed and when I saw the visuals of her I felt this rush of . . . something. It took me a bit to realize that it was desire. And I thought: *Oh my God!* All my adult life, I felt like a freak. Now I knew that I simply was drawn to a sexual type that didn't exist.

No, I didn't try to meet Timothy. Are you kidding? I knew she'd have staff to keep away the likes of me. That's okay. There's a wealth of black-and-white movies if you know where to look for them, full of those wonderful old-timey men. So I've got those and I've got my fantasies and sometimes I go to clubs where women dress up in Retromale suits. I guess that makes me a pervert. But at least now I know what I am.

Sienna Mars
Human Interest Journalist, Insight Hourly

Oh, the Timothy Years were golden! So much fun! She was always up to something. Drinking, drugs, and idiocy, well of course. Who doesn't at that age? That was a gimme. But every girl she kissed, every celebrity she dated, that was not only newsworthy but scandalous. Plus, the clothes were fabulous—the fedoras, vests, wingtips, Oxford collars . . . We kept a complete catalog of everything she was seen in, updated continually. Pretty good dancer, too. That disastrous attempt at a singing career? Eyeclicks went sky high. Everybody loves a trainwreck.

The poor girl's attempts at romance, ditto. There were so many hookups with publicity seekers who were secretly holding their noses. Or creeps who *liked* what she had to offer but in a way that made your skin crawl. Great stuff. She went into a group marriage and within the year every one of her wives had bailed on her. All five! She really went bananas after that. I hardly got any sleep, chronicling her antics. Oh, but Timothy was a wild one! But what could you expect? Her womb-mother was straight out of Cloud Cuckoo Land.

Then the merry-go-round stopped, and the world became a drearier place.

Kat Lee
Former Celebrity Handler

I thought it was going to be a delightful assignment. The itinerary was great. She was scheduled to meet with poets, musicians, cloud-sculptors . . . all kinds of interesting people.

But when I met Timothy at the airport, she was looking haggard and tense. My heart sank. I've had experience, I was sure she was going to be one of the awful ones—the divas, the complainers. We call them beasts. But when I'd summoned a car and it wrapped itself around us, Timothy leaned back, closed her eyes, and apologized for the state she was in.

It seems there was a woman on the plane. She came running up the aisle with a pair of scissors and ran them right up the side of Timothy's head. Blood went everywhere. Timothy thought she was going to die. Then the woman snipped off a lock of her hair. Can you imagine? The air stewards wrestled her to the floor, which I thought was a little excessive. Then they wiped off the blood and skin-sprayed the wound. Timothy told me one of them asked for her autograph.

Imagine my shock! I asked Timothy if she honestly thought that woman was trying to kill her. She sighed and told me it would have been the third time that happened.

I realized then I was going to have to find a new job. Something cleaner.

"Tisiphone" (Anne-Marie Smith)
Sexton, the Cathedral of Ste. Gianna Molla, Quebec

I wanted her. Physically, I mean. I wanted her to do to me all those filthy, disgusting things men used to do to women before the Rupture. I wanted it passionately. That's how I knew she was the Devil. That's why I knew I had to kill her.

Kill her and destroy all her dirty, degenerate, corrupt male genes. Turn the occasion of sin that is her body into scraps of flesh and splinters of bone. Bathe myself naked in her warm, sinful blood.

Kenese Tagaloa
Metropolitan Peace Officer, City of Boston

The Tisiphone bombing. I was there, doing crowd control. A lot of people had turned out because Timothy was getting an honorary . . . Well, to tell you the truth, I'm not clear on the details. Some award or other. Suddenly, there was this enormous noise and smoke billowing up from the theater. People were screaming and running away.

I ran toward. It was my job. When I got to the theater, there was blood everywhere. On the wall of the building, on the sidewalk, even on the red carpet, ironically enough. I saw limbs that had been ripped off. The people who'd lost them were still alive. I saw a woman with her hair on fire. I . . .

If you don't mind, I'm not going to say any more.

"Tisiphone" (Anne-Marie Smith)
Sexton, the Cathedral of Ste. Gianna Molla, Quebec

The bomb killed nine people and injured I don't know how many more. Timothy slipped into the theater seconds before it went off. The bitch escaped without a scratch. If that isn't proof that she's the Devil, I don't know what is.

Pray! Pray to Mary! Pray to Mary the Mother to vanquish evil from our genome! Let the wicked and the weak and the tolerant and all else who are not of the true understanding die! In agony and torment forever! Amen, amen, amen.

Lakme Bannerjee
Interventionist, New Dawn Services

Nobody can be saved from themselves unless they want to be saved. I told that to Timothy's parents when they hired me. Normally, the hardest part of my job is convincing someone that she would be better off without the habits and behaviors that are making her unhappy.

Not in this case. I never had a more cooperative client than Timothy. She desperately wanted out of the morass her life had become. She just didn't know how. Calmly, carefully, I laid out the road map for her. "First," I said, "you have to fire your agent and completely stop being a public personality."

That was when she hugged me.

L. L. W. Humboldt
Professor of Genomic Obstetrics, Stanford University School of Medicine

All right, yes, I sought out Ms. Moynihan. Or, rather, I sought out someone who would be ecstatic at the idea of giving birth to a male child. Yes, Nance is everything you say. But give me some credit. She was an adult in full possession of her wits.

There are a lot more women like her, too. You think Timothy's the only male out there? Hah! He's the oldest, to be sure. But I open coded my accomplishment. Any doctor competent to read a gene chart can do the same. There are many, many reasons a woman might want a son. And it's not an expensive procedure.

I guarantee you there are thousands of boys in existence at this very moment. With more coming every day.

Himari Watanabe
Director, Institute for the History of Science, University of Tokyo

In the long run, heteronormative structures are sure to return in one form or another. How long? More than a century, less than a millennium is a pretty safe guess. In evolutionary terms, the blink of an eye. What will these structures be like? We have no idea. In my field of study, culture trumps everything and there's never been a culture like ours before. That will shape what follows.

The fact that masculinity has returned doesn't necessarily mean we have to revert to the endless churn of warfare, predatory capitalism, and the oppression of every minority group we can dream up. Human beings are at root rational. I have faith in us.

I wish I were immortal, so I could observe and document whatever happens. It's going to be one hell of a ride.

Julia McIntyre
Postdoctoral Fellow of Male Studies, University of Edinburgh

We had made our way back into Eden and this time there was no serpent. So we took skin samples from our museums and cloned one. People are idiots.

Timothy

Who *was* I? Okay, I knew I was male, but what did that mean? The only people who could have told me were dead. The experts said all kinds of things about male women. All with absolute conviction. Meanwhile, I had no idea what a man was like—and I *was* one!

That was then. Now all that matters to me is being a good father to my child. Whatever that might mean.

L. L. W. Humboldt
Professor of Genomic Obstetrics, Stanford University School of Medicine

I never did get my Nobel.

ANNIE WITHOUT CROW

Annie and Crow were at odds.

Lord Eros had woven a dozen sets of sheets from sighs and orgasms he had collected in his avatar as Lady Incuba. A thousand times smoother than silk were those sheets and infinitely more sensuous. To touch one, however lightly, was to abandon reason for desire. Lust became one's master, one's purpose, one's all. Questions of gender or rank or appearance no longer mattered. So potent were these shimmering cloths that their effect could be felt through burlap.

Crow stole one of the sheets, wearing gloves made of Lord Eros's own hair, and then, for a prank, held a party for as many of the Peers of Creation as could abide his presence. As they entered, he sent them into an unlighted room to leave their coats upon a bed he had made up with the stolen sheet. Then he watched, laughing, as they rutted themselves to exhaustion.

Annie didn't think it was so funny.

"Look, babe, I played it straight with you. I told you what the sheet was and what would happen if you touched it," Crow said.

"The fuck. You thought you could leave something like that lying around without me trying it out?" She hit him hard in the stomach. Annie packed a lot more muscle than you'd expect in a woman so delicate-featured and slim-waisted. Crow waited until she had turned away in scorn before wincing in pain, then composed himself just before she spun back to confront him again.

"Th'art a vile, whore-mongering rogue!" Annie spat, eyes flashing like summer lightning. "Thou . . . thou . . . asshole!"

"Hey, hey, hey. You knew I was a trickster when you hooked up with me. This kind of behavior comes with the territory. It's a compulsion. I ain't got no say over it."

"So *you* say!" Annie grabbed her purse and flung it over one leather-clad shoulder. "I'm going to the Rite Aid for some tampons. Don't wait up for me."

She slammed the door behind her.

A few seconds later, Crow heard the world-shaking roar of his Harley starting up. "My hog!" Outraged, he ran outdoors and was just in time to see Annie's red hair flying behind her as she hit the road. For an instant the heat shimmering up from the highway mingled with the exhaust to make Annie, her hair, and the motorcycle billow and swell and snap in the air like a banner. Then she was gone, out of this gods-forsaken nation and century entirely.

"Shit," Crow muttered. This was really going to fuck up the timelines.

Annie was almost half a millennium deep into the Mountains of Eternity before she had to stop and take a leak. After she'd taken care of business, she checked the maps and saw that she was close to home. So she unstrapped the saddlebags and unpacked her silks, laces, and whalebone stays. She knew from experience that sixteenth-century England would accept a woman on a motorcycle a thousand times more readily than it would one in skintight jeans.

Men! she thought. With ill grace, Annie changed into clothing more appropriate to her destination, skimming her leathers onto the verge of the road. Then, perforce riding sidesaddle, she started up the Harley again. *Not just Crow—all of them!* They would have to be punished. Only how?

This would require some thought.

Half an hour later, she arrived at Maidenshead Manor in the depths of the Old Forest and had all her servants and ladies-in-waiting assembled for inspection in the main hall. Everything appeared to be in order when—

"What is *this*?" Seizing him by his ear, Annie hauled a young male—well-made and even handsome in his way—from among the servants. Turning to glare not at Mistress Zephora, her head-of-household, but at Mistress Pleasance, who was the most likely source of any mischief at Maidenshead. A glimmer of her aspect must have shown in her face, for all her ladies-in-waiting turned pale and a few backed away in fear. "Everyone here knows that my household has one unbreakable rule." Even before she had abandoned her husband for a gypsy trickster, she had maintained this one mansion free of men, so as to have a periodic refuge from their at times oppressive company. She was not anxious to see it defiled.

"That applies only to males of rutting age," Zephora said, adding with a dismissive flick of her fingers, "This pillicock is yet a boy."

"He came wandering out of the forest one day, cold and wet and miserable, and none of us had the heart to turn him away. Who knows where and into what year he would have emerged, had we done so?" Pleasance babbled.

Annie's nostrils flared. "By the smell of him, he won't be a youth much longer. A place for him must be found elsewhere. Account for yourself, lad. What skills hast thou? Ostler, footman, page?"

"Lady, I am a poet," the boy said with a short, stiff bow.

"May the Moon give me patience! Am I supposed to retain thee in order to tell me my eyes are the sun, my lips coral, my breasts as white as a January snowfall, my cheeks like roses, my bearing that of a goddess?"

"Your eyes are nothing like the sun—I can gaze direct at them without pain. Coral is redder than your lips and from what I can see of them your breasts are more dun than white and doubtless nowhere near so chill as snow. I have seen roses both red and white and they are not at all like your cheeks. Granted, I have never beheld a goddess, yet you show no signs of walking in the air rather than on the ground and therefore I doubt you are one." Thoughtfully, the youth added, "You are, however, far more beautiful than any woman I have erenow seen. That said, I am young and there are many women I have yet to see."

Zephora raised a hand to cuff the boy for his insolence. But, hiding a smile, Lady Anne forestalled her, saying, "Very well, you are a poet. If I can find you a post elsewhere before you mature, I won't have to kill you." Something about the pallor of his face prompted her to examine him more closely. "There is a fey look about thee, lad. Art dying?"

"Aye. Within the year, so the physician says."

"Best hope, then, that thy mortality wins the race with thy maturity." Annie turned away from the poet. "Are there any more unpleasant surprises awaiting me? Very well, I shall—" But the faces of her ladies told her that she had moved on too quickly. "What?"

"The child told a strange tale," Lady Zephora said, "of a man and a woman he encountered in the forest. They were in a carriage made all of metal and drawn by no animals that he could see. They stopped and asked him the year and when he gave it, one looked to the other and said 'Forty-three yet to go, then.' We grammar'd out the dates and it seems sure they headed for this very year. He said the two were tall beyond normal stature, dressed in black, and wore white masks."

Lady Anne turned to the boy. "The masks—were they white as chalk? Or white as lilies?"

The boy considered. "No," he decided. "White as bone."

"Crap. What's today's date?" Then, when Annie was told and had checked her PDA, "The king's bairn's christening occurs today at the Church of the Observant Friars. This can be no coincidence. Why are my best clothes not laid out? Why was I not given my invitation immediately upon arrival?"

Yet another uncomfortable silence fell upon the court.

Annie felt her lips go thin and white, and her heart correspondingly ruthless and hard. "Invited or no, we shall make a procession," she said. "Have the boundaries of the estate moved so that they border Greenwich."

The walls of the buildings leading to the church were lined with bright tapestries, and the street itself strewn with rushes, turning it green. A turbulent sea of peasants, priests, merchants, and other nonentities filled every open space and balcony and roof eave, waving scarves and roaring like an ocean squall.

Parked by the church was an ugly metal box of a vehicle, with thick black wheels, irregular sides, and windows of tinted glass. "Does't look familiar, poet?" Annie asked.

"Aye. 'Tis the conveyance I saw in the forest."

"That's an Ural Typhoon. It's a light troop carrier. Russian Federation, twenty-first century. Composite body armor and a KPV 14.5 millimeter machine gun mounted atop the cab. You have no idea what I'm talking about, do you?"

The boy shook his head.

"All that matters is the knowledge that none but Lord Vacant would have the bad taste to bring such a grotesque thing into Bluff King Hal's England."

The unwashed sea of celebrants froze immobile and silent as Annie's procession neared the church. It was the easiest way for her kind to deal with the rabble.

At the procession's approach, the crowds washed away from it like ocean waves parting—save for one, an old man who, unnoticed by the multitude, was pissing upon the church. Some flicker of motion made him look up. When he saw Annie, he blanched. "Lady Anne! You . . . You weren't supposed to be here." At her glare, he tucked himself in and buttoned his trews.

"Obviously not," Annie said. Laying a hand on his sleeve, she said, "Tell me, Papa Goatfoot—what's going on?"

Because the tale Papa Goatfoot told alarmed Annie greatly and because, technically, she was a party-crasher, she drew shadows around her entourage and slipped them inside the church unnoticed. Though all the pews were filled, enough new ones appeared to seat everyone. Such were the courtesies the universe provided those of her ilk.

"Looks like all the heavy hitters are present," she muttered to Papa Goatfoot. "I have half a mind to inflict a passionate desire for an unobtainable lover upon each and every one of them."

The satyr by now was sweating with fear. "Please. I'm supposed to be one of the godfathers—it wasn't my idea! I just agreed because I was in my cups when I was asked."

"As always. Never fear. You're too old and sozzled for me to bother with."

Papa Goatfoot breathed a sigh of relief. "I knew you wouldn't do that to a pal," he said, drawing a flask from an inside jacket pocket.

Taking the flask from him, Annie said, "Don't get cocky. You're not immune. I was the one who introduced Aristotle to Phyllis—and you know how *that* turned out." She took a swig, returned the flask.

At the front of the church was a baptismal font of silver, carved with symbols that were never Christian. It illuminated those standing by it, for it was filled with *uisce solais*, the water of light. Annie watched as one by one the Lords of Creation stood forward to proffer gifts to the babe.

First and most fearsome came Reverend Wednesday, old man Death himself. "Courage," said he. And sat down in the front pew, motionless as a stone. Then, solemn and richly dressed, as in a dumb-show, the other Peers advanced, each by turn, up the aisle to loom like storm clouds over the infant and bestow their gifts.

"Insight," said Lady Dale, sometimes called Lord Dale the Evasive.

"Restraint," one of Lord Silence's gray ladies said, and he nodded grave approval.

"Loyalty and the charm that inspires it," said Prince Mundus.

"Strategic brilliance," said Fata Morgaine.

"Ruthlessness," growled Lord Vacant, "and the sense to employ it sparingly."

There was a long pause. Finally, Annie jabbed her elbow in Papa Goatfoot's side and he popped to his feet. "Sobriety!" he squeaked, eliciting a ripple of laughter. Under his breath, he added, "But in moderation."

With each blessing, the infant was dipped quickly in and out of the luminous water. It bore the ceremony with surprising self-restraint, looking about alertly and making no complaint about the immersions.

Lady Anne waited until she was most of the way up the aisle before lifting the glamour that hid her and her ladies-in-waiting from the congregation. In her most commanding voice, she cried, "No one has asked *me* what gift I have for the infant."

Lord Vacant placed himself between her and the baptismal font, saying, "Stand away, upstart! You are but a weak archetype. Only the strong have the right to be here."

"Yet I have a blessing for the child. If I am as weak as you say, then you have nothing to fear from me, do you?"

For an instant, Lord Vacant hesitated. Then, with a brusqueness that was all but identical to rudeness, he stepped aside.

Lady Anne made her way into the circle of Peers surrounding the baptismal font. Then she dipped her hand into the water and dribbled a few drops on the infant princess. "My gift to thee is that thou shalt neither wed nor bed any man who is your inferior in wit or character." A pitiless smile rested complacent on her lips for a breath, and then she said, "After the gifts you have today received, I have good reason to doubt you shall ever find such a paragon. So, really, what I'm bestowing upon you is a lifetime sans husband or offspring."

A gasp rose up from the assembled Lords of Creation. Outraged, Fata Morgaine cried, "You would destroy the king's daughter's value?"

With a cold glee, Lady Anne said, "I would. Moreover, upon the babe's sire—who, I mark, did not bother to attend her christening—I visit the curse that his daughter will be ten times the king that e'er he was."

Elizabeth, princess of the House of Tudor and someday Queen of England, began to wail.

"There will be many changes made," the Lady Anne announced to the assembled women of her household, once they had returned to Maidenshead. "From this day onward, women shall not take lovers who are their emotional or intellectual inferiors. This will apply not only to the Princess Elizabeth but to every woman everywhere."

In horror, Mistress Pleasance cried, "We'll all die virgins!"

Heads swiveled to look at her and she turned red.

"But, milady, how is this to be done?" asked Mistress Zephora, who was always the most practical one of the household and, consequently, the least popular. "The world needs to be populated—under your terms, it will dwindle to nothing in mere centuries."

"Watch and learn. Oh, and clean the manor house from top to bottom and decorate it to a fare-thee-well. I anticipate guests. Erect tents and pavilions on the lawn and long tables covered by white cloths embroidered in silk with red hearts and yellow roses intertwined. Perfume the air and decorate the nearby woods with fairy lights and tame white harts. Set up targets for archery and prepare a lawn for tennis. Be ready to serve fruits and ices, roasted meats, crisp crudités, breads fresh from the oven with crocks of sweet butter, pâtés and mousses, Viennese pastries, and all manner of good things save only alcohol."

Appearing from nowhere, her new pet poet observed, "'Tis a strange feast that has neither flagons of ale nor goblets of wine. Wouldst have them drink dew, like mayflies?"

"No, still water, like carp. You wouldn't want to see this gang plastered," Lady Anne said. "When they get drunk, they break things." She clapped her hands and raised her voice. "Everyone! You are to make our visitors welcome. They may go where they please and do as they wish in all regards save one: Allow nobody male inside the manor house. No man may penetrate my chambers, whether from the front entrance or the rear or by any other ingress." Somebody tittered and she glared. "*What?!*"

No one dared say a word. "Very well," Lady Anne said. "You have your duties—see to them."

The women scattered like so many doves to the six quarters of the estate, and Lady Anne flung herself down on a couch. She caught herself drumming her fingers on its arm and stilled them. All her plans had been made in a trice, but if there was one thing she had learned from years with Crow, it was never to overthink matters. "Plot out your first seven moves," he had told her. "Then forget the last five." If things went awry, she could always extemporize.

"Poet," she said, "I require distraction. Recite for me 'The Bastard Queen of England.'"

The boy blushed.

The assault began with a flyover of combat jets, meant to intimidate the defensive forces Lady Anne did not have, followed by an all-out invasion of cavalry, infantry, and armored forces. War machines churned up the sod and crushed flowering topiary under their treads. Over the course of four hours, the grounds of the estate were secured, a task that could have been performed in an eighth that time had the invaders been capable of believing there were no defenders. Tanks and mobile guns were parked among the pavilions, latrines and defensive trenches were dug, rolls of barbed wire were unreeled along the perimeter, and guard stations were established by every gracefully winding road.

Servants offered lemonade and petits fours to their bemused conquerors. Lute music and diesel exhaust filled the air.

"Set up a chair in the croquet grounds by the great willow," Lady Anne told her handmaid Larissa. "Have a pitcher of martinis nearby, in case my guest decides to be reasonable." She did not think he would, but it was best to be prepared for all possibilities. Seated in what by no coincidence looked like a wicker throne, she waited for the head barbarian to come and announce that Maidenshead was no longer hers.

"If you die," said her poet, "I will write a ballad in your honor."

"Remind me again why I haven't had you strangled?"

"It will make all who hear it weep."

"Oh, go tell Mistress Zephora to find a hidey-hole for you, lest you be impressed into Lord Vacant's forces for the rest of your pathetically short life. Be off. Shoo!"

Shortly thereafter, he whom she awaited arrived. At his approach, she stood gracefully. "Lord Vacant," she said.

"Slut!" Lord Vacant backhanded her across the face. Fata Morgaine stood by his side, looking amused. "The royal brat was to give birth to a son who would conquer all of Europe and plunge half the world into a war that would last for centuries. You have undone a great deal of patient work today."

"I am glad to hear it," Lady Anne said, and Lord Vacant struck her again.

She was dragged to a sarsen stone at the edge of the Old Forest and there stripped of her ribbons and finery. Barefoot and clad only in her shift, Lady Anne was lashed to the stone. "Do not think to use your witchy wiles upon the guards," Lord Vacant said. "For they desire only men and are thus immune to you."

Then he left her.

There were five guards, Greek soldiers by their gear and outfits, and their faces were hard and stony. As an avatar, Annie could not be killed—not permanently, anyway. She could, however, be made to suffer. She was capable of enduring this captivity forever. It was a rare drawback to being what she was.

After a time, she began to hum "Arthur's Seat Shall Be My Bed" and soon after to sing the words aloud:

It's not the cold that makes me cry,

Nor is't the wet that wearies me:
Nor is't the frost that freezes fell:
But I love a lad, and I dare not tell.

She was not surprised to see the soldiers looking wistful and sad with old memories. She had the voice for the song and she knew how to deliver it. Soon, one of the large, stolid men began to weep.

Lady Anne hung down her head so that her long, loose hair hid her smile.

Weeks passed. Every now and then, Lady Anne would talk, as if to herself, of her life and sorrows, of the cruel husband Crow had stolen her away from, of how much she had given up and how little she cared. Then she would sing another ballad. By the time her long-awaited supplicant arrived, she and not Lord Vacant owned the hearts of her Greek guardsmen.

At last Fata Morgaine came striding out of the Old Forest. Shoving a guard aside, she removed her mask of bone and said, "I would parley with you."

"Morgi! How delightful to see you again. Timon, be a dear and send for tea."

Twin servitors—Hélène and Héloïse—fetched service, tea table, and a chair, then disappeared. At Lady Anne's nod, so did the guards. Fata Morgaine took a pro forma sip of Lapsang souchong and then said, "One of your whores is sleeping with my husband. This can only be your doing."

"It was my whim," Lady Anne admitted. "I put a geas on my ladies not to sleep with their inferiors. Being as they are, that drastically limited the number of potential bedmates. Who's the lucky lass? Pleasance, I presume?"

"Zephora." Outrage sharpened the Morgaine's tone. "I am an avatar of War, feared and revered in every culture there has ever been.

Wherever the bodies are piled high and their stench assails the heavens, there am I. How *dare* Lord Vacant prefer the company of a slattern over mine?"

"The ladies of my court are, when they choose, very close to irresistible. Since your husband insists on staying here, the outcome was inevitable."

"He is waiting for you to undo your curse on the child Elizabeth."

"You and I both know that's not going to happen. Just as we know that if Zephora keeps her hooks in your husband much longer, you will lose him forever. Now, given that you no longer have enough influence over Lord Vacant to get him to free me . . . what else can you offer?"

"Whatever you require. Ask."

The shift Lady Anne wore was sweat-stained and beginning to fray and her hair hadn't been washed in all the time she'd been kept prisoner. Yet, lashed to the stone as she was, she was able to look down upon the Morgaine. This psychological advantage was one of the reasons she had ordered a chair for her guest. "Wouldst kneel before me?"

Flustered, the Morgaine said, "I . . . yes. Yes, I would."

"Kiss my foot?"

"Yes, damn you!"

"Pledge your allegiance to me before all the world?"

"Anything! Anything! Anything!"

"None of that is necessary. By your words, you prove yourself my acolyte. All I require is that you borrow one of Lord Vacant's machines and drive it to the far side of the Mountains of Eternity. Then come back and tell your husband what you have seen. Do this and I promise he will never see Mistress Zephora's baubles again."

"That's it?" Fata Morgaine said in disbelief.

"That's all. And more than enough."

As soon as the Morgaine was out of sight, Lady Anne's boy poet appeared out of nowhere and began tugging at the knots of the ropes that bound her to the sarsen stone.

"What are you doing? Stop that."

"Lady, we have little time before the Greeks return. I have a set of men's clothing that should fit you stashed in the woods, along with a knife to hack your hair short, a leathern water flask, a wallet of food, and a bow and quiver of arrows. We can live off of venison and drink from forest pools until you have fled far enough to avoid recapture."

Lady Anne found herself strangely touched. "Tis a gallant but fantastical plan. I doubt any girl your age would be fool enough to come up with it. But there is no need. Tell Corydon—that's the curly-haired brute, the cute one—that the hour has come for my release. Then do thou follow me, a step behind and to the side, to the manor. I must look my best for the coming confrontation."

Walking point and trailed by her poet, guards, and a growing number of maidens, some of whom sang while others played lutes and pipes, Lady Anne made straight and sure through the enemy encampment for Maidenshead Manor. Soldiers started and stared, but without direct orders dared not interfere with one so obviously in command. She left her Greeks to defend the door, not because it needed defense, but for appearances' sake.

Indeed, they did look formidable.

A trip across the Mountains of Eternity and back, though objectively grueling, could be made in the subjective flash of an eye. So Lady Anne barely had time for a bath, fresh clothing, a new hairdo, a discreet touch of makeup, and a dab of Nuit de Titania behind one ear before Lord Vacant came howling to her door. Standing at the top of the steps (again, looking down), she turned the day in her hand so that the sun sank low and the light turned blue. It was twilight now, when her puissance was greatest. She left just a gleam of sunlight lingering on her face, so that all might admire her complexion.

Had anyone ever seen Lord Vacant as angry as he was now? Lady Anne doubted it. His bone mask crumbled in his clenched hand.

"What have you done?" he screamed at her.

One by one, the other godparents of the infant Elizabeth faded into existence behind him, for they all had a stake in this wrangling. Lord Silence looked stern and forbidding, Mundus and Dale looked alarmed, and Fata Morgaine was outright frightened. Even Papa Goatfoot, though obviously pixilated, looked as though he would be worried if he could just remember why. Only Reverend Wednesday appeared serene and untroubled.

"You came into my territory unannounced and without my leave, plotted to turn its queen into a broodmare for a would-be world warlord, and failed to invite me to a christening in which I had an obvious interest. The offense was not slight. I took appropriate action."

Gathering himself together with an obvious effort, Lord Vacant said, "You have killed off the human race, without whom we none of us have any purpose."

"I have killed not a single soul—slaughter is your prerogative. I merely assured that the species would quietly and without fuss dwindle over the coming centuries to nothing. As was my right and privilege."

"You have no privileges," Lord Vacant said with cold disdain, "and no rights. You are a songbird, whose sole purpose is to lighten the lives of drabs and housewives on their death march to the grave. Stick to your soap operas and confession magazines and leave the running of the universe to your betters."

So saying, he made a foul gesture.

Lady Anne hissed in outrage. Then she took on her aspect, so that she shone as bright as the moon. She yanked down her bodice. It helped that her seamstresses had access to elastics available to no one else in this century. "I am Romance, proud and fair—look upon my tits, ye Mighty, and despair. Thinkst thou mere brutality can stop me? Entropy? Desolation? I piss on you and all you stand for."

Lord Vacant sneered. "Such vulgarity, lady, ill suits you."

"You dare call me out on aesthetics? Fuck you! Do you imagine that Romance is neat and tidy? Meek, mild, and easily defeated? *Polite?*

It invades the heart like a conquering army and it takes no prisoners. Whatever stands in its way it lays to waste. Family, friends, duty, love of country, common sense—all fall before it. Decency is set aflame! Morality is tossed aside! Reason is trampled underfoot! Self-preservation? Don't make me laugh. There has never been a tyrant more ruthless or less prone to mercy than I. And I claim this era—nay, *all eras*!—for my own."

"I defy," Lord Vacant cried, "your every claim and throw them back in your teeth. You think to set murmured words and diadems of daisies against napalm and cold steel? Have at me! I am the lash that drives men on to greatness. You are a distraction for adolescent girls. Mine is the power that creates kings, destroys empires, and writes the lying histories afterward. What have you—"

"Enough."

It was Reverend Wednesday who had spoken. He raised a hand and Lady Anne found she could not speak. A coldness, like the first frost of autumn, touched her heart. "Your case, dread lady, has been made." He turned to Lord Vacant. "As has yours." Then, gesturing, "Come forward, little ones, and kneel before me."

Side by side, like children before a stern parent, they knelt. For the first time she could remember, Lady Anne felt small and unimportant. She did not much like the sensation. A quick sideways glance at Lord Vacant's face showed he felt much the same. "Lord of Discord, you have dissed a Peer and she has given you a taste of your own medicine. From this moment onward, you will treat her as your equal."

A choking noise came from Lord Vacant's throat and he nodded.

"Lady Anne, your trickster has not been a good influence on you, I fear. In extinguishing the human race, who are under my protection, you overstepped yourself. You will immediately remove the curse from them, so that they may thrive."

Lady Anne tried to speak and could only croak. So she, too, nodded.

"Nevertheless, you had cause. So I command that young Elizabeth be exempted from your lifting of the curse. Lord Vacant will have to create his world-encompassing war somewhere else, at some other time." He stroked Lady Anne's hair, as if she were a cat. "Now stand. This matter is over and done with."

Reverend Wednesday began to fade away, then became solid again. His eyes twinkled. "Oh, and do try to keep out of trouble."

Then he was gone.

Next to depart was Lord Vacant, taking his forces with him and leaving behind an estate that would be the despair of the groundskeepers for years to come. Fata Morgaine, hurrying after him, threw Lady Anne a look of what may have been gratitude. The others left in a more leisurely fashion.

Last to depart was Lord Silence. At his nod, one of his courtiers said, "All present capable of doing so will forget this day's doing and all that led up to it. The princess was christened like any other princess." Then Lord Silence flicked his fingers and the man said to Annie, "You have caused a great deal of trouble, lady."

"All of which could have been spared if you'd only sent me a fucking by-your-leave invitation to the christening. Remember that next time."

When the intruders were gone at last, Lady Anne's shoulders sagged and with all the sincerity in her body, she said, "Thank Whomever." Then, all business again, she said, "Pleasance. Take Master Shakespeare and put him back in his proper time and place. Oh, and he has an illness lurking within him. Give him the kiss of life so that he may have his two-score-and-twelve."

Eyes gleaming, the lady-in-waiting said, "Yes, milady."

"One kiss, no more, Mistress Pleasance. On the mouth. Nowhere else."

Eyes dimming, Pleasance curtseyed, saying, "As you will."

Annie kissed the boy farewell on his forehead. "I really should castrate you," she whispered in his ear. "Alas, I was always a sucker for a gaudy line of patter."

Because the Harley had disappeared—her ladies being no better than they ought to be, Annie was not surprised that one of them had nicked it in order to keep a tryst beyond her ken and reckoning—she left Maidenshead riding a white palfrey.

Not half a mile into the Old Forest, the path turned, and there was Crow, leaning against a tree. Annie did not ask how he had found her. By their very nature, it was hard for the universe to keep them apart. "Hey, babe," he said. "I brought you something more comfortable to wear." Neatly folded on the ground before him were a pair of jeans, a bomber jacket, a tank top, socks, and biker boots. Typical for him, the underwear was lacy and impractical. She was about to say something about that when he dropped a full carton of Kent menthols atop the pile. For that, much could be forgiven.

Crow watched appreciatively as Annie stripped out of her skirts and furbelows and pulled on the riding gear. The horse she set free, to brighten the day of whatever rascal found it. Casually, Crow mounted his new Norton Commando and started the engine. "So how was your little vacation?" he asked when she climbed on behind him.

"Dull," Annie said. She wrapped her arms around Crow so tight that it made his ribs creak. "Let's go the fuck somewhere else and stir things up."

UNIVERSE BOX

Out of the everywhere and nowhere the thief fled, quarks and galaxies crunching underfoot, vacuum rippling like a banner in his wake. Skipping nimbly in and out of space and time, he dropped down into the quantum slush underlying physical existence and then up again into the macrocosmic realms of which reality is but the tiniest province. Nightmares beyond human imagining howled and ravaged at his heels. Nihilism and despair sleeted down on his upturned face. But the thief couldn't have been happier. His grin was so mad and bright that it would melt granite.

His erection was shocking.

The thief—who was not really so mundane a thing as a thief but something far more intense and much less forgivable for which there was no word in any language, though he knew billions—had just pulled off the biggest heist in the history of existence. Even he *was impressed. For tucked under one arm was a box containing everything that anybody could possibly desire. Some of those anybodies were extremely dangerous, even by the thief's standards. There were no limits to what atrocities they might perform to wrest the treasure from his grasp.*

Which only made his flight all the sweeter.

Finally, in part because all other avenues of escape had been cut off and in part because that was simply the way the game was played, the thief went to ground. Compared to the other powers-that-be he was pathetically weak. But he had one tactical advantage over them all, which was that no laws had any hold over him, not even physical ones. So he could go where none of the others dared. He sought shelter in a place so fragile that his Opponent would not dare to follow him there, because doing so would burst it open and incinerate it and everything it contained, the box he had stolen most definitely included, to ashes and the memory of ashes.

This delicate soap-bubble of a world was called Earth.

In a low gray river port city, a former industrial center fallen on hard times, a dovecote of stenches and miasmas, a huddling-place of heartbreaks and miseries, a habitat of bad memories and unthinkable futures, indeed in the exact geographic center of that city, a young man who thought that he was happy checked his wristwatch for the seventh time that evening. Howard had on a new suit with front row tickets to a Valentine's Day concert at the Academy of Music tucked into one pocket and a tidy little box containing a rather expensive ring in another. A magnum of champagne was chilling in the fridge and a dozen red roses lurked in the shadows of the bedroom. There, the sheets had been changed and the bed freshly made, to create an attractive theater for the passionate sex he anticipated would fill half the night.

Mimi had promised to drop by after work. She suspected nothing.

There was a knock at the door—Mimi had a key but never used it—and Howard hurried to fling it open.

And froze.

Black fog filled the doorway, billowed, condensed, solidified, and then sprouted a striped scarf and the world's largest, roundest head. As Howard gaped, a crack appeared in that tremendous cheese wheel of a face and split it from ear to ear. "Aren't you going to say hello to your Uncle Paulie?" the apparition exclaimed, flinging its arms wide.

"Uncle . . . Paulie. Oh. Oh, yes, of course. Uncle Paulie? Come in, come in," Howard said, all in a fluster because an instant ago he would have sworn that he had never seen or heard of this man before yet now a lifetime's worth of memories of this dear and beloved relative coursed through his brain.

"What a lovely little place you have!" Uncle Paulie tossed his sable greatcoat onto the George Nakashima coffee table, dumped a cigar box atop it, and threw loop after loop of red-and-white scarf after them. "Charmingly Spartan. Is that a Picasso? So modest to have a print rather than an oil. But that's typical of you. I came as soon as I heard the good news."

"Good news?"

"Your engagement, dear boy, your engagement. Have you asked Mimi yet? No, of course not. Look at that bulge in your coat! Is that a ring in your pocket or are you just glad to see me? Hah! Don't answer that."

"You haven't changed one bit," Howard said with an embarrassed, perfectly pointless grin. "But I don't understand. I haven't told anybody yet, not even Mimi. So how . . . ?"

"That hardly matters, dearest of all nephews. Not one iota. Not one scintilla. Not one single charming quark. And do you know why? Because I am here." Uncle Paulie slapped his chest. "To help." He patted Howard on the head, two light taps. "You."

At which awkward moment, there came another knock at the door. This time it turned out to be Mimi.

Big scared eyes, waifish body, short-cropped hair. Mimi crept into the apartment, raised a startled paw to her nose, twitched her whiskers, and froze motionless at the sight of Uncle Paulie. "Oh!"

"This can only be little Mimikins!" Uncle Paulie lifted her up, whirled her around, set her down, and bussed her on the lips. Then he mock-scolded, "Nephew, she's exquisite! Why did you only say she was gorgeous?"

"I—"

"Never mind, if we don't get a hurry on, we'll be late!" Uncle Paulie snatched up hat, coat, and scarf, tossed all into the air, and was holding open the door, dressed to go. "Chop-chop, kiddies!" Exuberant, irresistible, he swept Howard and a rather dazed Mimi along before him, down the elevator, out of the Drake, several blocks down the street, through glass doors and up an elevator to the Top of the Tooz. Which was a rooftop revolving night club, and one that Howard had never been to because it had closed years ago.

"Have they reopened this?" Howard said. Surely, he would have heard.

"Nothing is ever closed," Uncle Paulie said, handing his things to a sullen hatcheck girl who tossed them over her shoulder onto the floor. "Not really."

The hatcheck girl accepted Howard's coat and, rummaging through his pockets, came up with a pack of Marlboros, from which she tapped a cigarette. Once she had extracted matches from Mimi's purse, she threw the purse and both coats onto the growing pile.

"Hey!" Howard objected, but Uncle Paulie, Mimi perched happily on one shoulder, was bulldozing him into the club, where they were greeted with abject enthusiasm by the maître d', the owner, several women who had spent a great deal of money on not very much clothing and considerably more makeup, and an elegant presence in a rose tuxedo whose hair was chopped in a blond slash that was either too long or too short for his or her gender, depending on what it might be.

With air kisses and squeals and declarations of eternal fealty from gushing strangers who had to be shooed away by the maître d', they were planted at a table with a splendid view of a city far too glamorous, it seemed to Howard, to be the one he had all his lifetime inhabited. Or perhaps it was the sunset slowly crawling by that granted magic to an otherwise drab world.

"Glasses! Caviar! A jazz band! Not overly advanced! Nor too loud! You'll waive corkage, of course." As his impromptu retinue scattered like pigeons to obey, Uncle Paulie turned to Howard and Mimi and said, "I have something special to show you both." He reached into an inner jacket pocket and pulled out an object which he solemnly placed on the table before him and patted with both hands. "There. What do you think?"

It was a cigar box.

Mimi clearly wasn't about to say anything. So Howard cleared his throat. "I don't want to hurt your feelings, Uncle Paulie, but I'm afraid I don't smoke."

Uncle Paulie looked shocked. "This isn't for you, child. No, no, no, I'm just going to let you *see* it."

"Oh. Okay, I guess."

Holding up a finger, Uncle Paulie made an owlish face and said, "Let me posit a question: What one thing does the world currently need most? Eh?"

"Um . . . love?" Howard ventured.

"World peace," Mimi said firmly.

"Pah! I'm disappointed in you both. A good bottle of wine, of course!" Uncle Paulie flipped open the lid of the cigar box and reached within. "As you doubtless know, the very finest collection ever assembled was the legendary Wine Cellar of Alexandria. Destroyed in that dreadful fire, such a pity. But no matter. I'll just have to dig deeper." A puzzled look came over Uncle Paulie's face as he reached within and further within and yet further indeed, until his arm had disappeared up to the shoulder. Then his expression cleared and, leaning back, he reeled in his arm, at the end of which was an unlabeled black glass bottle upon which were scratched archaic runes. "Ahh, Amarone della Lemuria! A 'sea-dark wine, half as old as time,' as that drunken sot Homer put it. There's never been a plonk like it."

Laughing, Mimi clapped her hands. Howard scowled and grumbled, "That's quite a trick."

"It is the single best trick ever performed, nephew—and I say that with no hyperbole whatsoever. May I burst into flames if I lie." A waiter cut away the lead, dug out the cork with a knife, poured the contents into glasses, faded to nothingness.

"A toast!" Uncle Paulie cried. "To the criminals, cads, con men, and perverts within us all!"

This struck Howard as being in very poor taste. But Mimi was already drinking so there was nothing to do but follow suit.

He took a sip. His eyes went wide.

A clarity that surpassed all understanding suffused his brain. The sun rose within the midnight of Howard's soul. A blindfold was ripped from his mind and flung to the wind. Everything that existed was right and holy, he could see that now—no, better than seeing, he knew it for a true thing down to the root of his being. The world was good, the universe better, and as for life—peanut butter and chocolate combined were tasteless by comparison.

"What's *in* there?" he gasped.

Howard meant in the wine. But misunderstanding him (whether intentionally or not, who could say?), Uncle Paulie held up the cigar box as if it were a window and opened the lid. "Everything you could desire: castles in the air, mountains on a plate, treasury bills, wisdom . . . you name it. Voluptuous goddesses, glass moons, methane seas. Dinosaurs, if that's to your taste.

"Look."

Howard looked. And beheld:

E*ndless clouds of diamond dust glittering on the deep, black velvet of infinity. Stars exploding above the frozen husks of sunless worlds. A herd of* Parasaurolophus *trumpeting and feeding in a grove of dawn redwoods. Wise machines drifting between galaxies, carrying in their bellies clusters of civilizations, each written on a silver disk smaller than a dime. A drunken Elizabethan poet singing and urinating from a third-story window. Nanowars being fought endlessly on the surface of a single mote of dust. A stray dog in Milwaukee gulping down a hamburger foraged from a dumpster. Trillions of integers, deep in the heart of an irrational number, pledging their love and obeisance to . . .*

Uncle Paulie snapped the cigar box lid shut and said, "Enough of that! Mimi and I are going to dance."

Howard blinked, gaped, and was back in real time. He wondered how many years had passed in stunned contemplation of the glory of . . . whatever it was in the box. Then he saw that his wine glass was still half full. He seized it and gulped down every drop. It made him feel better, so he refilled the glass and drank that down as well. The clarity this gave him intensified to such a degree as to be indistinguishable from a dizzy sense of genius.

He became aware that Lena Horne was singing "Stormy Weather." That his girlfriend and his uncle were slow dancing. That the bastard had his hand on Mimi's ass. And that, from the way she moved, she *liked* it there!

Intolerable. Howard was about to get up and confront his uncle when the personage in the rose tuxedo materialized before him, extended a hand, and said, "C'mon, sport." His head was reeling with the zodiac, and his tongue seemed to have climbed out an ear and slipped away. Meanwhile, the music demanded to be danced to. So he accepted the invitation with a nod.

At first, Howard thought that he was dancing with a woman in drag. Then, that his partner was an elaborately made-up man masquerading as a woman pretending to be a man. Or else a gender trickster made up to look at one and the same time like everything and anything that one might actually be. Or . . .

"You're not sure, are you?" the enigma leered. And, pressing up against him, murmured, "Slow dancing is your friend."

"I've, uh, never danced with, uh. You know. Before this." Giddy from the wine, Howard felt wondrously liberated. Ordinarily, he wouldn't have . . . But tonight everything was okay.

"That you know of."

Howard giggled. He must be a lot drunker than he thought. "I guess you've got a point," he said. Which sounded so witty that he giggled again.

By the time the song ended, the wine had done such a splendid job blurring the memory of looking inside the box that he was beginning to believe that he had suffered a momentary dream and nothing more.

When Howard returned to the table, Mimi looked flushed and happy while Uncle Paulie appeared uncharacteristically solemn. He handed Howard the cigar box, saying, "Take this, dear boy. Take it! Hide it! Don't tell me where. Don't tell anybody where. Don't even tell yourself."

"How do I do that?"

"Put the box on the table before you. Close your eyes. Open the lid with one hand. Then take the box in your other hand and place it inside the opening you just created. All of space and time will be accessible to you. Hide it wherever. Just be careful not to put it somewhere obvious. Excuse me. I have to change."

Uncle Paulie stood, winked, and plunged into the women's restroom.

"Hey! You can't—!" Howard started after his uncle, but was brought short by the door. If he went inside, women would scream. They might even throw things. Anyway, what could he hope to accomplish? No obvious answer presented itself. In an agony of indecision, he returned to the table, closed his eyes, and made the cigar box go away, as he had been told to do.

The woman who, minutes later, emerged from the ladies room was zoftig to an extreme. Tremendous breasts bulged out of a very tight dress that was obviously struggling to contain them. Everything else, belly and butt and who-knew-what, piled curve upon curve upon curve. But the huge round head was unmistakable and lipstick could not disguise that ludicrously long mouth. She descended upon Howard like an out-of-control tugboat upon a dock.

"Uncle . . . Paulie?" Howard said in a choked voice.

"Silly billy! It's *Aunt* Polly."

With that, she pulled his head down into those soft, warm breasts. Which caused Aunt Polly's dress to finally admit defeat and rip down the middle, revealing the biggest pinkest nipples any man had ever seen.

"Why, Howie!" Aunt Polly squealed, clutching him so close he could not breathe. "You spontaneous devil!"

Falling backward, Aunt Polly tumbled onto the pile of coats and furs, pulling Howard atop her billowing flesh. He heard the hatcheck girl sigh and unzip her skirt. People came in from the dance floor, chattering and laughing, giggling, kicking off their shoes, shedding their clothes.

And then, well, things happened.

Deep in the Pillars of Creation the Opponent, whom the thief had robbed, made itself manifest. Underlings, the least of which could have snuffed Earth's sun like a candle, cowered at the sight.

Commands were issued, which the underlings scurried to obey.

Sounds.

There was a murmur of voices and a scuffle of feet, as musicians packed up their instruments and waiters upended chairs onto tables. Closer by, revelers were buttoning and belting and pulling together their outfits, and slipping off into the night. By slow degrees, Howard found himself returning to what might well be described as consciousness. The orgy, he realized, was over, and he was lying in the cloakroom atop a diminished mound of jackets, wearing only one sock and a shirt missing half its buttons.

How on earth was he going to explain to Mimi what had happened? He couldn't even explain it to himself. He had done things that he'd never imagined people doing—and he had thumbed through a significant number of pornographic magazines in his time.

The coats stirred and Mimi crawled out from beneath them with a stunned expression on her face.

She was naked.

Howard's jaw dropped.

Howard and Mimi dressed in silence, neither capable of looking at the other. The streets outside were empty, dark, slick with rain, smeared with reflected neon. The hatcheck girl, fully dressed if a little rumpled, sneered as she locked the doors behind them. There were few cars out, so it had to be very late. Howard pulled his coat tight against the cold.

After a block or three, Mimi said in a small voice, "I didn't know you were into—"

"What? No! I only . . ."

"Oh." She fell silent. After a time, almost inaudibly, she added, "Because I liked it. A little, maybe. Sort of. I mean—" Mimi took a deep breath. "Howard, I was going to break up with you tonight. Because I thought, well, don't take this the wrong way but I thought you were the most predictable man on earth. I thought, how much more of this can I take? It's like going out with a robot. Everything laid out in the most obvious manner imaginable, a long straight road leading from this very instant to the grave with not one single surprise along the way."

Howard could hardly believe what he was hearing. "You're saying that I'm . . . boring?" Simultaneously, a painful sensation blossomed in the back of his head and he realized that the hangover he had confidently expected to arrive in the morning was tapping its toes in the anteroom, anxious to be recognized.

"You're going to laugh, but when you said you had concert tickets and I realized that it was Valentine's Day, I thought: Oh no, he's going to ask me to marry him! I could see a bottle of champagne in the fridge and roses in the bedroom and a cornball diamond ring and suddenly it was all too much for me. It literally felt like I was choking. I wanted to cough you up out of my life like a hairball."

"I . . ."

Mimi grabbed Howard's arm then and hugged herself against it. "But then—tonight. It was wonderful. The dancing! New people! In the cloakroom, I did things I thought I wasn't ready for. Things I was afraid I might never do."

"Mimi," Howard pleaded. "You can't mean that."

"They were all such interesting people, too. There was a rare book counterfeiter and a giraffe wrangler and a burglar and a garbage artist and . . ."

"Wait. What? Giraffe wrangler? Mimi, I'm not sure these are people I want you associating with."

Mimi stopped in mid-gush and let go of Howard's arm. In a voice grown suddenly cold, she said, "You were *screwing* them—and they're not good enough for me to see socially? Just what kind of a jerk are you?"

"Listen, maybe the sex was a mistake."

"Maybe you're the mistake. I—"

A car screeched down the street and leaped the sidewalk, headed right at them. Mimi shrieked and grabbed Howard, yanking him out of the way.

Crash! With a noise that would have made a corpse jump, the car smashed into the side of the building inches from where they had both fallen to the pavement.

For a small, still eternity, neither so much as breathed. Then they helped each other to their feet. "Well," one of them said. "That was—"

A second car crashed into the wall to the other side of them.

Fifteen car crashes later, Howard and Mimi tumbled into the Drake, fetching up against the elevators like two scraps of paper disdainfully blown in by the winter wind. "Well," Howard said. "Would you care to come up to the apartment?" There would be no proposal tonight, obviously, but he figured he could somehow explain away the roses in the bedroom.

"No. And I'll tell you why." Mimi was shivering with indignation. "All this time we've been going out, I had no idea that you might actually have a sense of fun. Finally—finally!—you show me a good time and then you scold me for enjoying it! How dare you judge me for liking a change from your dreary, dreary, dreary, predictable life?"

A low dark uneasiness spread itself across Howard's skull. It was not quite a throbbing but, now that he acknowledged its existence, he realized that it soon would be. "I . . ."

Mimi stomped (pip! pip! pip!) all but weightlessly across the lobby. Just before she disappeared through the door and down the street, without even turning to look back, she raised a hand, middle finger erect.

Slam.

Despondent, dejected, detumescent, Howard elevatored to his floor. With every foot the car rose, the incipient ache in his skull intensified, extending itself into his belly and his gastrointestinal system to form a chord of discomfort that grew steadily worse until, when the doors finally opened, his head clanged, his gut clenched, and he was afraid he might vomit. Stomach and bowels in a knot, he unlocked the door and scuttled into his apartment.

Where a stranger awaited.

"Speak of the devil, here I am!" the slim dark man said with unbearable chirpiness. "Dan Scratch, attorney at lawlessness." He presented a card which immediately burst into flames, then tapped the side of his nose, a gesture that Howard had previously only encountered in books. "I represent someone who wishes to remain anonymous but who is very powerful indeed. Powerful enough to destroy you, your fiancée, all that you value, and indeed the entire planet you're standing on with the Moon, Mars, and Venus thrown in for good measure. That's not a threat. Yet."

"Go away," Howard groaned. "Or else kill me, I don't much care which."

"Tsk." Dan Scratch went to a wall clock Howard had never seen before and moved its hands ahead eight hours. Sunlight flooded the room. "Is that better?"

Howard clutched his head in agony. "Oh God, no!"

"Big night, eh?" The attorney spun the hands around the dial so fast they blurred. Morning faded to twilight again and again and again before the dwindling light finally took with it the last remnants of Howard's discomfort. "Now. Let's talk."

Howard's emotions were divided. On the one hand, he was grateful to be rid of the single worst hangover he had ever experienced in his life. On the other, the imp with the pencil-thin mustache was still there. "How about let's you just scram?"

"Oh, sir!" When he grinned, Dan Scratch's eyes turned as yellow as his teeth. "You and I both know that's not going to happen. I'll cut to the chase: You have something my client wants. Frankly, you're in a very good bargaining position."

"Dear Lord. You're trying to buy my soul."

When Dan Scratch pursed his lips, his mustache disappeared entirely. "That shabby thing? Have you any idea of its Blue Book value? Of course not. Suffice it to say—negligible. However, for a certain cigar box . . . Well, idioms notwithstanding, the sky's no limit." From hidden pockets he deftly extracted small objects, lining them up upon the air before him. "A bell to summon mastodons, perhaps? A vaccine against sin?—you could inoculate the entire human race from this one vial. Lozenges of wisdom-come-too-late? A homunculus the size of your fingernail? It comes with a planet to keep it on. One of Abraham Lincoln's baby teeth? A crystal to relieve cramps and sharpen razor blades?"

Howard swept out an arm, scattering items about the room. The little silver bell bounced noiselessly on the rug. "Get out of my apartment!"

"Oh, you are a hard sell, sir," Dan Scratch said, bobbing up and down to retrieve his scattered possessions. "But I am confident I can break your resolve. What do you most want out of life? Deep down and for real, I mean. You can be honest with me. Whatever it is, I've heard worse."

The question caught Howard by surprise and, to his surprise, he heard himself answering it honestly: "Mimi left me. I want her back."

"Hmm. Tricky. Did she say why she was leaving?"

"She said I was boring," Howard said bitterly.

"I see. Did you ever break into her apartment while she was away and fill it with endangered lizards? Did you paint her nude on the side of a mountain over a major interstate and bring her to a high place to watch trucks collide? Did you kill the girl who humiliated her in high school and drop the bitch's head at her feet?"

"What? No!"

"Then she was right. Now that that's settled, sir, I'll see what I can arrange. You want her mind intact, I presume? Would you object to her becoming an addict? I can see you would. Not another word, it's as good as taken care of. Good day, sir."

With a jaunty little salute, Dan Scratch was gone.

Mimi was going through the adult classifieds in the weekly paper, reading each one carefully, when the doorbell rang. People certainly wanted a variety of different experiences! She wasn't sure that she was interested in half of them. Still, it was best to keep an open mind. She put down the paper, went to the window, and saw via the busybody that her caller was the giraffe wrangler.

She buzzed her in.

"Mimi! So good to see you again." The wrangler was as round as a pumpkin and twice as cheerful. She had a chubby, pleasantly open face and her hair was cut in a dyke do, shaved on one side and purple on the other. Her clothes were as nondescript as she was not.

"Gloria! How did you find me? Would you like some tea?"

"Kismet, chance, Brownian motion—take your pick. Yes, please."

While Mimi boiled the water, set out the milk and sugar, and filled the cups, Gloria grilled her on her breakup with Howard. It was odd that she knew so much, but then, it had been three days, which was more than time enough for rumors to spread.

"Bad feelings?" Mimi said. "Not really. Though I am a little peeved with my friends for setting me up with him in the first place. My so-called friends, I mean. Really, looking back I'm insulted they ever thought we were a good match."

"Forgive me, but maybe they believed you were a little dull yourself?"

Mimi laughed. "Touché. Only on the outside, though. Howard is boring to the bone, but inside I always had strange thoughts. So maybe this breakup was a blessing in disguise, a kick in the derriere to get me to stop being so timid." Gloria nodded, smiling. "But enough about me. I want to hear all about your giraffes."

"Oh, I'm not really a giraffe wrangler, dear. That's just my cover story." Gloria reached into her handbag and pulled out the most lethal-looking gun Mimi had ever seen in her life. "Actually, I'm an assassin."

As soon as the visitor was gone, Uncle Paulie emerged from the closet, commenting, "I thought he'd never leave."

"A minute ago," Howard said, "I'd have sworn that nothing could astonish me anymore. Were you here all along?"

"Of course, darling boy! Where else would I be in your hour of need?" Uncle Paulie opened the fridge. "You're out of mayonnaise. How is that possible? Well, no matter. Retrieve my box and I'll have this unfiascoed in a jiffy."

"Your box."

Leaving the door ajar, Uncle Paulie turned, hands on hips. Frowning as ominously as a thunderhead. There was a crackle of ozone in the air. The refrigerator softened and began to melt. "Yes," he said with terrible emphasis. "The one you hid for me, remember? To keep it safe? While we were partying?"

"I know which box you mean. I just don't know where I put it."

Uncle Paulie reached out one tremendous hand, grabbed Howard by the chest, and hoisted him almost to the ceiling. *"What?!"* His outraged mouth opened so wide that Howard could count every row of sharp triangular teeth. There were thirteen.

Terrified, Howard said, "You told me not to remember—remember?"

Putting Howard down, Uncle Paulie shook his head in chagrin. "The biter bit. The shark made sushi. The invading army killed by dysentery. This is certainly one for the books." He clapped his nephew on the shoulder. "Don't worry, I'm sure you'll get it back. The first order of business to rescue Mimi from her kidnappers."

"Kidnappers?! Who said anything about kidnappers?"

"Think, lad! You just told one of the Opponent's minions that you'd give up anything for Mimi. Of course he did the obvious thing."

"Oh, my God." For a long moment Howard processed this information. Then, because he had seen and learned too much to accept even his own memories, vivid though they were, he said, "Who are you, Uncle Paulie? What's your real name?"

"Name? Dear boy. Nobody who's anybody has a *name*. Call me whatever you wish. One label's as good a lie as any other."

The mad glitter in Uncle Paulie's eyes told Howard that this person or creature or entity, whatever he might be, was in no way his relation or, indeed, even human. Nevertheless, Howard said, "Before I do anything, I have to know what's in the box, who's trying to get it away from you, and why."

"You had only to ask," Uncle Paulie said, and began to explain.

Howard listened intently, all the while worrying about Mimi. God only knew what horrors she must be going through now.

"More cocaine?" Gloria asked.

"Oh, no. It's not really my thing," Mimi said. "I just did those lines to be wicked."

"How about if I open a wicked bottle of Chablis Grand Cru? Indulge yourself. Consider it my way of thanking you for coming along quietly. You'd be surprised how often I have to put a bullet into a client's leg before they'll take my kidnapping them seriously."

Mimi threw on a kimono, not to cover herself but just for the sensation of silk against skin. She went to the window wall and looked out over the snowy rooftops of the city. "You have such a lovely view of the Eiffel Tower," she said, and then, thoughtfully, "I always wanted to see Paris. And now it's my prison."

"Paris isn't your prison," Gloria said. "France is. That's a very important distinction, if you should happen to want to see Mont Saint-Michel, or Carcassonne. Berlin is *verboten*, however, as is Tokyo. And I really would have to kill you if you tried to escape."

"You seem so comfortable with . . . your profession."

"I am now. You should have seen what a mess I was when I began my spiritual journey." Gloria chuckled. "How many men did I have to kill before I achieved enlightenment? Ah, me. Youth!" She began pulling on her clothes. Item by item, that lovely body of hers disappeared, like the moon vanishing behind clouds. "But we've wasted almost all the day indoors. Get dressed, and we'll go out."

Mimi shed her gown and stood naked before the closet, lush with dresses and all of them in her size. A lot of care had gone into her kidnapping. "Where are we going?" she asked.

"Why, anywhere you like. There's a very amusing sex club I happen to know the password for. There's a show of embarrassing art at the Louvre. This being France, there are some highly regarded restaurants, of course. And there's always the Parc Zoologique."

Eagerly, Mimi said, "Do they have giraffes?"

"Wait," Howard said. "Wait. The cigar box you were carrying around contains the universe? Everything that is, was, or ever will be? And you stole it from its Creator? Who is not only pissed at you but at me personally as well?"

A little testily, Uncle Paulie said, "That is the gist of what I've just, at some length, told you, yes."

"I've made an enemy of *God*?!"

"Oh, pish. Don't be ridiculous," Uncle Paulie said in a tone that would have been reassuring coming from anyone else. "You couldn't expect an important fellow like God to do the actual construction work Himself. He sublet the job. To the Demiurge. Who built everything and therefore feels inappropriately possessive about it. So you haven't made an enemy of God but of somebody who is, for all practical purposes, as powerful as God without actually being Him. That's an important distinction. Though I can see where it might be a fine one for you."

"And the Opponent—the Demiurge—has arranged for Mimi to

be kidnapped? In order to put pressure on me? To reveal where I've hidden the universe? Even though I don't know that fact?" A dangerous look came over Uncle Paulie's face and Howard hastily said, "I understand everything now. Except . . ."

Uncle Paulie slammed his hand down on the kitchen table so hard it left its imprint half an inch deep in the oak. "*Stop talking!* Your own dear wee Mimi is in danger. Also, she was with you when you hid the box and must have seen where you put it. Go. Now. I'll wait for you here."

"You're not coming with me?"

That tremendous face folded in upon itself like so much pizza dough being kneaded into a ball, then reemerged—first mouth, then eyes, then nose and, last of all, ears—smiling in a manner which Howard no longer found endearing. "Alas," Uncle Paulie said, "I have to hide your doings from the Opponent, buy some mayonnaise, make a sandwich, oh there are not enough hours in the day. Why are you still here?"

"I . . . I don't know where to start."

"Start anywhere." Uncle Paulie thrust a hand as large as the blade of a shovel into his jacket. It emerged overflowing with kibble. "Let's see. A length of string, a rabbit's foot, the arrowhead I dug out of Abel's body, a vaccine against sin—where did that come from? Here, it's yours." He stuffed it in Howard's shirt pocket. "Ah! Any of these contacts would be particularly helpful."

Uncle Paulie thrust a rubber-banded bundle of calling cards at Howard. "Draw one at random." Howard did. It read:

[NAME WITHHELD]
UNDERPAID MINION TO THE STARS
BY APPOINTMENT ONLY

An icy knife of wind ripped through his clothing, skin, flesh, bones. Howard found himself before a turreted stone building completely surrounded by dark forest. The night was so cold that it drove all thought of Mimi from his mind. Desperately, he hammered on the door.

A sound that could only be the flapping of great wings came from inside. Then silence. Then the door opened. The hatcheck girl from the Top of the Tooz looked down at him. "Oh," she said. "You. Sorry. I'm busy. Cutting my toenails."

She shut the door in his face.

Howard threw himself against the door, drumming on it with fists and forearms. "Please! Help me! I can pay! Anything that you want!"

The door opened again. "Define 'anything,'" the hatcheck girl said.

Howard shoved past her and made straight for a baronial stone hearth in which crackled and roared a fire as big as all the Renaissance. Stretching out frozen hands toward its glorious heat, he began to talk. Turning a backside so cold that it stung to face the fire, he continued. Until at last he had explained all, his body had rotated a dozen times before the blaze, and that terrible cold had retreated bone-deep within his flesh, to become a memory he doubted would ever go away.

"So Polytreptos sent you out to slay dragons without giving you a sword or telling you where they live. Typical. Well, yes, I can help. In fact, I may safely say that without me, you're as good as dead. Now. My price. Anything, you said?"

"Mountains on a plate, if that's what you want. Or so I was told. Ask! It's yours."

The hat check girl raised her chin, staring off into infinity. "I was born in a city whose name you are not worthy of hearing. I was there when it fell to the armies of Uruk. Blood flowed in the streets, smoke assailed the heavens, vultures gorged on the corpses, the survivors were taken away in chains, the wailing went on forever. The usual. But I was a child and thought it was the end of the world. I was added to the slave coffles almost as an afterthought; a less greedy soldier would have killed me as hardly worth the bother. Long story short, I eventually signed on with the True Powers as a gofer, a waitress, a piano player, a clerk typist, or whatever else they might require. I had no idea promotions would be so scarce.

"My first two thousand years, I swore that if I ever achieved real power, I would humble the nation that destroyed my city. But that nation fell and will not rise again. The next two thousand, I vowed to raise up an empire that would outdo Uruk in its atrocities and teach all mankind a lesson. But I have seen atrocities beyond number forgotten before the corpses cooled." Her eyes, dark with eons of rage and resentment, lowered to Howard's. "Now you appear on my doorstep offering whatever I desire."

Overcome by an awareness of how far out of his depth he had swum, Howard hastily said, "Within reason, of course."

"Reason? You are already so far beyond reason that, without my aid, you couldn't find your way back if you dedicated your entire life to it." The hatcheck girl sat down at a table that had been planed from a single slab of oak and poured herself a glass of amber liqueur from a crystal decanter. "All I want is to escape. That's not too much to ask, I trust?"

"No! Not at all!" Howard cried, tremendously relieved.

"Good. My name is Shamkat. You probably won't need to know that, but just in case. Give me the cards." She riffled through them swiftly, handed him one.

"Him," she said. "He knows where all the bodies are buried."

THE BLACK LAMA.
KARMA ADJUSTED, RETRIBUTION DEFERRED, JUSTICE BAFFLED
HOLY AS SHIT

When he looked up, Howard and the hatcheck girl were in a swan boat like those in the Boston Public Garden. It floated in black waters within what looked to be a Gothic cathedral. Candles flickered and guttered and dripped wax in every stone niche and cranny, though he could not see how even the most agile climber could have set all of them in place. The leaded glass windows had patterns he could not make out because the glass was black.

"Even here I am found," someone sighed.

Howard twisted around in his chair. At the controls of the boat was he whom they had come to see.

At first glance, the Black Lama looked like every Oriental holy man in every racist movie ever made: wispy white Van Dyke, owlish expression, a robe with sleeves wide enough to hide an AK-47 inside. But when he met the ancient's eyes, Howard instantly whipped his head away, heart pounding furiously, for the lama was as much like a human being as a tiger was like a mouse.

Fighting back terror, Howard said, "We came here—"

"Please." The Black Lama held up a hand. "I know your banal little quest and how it will end as well. The universe indeed! When will one of you come looking for something worth having? Don't answer that, it was a rhetorical question. My price is stiff but I already know you will pay it. The one you seek is in Paris—the 7th arrondissement, to be precise. With the Giraffe Wrangler."

"Mimi said something about a giraffe wrangler."

"It is a code name. For a very dangerous woman."

"How dangerous?" Shamkat asked.

"When you unexpectedly materialize in her presence, she will without hesitation shoot the boring man twice—once fatally, the second time for insult. She will then immobilize you with bullets through your first and fourth chakras and report you to middle management, requesting that you be docked two weeks' pay."

"The bitch!"

"You are gambling for high stakes, which necessarily entails risk. As for the nonentity—were I in his place, I would simply go home." He addressed Howard directly: "There are plenty of fish in the sea, young man, and none of them love you. Your Mimi is nobody special. Find someone else to make miserable."

Howard flushed red. "You're the worst excuse for a holy man I ever met," he said.

"And you, I am sure, are the worst whatever-you-are. Your possession of the vaccine notwithstanding. But no matter. My work is done. You may hand me my calling card."

"Why?"

"For payment."

“Not yet,” Shamkat said. “First, I want your soul.”

“That old thing? I hid it in an egg in a hen in a well on an island in an ocean half the world away. It may not be easy to find. But I can give you the GPS coordinates, if you wish.”

“Yeah, right. As if you’d hide something that valuable where you couldn’t keep watch over it. Try again, boyo.”

The Black Lama snarled silently, then pointed. “Fourth candle to the right. Up seventeen.”

Shamkat scrambled, nimble as a monkey up the cathedral wall, tipped over a candle, and made a sharp cry of delight and pain. She held up a stone, gleaming darkest red in the candlelight. Blood dripped from her hand.

“Careful,” the Black Lama said, smirking, “it’s sharp.” Then, after Shamkat had climbed back down, “My payment.” When she handed over the card, he put it into his robes. “Let the bastard try to find me now!” he exulted.

And then the Black Lama was gone.

“That went better than I expected.” Shamkat tucked away the leaf-shaped gem and wrapped a handkerchief around her hand to stanch the bleeding.

“What did you want his soul for?”

“It’s sharp and pointy and that’s always useful when dealing with folks who are hard to kill.”

“Kill? Nobody said anything about killing anybody.”

Shamkat grabbed Howard’s shirt with both fists and lifted him just high enough that his feet didn’t touch the ground. “Do you love the girl? Maybe yes, maybe no. But if you’re *not* a man who loves a woman so much that he’ll sacrifice anything and anybody for her, then who the fuck *are* you? Eh?”

“I . . .”

“You ignorant little nullity. Without me, you don’t get your fiancé back. Without your fiancé, you don’t recover the universe. And if the universe stays lost for much longer, the Demiurge will come after it. Do you think your world would survive that?” The hatcheck girl let

Howard go. His feet hit the ground with a startled thump. "Are you following me?"

Unhappily, Howard said, "Yes."

Shamkat extracted a card from the bundle and handed it to Howard. "Last stop before the main event. Read!"

He read.

WAYLANDIA SMITH
ARMORER
PLEASE DO NOT CONTACT

Wherever they were now was uncomfortably warm. Shadows filled vast spaces lit only by the fires of an occasional open kiln or furnace. What walls could be seen were of rough stone.

A burly woman dropped an anvil at the sight of Howard and Shamkat. She wore work boots, leather trousers, a heavy leather apron, and nothing else. Her skin was scorched black and her head singed almost hairless. The muscles on her arms were beyond belief, as were the silvery scars crisscrossing her body. "No tours!" she barked. "No solicitors, no street artists, no questing, no wronged individuals looking for revenge, their own true love, or long-lost heirs. Beat it."

"It's not who we are," said Howard, who fancied he was beginning to learn how to handle such extravagant individuals, "but what we can offer you."

The giantess scooped up the anvil one-handed and flung it. If Shamkat hadn't grabbed Howard out of the way, it would have pulverized him. As it was, she nearly tore his arm out of its socket.

"You know me, armorer," Shamkat said as the anvil bounced and rattled to a stop. "Or, rather, you know who I work for. You will therefore not be surprised to learn that I know that the one thing you want most is the formula for Greek fire."

A wistful look entered the armor's eyes. "*Pyr thalássion.* I saw it burning on the water off the coast of Ruthenia once, but . . . How can you possibly know its formulation?"

"I don't. No one does. The secret was lost in the fall of Byzantium. But I know how to recover it." Shamkat began talking, steadily and convincingly, of Uncle Paulie's cigar box and the access it afforded to all space and time.

When she was done, Waylandia said, "I have better chemical weapons, of course. But the romance of Greek fire! There's never been a more beloved incendiary in all of history. Napalm doesn't even come close."

"We're going up against the Giraffe Wrangler," Shamkat said. "We'll need armor."

"Yes." The armorer turned to Howard. "Take off your shirt," she said.

Howard obliged. There was a silence.

"Huh," Waylandia said at last. "Not bad."

"I work out at the gym."

"Of *course* you do," Shamkat said. Waylandia snickered.

Howard's ears burned. "Hey! If you—"

"Hush." The armorer handed him a metal plate, padded on one side and the size of his hand, with straps attached to its three edges. "Place this over your heart." When he had done so, she tugged the plate half an inch to the left and strapped it in place. "Now, trousers." She strapped another piece of padded metal, very much like an athletic cup over Howard's vulnerable parts. "When she shoots you, it's going to hurt like hades and maybe splinter a few ribs. But you'll be alive, and her attention will be on Gofer Girl. Act then."

"He'll need a weapon," Shamkat said.

"The vaccine's not enough?"

"He doesn't know how to use it."

Waylandia shrugged and produced a gun. "This is a Glock 21. Reliable, lightweight, packs a .45 round. There are ten bullets in the clip, but if you don't take her down with the first, I doubt the others will matter. Tuck it into the back of your belt and put your shirt back on." She picked up two handfuls of chain mail and turned to Shamkat. "Strip down. These go over your undies and under your clothes. You dress shapeless, so it won't be obvious."

"A metal bikini. Really?"

"When she shoots you, ham it up. That will give Joe Sixpack time enough to take a shot at her." To Howard: "Make it count."

"How can you possibly know all this?" Howard asked.

"It's my business."

As she was donning her armor, Shamkat said, "One more thing." She held up the Black Lama's soul. "I want this placed in the tip of a dagger."

"Huh. Ain't seen one of these for a long time. Now where did I . . . ?" The armorer went into the shadows and returned with what looked like the skeleton of a knife. She snapped the gemstone into place so that it formed the cutting tip of a blade defined by gleaming arcs of silver. It looked lethal.

"What is that for?" Howard said. "Are you going to kill the Giraffe Wrangler with it if I fail?"

"Maybe." Shamkat riffled through the cards one last time. "Do your part, and you'll be a big hero to little Mimi."

"I honestly don't think that Mimi would like—"

Shamkat looked ready to kill him. "Your girlfriend is in danger, you twit! She's probably hysterical with fear. Weeping. Tied up with ropes." She paused for emphasis. "Sexy ropes. The kind men like." She handed him a pasteboard rectangle.

GLORIA WUNDERLY
GIRAFFE WRANGLER
RATES ON REQUEST

Howard found himself in an apartment with an obviously expensive view of the rooftops of Paris and, beyond them, the Eiffel Tower. A rotund but competent-looking woman was simultaneously turning to face him and raising a gun toward his heart. All he had to do was catch two bullets and, believing him incapacitated, she would turn away to confront Shamkat. There would be just enough time to snatch the Glock from his belt and shoot her. At this distance, he could hardly miss.

Or so he had been told.

But Howard had been thinking. He knew that no one, himself included, had ever believed him capable of serious thought. But danger brought out unsuspected qualities. So, instead of sticking with the plan, he flung out his arms in surrender and said, "I only want to talk."

Gloria held her gun pointed at Howard's heart, but did not shoot. In a pleasant voice she said, "You were in the orgy at the nightclub. I remember you made little grunty noises, like a pig."

Howard blushed yet again. "That was a mistake. I was drunk and—"

"Oh, piffle. You enjoyed it. I could tell. But let's get to business. You have a gun in your butt. Are you going to draw it and try to shoot me or is it just there for fun?"

Howard took a long, deep breath. "I'm going to draw it out slowly and place it on the floor." When he had done so, he said, "I have something you want."

"I don't want anything. That's what enlightenment is all about," Gloria said. Adding, "Shamkat, if you think you can kill me before I shoot you three times in the face, go ahead and try. But your bosses won't let you die, and the damage will take a long time to heal."

"Crap." Shamkat's dagger—the one with the Black Lama's soul in its tip—disappeared from her hand.

"You say you don't want anything," Howard said, talking fast lest Gloria lost interest. "But the universe is a big place and contains many things. For example." He showed her the vial he had just drawn from his pocket. "I happen to have a vaccine against sin. I can see that you want it. Let's make a deal."

Gloria clearly recognized the vial. "A specific against human folly? One that can be used to immunize the entire human race against all its worst impulses?"

Howard thought. Why not? "Sure."

"And all you want for it is Mimi?"

"Yes."

"Then it's a deal. She should be here in three . . . two . . . one . . ."

The door opened and Mimi rushed into the apartment, cheeks red from the cold. "I got the job!" she cried. Then, seeing Howard, "Oh."

Confronted with a Mimi so unlike the one he had conjured up in his imagination—no tears, no ropes, no look of newborn love in her eyes—Howard found himself too deflated to speak. But Gloria suffered no such disadvantage. "You've been rescued, dear. Your boyfriend offered me a bribe I could not refuse."

Arms crossed, Mimi listened. Then she said, "Let me see if I understand." She snatched the vial from Howard's hand. "No more sin, no more folly. No more free will, right? No more lust, no more children, is that it? Of course it is. What would be the point? You're talking about the extinction of the human race. Or have I misread the implications here?"

Howard flinched. "I, uh, I hadn't thought of that."

"Don't forget that we'll die off in a state of grace." Gloria smiled beatifically. "In the long run, that's all that really matters."

Mimi's lips grew thin and white. She marched into the kitchenette, placed the vial into the microwave, and hit High. A few seconds later, there was a quiet *pop* from within the machine. "Now," Mimi addressed Howard directly, "just what are you doing here?"

Realizing how little Mimi would like being told that he'd been expecting to rescue her, Howard said, "Well, I sort of . . . misplaced the universe, you see. It was in the box Uncle Paulie showed us in the nightclub, and he told me to hide it, and I . . . was maybe a little drunk. He, uh, sent me to find you."

"He did, did he? Why doesn't he just ask me himself?" Mimi went to a closet and opened the door. "You might as well come out, Uncle Paulie. I know you're in there."

Sheepishly, Uncle Paulie emerged.

"Not a word. Take us back to Howard's apartment," Mimi said. "Gloria can stay here. She's not needed anymore."

Shamkat handed the bundle of cards to Uncle Paulie. He handed one to Howard:

HOWARD PENDLETON

NOBODY IN PARTICULAR

PHILADELPHIA

So they were back where it had all begun. Mimi drew a sheet of paper from her clutch, crossed out something, scribbled a word above it, and laid the paper down on the kitchen table. "I was going to leave this for somebody else. But it fits you just as well," she told Howard. She went to the door. Over her shoulder, she said, "You hid it under your bed. It was the single most obvious place you could have put it, so of course that's what you did."

She left.

"That girl has spunk," Uncle Paulie said. "Am I the only one who noticed that?"

"No," Howard said glumly.

"Well, much energy and no matter." Uncle Paulie went into the bedroom, redolent of dying roses, got down on his knees, and groped under the bed. "Ah! Here it—"

Without warning, Shamkat leaped upon him, plunging her dagger into his back.

With all the grace of a side of beef falling off a truck onto the interstate, Uncle Paulie crashed flat on the floor, undeniably dead. By one outstretched hand, the cigar box lay, lid open. Galaxies and nebulae glimmered in its depths.

"What have you done?" Howard cried.

Shamkat turned a savage face on him. "All my life I've been trapped. In an empire that killed my family. In a job I hated. In a universe I despised. Now I have my cage before me. At last I can destroy it!"

She raised her foot high and brought it down hard on the box.

But as her foot descended, it grew smaller, and the rest of her leg with it. Thrown off balance, Shamkat toppled forward, tumbling, dwindling, into the box. She screamed and as her body diminished to the size of a pebble, a speck, a memory, so too did the scream, growing smaller in volume and higher in pitch until it was nothing but an unheard tension in the air.

Uncle Paulie got up, groped around his back, and pulled out the dagger.

Because he could think of nothing else, Howard said, "I thought you were dead."

"I was. Then I brought myself back to life. It's a thing I know how to do." Uncle Paulie's eyes twinkled. Then he tapped the folded paper sheet on the kitchen table. "I think it's time you read this."

Dear Gloria, the note had originally begun. But Mimi had crossed out the assassin's name. It now read:

> Dear Howard,
>
> It was pleasant enough spending time with you, but I'm moving on.
>
> Don't come looking for me. If you succeed, I'll have to kill you. I know you don't believe I could do that. But I'm not the woman you took me for. Not anymore. I have absolutely no doubt who would be left standing at the end of the confrontation. I know what you're thinking. If I'm so sure of myself, why aren't I making money off of it? No disrespect, but what is money?
>
> And wish me luck! I'm going to become a giraffe wrangler.
>
> Mimi

Howard had never read anything so blithe and final in his life. When he was done reading, he cried for a very long time.

"Ashes to ashes and tit for tat," Uncle Paulie said when he was finally done. "Do you remember playing London Bridge as a child? This is the price of being alive. We all fall down at the end."

"Not you," Howard said resentfully.

"Even me." Uncle Paulie put an avuncular arm about Howard's shoulders and squeezed. "Why do you think I behave the way I do? I'm as much a victim as you are. Only, in stark contrast to you, I'm having fun on the way down." He thrust two fingers into his mouth and whistled so loudly that Howard flinched. Something large and brown scuttled out from under the bed—the world's largest cockroach, Howard thought for an instant. But then it reared up on two of its four legs and revealed itself to be Dan Scratch.

"Did everything work out well, Boss?" he asked.

"Yes, yes, fine."

"And my service?"

"Impeccable as usual." Uncle Paulie handed the dapper little man the dagger that Shamkat had used to kill him. "Here's your payment. I know you'll put it to good use. Oh, and when you see him, tell the Black Lama I kept a duplicate of his card. He doesn't get free of me as easily as all that."

"Will do, Big Guy." The little man bowed deeply and was gone.

Now there were only the two of them, Howard and his uncle.

"This was all a put-up job, wasn't it? You were responsible for everything, from Mimi's kidnapping to Shamkat's falling into the box." It was all so obvious to him now. His uncle smiled benevolently. "Uncle Paulie . . . Aunt Polly . . . whoever you are . . . out of all the people in all the planets in the universe you could have descended upon . . . why me?"

"Opposites attract, dear child. You were dead inside. So I reached out to give you a spark of life. That's all. How could I *not* help you, loving you as I do?"

The world went still, black and white, grainy, unvarying, and tenuous. Then, just like all the others, Uncle Paulie was gone.

The adventure, if that's what it had been, was over. Howard's quest to win back Mimi had been an abject failure. And now, after all had been said and done, what was there for him to do? He looked at the clock. It was three a.m.

It was time—indeed long past time—for him to go to bed.

But before he did, Howard walked out into the city night, leaving his apartment door unlocked and open behind him, only to discover that in his absence it had begun to snow. The flakes came slanting down from the north, hurrying through the air, pausing in mid-flight to dance about the streetlights and traffic signals, creating white and red and yellow and green halos that diminished the farther away they were. But through some minor miracle of meteorology, though the clouds were heavy on all sides, a dwindling patch of sky overhead was clear as glass and thronged with stars. Howard gaped up at them, breathing in fugitive flakes, feeling tiny bursts of ice implode on his tongue and deep within his lungs, and in a moment of sudden lucidity realized that it didn't matter whether he ever got together with Mimi again or not. He could die right now and it wouldn't make any difference. Hearts were broken every day and mended themselves every bit as reliably. Lives went on, grew tedious, underwent unexpected renewals, changed direction for no discernable reason, lingered beyond their natural spans, came to abrupt ends. In the meantime, the night was cold and holy, the air as pure and exhilarating as antique wine, the stars as thick as snowflakes and every snowflake as large as any star.

Michael Swanwick published his first story in 1980, making him one of a generation of new writers that included Pat Cadigan, William Gibson, Connie Willis, and Kim Stanley Robinson. Since then, he has been honored with the Nebula, Theodore Sturgeon, and World Fantasy Awards and received a Hugo Award for fiction in an unprecedented five out of six years. He also has the pleasant distinction of having lost more major awards than any other science-fiction writer.

Roughly one hundred fifty of his stories have appeared in *Amazing*, *Analog*, *Asimov's*, *Clarkesworld*, *High Times*, *New Dimensions*, *Eclipse*, *Fantasy & Science Fiction*, *Interzone*, the *Infinite Matrix*, *Omni*, *Penthouse*, *Postscripts*, *Realms of Fantasy*, *Tor.com*, *Triquarterly*, *Universe*, and elsewhere. Many have been reprinted in Best of the Year anthologies and translated into Japanese, Croatian, Dutch, Finnish, German, Italian, Portuguese, Russian, Spanish, Swedish, Chinese, Czech, and French. He has also published several hundred works of flash fiction.

A prolific writer of nonfiction, Swanwick has published book-length studies of Hope Mirrlees and James Branch Cabell as well as a book-length interview with Gardner Dozois. He has taught at Clarion, Clarion West, and Clarion South.

Swanwick is the author of nine novels, including *In the Drift* (an Ace Special), *Vacuum Flowers*, *Stations of the Tide*, *The Iron Dragon's Daughter*, *Jack Faust*, *Bones of the Earth*, *The Dragons of Babel*, and *Dancing with Bears*. His short fiction has been collected in *Gravity's Angels*, *Tales of Old Earth*, *Cigar Box Faust and Other Miniatures*, *The Dog Said Bow-Wow*, *The Postutopian Adventures of Darger and Surplus*, and *The Best of Michael Swanwick*. His most recent novel is *City Under the Stars*, co-written with long-time editor and friend Gardner Dozois.

He lives in Philadelphia with his wife, Marianne Porter.